THE BONES OF VALHALLA

BOOK 9 IN THE BABYLON SERIES

SAM SISAVATH

Published by Road to Babylon Media LLC
www.roadtobabylon.com

Edited by Jennifer Jensen & Wendy Chan
Cover Art by Deranged Doctor Design

ISBN-13: 978-0997894608
ISBN-10: 0997894601

THE COMPLETED PURGE OF BABYLON SERIES

The Purge of Babylon: A Novel of Survival

The Gates of Byzantium

The Stones of Angkor

The Walls of Lemuria Collection (Keo Prequel)

The Fires of Atlantis

The Ashes of Pompeii

The Isles of Elysium

The Spears of Laconia

The Horns of Avalon

The Bones of Valhalla

Mason's War (A Purge of Babylon Story)

ALSO BY SAM SISAVATH

THE ALLIE KRYCEK VIGILANTE SERIES

Hunter/Prey

Saint/Sinner

Finders/Keepers

THE RED SKY CONSPIRACY SERIES

Most Wanted

The Devil You Know

ABOUT THE BONES OF VALHALLA

For every night, there is a new dawn.

One night. That was all it took for the world to be forever changed. Creatures that once lived in the shadows rose, spreading like a plague across the globe, swallowing whole cities and collapsing unprepared governments.

Survivors call it The Purge.

In the months since, every night has been a struggle against the supernatural terrors that thrive in the darkness. The days are no better, with constant battles against human traitors that have chosen to serve the new overlords.

But an end to the nightmare is finally at hand.

Mercer's army is in disarray, and Danny and Gaby have returned to the *Trident* with precious cargo. Meanwhile, Keo is a marked man behind enemy lines, and Lara once again finds herself tested as the answer she and the other survivors have been waiting for is finally revealed.

In the finale to *The Purge of Babylon* series, the future of mankind is at stake. Sacrifices will be made and heroes will be forged, and the road to Babylon will be paved with the deeds of the brave...and the Bones of the dead.

ACKNOWLEDGEMENTS

To everyone who picked up a copy of *The Purge of Babylon,* despite the fact it was written by a nobody, then decided to keep reading all the way up to *The Bones of Valhalla*, you're the reason I'm able to write for a living and I will never be able to fully thank you. But I'll try anyway: Thank you, thank you, **THANK YOU**.

Special thanks to George Bardmesser, Davis G., L. Chow, Stephen Schumacher, Tim Kilner, Naomi F., and Elizabeth Stang for everything you guys do.

BOOK ONE

WITH ENEMIES LIKE THESE

1

LARA

"Is it him?"

"Yeah, it's him."

"Are you sure?"

"Yeah."

"Danny, are you *sure?*"

"I've spent enough time in a foxhole with the guy—then there were all the times we were in the Stan. Bottom line? Sure enough to stuff him into an ancient-ass-looking chest and drag him all the way out here across the ocean. That sure enough for ya?"

"But you have to be *absolutely sure.*" *Because I don't want to go through this again. Not now, not after I've already accepted him being gone. I don't think I can do it, Danny; I can't go through it again. I won't.*

She stared through the open door into the cabin where Gage used to reside (*before I shot him and we threw his body overboard*). It was musty and smelled of abandonment, but maybe that had more to do with the window being sealed up and the lack of fresh air than anything else.

She couldn't pry her eyes away from the sole object in the

room. If she didn't know it was there—all thirty-by-eighteen-by-twenty inches of it—she wouldn't have been able to see it. They had deposited it—an old chest that looked like it might hold some unimaginable treasure—against the back corner. Even if they hadn't blotted out the window, it would have been difficult to make out the object from the shadows. It was constructed of thick, heavy wood, but that wasn't immediately obvious with all the duct tape mummifying it—Danny's way of ensuring not even the smallest ray of sunlight could penetrate it.

And he was in there.

Will.

She hadn't said his name out loud since the chest was brought onboard, and not when Danny led her down here while giving a rundown of what they (he and Gaby and Nate) had gone through last night in the small Texas town of Gallant. Maybe she was afraid of what would happen if she let his name slip out. It felt like another lifetime since she had last seen him, since she had held him and kissed him, before she finally surrendered to reality and forced herself to move on with the rest of her life.

And now here he was.

But he's not really Will anymore, is he? He hasn't been Will in a while. Out there, alone, while I gave him up for dead...

Next to her, Danny was picking at a speck of dirt clinging to his dirty blond hair. Danny, like Gaby and Nate, hadn't escaped Texas unscathed. They were bruised and battered and wounded, but Danny had managed to come through it mostly, well, Danny. The fact that he was here standing next to her onboard the *Trident* when there were so many nights where she didn't think she would ever see him again made all the difference in the world. It also greatly eased her mind, because if she'd lost him out there, it would have been her fault. After all, she was the one who had sent him back to Texas on a fool's errand in the first place.

How did you do it, Will? How did you manage so much with so little help from the rest of us for all those months?

"It's him, Lara," Danny was saying. "I made sure of it. He knows things only Willie boy would know."

"I believe you, Danny," she said quietly, and thought, *It's him, but is it really* him? *How long has he stopped being* him?

She didn't know what to do, what to say, or even what to feel at the moment. There was so much emotion roiling inside her, but she couldn't be certain about a single one of them. That uncertainty, more than anything, dominated her senses, though somewhere in there was the desperate urge to turn around and (*run*) walk away.

Is that really you in there, Will? After all these months? Have you really come back to me?

Danny was sure. Really, really sure. And yet, the ghouls could play tricks with your mind, make you do and think, even believe things that weren't true. But maybe the most painful part was that she wasn't sure if she *wanted* this to be true.

Will. Her Will.

Back, after all these months. Except it wasn't *really* him.

"You said he was hurt?" she asked, managing to keep her voice calm, even steady somehow. Her legs remained still, every inch of her fighting the intense need to flee up the hallway.

"Yeah, he took a real beating last night," Danny said. "A hell of a mess. Honestly, I didn't think he was even going to survive, but he pulled through. That's Willie boy for ya; he doesn't know the meaning of the words 'No means no.'"

"That's a phrase, Danny."

"Same diff."

"Okay," Lara said, and took a step back.

Danny did likewise, and she closed the door but didn't lock it. Since the mess with Gage, they had put a heavy deadbolt on the door with the intention of using it as a brig. She wished she could have said it was needless paranoia, but all she had to do was recall what they had gone through the last few nights, and she knew it wasn't. With so many people on the yacht now, the chances were good she was going to need it soon—she just hadn't counted on its first visitor to be someone she knew. Someone she had been waiting for. Even longed for all these months...

Will.

Is that really you in there?

She leaned against the hallway wall and wondered if he could still hear them out here through the thick door. The blue eyes were different from the black-eyed ones, according to everyone who had encountered them. They were faster, stronger, and hyperaware of their surroundings. Could they hear through walls, too? Could he hear the faltering beats of her heart right now? Or sense the doubt in every word she spoke, in her every movement?

You were dead, Will. And I accepted it and moved on.

Goddamn you, you're supposed to be dead.

"Who else knows?" she asked.

"I told the kids to keep it mum," Danny said. "But Carly knows. The BBs know it, too."

"BBs?"

"Blaine and Bonnie."

"Oh."

"Pretty much just the ones that came to get us when we showed up."

"Did anyone see you bring it onboard?"

"Unfortunately, yeah. I guess I underestimated the amount of civvies crawling all over the place. Carly told me the ol' tugboat's gotten a lot more crowded since the last time, and I didn't expect to get back onboard all ninja-like. Would have been better to wait until dark to bring it back, but..."

"Gaby and Nate needed Zoe's help."

"Yeah. Couldn't wait too long. Both those kids were touch and go there for a while."

"What about you?" she asked. She could still smell the gunpowder on his clothes, in his hair. He had brought her straight down here after returning to the *Trident*.

"Scratches, bruises, a few tender bones. Nothing to get too excited about. Just more character for the ladies."

"We need to keep it from Riley's people. They don't know him the way we do. We need to keep the circle tight—which means just us."

Danny nodded. "Agreed. But like I said, people saw us bring it onboard. They're liable to wonder about it. Curiosity killed the cat, and all that."

"We'll deal with it if it becomes a problem."

"Sounds like a plan," Danny said. Then, "What about you?"

"What about me?"

"It's a lot to take in. It took me a few days to just open the figurative door into the possibility of accepting it was even him, and I never slept with the guy—long, lonely nights in foxholes in the Stan notwithstanding."

I don't know, Danny. I had convinced myself he was dead, that he wasn't coming back and I had to move on.

And I did. I moved on, Danny.

God help me, I moved on...

"When did you know for sure?" she asked instead.

"Not until Gallant, but I had my suspicions before then," Danny said. Like her, he hadn't taken his eyes off the cabin door. "The first time was in the airfield outside Larkin. It wasn't him, then. Not really."

"Meaning?"

"It gets a little confusing, but bear with me."

"Go on..."

"He had taken over one of the black eyes in Larkin."

"They can do that?"

"Pretty easily, apparently. From what he tells me, the black eyes are like puppets moving on an almost base intelligence. Eat, sleep, stay out of the light. That kind of stuff."

"So how did you know it was him? Will?"

"I didn't, not back then. It's hard to explain, but I thought there was something different about those black eyes. Then came Starch, when he actually made contact. I still wasn't completely sure. At least, not until Gallant."

"That's when you talked to him..."

"Yup. We had a nice, long conversation. Hours and hours of gabbing. Well, mostly by me, but he eventually grew his lips back and contributed to the convo."

"What did he tell you?" she asked.

Did he say why he waited so long to make contact? Why he let me think he was dead all this time?

"He's been a real busy bee out there," Danny said. "Making a real nuisance of himself. So much so that the bad guys laid a mousetrap for him."

"At Gallant."

"Right-o. And we were the cheese. A very attractive and not-at-all stinking cheese, I might add."

"What else did he tell you?"

"A lot of things. You should talk to him, Lara. He can explain it a whole lot better than I can."

"Explain what?"

"He says he's found a way to win the war."

"Win the war...?"

"Yeah. Win the war. Save the world. Give humanity a second chance. You know, all the good stuff we've been waiting for."

"How?"

"The way he laid it out for me, it sounds doable. It won't be easy—hell, it's borderline impossible unless we get a lot more help

—but when have overwhelming odds ever stopped us before? I call it Plan G."

"What's the G stand for?"

"Really? You have to ask?"

"Oh," Lara said.

"I repeat: He can explain everything much better than I can. You know him; even his backup plans have backup plans. If I didn't know what I know or seen what I've seen, I wouldn't have believed a word of it."

"But you do..."

"Absolutely."

"How sure are you?"

"Pretty damn sure."

"All right."

"You want me to stay with while you talk to him?"

She shook her head. "Not yet."

"Lara, it's him. It's Will."

Maybe, she thought, but said, "I'm not ready yet, Danny," and turned and walked up the hallway, picking up her pace as she went, needing to get away—as far away—from the cabin as possible.

Behind her, Danny snapped the deadbolt into place over the door. Then a second later there was just her labored breathing dominating everything, even the roar of the engines grinding away around her.

She moved through the main deck, maneuvering around people whose names she didn't know and children whose faces she didn't recognize. Riley's people were everywhere, and eventually she would get used to it, but right now it didn't seem as if there was a hallway or room or turn where there wasn't a stranger waiting to almost bump into her.

Most of Riley's people stuck to the lower and main decks, but it was hard to keep track of everyone with so many onboard at the same time. The upside was that everyone seemed to be cooperating with the rules she'd laid down, and even the kids stayed away from the bridge and upper deck as ordered. She could make out pockets of conversation as she walked through them, but her thoughts were too jumbled to pay any attention.

By the time she reached her destination, Lara had shaken off some of the cobwebs that had lingered during the seemingly endless walk. She knocked on the strip of tan gaffer's tape someone had slapped on the door and scribbled *Dr. Zoe, M.D.* on it in permanent marker.

"It's not locked," a voice called from the other side.

Lara stepped inside. They had remodeled the place into something that actually looked like an infirmary, complete with cots and all the medical supplies and equipment they had been smart enough to stock up with before Song Island fell. The rest came from the *Ocean Star*.

Zoe was across the room, tapping on a tablet when she looked up. "Visiting time's not for another hour."

"I'm going to have to insist," Lara said.

"Hey, boss's prerogative."

Zoe nodded over at Gaby, who was lying on one of the beds with her shoulder wrapped. The teenager looked over and smiled, and Lara returned it.

They didn't have hospital gowns, but Gaby was in the next best thing—pajamas and a long-sleeve cotton shirt. She'd been cleaned up, but her eyes were glassy from the medication. The bruising and cuts along her face would stay for a little while longer, but they would heal along with the hole in her left shoulder. Or, as Danny put it, *"A going away present from this thoroughly unpleasant little midget we ran across in Texas."*

"How're you doing, kiddo?" Lara asked as she sat down on a stool next to Gaby's bed.

"Annoyed," Gaby said.

"Why annoyed?"

"Because I was shot and I'm lying in here, but Nate was shot too, and he's already running around out there."

"Your boyfriend didn't need me to pull a bullet out of him like you did," Zoe said. "And you're due for another dose soon, by the way."

"I feel fine. Better than fine, actually."

"For now."

"Zoe's right, you're stuck in that bed for at least all of today," Lara said. "Third-year medical student's orders."

"The two of you're ganging up on me, is that it?" Gaby smirked.

"It's for your own good. Besides, I wouldn't call what Nate's doing running around, exactly. More like limping around. Slowly. You guys did a good job keeping him alive out there."

"Danny did most of the work. I mostly just stood around getting blood on my clothes. What's he up to since he left me, anyway?"

"Looking for an available cabin. I had to tell him there wasn't any."

"What about Gage's? I heard he doesn't need one anymore."

"I had to convert it into a makeshift brig."

"That's too bad. He's been really looking forward to that room. Mostly he's been looking forward to us doing things down there where no one can hear us."

"Spare me the details."

"Heh."

"The good news is, it won't be like this for too much longer."

"The Bengal Islands?"

Lara nodded. "We'll be back on course soon, and we have all the fuel we need to get them there."

"And assuming there are no bad guys waiting for us there...?"

"Then we'll say our good-byes to Riley's people and we'll have the *Trident* all to ourselves again."

"What about...," Gaby said, but didn't finish. She made a downward motion with her head instead—difficult to do, since she was flat on her back.

But Lara knew what she meant: *Will.*

"I don't know yet," Lara said.

"Did Danny tell you? About why he came back?"

She nodded.

"But you haven't talked to him," Gaby said. It wasn't a question.

"No. Not yet."

"Danny's convinced it's him."

"What about you?"

The teenager shook her head. "I never got the chance to really talk to him. It. Him? Are we calling it—him—a 'him' or what?"

Lara shook her head too, and didn't know whether to laugh or cringe...or cry. She said instead, "I don't know."

"It's crazy, huh?" Gaby said as she reached over and squeezed Lara's hand.

"Which part?"

"All of it." She pursed her lips. "You're scared. That's why you haven't talked to him yet."

Lara managed a smile back at the girl. (*No, not a girl. Not anymore. She hasn't been a girl in a long time.*) "What happened to you out there?"

"What do you mean?"

"You've gotten smarter."

Gaby grinned. "It wasn't easy, being around Danny for all

that time, but I managed." Then she was serious again—and stronger than Lara remembered. "You need to talk to him, Lara. He fought his way to get back to us. To get back to *you*."

She nodded. "I will. In time."

"So it's really him," Zoe said from the foot of Gaby's bed.

Lara and Gaby both turned to the doctor. They had been so caught up in their conversation Lara realized they had both forgotten Zoe was even in the room with them.

"Will," Zoe said. "It really is him down there. In that chest that Danny brought back with him."

"Yes," Gaby said.

"And he's...?"

Gaby nodded.

Zoe seemed to lapse into her own thoughts, and Lara had to remind herself that she wasn't the only one who shared a past with Will. Zoe had, too; even if Lara never pried into the specifics, she always suspected something had happened between the two of them out there. But by the time Zoe had shown up on Song Island, alone, it hadn't seemed to matter.

But now, as she watched the other woman struggling with the thought of Will's return, Lara couldn't help but wonder all over again.

"We have to keep this between us," Lara said instead. "Understand? No one can know about what's down there. Especially Riley's people."

Zoe nodded. "I understand."

"You need to talk to him," Gaby said. She was staring at Lara, and might have been for some time, but Lara just now noticed. "You need to talk to him, Lara. You need to hear what he has to say. What he came all the way back here to tell us."

"I will." Lara nodded, and thought, *I'll talk to him. I'll go down there and open the door and pry open that chest and I'll watch him climb outside—not as the man I remember, but as a creature.*

A monster.

You're supposed to be dead, Will. Why the hell aren't you dead?

You goddamn bastard, you left me alone and I moved on. I moved on...

"There you are," Carly said, leaning against the railing next to her. "I was beginning to think you were avoiding me on purpose."

"Don't take it personally," Lara said. "I've been avoiding everyone since the infirmary."

"Great. Now I don't know whether to be pleased or insulted."

Lara smiled but didn't take her eyes off the group of strangers milling around on the floor below them. There was a steady stream of heads coming out and disappearing back into the deck, a mixture of civilians and soldiers. At one point she was sure she saw the familiar, faded ball cap belonging to Peters.

The Gulf of Mexico flashed by around them, the endless horizon a constant companion on all sides. She could look for miles and only see crisp blue water, which was the only thing keeping her mind even a little bit at ease, because an empty ocean meant no one was trying to sneak up on them. She'd had enough of that to last a lifetime. Except for the smaller refueling ship keeping pace nearby, she could almost believe the *Trident* was the last seafaring vessel in the world at this very moment.

Of course, she knew better. But it was nice to pretend, even for a short time.

Every now and then she found herself peeking up at the open skies, waiting for the plane she had seen last night to come back. After hearing all the stories about Mercer's warplanes bombing collaborator towns in Texas, she had been expecting the worst, but the plane had simply abandoned its pursuit (*if* it had even been pursuing them in the first place) and vanished. It had never gotten close enough for them to make out what kind of aircraft it had been, so she couldn't even be sure if it was one of Mercer's.

It saw us. It was searching for something, and it saw us; then it turned around.

So why did it just leave?

Just one more question to fill her head and make her nights more troubled, as if she didn't already have enough even before she ran into Riley and his rebellion.

"You're avoiding him too, I hear," Carly was saying beside her.

"I'm not ready yet," Lara said.

"I can dig it."

"Can you?"

"If Danny died, then came back as a ghoul? Oh, yeah. I can dig it."

"Danny's one-hundred percent sure it's him."

"Danny was one-hundred percent sure he had an alien baby growing inside him two weeks ago, but it turned out to just be a case of bad seafood."

"What do you think?"

Carly shrugged. "The jackass wouldn't even tell me what was inside that thing until we were halfway to the *Trident*. I guess he didn't want me to freak out."

"Did you?"

"Maybe a tad. I mean, I've never been that close to one of them before." Carly went quiet for a moment. Then, "But if it is him, it would be nice having him back. Even if he's not really...*him* anymore." Carly sighed. "Is all of this as confusing for you as it is for me?"

"It's going to take a lot of getting used to."

"Glad it's not just me, then. I haven't told the kids, of course. Man, they are going to *freak*."

"We need to keep it in-house. Riley's people aren't ready. I honestly don't know if they'll ever be ready to find out what's down there in the engine room."

Carly shot a quick look behind them before turning back around. "Do you think it's him? You think Danny's right?"

"I don't know," Lara said, surprised that the answer came out so quickly. The three words had simply tumbled free, but she didn't try to take them back.

Because it was the truth: *She just didn't know.*

"It's complicated, I guess," Carly said.

"Yeah. It's really complicated."

Carly reached over and put a hand on Lara's shoulder and squeezed. "Whatever you decide, it'll be the right decision."

"You sure about that?"

"Yes."

"Why are you so sure?"

"Because you're Lara. You're the boss lady. That's why."

Lara gave her friend a half-smile, wishing she could be as confident.

They didn't say anything for a while and were content to just lean against the railing in silence and look out at the endless ocean, turning their faces into the cool wind. The peace and tranquility temporarily dampened her chaotic thoughts, though it didn't come close to washing away her problems. Right now, that was an impossibility, and she accepted it.

The serenity was finally broken when the radio clipped to her hip squawked and she heard Blaine's voice: "Lara, come in."

"Just like Blaine to ruin a good moment," Carly said.

Lara unclipped, then keyed, the radio. "I'm here, Blaine."

"You're needed on the bridge," Blaine said.

"Problem?"

"Something you need to hear."

"I'm on my way."

Lara nodded at Carly, and they headed back into the upper deck.

"I didn't know Blaine was back on the bridge already," Lara said.

"You kidding me?" Carly said. "He practically ran up there as soon as he climbed back onboard. Also, I think he and Sarah are done."

"What happened?"

"Don't know. I didn't want to pry." Then, when Lara flashed her an amused look, "Hey, I can be really sensitive and shit, if I try."

"I never doubted it," Lara smiled.

Blaine was standing behind the *Trident*'s helm as if he'd never left with Carly to go rescue Danny and the others at all. Riley was inside with him, one arm in a sling, and looking brighter and healthier than in all the other times she'd known him. The irony was that it took getting shot for the man to finally get some of the sleep he had denied himself for so long.

"Shouldn't you be resting?" Lara asked Riley as she entered with Carly.

"I got plenty of that already," Riley said.

Lara turned to Blaine. "What did you want to show me?"

"Tell her," Blaine said to Riley.

"Tell me what?"

Riley said, "After you spotted that plane in the sky, I asked Marsha—"

"Maddie," Lara said.

"Right, Maddie. I asked her to keep an ear on the radio

frequency that Mercer's people have been using since the attacks began. The transmission is supposed to be all in code, in case someone stumbled across it by accident."

"You said 'supposed to be.'"

"I did." He nodded at Blaine. "Show them."

Blaine flicked a switch on the dashboard. "It's a recorded message."

A male voice came through the speakers along the bridge's walls. She didn't recognize it, but the man sounded slightly...what was the word...hesitant? But tone was hard to decipher over the radio, and she could have been far off, for all she knew.

"*This is* The Tide," the man began, "*to every unit still in the field. Effective immediately, you are to stand down and cease all operations. If you're already on your way home, continue doing so. I repeat: If you're in the middle of operations, you are to abandon them and fall back and await further instructions.*"

Blaine hit another button and the voice shut off. "That's it. The same short message on a loop."

"How long has it been broadcasting?" Lara asked.

"I don't know when it first started, but it's still broadcasting as we speak."

"What's it mean?" Carly asked. "Are they pulling back? Giving up? That sounded pretty important."

"Messages don't get any bigger than telling the kill teams to stand down and for people to come home," Riley said.

"So back to my original question," Carly said. "What's it mean? Specifically for us? Call me selfish, but I just care about our own necks."

Lara stared at Riley. She could see it on his face: He had been asking himself that very same question since he'd heard the message.

"Was that Mercer?" Lara asked him.

Riley shook his head. "No. It's Rhett."

"*Gone with the Wind* Rhett?" Carly asked.

"You told me about him before," Lara said. "Rhett. He was one of Mercer's original Four Horsemen. Along with you, Erin, and another guy."

"Benford."

"Right. Benford. So what's it mean that it's Rhett and not Mercer telling your people in Texas to stand down?"

"It could be any number of things..."

"Are any of them good for us?" Carly asked. "That's all I care about right now."

"I don't know. It would almost entirely depend on what happened to Mercer."

"What makes you think anything happened to him?" Lara asked.

"Because the only way Rhett would be in any position to order a stop to the war effort is over Mercer's dead body. I didn't risk everything to mutiny because the man was stable, Lara. Like all fanatics, he's committed to the war to the very bitter end. Rhett, on the other hand..."

"Keo," Lara said.

Riley nodded. "It's a possibility. It was a long shot, and I didn't want to invest too much energy in it, but if he's either killed Mercer or he's incapacitated him to the point where Rhett was able to take over... That opens up opportunities that didn't exist before."

"Keo," Carly said, breaking out into a big grin. "Good ol' Keo, always causing trouble. I love that guy."

"You asked me before what I would do if Keo succeeded," Riley said, looking across the room at Lara. "I told you I never really thought about it, that getting the hell away from Mercer was always my primary goal. I wasn't lying. I really hadn't thought that far ahead, because I didn't think it would ever happen."

"And now?" Lara said.

"If Keo somehow actually did it, maybe we don't have to flee to the Bengal Islands after all. Maybe the answer isn't out there, but back home."

"Where is home?" Carly asked.

"Black Tide Island," Riley said.

2

WILL

He could hear them talking through the thick chest that kept the sunlight at bay. They were keeping their voices low enough that if not for his heightened senses, he wouldn't have been able to distinguish their words from the loud roar of the engine that tried to drown out everything. The walls of the chest vibrated constantly around him and had been since they carried him onto the boat. The cramped space was a nonfactor because he had no uses for comfort anymore.

He was awake, in the daylight. The reality of sunlight inches from his exposed skin, already so weak after his encounter with the blue eyes in Gallant, had been overwhelming at first. He couldn't really call it fear because he was beyond that; he remembered what fear was, but to actually *feel* it again was something else entirely.

He could hear them just fine, just as he could hear and feel the *sloshing* of the waves underneath the moving boat and taste the bitterness of the ocean on his tongue. He'd traversed it once before on a much smaller craft, but he would never become used to it. It made him uneasy being this close to something that could end him with so little effort, especially with so many things left to do.

Mabry.

He was there, waiting.

And vulnerable, so vulnerable.

"But you have to be *absolutely sure*," he heard Lara say now.

"It's him, Lara," Danny said. "I made sure of it. He knows things only Willie boy would know."

How many times had he played this scenario over in his mind, during all the nights and days since his transformation? Too many, and each time the outcome was always different...and always the same.

You're not a man anymore. Don't fool yourself.

But he wasn't fooling himself. He didn't come here in a delusional attempt to regain his humanity. The only thing left now was action, to strike back at the enemy. To save them. Everyone.

But mostly her...

The grind of the door closing, then Danny, his voice clear as day even through the thick metal: "It's a lot to take in. It took me a few days to just open the figurative door into the possibility of accepting it was even him, and I never slept with the guy—long, lonely nights in foxholes in the Stan notwithstanding."

"When did you know for sure?" Lara asked.

"Not until Gallant, but I had my suspicions before then..."

He let their conversation drift into the background in order to focus on healing.

He was weak. Much, much too weak to do anything for them right now. If they wanted to, they could come in here and kill him. A bullet to the head. That was all it would take. It was ironic that for all the benefits of being turned, he didn't have the near-invulnerability of the black eyes. But he didn't have all of their weaknesses, either.

He had reclaimed a lot of what made him *him*, but he

would never be whole again. There were moments when the simplest things still eluded him—like the name of a book he used to love reading as a child, his favorite movie, a joke that Danny liked to tell even though it had gotten old a long time ago...

Concentrate. He needed to concentrate on healing.

Even with his pain receptors turned off, he could still tell how bad the injuries were. The muscles were torn and bruised and ripped, the tendons and sinews stretched beyond their abilities. There was no pain, but their current fragile state weighed heavily on his mind. Ironically, all the broken bones made lying inside the chest, crumpled up like a marionette with its strings cut, simpler.

Irony? Or was that tragedy?

Not that it mattered, but it would come to him eventually.

It always did...

———————

"Where are you?"

He woke up to soothing darkness, the blue glow from his eyes the only thing keeping the narrow universe around him from being completely pitch black.

"You're running again."

The voice echoed inside his head, reaching out to him from the vastness of their connection with a calming hand. He had to resist the instinct to grab it, to beg for forgiveness, to give in and slip back into the hive like a good little boy.

"I know what you're planning."

No, that was a lie. A trick. The enemy didn't know his plans.

"It won't work."

Are you sure about that? he wanted to ask, wanted to pull down his mental defenses—they were stronger now, with the extra day's rest—and reveal his defiance. But he didn't. Not yet. Not until the time was right.

"You can still come home."

More lies. There was no home for him. There had never been. Not with *them*.

His home was with her. Lara. It had always been. Even if she turned him away...

Would she?

Maybe. Maybe...

"They'll never accept you. But I will. What you are now, what she made you, this is the new world. Why won't you accept it?"

Lies. The blue eyes had tried to kill him in Gallant. They had lured him there, with Danny and Gaby (and the boy, what was his name again?) as bait. They hadn't brought him there to be embraced as one of them. No, they had meant to destroy him. He still remembered their conversation, crowing about how pleased *he* would be.

"Now you're going to die."

"Again."

"But this time..."

"...for good."

"And he'll be pleased..."

"...that we finally ended you."

"...so pleased..."

He closed his eyes and let the movement of the vessel calm him. He resumed healing even as the voice continued. He couldn't have silenced it if he wanted to, because the voice prowled the river of thoughts that flowed through the consciousness of the brood that they were all a part of. It was an intimate connection, only possible because they came (*were born*) from the same blood. His life force flowed through their veins. Through his at this very second. They were as much a part of him as he was of them, and it would always be so.

Always...

"*Come home. This is where you belong. This is where you've always belonged. In another year, in ten years—a century—you won't remember the old world. The old you. This is the way of things now. The new order. It's fate.*"

I don't believe in fate, he wanted to answer.

"*It's destiny.*"

I don't believe in destiny, either, he wanted to shout.

But he kept quiet, because it was a trick. Once he reacted to the voice, he wouldn't be able to stay hidden from it, and then all would be lost.

"*It's her, isn't it? You still long for her. Even now, after everything that's happened. You hold onto the delusion you can be together again.*"

No. He hadn't come here for that. He hadn't...*right?*

"*Lara can be yours, and all you have to do is come back.*"

Lies. More lies.

"*Years, decades, generations from now. You'll always be together, just the way you want it. You won't have to worry about disease, or age, or death.*"

Ignore his lies. It was all a trick.

"*All you have to do is make the choice, and you'll be reunited again. Just make the choice to come home.*"

The choice...

"*She'll thank you for stripping away the pain. No more running, no more suffering. And you'll be together again. Reunited. Isn't that what you want? Isn't that what you've always wanted?*"

Yes, he thought, *Yes*...

"A priest, a rabbit, and a horse walk into a bar..."

Medical ointment passed through the chest's walls, and though Danny wasn't talking very loudly, he had no trouble hearing him. He almost smiled, and maybe he did, but simple tasks like that were harder to accomplish these days.

"Stop me if you've heard this one before..."

He didn't stop him, even though he had heard it many times before. The exact number escaped him, but that was nothing new. Information he didn't need to survive was buried deep down in his mental recesses. Maybe one of these days he would release the box and let them all out, or maybe he would fling the lid open only to discover there was nothing left, that they had all dissolved away.

One day, he hoped to find out.

But that day wasn't here yet.

"Ah, never mind. It's just not the same when you can't see the absolute joy in the other person's face as I present the joke to end all jokes," Danny was saying. "I'd open the lid, but I'm thinking you would have done it yourself if you wanted to. Surely those little strips of duct tape aren't holding you back, are they?"

No, they weren't.

"And that door... I bet you could breathe on it and bust it down, huh?"

It wasn't that easy, but Danny wasn't wrong. He could take it down with little effort.

"I would offer you something to eat, but I'm not sure if you even eat anymore. Or is it just a liquid diet these days? Food through a straw?"

This time he was sure he must have smiled. Maybe.

"She'll be down here to talk to you soon. I don't know when, so don't ask. She just needs time. Can't say as I blame her. The first time you dropped in on me... Well, you're not exactly your old self anymore, are you?"

No, he wasn't. He wasn't sure how much of his "old self" was even still left after the transformation. He had done things that he wouldn't have before, things that would have turned his stomach back when he was...still human.

"Something's come up, too. Our mutual buddy Mercer? He's either dead or dead-ish. Or, at least, that's the going theory."

Mercer. The name hung like a sword over the hive and made the blue eyes frantic. Mercer was the human who had brought death and destruction to the food supply, and in doing so, introduced doubt about the future. Just a sliver, but it was there.

"The food!" the ghouls shouted day and night. *"Save the food!"*

"I'm of two minds on the guy myself," Danny was saying. "While on the one hand he's a murdering sociopath, but we might not have made it out of Gallant without that little Hog of his showing up. So there's that."

Mercer's warplane had saved them, though not on purpose. He was sure of it. It had come there to burn the town down, wasting its armament in what amounted to a revenge attack. Even if there were ten of them—or a hundred—it wouldn't have mattered. The ghouls were endless, and there was only one way to defeat them...

"You said we were going to need a hell of a lot of luck to make this plan of yours work. Maybe this little revelation can help with that. What do you think?"

Yes. Yes, it could. He hadn't considered it because it wasn't something he had any control over, but if Mercer was gone, if there was an army out there...

"The more the merrier, right?"

Yes. The more the merrier. The more, the better the chances of success. He was ready to do with less, but if there was a choice...

His mind churned, processing the new information.

"Anyways, thought you'd want to know. Maybe you can do

something with it." A slight grunt and tired knee joints popped as Danny stood up. "I hate to chat and run, but the redhead's expecting me topside. Nice talking to ya as usual, buddy. I don't suppose I should call you Will anymore, huh? You got a new name you prefer?"

Frank. Someone had once called him Frank.

Who was it? It hadn't been that long ago since he saw him, but the man's face was starting to fade from his memory, pushed into the background to make room for the here and now.

"Sit tight; I'll be back when I can."

Footsteps, then a door opening and closing. The scent of two additional people outside, mingling with the oil and grease from the machines. A man and woman.

Silence again, except for the *sloshing* of the ocean under him, the roar of the engines. Footsteps moving around above him, men and women and children talking, laughing. He listened for Lara, but she wasn't among them.

"What'd he say?" a voice asked in the hallway. Young, but familiar.

"Is he still inside that thing?" another voice asked. This one was female and she spoke haltingly, quietly, as if afraid he would hear.

"Nothing, and yes," Danny said. "Eyes open, kids. No one goes in there that isn't me or Lara, understand? When in doubt, buzz the radio. That's what they're for."

"But it's him?" the young man asked. "For sure?"

"It ain't Santa Claus."

"Nate said it could bust through that door if it wants to," the woman said. "So what are we doing down here exactly?"

"What, you got something else better to do?"

"That's not what I'm saying..."

"Stay frosty," Danny said.

Footsteps, as Danny left, leaving the boy and woman behind to shuffle their feet. Nerves, but steely resolve.

He closed his eyes and concentrated, willing the bones to mend faster, for the muscle tissues to regrow. He needed to be at full strength for what was to come. And maybe even that wouldn't be enough.

"Something's come up, too," Danny had said. *"Our mutual buddy Mercer? He's either dead or dead-ish. Or, at least, that's the going theory. You said we were going to need a hell of a lot of luck to make this plan of yours work. Maybe this little revelation can help with that. What do you think?"*

A new development that he continued processing, adding to what he already knew, what lay ahead for them. For him.

The news was unexpected but not unwelcome, and he did what he did best—he adapted.

But even as he shifted the plans around in his mind, he reached out with his senses, throwing them outward and beyond the lower deck, searching for the snippets of conversation, the hushed whispers.

"Is he dead?" someone said. *"Is he really dead?"*

"I don't know," someone else said. *"Rhett's in charge now..."*

It was dark outside the boat, and had been for a few hours. He knew without a doubt because he existed on two simple measurements of time—day and night.

And right now, it was the latter. He didn't need a watch to know. It was in the way the air changed, even inside the tight confines of the chest. The gradual drop of temperature in the room, digit by digit, and the dramatic plunge in degrees beyond the boat's thick walls.

His guards, who had been talking on and off, had gone quiet.

The boy and the woman. Their names still escaped him, but he reasoned if he didn't recall them then they probably weren't important enough to his survival.

His body responded to the shift from day to night by cranking up, the blood in his veins flowing faster and freer, the mutated cells coming even more alive as they targeted and closed the wounds and repaired his injuries. He always healed faster at night because darkness was where he belonged. If traveling with Danny in the day had been nauseating, he was in bliss now as—

The boat. It had stopped moving.

How did he miss that before? The vessel was adrift under him and would be still, except for the occasional swaying against the waves. Why had they stopped? They were far from land; he knew because he could taste nothing but salt water all around him. So much of it that he grew agitated and had to refocus on something else.

There. Footsteps.

So many footsteps above and around him. Men and women of all sizes, and children. They were on the upper decks moving around. And talking. The buzz of excitement he had picked up earlier was still there.

"*Is he really dead?*" someone said.

"*Maybe,*" someone answered.

"*What does it mean?*" someone else said on another part of the boat.

Mercer. They were still talking about Mercer.

The new development, and the reason he'd had to restructure the plan.

"*Adapt or perish,*" someone had once said.

Had it been him? Lara? Or Danny—

A very distinct pair of footsteps intruded on the hushed conversations around the boat.

Heavy. Male. With *purpose*.

They were moving through the now-silent engine room toward the back. Toward him.

He shut out the rest and zeroed in on the new arrivals.

"What are they doing down here?" one of his guards said. The boy whose name he couldn't remember.

"You know them?" the woman asked.

"Riley's men. I don't know their names, but I know they're not supposed to be down here."

"We should radio Danny..."

"Wait, let me talk to them first," the boy said, even as his heartbeat accelerated slightly.

The woman was calmer, but not by much. "You sure?"

"Yeah," the boy said. Then, "You guys aren't supposed to be down here."

"Hey, Benny," a new voice said. Male. Older.

"You're not supposed to be down here," the boy named Benny said again.

"Lara sent us."

"No one told us," the female guard said.

"Radio her yourself," a third male voice said. He was softer spoken than the first. Easygoing.

"Why'd she send you down here?" Benny asked.

"Backup, I guess."

"We don't need backup."

"You'll have to take it up with the bosses. We're just following orders."

"Is it in there?" the first newcomer asked.

"Hey, get away from the door," the woman said.

"I've never seen one in person before."

"I said *get away from the door*."

"Okay, okay..."

"Stay right there while I radio Lara."

"Be our guest," the second new arrival said.

The sea clung to their skin, and fresh fish expelled from their breaths. They were breathing heavily even though they were doing everything possible not to show it. Their heartbeats were erratic, and one of them was on the verge of hyperventilating. Adrenaline coursed through their veins like sledgehammers against his eardrums.

They're lying.

The *click* of a radio, then the woman saying, "Lara, this is Carrie. Come in."

His nostrils suddenly filled with the smell of oil rubbing against leather, followed by the boy shouting, "Don't—," but he never got the rest of it out before two gunshots boomed in the narrow confines of the hallway outside his door.

Bodies falling to the hard floor, the clatter of weapons. Racing heartbeats and sweat flitted into the air as the deadbolt was pulled aside.

The door opening and a voice—one of the two new arrivals—saying, "Is that it? Is it inside the chest?"

"I think so," the other man said. The one with the softer voice. "Should we open it?"

"Fuck opening it," the first one said.

The air shifted as a long object was raised and a single finger moved. The smell of discharging gunpowder overwhelmed his senses, even as the bitter taste of silver licked at his lips and tried to force their way down his throat.

He bit back the bile and pushed through the discomfort as the impossibly loud crashing of automatic gunfire filled the room.

3

GABY

She blamed it on the meds, because there was really no reason why she should be so tired or drowsy, or had no incentive to get out of bed when she finally woke up from what seemed like a year's worth of sleep. It wasn't nearly cold enough inside the infirmary for her to need a blanket, but she just couldn't find the inclination to whip it off. The room was noticeably darker than the last time she had her eyes open, though she didn't have a prayer of telling time at the moment.

Conclusion: Getting shot was a real pain in the ass, and it was something she would definitely say no to if given the choice in the future. Of course, no one had given her the choice back in Gallant. Mason certainly hadn't.

I hope you get yours soon, Mason, you prick.

She didn't recall when Lara had left, because there was just her and the doc, who looked busy with a tablet across the room. Gaby didn't feel any pain, just that annoying fog rolling around in her head, making everything difficult to grasp. She'd only been asleep for a day, right?

And what had she and Lara been talking about? Oh, right.

Will.

He was alive, despite all the odds. There was a time when Gaby thought he was indestructible, that even if you could knock him down, nothing could keep him from leaping right back up to his feet. If all else failed, his love for Lara would bring him home. Naively, she had always believed that.

Until now.

She was thinking about Will, trying to remember the last time she saw his face (his *real* face), when Zoe was suddenly replaced by Nate. Gaby blinked, trying to understand how that had happened as Nate walked over and sat down (gingerly, she noticed) on a chair next to her bed.

"Hey there," she said.

"You look good," he said.

"Do I?"

"Well, sort of."

"Not what I wanted to hear."

"You still look better than every girl on this boat."

She smiled. "That's the one."

"Glad to be of service. Anyway, I got good news and bad news."

"Tell me the good news first."

"We got a whole lot of new chumps to whip at the next game night."

"Sweet. So what's the bad news?"

"There are way too many chumps onboard, and they're taking up a lot of space. And you know about..." He nodded toward the floor.

She almost laughed, because she had done the same thing when Lara was here.

"Are you afraid to say his name?" she asked.

He grunted, but then glanced quickly over at the door. "Lara made it pretty clear we can't go around blabbing about him. I think that's a good idea. It's hard to predict how the others will take the news."

"Lara's always been the smartest person in the room. It pays to listen to what she says."

"You won't get any disagreements from me," Nate said as he leaned over her, looking her up and down.

"Take a picture, why dontcha."

"Zoe really doped you up, huh?"

"Is it that obvious?"

"You're still the hottest thing on this boat. Have I mentioned that?"

"Yes, but you have my permission to keep saying it."

He grinned before glancing at the window across the room.

"What is it?" she asked.

"He's still out there..."

"Who?"

"Our pal Mason."

She frowned. Mason brought out the worse in her, and she couldn't picture his beady little eyes without getting angry. Not just at him, but at herself for not pulling the trigger when she'd had the chance.

"We should have shot him," she said.

"As Danny would say, shoulda, coulda, woulda, but didnta."

"You've been hanging around Danny too much."

"I know," Nate said, and flicked the remains of his Mohawk over to one side. "I'm even losing my sense of style."

"So what's the negative side?"

"Oh, below the belt, lady."

She smiled. This time it came out better. Or, at least, she thought it did. She was so groggy it could have looked awkward and freakish, for all she knew.

"Strangely enough, I miss it," she said.

"What's that?"

"Your dumb Mohawk."

He flashed a triumphant smirk. "I knew you'd come around." He ran his fingers through his hair. "I'm making an appointment with Carly tomorrow, just for you."

"I said I missed it, I didn't say I wanted it back."

"Hey, make up your mind."

"Come here," she said.

"Why?"

"Just come here."

He leaned over her and she reached up, took his face in her hands, and pulled him down. There should have been stabbing pain from her left shoulder where she was shot, but she hardly felt anything and had no trouble directing Nate until their lips touched. He tasted both sweet and salty, like most things out here on the ocean.

She didn't know how long they kissed and wasn't all that concerned about the passing time until someone cleared their throat.

Nate pulled back and smiled across the room at Zoe. "Hey, doc."

When had Zoe come back? Or had she been here the entire time?

Gaby couldn't tamp down—and really, didn't want to—the flair of annoyance with herself for her lack of focus on her surroundings.

What would Will say?

"Seriously, guys, I just came back from lunch," Zoe said. "Go easy on the lovey dovey stuff when us single people are around."

"Give us a break," Nate said. "We almost died out there. Twice." He looked back at her. "Twice, right?"

She thought about it. "Three times?"

"You sure?"

"Larkin, Starch, then Gallant."

"So we're not counting when that Warthog strafed us on the road?"

"You think we should?"

"A hog tried to do what to you on the road?" Zoe said.

"Warthog," Nate said. "It was one of Mercer's warplanes."

"Christ. What else does that psycho have flying around out there?" Zoe looked down at her watch. "Five more minutes; then you need to let her get some rest."

"I've had plenty of rest," Gaby said.

"Hey, who's the one with the medical degree here?"

"Can I sleep in here with her?" Nate asked. "It's pretty cramped out there with all the new faces around. You can't go around a corner without running into people. And you have the other two empty beds..."

"Okay," Zoe said, "but you need to let her rest. You'll be able to talk to your heart's content tomorrow. Five more minutes of chatter, then it's night-night for her. And that goes for you, too. I see you barely getting by out there."

"I'm fine, doc."

"Bull. Your wound's going to take longer to heal than hers. By tomorrow she'll be running around and you'll still be limping along."

Nate sighed, but said, "Thanks, doc."

Zoe returned to her work at the far counter while Nate looked back down at her.

"How's your side?" Gaby asked.

He shrugged. "I won't be playing hopscotch with the kids anytime soon, or cannonballing into the Gulf of Mexico, but it's getting better. I've already asked Lara to put me on guard rotation outside Will's room."

"And she said yes?"

"Well, no."

"Good."

"Why, you don't think I can handle it?"

"Not yet."

"I handled it pretty well in Gallant."

"No, you didn't."

"What are you talking about?"

She sighed. "Real talk?"

"I don't know what that is."

"The truth."

"Always."

"I thought you were going to fall down and die on me every time I looked at you."

He raised both eyebrows. "Was I really that bad?"

"Worse."

"Damn."

"Yeah."

He leaned down and kissed her on the forehead. "Thank God you were there, then." He smiled again, and in that moment Gaby realized she would never get tired of seeing it. "But then I thank God every day that you came into my life."

"Corny," she said, but couldn't help but smile back up at him anyway.

"Corn on the cob?"

"Maybe on a stick."

"You love my stick."

"I heard that," Zoe said from behind them.

Gaby stifled a giggle. She couldn't remember the last time she had done that, and it should have embarrassed her, but it didn't. Not here, now, with Nate sitting next to her. The fact that they had survived Texas, gotten through the nightmare of Gallant, only made her appreciate having him at her side more.

"We really need our own room," she whispered.

"What I've been saying," Nate said. He gave her a peck on

the cheek, then whispered, "The things I'd do to you when we're finally alone again..."

"And healed up first, right?"

"Sure, if you wanna be all cautious about it."

"I prefer not dying while doing the...you know."

"Oh, I know," he said, and grinned widely, though for some reason his head, followed soon by the rest of his body, started to become a little blurry. He must have seen her reaction, because he frowned. "You okay?"

"Meds are kicking in again..."

He reached down to stroke her hair gently. "Go to sleep. I'll be here when you wake up."

"Promise?"

"Always."

"And no Mohawks."

He let out an overly dramatic sigh. "You never let me have any fun."

She smiled and drifted off...

It was fully dark when she opened her eyes again, but she didn't have a lot of trouble seeing the two figures moving around the room. At first she thought it was Zoe and Nate—maybe he was helping her with something—but no, because the two silhouettes separated and became three, then four, in all.

Gaby recognized Zoe's outline as a bigger, taller shape directed the doc from one side of the room to the other. Gaby's instincts snapped to attention and the words *Ghouls. There are ghouls on the* Trident! flashed across her mind, but it didn't take very long before her eyes adjusted to the semidarkness, and what once looked like a black-eyed ghoul instead turned into a man wearing jeans and a plaid working shirt.

But her alarms didn't stop completely, because the man was holding a handgun in his right fist as he pushed Zoe forward with his other hand, and Gaby woke up to him in mid-sentence saying, "—it'll be over soon. All you have to do is not get in the way."

"Why are you doing this?" Zoe asked.

"We don't have a choice," the man said.

"Need-to-know, Bray, remember?" a voice said.

Gaby turned her head slightly to look at the silhouette that had spoken. He was shorter and thinner than the first, and holding a pistol on a fourth figure—

Nate.

He was standing at the foot of a bed, hands folded behind the back of his head, and he was *looking directly at her.* When he saw that she had seen him, Nate shook his head—just barely. The man with the gun behind him wouldn't have picked it up, and she wouldn't have either, if she hadn't been staring right at him.

No? Why is he telling me no?

She understood as soon as the second man leaned out from behind Nate and zeroed in on her. Gaby closed her eyes and lay perfectly still, and though she didn't do it on purpose (or, at least, she wasn't aware of having done it on purpose), her heartbeat slowed down and she slipped back into a relaxed state, the kind that someone sleeping would be in.

"What's wrong with her?" the second man asked.

"She was shot," Nate said. "She's not going to give you any trouble. Zoe's got her all doped up."

"Is that true?" the man named Bray asked.

"Yes," Zoe said. "She's unconscious. Just leave her alone."

"Check her, just to be sure," Bray said.

"Stay here," the second man said, though Gaby didn't know whom he was talking to. It was probably Nate.

Quick footsteps as someone approached her bed; then the heat of a body leaning over her, along with the strong aroma of fried fish on the man's clothes and breath. A (cold) pair of fingers pressed against the side of her neck, then gripped her chin and turned her head from side to side.

"Well?" the first man said.

"She looks asleep," the second one said.

"Maybe she's faking it."

"I don't think so."

Fingers pried open the lid over her right eye, and Gaby stared back at a man with short blond hair. He looked to be in his late twenties and may or may not have been sporting facial hair; it was difficult to see a lot of details with only the moonlight splashing across different parts of the room for light.

Gaby willed her eye not to blink, or move, or for her pupil to dilate. Was that possible? Could you even force something like that?

The man tapped lightly on one of her cheeks, and she let out a soft, annoyed groan and opened her other eye.

"She's awake," the man said. "But she looks pretty out of it, like the kid said. Shouldn't be any trouble."

"You gotta make sure," Bray said.

"I'm sure."

The man let go of her eyelid, and she let it slide shut and turned her head slightly while continuing to lie still.

"What did you give her?" she heard Bray asking.

"Sedatives for the pain," Zoe said. "I had to take a bullet out of her. She'll sleep through this whole thing and wake up tomorrow thinking it was all just a bad dream."

Gaby didn't know if that was true, but Zoe must have sold it well enough, because Bray said, "Let's keep an eye on her anyway."

"Yeah," the other man said.

Nice work, doc.

"You're making a mistake," Zoe said. "You shouldn't be doing this."

"No, *you* made a mistake when you brought that *thing* onboard," Bray snapped back.

"Thing?" Gaby thought.

Will. They're talking about Will.

How did they know?

"We have to keep this between us," Lara had said when she was here earlier. *"Understand? No one can know about what's down there. Especially Riley's people."*

So how did these two know? They had to be a part of Riley's group, because she didn't recognize either one of them. It didn't help that there were a lot of new faces onboard the *Trident* these days.

"What now?" she heard Nate asking.

"Sit down," the one who wasn't Bray said. There was just enough menace in his voice to let them know he meant business.

"And then what?" Nate asked.

Before someone could answer Nate, a radio squawked and Bray said, "We've secured the infirmary."

"Any trouble?" a voice asked. It was muffled, clearly coming through the radio.

"Nothing we couldn't handle."

"Good. Because if this thing goes south, we're going to need the leverage."

"So we're proceeding?"

"Yeah, we're proceeding," the new voice said.

Proceeding with what?

Gaby resisted the temptation to move or open her eyes, and it took all of her willpower to keep her arms and legs from making any sudden movements that would draw attention. She continued to breathe, because sleeping people did that. She had to be content to listen and use what she heard to sketch out the room to the best of her ability.

Bray and Zoe were to her left at the wall with the windows, while the second man whose name she didn't know remained on the right side with Nate. They had smartly split up the room's two occupants (not counting her) for easier control and had no doubt locked the door as soon as they entered. She expected them to start barricading the door, but maybe they had already done that before she woke up to the sounds of their movements.

"Sit down," Bray said from her left. Then, a few seconds later, *"Please."*

It almost sounded as if he was really asking Zoe, which didn't make any sense. Men with guns, especially ones that had taken hostages, didn't ask—they ordered.

"You're making a terrible mistake," Zoe said.

"You already said that," Bray said. "You should be quiet."

"Things were going well; we would have taken you straight to the Bengal Islands," Zoe pressed on. "You shouldn't have done this."

"You don't even know what we're doing."

"I don't have to. I just know what you've done. Which is come in here with guns and taken me and my patients hostage. That's enough."

"Enough for what?" the second man asked.

"To get you killed," Zoe said.

Someone snickered. It might have been Bray, but she reconsidered when the second man, on her right, said, "We outnumber you almost five to one on the boat. And half of your number are kids and an old lady. I think we'll take our chances."

"This is all your fault anyway," Bray said.

"What is?" Nate asked.

"Bray, need-to-know," the second man said.

But Bray ignored him and said, "That *thing* you brought back onboard with you this afternoon. Did you think we wouldn't find out? Did you really think you could keep it a secret forever?"

There was a brief moment of silence, and she imagined Nate and Zoe trying to come up with a response.

They know about Will. Jesus, how did they know about Will?

"We trusted you," the second one was saying.

"Says the man with the gun," Nate said. "Besides, it's not a threat."

"What the hell are you talking about, it's not a threat?" Bray said. "That's a ghoul down there, kid."

"It's...different," Nate said. He seemed to be struggling with his words. "You don't understand—"

"We understand plenty; you brought one of those things into our midst and you didn't tell us about it," the second man interrupted. "True or not true?"

Silence again.

"That's what I thought," the second man said.

"You can still stop this," Nate said. "No one's been hurt yet. Turn around now and leave the room, and—"

"What, you won't tell anyone?" Bray said, the mocking in his voice clear as day. "Too late for that now, kid."

"Stop calling me that."

"What?"

"Kid," Nate said. "Do I look like I'm a goddamn kid?"

Someone chuckled, before the man who wasn't Bray said, "Bray's forty going on sixty. Everyone's a kid to him."

"You got a name?" Nate asked.

"Ethan," the second man said.

"Like I said, Ethan, this doesn't have to go any further. We can still salvage this. But that option goes out the window when someone fires the first shot—"

Pop-pop!

Two shots, close together, and it came from below deck.

"Too late for that now," Bray said, and Gaby thought there was something that almost sounded like regret in his voice.

"This was the plan, remember?" Ethan said.

"I know..."

"What's happening?" Zoe asked.

"We're doing what you should have done when you found that thing in Texas," Bray said. "After that, we're taking over the boat."

"Over our dead bodies," Nate said.

"Yeah, well, if it comes to that," Ethan said, and like before with Bray, Gaby thought she could hear the regret in Ethan's voice also.

The two shots were followed by silence—maybe it was ten seconds, or thirty, or possibly even a minute (though she didn't think that last part could possibly be true).

But it didn't last, and soon the *pop-pop-pop* of fully automatic rifle fire exploded from below her...before it was joined by gunfire from seemingly all across the boat.

4

LARA

"No wonder you spend all your time in here," Bonnie said as she stepped inside the cabin. "Compared to the zoo out there, this is paradise."

Lara smiled and finished drying her hair with the towel. She couldn't remember the last time she had a moment to herself where she could take a shower and spend more than just a few perfunctory seconds in front of the mirror. "Is that what you came here for? To make me feel guilty about having this penthouse suite?"

"Well, yeah. That, and Riley requested the presence of your company."

"He said it just like that, huh?"

"Just abouts."

"Did he say why?"

"No, but he looked pretty serious."

"He always looks serious," Lara said. She took a moment to breathe in the cool air; it was like stepping out onto the exterior deck at night after the scalding hot shower. "And since when did you start doing Riley's bidding?"

Bonnie shrugged. "Well, he is pretty cute. You could even mistake him for handsome, if you were so inclined."

"There is that."

"And oh, word's getting around. Everyone's talking about it."

Lara gave her an alarmed look. "About what?"

"Mercer. People are talking about the radio message that we intercepted earlier." Bonnie paused and gave her a curious look. "What did you think I was talking about?"

"The chest."

The other woman shook her head. "As far as I know, that's still just a secret between us. Danny, Carly, and everyone else I've talked to has been driving that point home. I think we're safe on that front."

Maybe, she thought, but said, "I'm sure we are."

"Have you gone to see him?"

She nodded.

"Talked to him?" Bonnie asked.

No, because I'm afraid. God help me, I'm afraid.

"I will," she said instead.

"I know it can't be easy for you. I thought he was gone, and then he shows up..." Bonnie gave her a pursed smile. It was probably meant to be reassuring, but didn't quite get there. "Not that I know what it's like for you. None of us really do."

"It's okay, Bonnie."

"I'll be honest with you, kid..."

"Kid?" Lara said, giving her an amused look.

"Well, you are younger than me."

"Not by much."

"Still technically younger."

Even though I feel like sixty going on ninety.

"You were saying?" Lara said.

"I don't know how you do it."

"Do what?"

"Everything." She shook her head. "It's like you were born for this."

Or maybe I'm just a very good liar, she thought, tossing the towel onto the bed and picking up her gun belt and slipping it on.

Bonnie watched her from across the room. Lara could tell the other woman had something else on her mind, but for whatever reason she was reluctant to say it.

"What is it, Bonnie?" Lara asked.

"If Mercer's dead, what does that mean for Keo?" Bonnie said.

The question caught her by surprise, and Lara actually had to take a moment to think about it. The truth was, with everything happening today—Danny and Gaby's return, the chest, *Will*—she hadn't had time to think about anything else. Or anyone else. Not even Keo, who had gone to Black Tide Island to kill Mercer.

You still alive out there, Keo?

If Mercer was dead—or as Riley hypothesized, somehow incapacitated—then someone would have had to put him that way. Keo had the motive and the skills to be the culprit. So what did that mean for him?

She still remembered the last (the last, *last*) conversation they'd had on the *Ocean Star*:

"Don't be an asshole, Keo," she had told him. *"If you won't stay with us, if you won't come back to the* Trident *with me, at least promise me you're not going out there just to get yourself killed. Tell me you'll at least try to make it back, and mean it."*

"What if I can't?" he had answered.

"You can. You just have to make the choice."

"Okay."

"Okay, what?"

"I'll do my best. How's that?"

She had nodded, and said, *"Good enough."*

So had it been *good enough*, after all? Had Keo reached Black

Tide Island with Erin's help and done what he had to? Was he on his way back to them right now?

That last part was a stretch because he wouldn't know their current location. The last time he had seen them was on the oil rig, preparing to leave. But Keo would know not to go there after last night. So where would he go instead? What would he do?

"He hasn't radioed?" Lara asked.

Bonnie shook her head. "Blaine's keeping the emergency channel open, but so far there hasn't been a peep."

"With Keo, you can never tell. How many times have we given up on him only for him to pop up again? That guy has nine lives."

"So how many has he used up so far?"

"I don't know, but let's hope he has a few left to spare."

"Hope springs eternal, is that it?"

"Have faith, Bonnie."

The other woman sighed. "Hey, it's not like I'm married to the guy or anything. We haven't even done the horizontal dance. I'm just worried about him, that's all."

"We both are. But Keo can take care of himself." She picked up her Glock from the nightstand and slid it into the holster. "I need volunteers to relieve Benny and Carrie in a few hours."

"Gwen and Jo have already offered. Though from everything I've heard, we could have everyone down there and it still wouldn't do any good. I've never actually seen them in person—one of those blue-eyed types—but I was talking to Nate and..." She actually shivered. "I don't think I want to, after hearing what they can do."

"I know," Lara said, heading for the door. "But the guards aren't down there to keep him inside the cabin. They're there to keep people *out*."

They found Riley back on the bridge with Blaine and Hart. Besides her cabin and Zoe's infirmary, the bridge was the only other place on the yacht that wasn't constantly filled with people, the din of which faded as soon as Bonnie closed the door after them.

It was already dark on the other side of the wraparound windshield, and the bright floodlights around the boat were the only thing visible for miles around. She might have been slightly alarmed at how lit up they were (*Like a Christmas tree, right, Will?*) if not for the fact that the vessel was still moving. Their speed, just as it had been since they left the *Ocean Star*, was hampered by the refueling ship following closely behind them.

"You wanted to talk to me?" Lara said as Riley and Hart glanced over.

Riley nodded. "We just came from a meeting with our people. We had a long talk about what to do next."

"That was fast."

"I didn't think we had time to waste. We'll be at the Bengal Islands soon if we keep on this course."

"Okay," Lara said, and waited for him to continue.

Riley and Hart exchanged a look. She tried to read their faces, but came up with very little, except that they both seemed uncertain.

"Guys," Lara said, "you called me up here. Let's get on with it."

"We're leaning toward going back," Riley said.

"Going back where?"

"Black Tide."

Bonnie laughed. "You want to go *back?* You're crazy."

"Not with Mercer out of the equation," Riley said.

"You don't even know what really happened to him, or *if* anything happened at all," Lara said.

"Rhett wouldn't have given the stand-down order if everything was status quo."

"But you don't know that for sure, Riley. This is all just conjecture."

"That's where you're wrong. I've been with him long enough —almost since the beginning—to know how he works. And I'm telling you, the kind of order Rhett gave this morning is something Mercer would never have allowed. Or if there was a reason behind it, Mercer would have given it himself. The fact that he didn't speaks volumes."

"You *hope*," Bonnie said.

"I *know*," Riley insisted.

Just like you knew Andy was "all-in" with your mutiny? Lara wanted to ask him, but she refrained for the simple reason she didn't feel like arguing the point. It was done, in the past, and bringing it up again wouldn't have helped either one of them.

Besides, she wished she could force herself to care about what happened to Riley and his people once they left the *Trident*, but she couldn't. She had other things on her mind right now, and the fate of Riley's group was not at the top of her list of priorities.

Lara looked over at Hart. "You've been quiet."

Hart shrugged, but didn't say anything right away. He might have been the oldest man on the bridge at the moment, but he looked reinvigorated since the *Ocean Star*. She could almost believe he was in his late thirties, if not for those streaks of gray.

"No opinions?" Lara asked.

"I got lots of opinions," Hart said.

"So spill it."

"The honest truth is, I don't know. But if there's a chance Mercer could be gone, and Rhett or someone else is now in charge..." He shook his head. "Maybe this is our only chance to go home. It's not about the island but the people on it. We left a lot of good friends behind. We didn't agree with them on the war, about Mercer's plans, but they're one of the reasons we ran instead of fighting."

"You didn't want to have to kill your friends."

Hart nodded. "If we couldn't avoid that, I'm not sure how many people Riley could have gotten to sign up for this. I know I wouldn't have."

"But people are already dead, Hart," Lara said. "Did you forget about Andy? What about the group that came through the *Ocean Star* with Erin?"

"And I wish none of those things had happened," Riley said. "But that's the past."

"So what's the future?"

"I don't know yet. I guess it'll depend on what's waiting for us at Black Tide." He sighed, the decision clearly weighing heavily on his mind. "I told my people about what's happened, what we think's happening right now. But I'm not going to force them to do anything they don't want to. If the majority of them want to stay on course to the Bengal Islands, then that's what we'll do. I'm not Mercer. I'm not going to strong-arm people into doing something they don't want to. I'll lay out everything we know—everything we *think* we know—and let them make their own choices."

"What if the majority wants to head back, but a few wants to stick to the original plan?"

"Then I'll have to do some begging to get the captain of this boat to let them stay on and help them get to where they want to go."

"No promises. The deal was to take you all there, not to take one group to Destination A and the rest to Destination B."

"I understand."

"Wow, democracy on the high seas," Bonnie said. "Who would have thunk it?"

"Can I have it?" Riley asked. "Can I get more time?"

"How long is it going to take?"

"A day. Maybe two. This is a big decision. Almost as big as when we decided to mutiny."

"Two days at the most," Hart added.

Instead of answering them, Lara turned to Blaine. "Shut her down. There's no point wasting fuel until they've made up their minds."

"Thank you," Riley said.

"One day," Lara said, looking back at him. "I'll give you one day to decide what you want to do, but that's it. Make your decision, and this time, stick to it."

The *Trident* was about half the length of a football field—not that Lara ever sat down to measure every inch of it or dug out the manual and looked over the specs. The yacht had seemed endless in the beginning, but that distance shrunk as she familiarized herself with its nooks and crannies. Now with Riley's people onboard the boat felt endless again, mostly because she couldn't go a couple of steps without almost walking into someone, or had to go around a throng of civilians blocking the narrow hallways.

She thought about detouring to Carly's room to fill Danny in on what had transpired on the bridge, but decided to keep going to her cabin instead. Her friends needed time alone after all those days apart, and she didn't want to ruin that reunion. They would have done the same for her if Will had come back.

But Will did *come back, remember?*

Except it wasn't Will. Not really.

Or, at least, not anymore.

So what was he then? Something else? Yes. Exactly.

Some*thing* else.

The realization that Will had been out there all this time left an even bigger hole in the pit of her stomach than when she thought he was dead. Will coming back changed was the most terrible thing that could have happened to her, something she couldn't have imagined in her wildest nightmares.

But here it was. Here *he* was. Down there, waiting for her, maybe wondering why she hadn't done more than just enter the cabin and looked at the chest before fleeing. And that was exactly what she had done.

She had fled. Ran away from him. *From him.*

You fucking coward.

You fucking, selfish coward. He deserves better than this.

Her door was never locked, and except for a *Captain's Cabin* plaque (though the *Captain* had been scratched out and *Lara* scribbled over it), there was nothing to keep anyone—not even those two kids she had just walked past—from going inside. The fact that no one had yet was a minor miracle—

Something was wrong.

She couldn't explain it, but she knew there was something different about the room as soon as she stepped inside and let the door *click* back into place behind her. It was pitch dark, with only a small pool of moonlight spilling in from the window on the far wall.

A second after she sensed it, she smelled it—sweat that didn't come from her own skin, but from someone hiding in the shadows.

Someone's in the room.

God, she hoped it was someone, because the only other option was some*thing* being in the room with her right now—

She reached for her gun, got her fingers around the grip, and was lifting it out of the holster when the barrel of a weapon pressed against her right temple. The cold contact of the metal against her skin sent a sliver of electricity through her body.

"Don't," a voice said, the sound freezing her hand—and the gun—in place.

A strangely warm (and large) hand grabbed her right wrist and yanked away the Glock. The cold of the gun barrel abandoned her temple as a tall figure shuffled in the shadows and there was a *clack!* from behind her as the door's lock was twisted into place, followed by more movements as her cabin's intruder traveled the short distance from her side to stand in front of her.

Despite the semidarkness, she recognized the face looking back at her. She had first seen it on the *Ocean Star*.

"Phil," she said, "what are you doing?"

He had some kind of submachine gun pointed at her face. She wished she could have said his hand and the weapon in it were shaking, but they were as calm as could be. With his other hand, he shoved her Glock into his front waistband before taking a step back and then, and only then, letting his weapon lower —slightly.

"Sit down, Lara," he said.

"Phil—"

"*Sit down,*" he said through clenched teeth.

She walked over and sat down on the side of her bed and watched Phil walk to the door and lean against the wall next to it. Now that her eyes had adjusted somewhat to the darkness, she could just make out the MP5K with the pistol grip hanging almost nonchalantly at his side. Besides her Glock stuffed into his front waistband, he had only come here with just the submachine gun as far as she could tell.

"Just the submachine gun?" That's more than enough.

"What's this about?" she asked.

He didn't answer her, and instead unclipped a radio from his hip and held it in his left hand, while the right continued to clutch his weapon. A sudden spurt of footsteps from the hallway made him turn his head, but he quickly relaxed and resumed his stance when the noise faded.

"Phil," she said. "What are you doing here?"

He didn't respond or even look back at her. Had he even heard her?

"Phil," she said again, louder this time.

"What?" he said, sounding agitated.

You're the one with a gun hiding in my room, asshole, she wanted to snap back, but said instead, "What are you doing?"

He finally trained his eyes on her, and even without any real light in the room, she could make out the penetrating stare he had pointed back at her. "You know why."

"I don't."

"The creature. The *ghoul.*"

Oh, goddammit. He knows. He knows.

"I don't understand," she said anyway. "What ghoul?"

He smirked. "You can stop pretending. We know all about it. The creature you have locked away in a chest down in the engine room." He sneaked a peek at the glowing neon hands of his wristwatch. "But don't worry, Lara, we're going to take care of it for you."

"What do you mean, 'take care of it?'"

He didn't say anything.

"Phil..."

"You shouldn't have brought it onboard," he said. "You should have known better. Riley might have made that mistake, but not you. You should have *known* better."

I didn't bring him onboard. Danny did. He didn't tell me what was in the chest until after it was already in Gage's old room.

Of course, she didn't tell Phil any of that. She didn't think it was going to matter anyway. The man with the gun glaring at her from across the darkened room right now didn't care about the truth. He had come here to do a job, and he was doing it.

But if Phil's job was in here with her, then what was happening outside? Because she didn't believe for a second this was a one-man job. And she had absolutely heard him say, *"But don't worry, Lara, we're going to take care of it for you."*

"We." He said *"we."*

"Was this Riley's plan all along?" she asked. "Trick me into bringing you onboard with some sob story about wanting to leave Mercer's war, then take over the boat when we let our guards down?"

Phil might have chuckled. If he did, it was very quiet and short. "Riley has nothing to do with it. He's a good man, but he was never really meant for leadership. I could think of twenty people off the top of my head who are more qualified. Still, he got us out of Mercer's insanity, so we owe him that much."

Your mutineers are mutinying again, Riley. Why am I not surprised?

"What are you going to do, Phil?" she asked.

He might have answered her, but before he could the radio in his left hand squawked and a voice she didn't recognize said, "We've secured the infirmary."

Phil lifted the two-way to his lips and keyed it. "Any trouble?"

"Nothing we couldn't handle," the voice on the radio said.

"Good. Because if this thing goes south, we're going to need the leverage."

"So we're proceeding?"

"Yeah, we're proceeding," Phil said. He let go of the transmit lever for a second, seemed to take a breath, and then pressed it again. "You heard all that?"

"Yeah," a new voice said through the radio. It sounded...hesitant?

"Do it."

"Wish us luck."

"Good luck," Phil said.

He lowered the radio and stared forward. She followed his

gaze, trying to see what he was looking at, but there was just the wall next to the window and nothing else except the ocean on the other side.

"Phil," she said, "you're making a mistake."

"I'm fixing your mistake, Lara," he said.

"It wasn't a mistake. There's a reason it's onboard."

"There's no reason in this universe that justifies bringing one of those things here. Jesus Christ, we have kids on this boat."

"There is a reason. If you'll let me explain—"

"I don't want to hear it."

"Phil..."

"I said *shut up.*"

She sighed, and was thinking about the spare Glock she had stashed in the room—and more importantly, about how to get to it —when Phil's form shifted alarmingly and she saw the MP5K moving at his side.

"Don't," he said.

"Don't what?"

Phil came out of the shadows and pointed the submachine gun at her. "Don't test me. I know you're thinking about doing that right now. I like you, Lara. I respect you. Hell, maybe even more than Riley. But I'll shoot you if I have to. So don't test me."

She stared back at him, feeling the annoyance growing. And it was that, and not fear. She didn't know why she wasn't more afraid; maybe it was the fact someone was in her cabin—her own private space, the only place she could count on to have all to herself these days—with a gun in her face.

"Hands," he said.

She hadn't been aware of it, but her hands were pressed against the mattress behind her. She brought them out and put them in her lap.

"Good," he said, and lowered the weapon and took one, then

two, steps back into the shadowy parts of the room. "I know it doesn't look like it right now, but we're still on the same side. At the end of the day, we both want the same thing—to stay alive. Our chances are better with that thing down in the engine room dealt with."

That "thing" used to be the man I love, asshole, she wanted to spit back at him, but said instead, "You said Riley doesn't know about this."

"No. We couldn't risk him not going along with it."

"So who's the ringleader?"

"You're looking at him." Phil shrugged. "I guess you could say I'm taking a page out of Riley's playbook. I only recruited the guys I knew I could trust, who wouldn't like the idea of a ghoul on the same boat as them, either. We're going to take it too, by the way. The *Trident*."

"And you think I'm just going to let you have it?"

"You won't have a choice." He tightened his fingers reflexively around the MP5K's grip. "I didn't want to do this, you know, but you left me no choice. That thing down there is an abomination. It needs to be killed. They all do."

"Talk like that makes me wonder if you don't belong with Mercer after all."

"Maybe, but the difference between me and him? I don't kill civilians. At least, not on purpose. I would never do that. Why do you think I'm here? We're going to use you and the doc as leverage. I'll get Riley to come around, and when he does, we'll go to the Bengal Islands just like we planned. No more of this going back to Black Tide bullshit."

"Just like that?"

"Just like that."

Over my dead body, she was going to say, but she had a feeling she already knew what his response to that would be.

Instead, she kept quiet when there was another squawk. Phil

tensed, because it hadn't come from his radio, but from the one still clipped to her hip:

"Lara, this is Carrie. Come in."

She didn't get the chance to answer it, because there were two distant *pop-pop* from below them. They were little more than faded echoes, the noise greatly affected by the decks of the yacht, and she might not have even heard them at all if the *Trident* wasn't currently drifting on the ocean.

"It's started," Phil said. "It'll be over soon—"

There was a loud *boom!* from outside the cabin just before a big chunk of the wooden door showered the room, leaving behind a gaping hole where the doorknob (*and lock!*) once were. Bright lights splashed through the hole and over a section of the floor—

Phil was turning toward the door, raising his gun hand, when Lara took advantage of the distraction and let herself fall backward onto the bed. Even as she fell, she stuck out her right hand toward the pillows and reached underneath one of them.

She had no delusions Phil wouldn't know what she was doing as soon as she did it. They were just too close for her to hope she could get away with it for more than a few seconds—two if she was really, really lucky. And she almost got those two seconds before Phil abandoned the door and turned back toward her.

There was a flurry of movement from the corner of her right eye as the door flung open, allowing even more light to wash across the previously darkened captain's cabin. She ignored it—or tried to as best she could—and focused on swinging her right hand forward and up, revealing the gun in it, even as her forefinger struggled to find the trigger.

Phil's eyes went wide just before she shot him in the chest. He seemed to stumble for a second and had just enough strength left to squeeze the trigger, sending maybe a dozen rounds into the ceiling before collapsing. Because she was still mostly lying on the bed on her back, he disappeared out of her view at about the same time a figure burst into the room, the sound of a shotgun racking like an explosion in the suddenly bright cabin.

Danny appeared in front of her like a wraith, sweeping the room with his weapon before locating Phil's body on the floor. He looked up at her, a slight grin forming on his lips, and he was probably about to say something stupid when a torrent of gunfire filled the *Trident*.

Unlike the first two earlier shots, these kept going for some time.

"Will!" Lara shouted, even as she scrambled up from the bed. "They're going after Will!"

5

WILL

The hasps snapped first, then the clamps along the edges, followed by the strips of duct tape that covered up nearly every inch of the chest's exterior. The lid flung open with ease, and it hadn't fully raised ninety degrees before he was up and out, the cold air inside the room brushing against his skin and through the still-exposed wounds.

There were two of them. Men. Their rifles sending stabs of flame in his direction. They reacted instantly to his presence, eyes widening at the sight of him emerging.

What did they think was inside the chest, he wanted to ask them. Didn't they already know it was him? Wasn't that why they had come here prepared, their weapons loaded with silver bullets?

One of those rounds punched through his chest and out his back, hitting the wall behind him with an echoing *ping!* Other bullets missed their mark, and if they knew to aim for his head (all his strength and speed, and all it would take was one bullet in the right spot to end him, end his mission) they didn't show it in the way they swung their weapons left and right, trying desperately to draw a bead on his moving form.

The room was small and the limited space made it easier (not that he really needed the advantage) to reach his targets. One of them screamed something incoherent as he scrambled to reload, reaching behind his back for a spare magazine. He smashed into the man feet first and drove him to the floor. A slight grunt of shock as the man went down, his spine snapping on impact.

The second one dropped his rifle and stumbled back, reaching for a handgun in a hip holster. The pistol was halfway out of its housing when he twisted and snatched the man by the throat, then threw him across the room. His would-be assassin sailed over the opened lid and crashed into the wall, followed quickly by the loud *cracks!* of bones, and disappeared behind the chest.

He set his feet to both sides of the unmoving figure below him and went into a slight crouch. There was no point in attacking a second time. His victim wasn't going to fight back. He couldn't, even if he wanted to.

A flicker of movement—sudden scurrying—drew his attention, and he looked up and out through the open door and into the hallway.

The boy whose voice he had heard (*"Benny,"* one of the would-be killers had called him) was sliding across the floor in the narrow passageway outside, one hand holding to a bloody red patch in his side. He was having difficulty breathing as he moved, blood oozing out between his fingers. His face was covered in a film of sweat and he grunted the entire way, until finally making it to the other side and leaning against the wall to keep himself from toppling over.

Then the boy looked up and their eyes met, and Benny might have screamed if he had the strength. Or, if he could, get up and run away. But the boy did neither of those things, either because he couldn't or he was too terrified to try.

He didn't so much as see Benny as he *smelled* and *heard* the blood dripping from the wound in his side. The wetness was fresh and thick and sweet, and it had been so long since he had allowed himself to taste the glory. There was such a difference between the life force that flowed through humans and those that came out of animals. He knew, without a doubt, that he would heal faster with a fresh supply.

No. Not again.

You promised. Never again.

He pried his eyes off the boy and returned it to the man on the floor. His would-be killer blinked back up at him, pale lips quivering as if he wanted to say something but couldn't find the words. The man moved his head slightly from left to right, but that would be the full extent of his movements, now and forever.

A mechanical squawk from the hallway, before a voice that was all too familiar filled the air: "Benny, Carrie! Come in! Are you guys there? Come in!"

The boy reached for the radio on the floor, the slight movement helping the blood to *drip-drip-drip* farther out of his wound.

No. Look away.

Look away!

"This is Benny," the boy said into the radio.

"Benny, thank God!" Lara. She was out of breath, her voice shaky from running, but somehow still in control. "We're on our way down there now! What happened? Are you okay?"

"I've been shot, and I think Carrie's... I think she's dead, Lara."

"We're almost there! Hold on just a little longer!"

He stood up, and the boy's eyes widened in response before his hand scrambled to his empty holster.

"Oh God," the boy whispered breathlessly.

No, not God.

He took one step, then two—the boy flinching with each one —and grabbed the door and swung it shut. Relief flooded Benny's face for the split second he was visible, just before the door closed on him.

He turned around.

You promised you wouldn't do it again.

Don't break your promise. Not here. Not now!

His nostrils flared at the smell of fresh blood. How long had it been? So long. He couldn't even remember.

Lara's coming. She's going to see!

But he was still so weak despite the last twenty-four hours of healing. Could he afford to stay this way if more came for him?

You have a choice.

And there was so much still left to do. So, so much...

You said you wouldn't do it again!

He focused on the precious liquid pulsing through the paralyzed man's veins, from his arms and legs and neck.

Not here! Not now!

And behind the chest was the other one. Not quite dead, but he might as well be. Both of them. They were useless now... except to him. Except to the greater cause.

Keep your promise!

He needed it. To heal faster. To grow stronger. He needed it in the worst way.

He crouched over the man with the broken spine. The eyes— dark brown, like his own once upon a time—continued to stare up at him, and bloodied lips quivered and sounds that might have been attempts at begging came out as gibberish instead.

She'll know what you've done. She'll know.

He wished he could have said it was horrifying and the mere thought of committing the act turned his stomach, but it would have been a lie. He bathed in the man's plasma and could feel the cells in his body reacting, mobilizing, coming even further alive to tackle his remaining wounds and mend him from the inside out.

You lied.

He made a mess, but he didn't care.

You made a promise, and you lied.

When he finished with the first one, he got up and walked around the chest and started on the second.

So what else is new?

"Will."

No, not Will. He hadn't been that for a long time now.

It seemed like years ago—decades—since the last time he saw the true color of her eyes. He longed to reach out and run his fingers along the supple curves of her skin and wallow in the taste of her lips. Those lips were pale and dry tonight, as they had been for the last few weeks and months since...

I died. Ever since I died.

She looked into the room, the light from the open door behind her washing across portions of the cabin while leaving the rest shrouded in darkness. He had left the body of the first man where it lay, in front and slightly to the left of her. There was a slight shift in the air as she looked down at the dead man, accompanied by her slightly accelerating heartbeat. He could almost taste the wetness of her saliva as she forced them down her throat and did her best to orient herself to the horrors of what he had done, what he had been doing for the last—

How long had it been since the men came into the room to kill him?

Seconds? Minutes? Maybe hours.

It was always difficult to tell time when he fed, and it had been such a long time that he might have lost himself in the act.

Exhilaration overwhelmed him, and he was as alive now (*Ha!*) as he had ever been since the transformation. The bones were healing, the skin reforming, and every inch of him bristled with new flesh.

He stayed in the shadowed back part of the room, with his second would-be killer lying nearby, the man's blood forming a jagged circle at his feet. If he wasn't already bloated from his feeding, he would have lapped up the precious fluids no matter how uncivilized it might have looked. What did civilization have to do with it anyway? He was no longer human. It didn't matter how much he held on, because he could never go back. He could never have her back.

Never...

"Will," she said again, his name (*No, not your name now, your name* then) almost painful as she forced it between her lips.

Her legs were unsteady and her arms were tense at her sides. There was blood on her clothes, but it wasn't hers.

"It's you," she said. "It's really you, isn't it?"

"No," he said. Or hissed. He hated the sound that came out, reminding him of the abomination he had become and how far he had drifted from himself, from her.

They were alone down here, in the lower bowels of the boat. She had sent the others away with the body of the woman and the wounded boy. (*Benny. His name's Benny.*) She had the radio on her hip, but he'd heard the *click* as she turned it off.

It was just the two of them now. Here, in this room, with two bodies between them and blood everywhere.

God, he really did make a mess.

"No?" she said.

"Not Will," he hissed. "Not anymore."

"What should I call you, then?"

He didn't answer.

"*What should I call you, then?*" It was a good question. He had been asking himself that ever since Kate transformed him outside that nothing gas station in Louisiana.

He remembered a little girl in a rotting barn back in Texas asking him the exact same question: *"What are you, mister?"*

I don't know, he had thought then, and he thought it again now: *I don't know.*

When he didn't answer, Lara said, "I have to call you something."

"Frank," he said.

"Frank," she repeated. Then something that looked like recognition sparkled in her eyes. "Frank," she said again.

She tried to peer into the shadows, to get a better look at him. It would have been difficult without light, and he imagined her fighting the urge to reach back and hit the light switch. But even if she couldn't really see him, she would have no trouble seeing the blue of his eyes. Their glow were beacons in the darkness, at once bright and unnatural.

"Keo," she said. "He once told me he had someone he wanted me to meet. Someone who knew how to defeat the ghouls." She paused, then, "That was you."

"Yes..."

"But you left him before we could meet."

"I had no choice."

"Why?"

"Danny and Gaby were in trouble."

She seemed to think about it. "When they were trapped in Starch?"

"Before..."

"Larkin. In the airport."

"Yes."

"Mercer."

"Yes..."

Her shoulders drooped slightly, releasing some of the tension she had come into the room with and held onto until now.

"Can I turn on the light?" she asked.

"No," he said.

"Why not?"

"Not yet..."

"I know what you look like."

"You don't...know."

"Don't I?"

Why did she want him to explain it? Didn't she understand why he didn't want her to see him like this? This...*monster?*

"Not yet," he said.

"But soon."

Maybe, he thought, but said, "Yes."

"You fed on them."

She was staring at the feet of the dead man sticking out from behind the bullet-riddled chest. Splintered pieces of the furniture were scattered in and out of the shadows, sprinkled among the puddles of blood.

"I had to," he said.

"Because they tried to kill you..."

"No."

"No?"

"I was too badly injured. The injuries weren't healing fast enough."

"And feeding on them...helped?"

"Yes."

"They were Riley's people," she said, and glanced back at the open door as if afraid of being overheard. "I don't know how they knew about you, but they came down here to kill you. There was another one in my room. I had to kill him." A look of sorrow, there and gone in a flash, replaced by steely determination. "They killed one of us. Carrie." She returned her gaze to him. "But you never met her, did you? She came to the island while you were gone."

"No," he said. *Hissed.* He hated the sound.

"What about Benny? Do you remember him?"

Maybe. He knew the name, because one of the assassins had said it. He dug into his memory reservoirs, but he couldn't find the boy in there.

"No," he said.

"Danny told me you have trouble remembering them. Names and places. But you remember the important things. Like him, and Gaby...and me."

I'll always remember you.

"Yes," he said.

Emotions flickered across her face. Happiness, sadness, and resignation. Back and forth they went, reminding him again that he should have been there for her during all those hard days and dark nights. She had been alone because he had failed to come back to her like he had promised.

He saw all of that in her eyes now as she stood before him, unsure whether to turn and run out the door or stay.

"I'm sorry," he said quietly.

"For what?"

For everything.

"For feeding on them," he said.

"You said you needed it."

And it's been so long...

"Yes," he said.

She stood taller, her growing resoluteness manifested in the visible strength along the lines around her eyes and mouth, in her steady stance. This wasn't the Lara he remembered. She wasn't the same woman he had left behind and failed. That Lara was younger and less decisive.

We've both changed so much.

Her, for the better.

And me...

He didn't know. Even now, after all these days and weeks and months, he still didn't know the answer.

"What are you, mister?" the child had asked him.

"You took a risk coming here," Lara said.

"I had to," he said.

"Because you had something to tell us."

Because I needed to see you.

"Yes," he said.

"You know what's out there. Keo said you had information. Not just about the ghouls, but about the ones pulling the strings. The blue eyes. You're one of them...but not. You know their secrets. That's why they tried to ambush you in Gallant."

"Yes..."

"You think we can win this war. Turn everything around and end this nightmare, finally."

"Yes..."

"How?"

"You stopped the boat."

She gave him a puzzled look, caught off guard by his change of topic. Then, nodding, "I did."

"Why?"

"Riley's people—before all of this—were considering going back to Black Tide Island. They think he's dead. Mercer. You know about that?"

"Yes," he hissed. "Danny told me."

And he had heard the conversations across the boat. The hushed whispers in secret and the rising voices in the open. They were all full of uncertainty and exhilaration and hope.

"He may or may not be dead," Lara said. She watched his face intently, though he wondered how much she could really see without coming closer. "Some of them want to go back to find out for sure."

"Let them."

"Go back?"

"Yes."

"Why?"

"You'll need them."

"Who?"

"Mercer's army. We can use them."

"Were they always part of the plan?"

"No. But the plan's changed."

A flash of amusement. "Backup plans for your backup plans. That's what Danny said."

Not quite, but close. It was more like adapt or perish.

Who had said that? He still couldn't remember.

"So what do we need Mercer's army for?" Lara asked.

She moved closer, kicking at a couple of bullet casings on the floor. She stopped briefly, as if coming to her senses—but then started forward again.

She's so much stronger than before. So, so much stronger.

He wanted badly to reach out and brush his fingers against her cheeks, to taste her lips. But he resisted and didn't move, and let her come to him—into the shadows where he resided. He could sense the fear slipping from her little by little.

"Tell me," she said, and leaned forward into the shadows.

"It won't be easy, and people will die."

"A lot of people have already died."

"More will die."

Maybe some friends...

She nodded. "You risked a lot to reach me. And here I am. So tell me everything."

"There's a way to reverse the infection."

"How?"

"Mabry is the key."

"I thought he was just another blue-eyed ghoul."

"He's more than that. He's always been more than that. He's the beginning..."

"The beginning of what?"

"The beginning of everything."

"I don't understand..."

"It won't be easy..."

She smiled. "And when have things being hard ever stopped us before?"

6

LARA

Her hands were still shaking ten minutes after she stepped outside the cabin. She leaned against the wall next to where Carrie and Benny had lain after being shot. She willed her breathing to slow down, afraid someone might hear and realize she was just as scared and wholly unprepared for all of this as they were. Without the engine running or any movement at all above and around her, the yacht was ghostly quiet, leaving just her slightly labored heartbeat to fill in the noise.

She found herself staring at the blood on the floor and a bullet casing frozen in the congealed liquid. There was a lot of blood, most of that coming from a bullet that had severed Carrie's femoral artery. If she had any desire at all to give the shooters the benefit of the doubt (maybe they never meant to kill her), she didn't anymore. The two men had come down here to kill Will, and they had been willing to do anything—and did—to get that done.

One gone and one down. How many more before tonight's over?

She looked up at the closed door.

He was in there. Will.

No, not Will. Not anymore. He hadn't been her Will for a while now. If only she hadn't let him leave with Gaby and Jen in that helicopter...

I shouldn't have let him go. Why did I let him go?

Because she had no choice, that's why. She wasn't the woman she was now. She could have no more stopped him from leaving than she could tell Danny not to bring Will (*Not Will, not anymore*) onboard even if he had told her what was in the chest before he actually showed up.

Even now, a part of her wondered if it wouldn't have been better if he had stayed dead. For him, for them, for *her*. It was selfish, and she hated herself for even thinking it, but it had always been at the back of her mind. It came to the forefront now, stronger than any other emotion, followed quickly by guilt.

But there was no denying it: His presence on the *Trident* had complicated things, and not just with Riley's people. It had turned her world upside down and made her start to doubt herself again. Without Will, she had been forced to act, to make decisions for everyone, and follow through on them.

He had never left the shadowed corner while she was inside the cabin, the blue of his eyes like twin crystals looking out of the darkness at her. But she hadn't been afraid—not really—and maybe that was because she knew it was him in there.

Except it wasn't him. Not really.

Her hands were still trembling, though it had lessened noticeably as she unclipped the radio and brought it to her lips. "Danny..."

"Boss lady," Danny answered through the two-way.

"What's the situation?"

"They're still inside and we're still outside. Other than that? Everything's peachy."

"Riley?"

"He's here with me right now, trying to talk his wayward sheep off the cliff. I told him he should have just prodded them with his shepherd's stick. What do you call those things?"

"So it's not working?"

"Not so much." Danny paused, then, "How did things go on your end?"

"Where are you right now?"

"I got the earbuds on. It's just the *dos* of us."

"You were right," Lara said. "It's him. It's Will. Or it used to be him. You know what I mean."

"Yeah, I know. It'll take time to wrap your head around the whole thing. It did with me, but then I've always had a bigger-than-average size head."

She pursed a smile at the empty hallway. If anyone knew what she was going through, it would be Danny.

"Did Bonnie find out what happened?" she asked. "How they knew about him?"

"It was Annie," Danny said. "Apparently she spilled the beans to Phil, and he decided to make himself judge, jury, and dickhead. Convinced the other four to go along with it."

Annie. She had come to them with Gaby and Nate back when they still had Song Island. She'd become a valuable member of the group, spending most of her time helping Sarah in the galley and Carly with the kids. Unlike Bonnie and the others, who had taken to their weapons training with enthusiasm, Annie had always done so reluctantly, and even then only because Lara insisted everyone learn how to handle a firearm.

"How did Bonnie find out it was her?" Lara asked.

"She didn't," Danny said. "Annie confessed."

"Why?"

"You'll have to ask her yourself. Let me know if you need a hand with the enhanced interrogation techniques."

"What about Riley? Do you think he knew?"

"Didn't you tell me Phil said he didn't?"

"He did..."

"But you don't believe him?"

"I just want to be sure."

"I don't think he knew," Danny said. "You should have seen the look on his face when I told him. You would have thought I'd kicked his cat and tossed his nana out the window, then tried to light his double-wide on fire."

"Was this Riley's plan all along?" she had said to Phil. *"Trick me into bringing you onboard with some sob story about wanting to leave Mercer's war, then take over the boat when we let our guards down?"*

"Riley has nothing to do with this," Phil had said. *"Riley's a good man, but he was never really meant for leadership."*

First Andy on the *Ocean Star,* then that hiccup with Lang and Ezekiel, and now Phil and the others.

Jesus, Riley. How many other bad choices did you make that's going to come back and haunt me?

"All right," Lara said into the radio. "I'm coming to you."

"I await with bated breath," Danny said.

She put the radio away and gave the cabin door one last look. She wondered if he could hear her in there, through the door and walls. Besides their unnatural (*So what's natural about any of this?*) speed and strength, the blue eyes also had heightened hearing, according to Danny and Gaby.

Because that's what he is now. He's a blue-eyed ghoul.

But that wasn't entirely true, either. He was, but he also wasn't.

So where did that leave him?

She didn't know, and she suspected he didn't, either. They were in uncharted territory, that much was clear. There was nothing normal about this. Even in a post-Purge world, this was something...else.

She headed back up the corridor. She passed the machinery, went up the stairs, and pushed through the door onto the lower deck, where Gwen and Jo were waiting with M4 rifles on the other side. The two women were alert, their bodies tensing as she emerged from the hatch.

"No one goes down there," she told them.

They both nodded and gripped their weapons tighter. She didn't have to tell them to stay alert, because they already knew about Carrie and Benny. But especially about what had happened to Carrie.

One gone and one down. How many more before tonight's over?

"Why did you do it?" Lara asked.

"You don't know?" Annie said, as if the answer was so obvious she couldn't comprehend why Lara didn't already know.

"Tell me."

"Because it's dangerous. You shouldn't have let Danny bring it onboard. It's *dangerous*, Lara."

She stood across the room from Annie, who sat on one of the small cots they had put into the crew cabin. Three people shared the room—Annie, Lorelei...and Carrie. If the irony of being locked in here with Carrie's personal belongings—her clothes, keepsakes, even her weapons—did anything to Annie, the woman didn't show it. Not that Annie was a stone in front of her. Lara could see something that might have been sorrow in Annie's eyes, but how much of that was real and how much an act?

There was nothing separating them but empty space, not that Lara was afraid Annie would do something stupid, like try to lunge for her holstered sidearm. The woman sat with her hands in her lap and stared back at her, and hadn't tried to avoid Lara's eyes when she stepped inside the room.

"You know that, right?" Annie said now, when Lara didn't respond. "You shouldn't have brought it onboard, Lara. It's too dangerous to have around us, the kids..."

"It wasn't dangerous to anyone...until it had to be."

"You don't understand. I've been out there, Lara. I know what those things can do. I've *seen* what those things can do."

Lara knew all about Annie's past, about what had happened at the farmhouse in Louisiana. That was also the first time Gaby had come face-to-face with the blue-eyed ghouls. Everyone had survived the encounter...except for Lance, Annie's boyfriend.

"So this is revenge?" Lara asked.

"Revenge? Why would you think that?"

"Because of what they did to Lance."

"No. This isn't revenge, Lara. I'm trying to protect us. I'm doing exactly what you would have done if that thing down there didn't use to be Will."

Lara sighed. She didn't know what she was doing here in the first place. There was nothing Annie could tell her that would help resolve what was happening above them at this very moment. She could hear it in the other woman's voice—Annie believed everything she was saying, even if the outcome of her actions hadn't been what she wanted.

"You still shouldn't have done it," Lara said.

"I had no choice."

"You could have come to me."

"And would you have listened?"

"Yes."

"Maybe, but you still wouldn't have acted any differently, would you?"

Lara didn't answer right away.

"Of course not," Annie said. "That's why you didn't give me any choice."

"We always have choices, Annie. You just chose the wrong one."

"I didn't..." She shook her head. "I did what I had to do to get rid of that monster."

Will. His name is Will. Whatever he's become, he's still Will. ...mostly.

"All right," Lara said, and turned to go.

"Carrie..."

Lara, with one hand on the door lever, turned back. "What about her?"

"I'm sorry about what happened. They told me they wouldn't hurt anyone. They were just going to go down there and kill it."

"What about Zoe and the infirmary?"

"They didn't tell me anything about that."

"Would it have made a difference if they had?"

Annie opened her mouth to answer, but no sounds ever came out.

"Right," Lara said, and opened the door and stepped outside.

Bonnie was waiting for her in the narrow passageway, and the other woman padlocked the door as soon as Lara stepped out. "Talk about a waste of a whole room."

"We'll move her when everything's calmed down," Lara said.

Bonnie pocketed the key as they headed up the hallway. Without constantly bumping into someone from Riley's party, they could walk side by side without a problem, a luxury Lara didn't think she would ever get back.

"Where is everyone?" Lara asked.

"Riley ordered his people into their cabins, and the rest are securing themselves in the lower deck. The doors are locked and I have Lorelei walking around down there to make sure they don't stray."

"Lorelei?"

"She wanted something to do after what happened to Carrie. Keep herself occupied. The kid's suffering, but she's a trooper."

"She's by herself down there?"

"She has a radio. The only other able body we have left is Blaine, and I didn't think it was wise to take him away from the bridge."

Lara nodded her approval. "What's Benny's situation?"

"The vet says he's stable."

"The vet" was George, the veterinarian who had been a part of Riley's crew on the *Ocean Star*. With Zoe stuck in the infirmary, he was the next best option.

"A hell of a mess," Bonnie said. "You really think Riley didn't know about any of this?"

"I don't think he had any idea."

"He's cute, but he's all kinds of clueless, isn't he?"

"I don't think *clueless* is the word. Maybe..."

"What?"

"Too trusting."

"Yeah, that can definitely get you shot these days."

The old her would have vehemently disagreed, but if the last year had taught her anything, it was that people you couldn't trust with absolute one-hundred percent certainty were best approached with a gun at the ready.

I bet Mom would have loved to hear me say that.

They took the stairs, and on the way up Bonnie said, "What did he say?"

Bonnie didn't have to elaborate on who *he* was. Lara didn't answer right away, mostly because she still didn't know how to process all of it. There was so much information, so many *ifs* and *whys* and *hows* that it made her head hurt.

It's a suicide mission, she remembered thinking when he told her his plan, what Danny called Plan G.

At the same time, she couldn't help thinking, *But what if it worked? Then it would change everything. It would change everything.*

But that was the problem. It *could* work, but it could just as easily *not*. There were so many possibilities, so many pieces that still needed to fall into place. And at the very center of it was Will...and her.

Always the two of us, Will. Even now, after everything that's happened, why does it still have to fall on our shoulders?

"Lara?" Bonnie said next to her. "What did he say?"

"I'll tell you and everyone else later," she said. "Right now we have more immediate problems."

With Riley's people confined to the lower deck, Lara and Bonnie made good time reaching the floor with the infirmary. Danny was there to meet them when they climbed up the stairs. He was leaning against the wall, sipping from a ceramic mug with steam rising above the rim. Danny had slipped on his old SWAT comm gear with the throat mic and earbud and a tactical vest.

"Kendra was in the armory, counting the hardware," Danny said when he saw them. "She said they swiped the mags with silver loads, the sneaky little buggers."

"I guess they didn't know about silver not affecting him," Bonnie said.

"Oh, they affect him, all right. They just don't put him down. It's all about the ol' noggin," Danny said, tapping his temple with his free hand for effect. "It works on the black eyes so they probably assumed it was the same with the blue eyes, and you know what happens when you assume. Assholism."

"What's the situation?" Lara asked.

"Same-o, same-o." He turned around and led them through

the hallway. "O-O-O-O'Reilly hasn't had much luck talking his boys down, before you ask."

"There's two of them?"

"A Bray and an Ethan."

"What kind of name is Bray?" Bonnie asked.

"Redneckian, would be my guess," Danny said. "As far as we can tell, they haven't harmed anyone yet. The *mucho importanto* part being *yet*."

"You think they will?" Lara asked.

"Dunno. They shot Benny and killed Carrie, didn't they?"

"I don't think they meant to kill Carrie. The bullet hit her femoral artery. It probably wasn't on purpose."

"You sure about that?"

"No, but it doesn't matter. She's dead and they're dead."

"Dead used to be dead," Danny said. "Not so much anymore."

No, not anymore. Will's further proof of that.

The others were at the end of the hallway, gathered around the closed infirmary door. Riley and Hart were there with empty gun holsters, and she had expected resistance when she ordered Danny to disarm them, but Riley had capitulated without putting up much of a fight.

Hart and Riley being present wasn't a surprise, but Jolly was. The young man nodded when he saw her, and said, "Ma'am."

"I told you not to call me that, Jolly," Lara said.

"Sorry, ma—I mean, uh, Lara."

"You can call me *ma'am* all you want," Bonnie said from behind Lara.

Jolly flashed a shy smile.

Riley and Hart glanced over as she approached them. The two men were leaning on opposite sides of the infirmary door, and Lara wondered what exactly they were going to do if Bray and Ethan decided to come out, guns blazing, at that very second.

The only one with a weapon was Maddie, who stood slightly back in the hallway, with her M4 at the ready.

"No luck?" Lara asked.

Riley shook his head and frowned. "No."

"They're stuck between the proverbial rock and a hard place," Hart said, his voice purposefully low. "They might have had some semblance of a plan when Phil was still around, but after he left this mortal coil, along with those two idiots in the engine room, they don't have any idea what to do next."

"That makes them even more dangerous," Maddie said.

Lara nodded. She was right, but so was Hart.

"Gaby, Nate, and Zoe?" Lara asked.

"As far as we know, they're okay," Maddie said. "I don't know how long that's going to last, though."

Lara could read it in Maddie's eyes—the small Texan wanted to go in there and get it over with. She could tell that much just by the way Maddie gripped her rifle, clutching and unclutching the pistol grip under the barrel.

She turned back to Danny, casually braced against the wall nearby with his steaming mug. She walked over to him to get some privacy, even though there wasn't really a whole lot to be had given the narrow confines of the hallway and all the bodies jammed inside it at the moment.

"What do you think?" she whispered.

Danny shrugged, as if he hadn't given it any thought at all, but of course she knew that wasn't true. Danny, like (*the old*) Will, was just good at hiding it.

"What do I think?" Danny said. "Mostly that I'd love to be cuddling with the redhead in our cabin right now."

"You can do that later. What about here, now? You've been in this situation before, back when you were with SWAT."

"Once or twice. Though, usually the guy on the other end

was either naked or on meth. And sometimes when we were really good boys, both."

"So what do you think?"

Danny sipped his mug for a second. Then, "Wait till morning and see what we see. Everything looks better with a little sunlight. All shiny and shit."

"You want to wait it out?"

"Sure, why not? There's nothing to be gained from going in now. Put our people here in case they try anything in the meantime."

"We're running out of people, Danny."

That wasn't entirely true, but they were running out of gun-carrying adults. The idea of letting the kids get involved—like Claire, who had shown up with Gaby and was probably the most ready next to Dwayne—made her nauseous. And Carly, Sarah, and the others had their own jobs to take care of that couldn't be ignored, even now.

"Not necessarily," Danny said. "Give the kid"—he glanced back at Jolly behind them—"a gun and sign him up."

Lara looked down the hallway at Jolly, watching them back from about twenty feet away. It was so quiet and the passageway was so narrow it wouldn't have taken him very much to overhear their conversation. If he did, though, the young man did a good job pretending he wasn't eavesdropping.

"Jolly?" she said doubtfully.

"Sure, why not?" Danny said.

"He's just a kid himself." She pictured Riley and Hart listening in behind her when she added quietly, "And he's not one of us."

"No, but he worships me."

She gave Danny a wry look. "Since when? You've only known him for a day."

"A day's all you need. Plus, the kid always wanted to be a

Ranger. Was going to apply for it before the world went kaput. Trust me, he'll do what I tell him."

Lara remembered Jolly's actions on the *Ocean Star*, how he would always move ahead of her when they were approaching a corner so he would be the first one to encounter any dangers.

She looked past Danny at the young man again. "Jolly."

He hurried over. "Yeah."

"Go with Bonnie and get geared up. You're with us now."

A big, effortless grin spread across his face. "Yes ma—I mean, Lara."

"Come on, kid," Bonnie said, and led Jolly down the hallway.

"See?" Danny said.

Lara looked back at him. "See what?"

"You could practically feel the unrestrained man crush he's got for me emanating from every pore."

"You're right; it's so obvious I don't know how I missed it." She looked back at Riley and Hart. "You guys should go get some rest."

"We're okay," Riley said.

"You should go anyway. You don't want to be here if something happens between now and dawn."

The two men exchanged an uncertain look, but if they had any objections, they swallowed them and nodded back.

Lara said to Danny, "It's your show."

"Sure, who needs sleep?" Danny said. "And where are you going?"

I have to clean Phil's blood off the floor in my cabin, she thought, but said, "To fix my door, no thanks to you."

"Boy, you save someone's life and they won't let you live it down," Danny said after her.

7

GABY

Bray and the second man, whose name turned out to be Ethan, didn't do or say very much after the burst of gunfire shattered the peaceful night. Gaby eventually let go of the façade and sat up, while Nate was allowed to come over and sit on the bed to her right, with Zoe taking the one to her left. She guessed their captors realized the real danger was outside the room and not inside, and the less they had to deal with—like keeping Nate and Zoe under control at gunpoint—the better.

They were right to ignore her, because she wasn't in any position to pose a threat. Whatever pain she had arrived on the yacht with was numbed thanks to the meds, but it also limited her movements. The men also didn't have to worry too much about Nate; even though he was much better off after being shot in Gallant, he was still far from 100%, and Riley's men knew it just by the way he walked gingerly back and forth.

The night came and went, and the only sound was Riley's and Hart's voices through the door, trying to communicate with Bray and Ethan. Gaby was at least glad to know that Riley wasn't involved in the attempted yacht takeover, which meant this was more of a rogue mission with a limited number of personnel. That provided some comfort—fewer men meant an easier time for Lara and Danny to deal with—but of course it didn't do anything for her, Nate, and Zoe as they sat in the dark and watched Bray and Ethan guarding the door with weapons at the ready. She couldn't quite see their faces from across the room, but their body language didn't suggest they were any closer to surrendering.

A pool of moonlight filtered in through the window to their left and splashed across the middle of the room, as if symbolically separating hostages from captors. The whole thing was almost romantic...if people weren't holding her at gunpoint.

"You think he's okay?" Zoe whispered.

She looked over at the doctor, and matching her pitch, "Who?"

"Will..."

Gaby didn't have to think too much about it. In fact, she didn't have to think at all. After the loud cracks of gunfire there had been only silence, both throughout the boat and from the radios that Bray and Ethan carried. As far as she knew, there were three others in on the plan, and all three had gone silent. That didn't bode well for the mission, and she suspected both of the surviving conspirators knew it.

"Yes," Gaby said without hesitation.

Zoe glanced over, clearly surprised by the absolute certainty in Gaby's voice. "How can you be so sure?"

"He's not...Will anymore."

Just saying the words out loud made her wince, because it meant embracing the reality that Will wasn't really Will anymore.

"He's something else now," Gaby whispered.

"So how are you so sure it's really him?" Zoe asked.

"The same reason Danny is. He didn't have to do any of the

things he did for us when we were out there. You should have seen him in Gallant. He risked everything that night to come save us."

Zoe didn't say anything else and seemed to drift off to be with her own thoughts. Maybe some of those were about Will. Gaby always suspected something had happened between them back in Louisiana, but she'd never asked about it. Neither had Lara, who Gaby knew had the same suspicions. But after Will went missing, it didn't seem to matter anymore.

And it still doesn't matter now.

She focused on the two black silhouettes stationed in front of the door on the other side of the infirmary. Their faces were hidden, along with their expressions, but she could just barely pick up that they were whispering back and forth. She wished she were closer so she could eavesdrop, because she had a feeling what they decided was going to affect everyone in the room.

"How are you doing?" Nate asked. Unlike Zoe, he hadn't bothered to lower his voice, probably because the question wasn't something worth hiding.

"I'm okay," she said. "You?"

"A little throbbing here and there, but okay." He looked past her. "Hey, doc, I might need a refill on those meds soon."

"Remind me again when this is over," Zoe said.

"Thanks." Then, returning to Gaby, "What a night, huh? And here I thought getting back here would translate into fun times in the sun and a whole lot of bikini-clad boredom."

"Bikini-clad boredom?"

"Well, you'd be wearing most of it, and I'd just be enjoying it."

"Shows what you know," she smiled back.

He snorted. "That's me, Captain Optimism, as Danny would say. Speaking of..." He glanced over at the door, at Ethan's and

Bray's shadowy forms. This time he did lower his voice to almost a whisper when he said, "I bet we could take them."

"In your pain-induced dreams," she whispered back.

"I'm serious."

"So am I. Leave it alone. Danny and Lara don't need us mucking things up." Nate didn't look convinced, so she added sharply, "*Nate.*"

"Okay," he whispered. "Okay. Sheesh. When did you get so bossy?"

"Since I saved your life back in Gallant."

He sighed. "How many times are you going to bring that up?"

"Whenever you come up with a stupid plan."

"So...always?"

She pursed a smile at him.

"It's quiet out there," Zoe said. She was looking up at the ceiling for some reason. "I don't think I've ever heard the boat this quiet."

The calm after the storm. Or maybe it's the calm before the storm.

The fact that no one had tried to breach the room wasn't surprising. There simply was no advantage to something like that, not with two captors and three hostages. Even though the two men only seemed to be armed with handguns, that was still two too many weapons against her, Zoe, and Nate's zero.

The night dragged on and her eyelids grew heavy, and the final straw was when Nate started stroking her forehead. That made her close her eyes, and despite telling herself to stay awake, she eventually drifted off.

"Geez, I thought you were going to sleep through the whole thing," Danny said when she opened her eyes.

"Danny?"

"It ain't Elvis, though I have been mistaken for the King of Rock 'n' Roll once or twice. Must be the blue suede shoes."

"What...?" she said, but couldn't find the will to finish.

Her voice sounded overly groggy to her own ears, and maybe that was because— She saw the clock on the wall and groaned.

It was almost noon.

"You slept through all the fun," Danny said.

Danny wasn't alone. There was a man with a crew cut, and despite his intimidating size—he was taller than Danny and built like a football player—he might have been just a few years older than her. The stranger had an M4 rifle slung over his back and was wearing the same kind of tactical vest and comm rig that Danny had on.

She glanced about the room, but Zoe was nowhere to be found. On her right was an empty bed where Nate should have been.

"Don't worry; your boyfriend's outside getting some rays," Danny said. "And the doc's seeing to Benny. Can't very well leave your ex to some animal doctor. He probably has cooties or some such."

She slid up the bed and propped a pillow behind her, wincing at a small jolt of pain. Her shoulder was hurting a little bit more than usual, maybe because whatever Zoe had given her was starting to wear off. After all, she had slept through almost all of yesterday and the entire morning today.

"My ex?" she said.

"Benny," Danny said. "You forgot the poor kid's name already?"

"What happened to Benny?"

"He got caught in last night's crossfire."

"Is he okay?"

"He's alive." Danny nodded at the big guy behind him, and said, "Head on out. I'll be along in a few."

"Yes, sir," the man said, and turned and left.

Gaby scooted into a better sitting position while Danny adjusted his seat on a stool at the foot of her bed. The infirmary didn't look any different than the last time she was awake—except there were no strangers with guns, and she didn't see anything that looked like collateral damage. She also let out a sigh of relief at the visible lack of blood and bullet holes around her.

"What happened last night?" she asked. "I heard a lot of shooting..."

Danny told her, filling in the pieces she was missing from being stuck up here during the whole ordeal. The two (dead) men in the engine room, the attempt on Will's life, and Benny and Carrie caught in the middle.

Gaby frowned. "They killed Carrie?"

"Maybe not on purpose, but same shitty result."

"And Zoe's with Benny now?"

"He's stable, and the doc's got it handled. The kid bled a lot before we could get him up here, but there's more where all that gooey red stuff comes from. Speaking of which, I'd like to be handled by Zoe. That's one fine-looking woman."

"You're already taken, remember?"

"*Shhh,*" Danny said, putting a finger to his lips, "don't tell the ladies. Or Carly. That redhead just don't understand that I'm a man and men need to spread their seed around. It's like biology or sumthin'."

"Ugh, spare me the visuals." She looked past him at the empty room again. "So what happened while I was asleep?"

"They gave up about two hours ago."

"Just like that?"

"I guess with their pals dead and all their friends—including their COs—telling them to come to their senses all night long, they finally buckled. It was all very anticlimactic, to be perfectly honest with you. Me and Jolly were ready to bust the door down and come in shooting like Rambo and his mini Rambo. It totally ruined our morning. Heck, we could barely keep our breakfast down afterward, we were so disgusted."

"What's a Jolly?"

"The big kid that was just in here with me."

"Who is he?"

"One of Riley's guys."

She gave him a surprised look. "And you gave him a rifle after what they tried to do last night?"

"The kid's cool."

"How do you know that?"

"Trust me, cool knows cool, and Jolly Green Giant's cool as a cucumber." Danny got up. "But back to you. You gonna lie in bed all day, or what?"

"That depends. What's happening out there?"

"Well, we're not going to the Bengal Islands after all."

"When did that happen?"

Danny told her about the radio broadcast from Black Tide Island, about the stand-down order that had been issued to Mercer's army back in Texas.

Then Danny smirked. "You remember ol' Benford? Back in Gallant?"

"How could I forget?"

"Apparently he was one of the big cheeses. Big dead cheese now, anyway."

"Fuck him," Gaby said.

"Harsh," Danny chuckled.

After Danny left, she quickly grew tired of being in the room all by herself and swung her legs off the bed and sat up for a moment, just to see if she could. It wasn't nearly as bad as she had been expecting, and she found that moving actually helped with the occasional slight pain.

She stood up and looked around for her clothes. There was so much light in the room now as opposed to last night that she had no trouble finding a fresh pair of khaki cargos draped over a chair along with a thermal sweater from her personal effects clearly waiting there for her. She smiled, thought *I love you, Nate,* and made sure the door was locked before stripping out of her "patient" clothes and pulling on her own. She only grimaced three or four times during the whole thing, and once she (very) carefully slipped her left arm through the sleeve, was feeling like herself for the first time in seemingly weeks.

Walking was easier than moving any part of her upper body around, and with her left arm (and everything attached to it) basically immobile as a precaution under the sweater, she opened the door and stepped outside and headed down the hallway. There were plenty of footprints immediately outside and around the infirmary—evidence left behind by Danny and the others as they moved around last night—but no actual people.

She slipped outside using the nearest door, drawn forward by the rays of light on the other side. The sun and cool weather against her face was a monumental relief, and she hadn't realized how much she needed the fresh air until she was standing in the middle of it. The old Gaby would have loved to lie in bed for days being tended to, but Gaby 2.0 needed to move even when there was nothing to do.

The *Trident* was almost as quiet outside as it was inside, with just the waves slapping against the hull and the occasional howl of wind gusts. It was a nice (ridiculously nice, in fact) cloudless sky, and she had the urge to keep going rather than retreat.

She ended up down the side of the boat until she was on the

lower deck. She didn't know how she got there, but soon she was walking toward the engine room and spotted a lone, small figure standing guard in front of it.

Maddie heard her approaching and glanced over. "She lives!"

Gaby smiled. "Hey, Maddie."

"What are you doing out of bed?"

"Bed was getting boring."

Gaby glanced past her at Lorelei, who was moving up and down the deck behind Maddie. The girl looked as if she were moving in slow motion, or maybe she just wasn't certain where she was going, if anywhere at all.

"Kid's all messed up," Maddie said. "Fighting through it like a champ, though. Good for her."

"I heard about Carrie."

"Yeah. It sucks. But at least Benny's going to get through it."

"Thank God for that." Then, looking past Maddie at the engine room door, "Is he alone down there?"

"Yes. Why?"

"I haven't really gotten the chance to...talk to him."

"You sure you wanna go down there? The last two people who did didn't come back up."

"I'll be fine," she said, and managed a forced smile while thinking, *She's right. Stay up here where it's safe. You don't really want to go down there, do you?*

Well, do you?

She hadn't turned around and left by the time Maddie pulled the hatch open, so Gaby gave the small Texan a pursed smile and stepped inside. She moved on automatic pilot through the machinery, not sure what she was doing down here or if she really wanted to see what was waiting at the other end—

She smelled the blood before she actually saw it on the floor toward the end of the narrow hallway. She stepped cautiously over and around the dry puddles until she was in front of the cabin door. Gage had been using the room until Lara dealt with him, and once upon a time it was supposed to be hers and Nate's. But now it had become a makeshift brig, though at the moment there was nothing to fear from its only occupant.

Keep telling yourself that; then maybe your hands will stop shaking.

She managed to calm down enough to pull the lever and yank on the door, relying entirely on her good right arm. Artificial light from the hallway glinted off spent shell casings that still littered the floor, many of them held in place by the plentiful blood that had been spilled last night. She tried to look for the black among the red, but if Will had been injured and bled out, she couldn't spot the evidence.

Gaby didn't close the door behind her as she stepped inside. She told herself that there was no point—because sunlight didn't reach this far down and the cabin's only window was covered from the outside world—but the truth was she wanted an easy way out if she needed it.

I won't need it. Not down here, not with Will.

Not with Will...

There was a slight movement in the corner of the room as a figure—tall and skeletal—stood up in the shadows, piercing (*pulsating*) blue eyes watching her back from the blackness. The hairs on the back of her neck went straight, and a shiver snapped up and down her spine. Memories of the farmhouse, of the nights in Gallant, rushed back in a tidal wave.

Gaby pushed through the overwhelming uncertainty (*What are you doing down here? Are you crazy?*) and the fear, and stood her ground. Her legs weren't shaking nearly as much as she expected, but she hadn't moved any closer toward it, either.

Him. It's a him, not an it.

It's Will.

Mostly...

"Will," she said, his name coming out softly, as if she were afraid to say it too loudly.

There was no answer, and the shadowy form in the corner continued to watch her back in silence. For a moment she wasn't sure if she had actually spoken his name, that maybe it was all a figment of her imagination. Maybe she was actually back in the infirmary, sleeping off another round of meds-induced haze—

"Frank," it said, the word coming out as a soft hiss, as if it was doing everything possible to hide it.

"Frank?" she repeated.

"Will's dead," it hissed. "He's been dead for a while now."

"Danny says you're Will..."

"I was..."

"But not anymore."

"No."

"Then what are you?"

It—no, not *it*, but *he*—didn't answer right away. Maybe he was thinking about the answer, or maybe he just didn't feel like talking. It was hard to tell, because she could barely make out the tight contours of his face or the smooth dome of his head. The only thing she could be sure of were the eyes, like twin solar flares in a galaxy devoid of life, focusing in on her.

"Do you know who I am?" she asked. "Danny says your memories come and go."

"Gaby," he said.

Her heart leapt in her throat and the smile came out unexpectedly. "You remember me."

"Yes..."

"Are you...okay?"

Something along his face moved. Did he just...*smile?*

"Yes," he said (hissed). "I'm healing."

"Will you be okay?"

"Yes..."

Gaby looked down at the dried puddles of blood that covered the floor. The chest they had stuffed him in before leaving Gallant was riddled with bullet holes, pieces of the lock and clamps scattered across the room.

She looked up and tried to see him through the shadows. "I'm sorry."

He didn't respond. Maybe he didn't know why she was apologizing (Did *she* know?) or maybe it was something else entirely. And maybe she didn't know what she was doing down here after all.

It's Will. You don't have to be afraid.

It's Will.

"We left you back there," Gaby continued. "In Louisiana. We should have gone back for you."

"You...had no choice," he said. "That was the plan."

"It was a stupid plan."

"Maybe..."

"We shouldn't have left you. We should have gone back for you."

"There were too many..."

"We should have risked it."

"No."

She shook her head. "We should have tried, instead of just leaving you out there by yourself. All this time, we've wondered what had happened to you. What your last moments were like..." It was suddenly very cold in the room and she wrapped her arms across her chest, ignoring the stab of pain from her left shoulder. "I'm sorry. God, I'm so sorry for abandoning you."

He didn't say anything, but if she thought he was ignoring her, the glowing blue eyes that hadn't left her face since she set foot into the cabin said otherwise. Maybe he just didn't know what to say or how to respond to her all-too-human confession.

Was that it? Was he beyond (*human*) things like that now? Maybe this wasn't the Will she remembered after all—

"I forgive you," he said finally.

She started to cry. It was stupid and girly, and she despised herself for it, but the first tear sneaked its way down her cheek and it was quickly followed by another, then another. At least she could say she never went full Gaby 1.0 and bawled her eyes out in front of him, in this dark room covered in blood and death. If she was going to cry, at least they were silent tears.

"Gaby," he said.

She looked up at him, the tears coming faster now.

"You saved her," he said, his eyes never wavering from hers. "You saved Lara. I would do it again, a hundred times over, for the same outcome."

She fought through the emotions, wondering if she looked as silly and childish as she was feeling. But she didn't care, and didn't try to stop any of it. Instead, she wiped at the tears with the back of her hand, only to make room for new ones.

"I don't know if we saved her or if she saved us," Gaby said. "You should have seen her that night. She was amazing. We couldn't have done any of this without her. Or gotten this far. You picked a good one."

"I know."

"Has she been down here?"

"Yes."

"You've talked."

"We have..."

"And you told her everything?"

He nodded. Or she saw his head bob slightly in the shadows. "She knows what she has to do. The only thing left is to do it."

"That's the trick, isn't it? Knowing what to do is the easy part. Getting it done, that takes a little doing."

"Yes."

She managed a smile. "So. Frank?"

"Yes..."

"That's a stupid name. You don't look like a Frank at all."

He made a sound—it might have even been a snort, though she couldn't be entirely certain—and said, "I know."

8

LARA

"I don't agree with what Phil and the others did, but you can't blame them," Riley said. "One of those things, on the boat with us..."

"He's not just 'one of those things,'" Lara said. "He's a friend."

"That's the third time you've said that. *He*. You keep calling it a *he*."

Because he used to be Will. Because he used to be my everything. And because I have faith that he's here to help me, to help all of us.

God help me if I'm wrong.

"He's an old friend," she said.

"It *used* to be," Riley said, looking at her intently from across the bridge of the *Trident*. "It's not anymore. You have to accept that."

"You wouldn't be saying that if you'd been in Texas with us," Gaby said.

The teenager (though it was hard for Lara to think of Gaby as one anymore, her age notwithstanding) stood next to Blaine, and if Lara was concerned about her being up and about after only a full day's rest, Gaby didn't just look okay; she looked energized.

There were six of them in all inside the room, with Hart and Danny making up the other bodies. They had been there for a while, trying to come to terms with what had happened. Not just with Phil, but the *why* behind his actions.

"He might not be Will anymore, but he's still our friend," Gaby continued. "And he didn't come here to hurt us, otherwise he wouldn't have let us lock him inside an old chest and transport him across water that could kill him, in the daylight."

"You ever been stuffed inside a wooden chest?" Danny asked. "Granted, he's all spindly and such, but it's still kinda a big deal."

"You said it was hurt back in Gallant," Hart said. "Maybe it didn't have any choice."

"Oh, it had a choice, all right."

"You don't know that for sure."

"But I do, Hart to Hart, I do."

"Hart to what?"

"It's his thing," Blaine said. "Just roll with it."

"Thanks for that, *Capitan* Blaine-o."

"You're welcome."

"Bottom line," Danny said, turning back to Hart and Riley, "he didn't have to come here. He didn't have to do any of the things he did. That means a lot in my book. And trust you me, people don't get into my book just willy-nilly."

Maybe Danny's and Gaby's words didn't completely convince Hart and Riley, but Lara thought it might have softened the duo a bit. Even if they weren't there yet, it was a good start, and after the night she'd had, she could work with it.

"I know how all of this sounds," Lara said. "You didn't know him like we did. But as hard as it is for you to grasp, imagine how much more difficult it is for us, to have him come back after we had given him up for dead. It's him, but at the same time it's not.

It's...not an easy concept to just accept at face value, but it's the truth."

"You're right," Riley said. "To us he's a stranger, but to you it's possibly an old friend coming back after...dying?" He shook his head, struggling for the right words. "It's not something that happens every day, even these days. We're going to need some time."

"And this plan of his," Hart said. "What did you call it?"

"Plan G," Danny said. "I came up with the name, by the way. Brownie points if you can guess what the G stands for."

"Georgia?" Blaine said.

"Close, but no cigar."

"I think we all know what the G stands for," Gaby said.

"It's not you," Danny said.

"No shit."

Lara focused on Riley standing across from her. If she had any hope of advancing Will's new plan, it would have to be through Riley. As much as she doubted the man's decision-making ability, Riley was her best shot at the moment.

"This is what he does," Lara said. "Will has always been a strategist. His mind is the reason we stayed alive through the first few months of The Purge. The reason we're still standing here."

"It's what he *used* to do," Riley said. "You said it yourself, Lara. He's not the man he used to be. He's not even a man at all."

"But it's still him."

"Are you sure about that?"

"I spent an hour in a room with him. I looked into his eyes. Turning into that... Turning didn't take away his ability to think. If anything, he's even more capable now. And he's been out there, deep behind enemy lines, absorbing everything that makes them, *them*. How many of us can say that?"

"Bottom line?" Danny said. "You can take the boy out of the Ranger, but you can't take the Ranger out of the boy. Ol' Will did what he did best when we thought he was gone. He infiltrated, collected intelligence, and came up with a way to save everyone. Pretty friggin' impressive, if you ask me."

"Maybe, if he's right," Hart said.

"That's the big question, isn't it?" Riley said. "*If* he's right. Just to find out is going to take a lot more than what we have on this boat."

"There's nothing we lack that Black Tide can't provide," Lara said.

"It won't be easy," Will had said, *"and people will die."*

People have already died, Will. Too many people. Good and bad, and everyone else in-between, too. And people will keep dying...unless we stop it.

"It's not an easy thing, what you're asking," Riley said.

"Who says it was going to be easy?" Gaby said. "We're talking about ending this once and for all. Even if it's the hardest thing we ever do, shouldn't we do it anyway? The entire human race is on the line."

"Not nearly dramatic enough, kid," Danny said. "But Kid Ranger's right. It's now or possibly never. Maybe it's just the old fart in me, but I don't much like being at the bottom of the food chain. I like it better on top—and yes, that's what she said."

Lara was doing her best to read Riley's and Hart's faces, and she thought she saw flares of agreement, especially from Hart. Riley appeared more reluctant, maybe the result of having so much gone wrong since his mutiny.

She decided to help him along: "You left Mercer because you didn't want to kill innocent people, but you can't run forever. Sooner or later, you have to come face-to-face with the monster. The *real* monster. This is our best chance to do that, but we can't do it alone. We need Black Tide."

Riley sighed. "All of this talk about saving the world will be a moot point if they open fire on us as soon as we show back up there."

"Which is why we're not just going to show up out of the blue," Lara said. "First, we have to make sure Mercer's not in charge anymore. This whole thing doesn't work if he's still calling the shots over there."

"Agreed," Riley nodded.

"So how do we make sure?" Hart asked. "We can't just call them up and ask, can we?"

"Why not?" Lara said. "Why can't we just radio Black Tide? They don't know where we are right now, or that we intercepted their stand-down order. The only way to find out for sure what's happened to Mercer without exposing ourselves—"

"Is to ask for Mercer," Hart finished.

Lara nodded. "Give them any excuse. You just want to talk. You had a change of heart. Whatever it takes. Either Mercer will come to the radio or he won't."

"You're right," Riley said. "We don't actually have to be there to get what we need." He nodded, though she thought it was more for his own benefit. "We just have to be careful."

"Very careful," Lara said. "We don't give away our position. As far as they know, we could be across the globe by now."

"Jesus, if Keo really did it," Blaine said. "I always knew that guy was dangerous."

"I met him back at the *Ocean Star* when he was there," Hart said. "He came across as more crazy than dangerous to me."

"You mean there's a difference?" Danny asked.

"That's another thing," Lara said to Riley. "Try to find out what happened to Keo, if he's still alive."

"It's been two days," Riley said. "What are the chances of that?"

"I've learned never to underestimate the man," Lara said. "Keo's been known to buck the odds once or twice."

"Or twenty," Danny chimed in.

"I have to leave."

"And go where?"

"Texas."

"Why? Is it the water?"

"No."

"Tell me why."

"I have too many miles to cover. I have to start now, or I won't be ready."

"Why does it always have to be you?"

"Because it has to be."

She shook her head, not that it did any good. Transformed or not, he was still Will, and once he made up his mind...

"What if I can't convince them?" she asked.

"You will," he said.

"But what if I *can't?*"

"You *will.*"

"Maybe you have more faith in me than I do. Than other people will."

"You're wrong," he said, and there was a tenderness in his voice that belied the hissing that accompanied every word, every sound he made. "I've always known you were stronger than you realized. Even now, as strong as you've become, you're still capable of so much more. You were born to lead, Lara. So lead. Do whatever you have to to convince them. Mabry won't be there forever. This is our chance. It might be our only chance."

She sat in the chair and stared across the semidarkness at him. If she still had any doubts that this Will wasn't the same one who had left Song Island all those months ago, his tall, elongated form curled up into almost a ball in the corner of the room ended that. It was her Will, but it also wasn't. Even so, the thought of him leaving her again so soon after coming back into her life was like a knife in the back.

Not again. You can't just leave me again, you bastard.

She was angry with him, even though she knew things would never be the same between them—*could* never be the same. There had been a part of her that held out hope he wouldn't abandon her once more, that he would stay and protect her this time, like he had promised. She wanted desperately to go back to being his girlfriend and marveling from the background as he led everyone to safety and always had the answers to all the problems.

She wanted all those things badly, but she also knew she couldn't have them. Not anymore. Because the Will she knew and loved and missed, and eventually accepted as being lost was, for all intents and purposes, gone. Kate had taken him from her.

But she could still see enough of him left in the blue-eyed creature that looked out from the shadowed corner at her now that she found herself hating him for wanting to leave her all over again.

You promised me. You promised *me.*

"Do you remember...us?" she asked.

"Yes," he said (*hissed*).

"Everything?"

"Most of it."

"What do you remember?"

"It comes and goes, but if I focus... I remember that I love you. I remember that I would rather die than disappoint you. I remember..."

The smile came to her lips easily, and with it too much wild emotion that she had to shove it all back because she wasn't sure she could control it. And right here, right now, she didn't want to break down in front of him.

"I'm sorry," he said.

"For what?"

"For everything. For not coming back..."

"You didn't have a choice."

"I tried..."

"I know you did. I never doubted that you would."

Except for all those days and nights when I did have doubts. When I lay in bed and wondered if you had abandoned me.

I was wrong.

I was so, so wrong.

"But you finally made your way back," she said. "And now you want to leave again?"

"I have to, or the plan doesn't work."

"Is that the only reason?"

His eyes shifted as he looked away, and the sudden absence of his pulsating blue eyes left her feeling strangely empty.

"No," he said.

"What's the other reason?"

"I don't belong here."

"With me..."

"With people."

"Your friends..."

"With people," he said again.

She leaned forward. "Will..."

"Frank."

"No. You're Will. You'll always be Will."

He lifted his head back up, blue eyes reappearing in their fullness. They were soothing and calming, and nothing like the souls of mindless monsters that she envisioned the blue-eyed ghouls as being when she had heard the stories.

"You'll always be Will," she said. "Maybe you're not the man you once were, but you'll always be the man I love."

"Man," he said, and there might have been something that

almost sounded like...amusement (?) in his voice. "I'm not even that anymore, Lara."

"That doesn't matter."

"It matters."

"No..."

"It matters," he said, so softly she barely heard it. "I have to go. I have to go back."

"You're going to leave me again," she said, regretting the words as soon as they left her lips.

"I'm sorry."

"Are you?"

"More than you'll ever know."

"Then promise you'll come back when this is over. Promise me, and this time you better goddamn keep it."

He nodded. "Yes..."

"Say it."

"I promise."

"Good. We'll figure the rest of it out later. Together."

"Yes," he said, again so softly she had to strain to hear him. Then, "Lara..."

"Yes, Will?"

"Can I..."

"What is it?"

"...Touch you?"

She stared at him for the longest time. His eyes pulsed in the shadows, watching her back. She couldn't have begun to read his face even if she could see it. He barely moved in the corner, and whenever she heard anything at all coming from him, it was the unnatural *clacking* of joints.

"I want to remember," he said.

"Remember?"

"You. They're fading. My memories of you. Each night, they fade a little more. I want to remember..."

"Yes," she answered before he could finish, surprising even herself.

"Close your eyes."

"Why?"

"I don't...want you to see me like this."

"I've already seen you."

"Not...like this."

She didn't move, but closed her eyes like he asked. The wait was excruciating, and she exerted every ounce of willpower she had to sit perfectly still on the chair and not get up and run away—

His touch was cold against her left cheek, and she startled but didn't pull away because she knew without a single shred of doubt that he wouldn't hurt her. If he wanted to, he could have done it a dozen times now. Even the guards outside the engine room door were there just to keep people out. Nothing could hold him in here if he didn't want to stay. Those two men Phil had sent down last night had found out just how dangerous he could be when—

She sighed out loud, involuntarily, when warmth spread through his fingers and against her skin and chased away the coldness. His entire body must have been closer than she realized, because she could sense the strange aura of chill and heat that Danny and Gaby had told her about. It was an impossible balance of winter and summer radiating from every pore of his skin.

She wanted to open her eyes, to look at him up close and see every inch of him the way he was doing to her, but she didn't, because this wasn't for her.

A second hand touched her right cheek, and this one was also ice cold at first, but the sensation quickly faded and was replaced by warmth. He traced her face with his fingers, as if trying to remember every inch of her, every imperfection, like a blind man would in order to "see" what someone looked like.

She expected her heartbeat to continue accelerating, but after the first ten or so seconds of contact, it plateaued and returned to a normal rhythm. Her breathing came out in even spurts, defying all logic. Her entire body seemed to almost slow down, her perception of time and space and senses moving in molasses, almost as if she, and not him, were trying to prolong this moment.

"Lara," he whispered, and his voice sounded almost human, almost like Will again. The Will she remembered, not this new Will that had come back to her changed. But that was impossible, and she was almost entirely certain it was her mind trying to deceive her in an attempt to keep her still as she allowed a blue-eyed ghoul to touch her—

Will. She was letting *Will* touch her.

"Lara," he whispered again, as one of his fingers touched her lips and traced them from side to side, then up and down. The cold followed by the warmth, then back again, until there was that strange, impossible balance of heat and freeze that defied nature.

"Will," she whispered back.

"I'm sorry," he said.

"Don't be sorry."

"I'm sorry," he whispered again. "I'm sorry...I'm sorry..."

Then he was gone.

His touch faded, and so did the cold and heat that came from him.

When she opened her eyes, he was back in the shadows, huddled in the corner, and his head was downcast so she couldn't lose herself in his blue eyes.

"Will," she said.

"I have to go," he said.

"Will..."

"I have too many miles to cover."

"Will, please look at me."

"...And you have too much work ahead of you."

"Will, please..."

"We have to succeed, because we won't get another chance," he said quietly. "We won't get another chance..."

"Will," she said again, pleading with everything she had in that one word.

"I have to go back," he said, still not looking up at her. "I have to go back..."

She left the cabin, but she didn't leave the engine room. Instead, she leaned against the wall and let the loud grind of machinery camouflage her tears. There were a lot of them. She didn't know where they came from, but maybe they were always there, waiting for the dam to finally burst.

And they did, now.

She was just glad she was alone, with only the engine to bear witness to this weakness she had spent so much time and effort to hide from the others. She didn't know if she was actually crying too, because the noise around her was so loud she could have been screaming at the top of her lungs and never heard a single sound.

But she could be absolutely certain of the tears. They rolled down her cheeks and dripped from her chin to the floor and there was nothing she could do to stop them—not that she wanted to. She slid down and put her arms over her knees and closed her eyes, remembering what it felt like to be young and afraid and helpless for the first time in such a long time.

Her body ached—every inch of her. Her chest was tighter than it should have been, and just breathing hurt. It was as if her entire being were being ripped apart from the inside out, as if her soul were being crushed inch by inch by inch.

All those times she pushed through the emotional and physical pain so the others wouldn't see, so they'd have at least one person to look to with Will gone.

But not anymore. Not anymore.

She looked down the hallway, toward the cabin.

He was in there.

Will. Her Will.

But not really.

No one could possibly understand that concept except for her and Gaby and Danny, and just a small handful of others. To everyone else, he would be just another blue-eyed ghoul. Phil and the others had proven that.

Eventually, she found the strength to stand up and wipe away the tears with her sleeves and used the shiny machines to make sure her eyes weren't still red and puffy. She hadn't worn makeup in so long she didn't have to worry about smearing it across her face.

Only when she was certain no one would know what had happened by looking at her face did she finally go back topside.

Bonnie was standing guard on the other side of the door when she came out. "How'd it go?"

"It went," Lara said, hoping her voice didn't crack, but it was probably not as strong—or steady—as she had hoped, because Bonnie gave her a questioning look.

"Lara," Bonnie started to say, but Lara turned around and started walking away. "Lara," Bonnie called after her.

Lara ignored her and kept walking, then faster, and faster still.

BOOK TWO

9-8 SUITED

9

KEO

Rhett hadn't returned. Of course, it had only been a few hours and it wasn't as if Rhett were in any hurry to take Keo's offer to the higher-ups. That is, if there were higher-ups now that Mercer was gone. It was hard to figure out who was in charge at the moment, if anyone at all. It would have been nice if Erin were still around to fill him in on the island's hierarchy.

But of course Erin was dead, and he should have been, too. The only reason he was still breathing was because Rhett and the others didn't know what to do with him. That, and the fact that apparently more than just Riley had thought about rebelling against Mercer's rule, but just hadn't had the balls to go through with it. Keo had never actually met Riley—he didn't consider seeing some guy lying in bed on an oil rig's sickbay as "meeting"— but he had to admit, knowing what he knew now, he had new respect for the guy. Riley had done what so many others wanted to, but hadn't. That took some brass ones right there.

At least Rhett had done him a solid and opened the high window to the left of the holding room so Keo could, once again, enjoy the natural and very airy upside to being held prisoner on an island. So if nothing else, there was that.

That's it, pal; look on the bright side.

He sat on the floor with his back against the wall so he could face the window on the other side of his cell bars. After three days of soaking in his own BO, it was as close to paradise as he was liable to get. Now if only he could get them to give him something to eat that wasn't mush or tasted like something someone gurgled out—

Clank! as the door across the room opened.

Keo looked over as two men stepped inside, while a third stood back holding the door with one hand. Keo only recognized the third guy—his afternoon jailer, who swapped places with two others in eight-hour shifts.

He had never seen the other two newcomers before.

"Visiting hours?" Keo asked.

The men didn't bother answering him, and while the first two walked over to Keo's cell in the back, the third guy remained standing in the hallway looking in. Keo had never actually seen his jailer's face before today, and in fact this was the most the man had ever exposed himself: Keo glimpsed his name tag and the word *Donovan*.

Keo focused on the two approaching him. One was six-five and built like a truck (*Calvin* was written on his name tag). The second one was around six foot, skinnier, and African-American (*Bellamy* was scribbled across his chest), and by just the way they were walking, with Calvin always a step behind, it wasn't hard to guess who was in charge.

"On your feet," Bellamy said.

"I like the view from down here," Keo said.

"On your *feet*, soldier."

Keo grinned. "Now that's just mean. I spent an awful lot of time and effort avoiding that title."

The two men had stopped in front of the cell bars and Calvin's hand dropped to the Sig Sauer at his hip, but Bellamy didn't make any moves toward his holstered Glock.

"Rhett sent me to come get you," Bellamy said. "They've made a decision."

"You should have started with that," Keo said.

He stood up and brushed at his stained slacks and shirt, even though it didn't do any good. Besides three days in here without an open window, he'd dripped (then had to wipe off) what passed for "food" on his clothes since they hadn't bothered to give him utensils, not even those flimsy plastic ones.

"What's the verdict?" Keo asked. He directed the question at Bellamy. If Calvin was bothered by that, he didn't show it.

Someone knows his place.

"You'll find out when we get there," Bellamy said. He took a step back and nodded at Calvin, who moved toward the gate. "Hug the wall."

"Could you at least buy me dinner first?"

"Do it." This time, Bellamy reached for his gun for effect.

Keo gave him a wry smile and turned around, then pushed up against the wall until his chest touched the jagged brick surface. The gate *clinked* and *clanked* behind him as Calvin opened it with all the dexterity of an ape who had just learned how to use his opposable thumbs a day ago.

"Did you guys make contact with the *Trident?*" Keo asked.

"Ask Rhett when you see him," Bellamy said.

"How did it go?"

"Ask Rhett when you see him," Bellamy said again.

"Oh, come on—" Keo started to say when a pair of incredibly strong hands grabbed his arms and bent them behind his back, followed by the rubbery sensation of plastic handcuffs slipping over and then tightening around his wrists. Keo was momentarily surprised by not just how strong but quick Calvin had been.

Who knew the Yeti could move that fast?

Calvin took a step back and turned Keo around, then put one massive hand around Keo's right arm and located a good grip.

"Easy there, Tex," Keo said. "It's our first date. Let's take it slow and steady with the PDA, huh?"

Calvin ignored him and marched him out of the jail cell. Bellamy stepped back to let them pass. Keo breathed in some more of the fresh air as they walked across the room, then expelled it slowly.

"Must be nice living on an island," Keo said.

"It has its moments," Bellamy said as he followed them to the door.

The third man, Donovan, hadn't moved from his spot, but it wasn't where Donovan stood that caught and held onto Keo's attention. It was the man's face. He looked...conflicted?

Aw, shit. And everything was going so well, too.

Okay, maybe not "well," exactly, but better-than-I-could-have-hoped-for-ish.

But maybe he was wrong. Maybe he was reading too much into one man's facial expression. After all, he'd never been particularly good at reading faces. Every woman he had ever met or dated or been locked in a room with for more than a few minutes could have told him that.

Then again, this wasn't about a single look on Donovan's face. It was also about his body language, the way he was gripping the lever—way too tightly, as if he were afraid it would slip from his hand if he relaxed even for a second.

Donovan looked away as Keo and Calvin neared him, and by the time they reached the door the jailer had slipped behind it so Keo couldn't see him anymore.

Shit.

"So, Rhett sent you guys to get me?" Keo asked as he was led into the hallway.

"That's right," Bellamy said. From the sound of his voice, he wasn't very far behind them; Keo guessed only about five feet.

The door *clanged* shut; then he heard the *click-clank* of the lock turning into place. That last part made Keo smile to himself.

Why bother locking it, Donovan ol' pal? There's no one in there anymore, remember?

But of course that thought didn't last for very long, because he was too busy concentrating on what lay ahead of him—or as far ahead as he was going to make on this particular trip, anyway. He didn't think it was going to be very far at all.

Captain Optimism, amirite, Danny?

"Rhett said he'd come to get me himself when they finally made up their minds," Keo said.

"He's a busy man," Bellamy said. "He's running the place now."

"Is that right? He never told me that."

"I guess he didn't think you needed to know."

"Yeah, you're probably right. Why tell a condemned man anything?"

"Exactly."

Keo glanced sideways to his right, at Calvin. The big guy hovered over him, much taller up close than the six-five Keo had pegged him at earlier. More like six-six. One inch might not have seemed like a lot, but it factored into Keo's calculations. Just as he took into consideration Calvin's size and possible weight. The guy was practically busting out of his uniform, so much so that his name tag actually wrapped around his pecs.

And what have they been feeding you, big boy?

Keo was sure of one thing: Whatever Calvin had been surviving on, it was probably not the slop they had been giving him while he sat in his jail cell.

Behind them, Bellamy followed in silence, the only noise coming from the *tap-tap-tap* of their boots against the hard floor.

Keo had no clue where his prison was located in terms of the building's blueprint, because he hadn't bothered to memorize all the turns and hallways they had led him through after the Comm Room. For all he knew, he could have been in an entirely separate building. He regretted the lack of forethought now because he had absolutely no idea where they were going—one gray wall looked like the last one—or why there didn't seem to be anyone around.

Up a creek, and me without my hands for paddles.

He wanted to tell himself that he'd had to deal with worse situations. There was that whole mess with Pollard's army in Louisiana, surviving Song Island, then going toe-to-toe with a blue-eyed ghoul. Compared to those trying times, he was only dealing with two guys here. Two *human* guys, at that. Of course, he had free hands in all those other incidents, so maybe that had a little something to do with his successes.

Oh, stop your whining and get on with it. You shouldn't even be alive anyway. Everything after this is a bonus.

Shit, almost convinced myself that time!

"So, the big boys finally made up their minds, huh?" Keo said.

"Yup," Bellamy said from behind them.

"And you don't know if they've radioed the *Trident* yet?"

"Nope."

"A man of few words, I see."

"Uh huh."

"Two words that time. Eureka!" He snapped Calvin a grin. "Is Bellamy your boss or something?"

"Or something," Calvin said in a deep baritone.

"Listen to that voice! You ever thought about doing soul music?"

"What?"

"Soul music. You got the voice for it. Right, Bellamy?"

A mild chuckle from the back of their little caravan. "Sure, why not?"

Keo was hoping they would eventually run across people in the hallway, but after the third turn they still hadn't seen anyone and he was starting to get a feel for just how big the facilities on Black Tide were. Of course it made some sense why they hadn't seen anyone yet. Who would put the brig close to the living quarters?

Even so, he expected to see *some* faces, not a big fat nothing.

"Where are we going?" Keo asked.

"You'll see when we get there," Bellamy said.

"I didn't realize the brig was on the other side of the island. How big is this place, anyway?"

"Big enough."

"Not much of an answer."

"It's all you're going to get."

"Tell me something..."

"What's that?"

"You guys manage to scrape Mercer's brains off the Comm Room floor yet?"

Calvin was the first to react—he actually twitched with his entire body, and the fingers gripping Keo's right arm tightened even further.

Now now now.

He threw his entire body into Calvin, and despite all the big man's impressive bulk, the sudden shock of being rammed into knocked him off-balance. He stumbled and crashed into the wall, while somehow still managing to hold onto Keo's arm and dragging him along.

Keo didn't mind being pulled, because that just allowed him to twist sixty degrees until he was facing Calvin, who had *thumped* into the wall with his back, having turned at the last second until they were face-to-face. Keo saw the flash of confusion on the other man's face, but if Calvin didn't know what was about to happen, he figured it out pretty fast when Keo smashed his forehead into the bigger man's face. There was a satisfying *crunch!* as Calvin's nose turned to mush, his blood spraying the hallway.

Stars flooded Keo's eyes and his head rang, and he was almost sure that a piece of Calvin's pulverized nose was jutting out of his own forehead (*That's what you get for using a part of your head as a battering ram!*), but he fought through all of that—or as much as he could—and staggered back and spun around. He blinked through the blood coating his eyes (his, Calvin's, but mostly Calvin's) as Bellamy stood five feet from him.

"Jesus Christ," Bellamy said even as he backpedaled, the look of shock frozen on his face.

For some reason, Keo grinned and wondered what he must look like with his face coated in a film of Calvin's plasma while the man himself was sitting against the wall, large body tilted dangerously over to one side as blood *drip-drip-dripped* from his chin like heavy raindrops. Calvin was still alive, because Keo could hear him breathing. Or wheezing, anyway, because the air was clearly going through that bloody hole in the middle of his face that used to be his nose. It was a grotesque sight, but at the moment Keo couldn't be bothered to feel any sympathy for the man.

Keo didn't so much as run at Bellamy as he threw himself like some human missile at the man. His aim was true and he crashed into Bellamy's chest, turning his body slightly at the last second so that his shoulder buried itself into the other man's sternum just as Bellamy managed to get the Glock out of its holster.

He collapsed back down to Earth on his shoulder and let out a pained grunt, even as Bellamy landed on his back farther up the hallway. For some reason Keo thought his luck might have been good enough to jostle the gun loose from Bellamy's hand, but he was wrong. Very, very wrong, as it turned out, because he found himself staring at the wrong end of a gun barrel.

Keo gritted his teeth and waited to eat a bullet, but for whatever reason Bellamy, sitting on the hallway floor on his ass, didn't fire. Instead, he just stared across the iron sights of his weapon at Keo, that look of shock still present on his face.

After what seemed like an eternity—though it was probably more like two or three seconds—Keo let out a resigned sigh and slowly picked himself up from the floor and onto his knees. He was breathing hard, but that was more from exertion and the throbbing pain originating from his forehead than fear.

Bellamy stood up, the gun never wavering from Keo's head for a single heartbeat. After a moment, he smirked.

"I had to give it a shot," Keo said.

"Nice try," Bellamy said.

"So what was the plan?"

"Take you outside, shoot you, then say you were trying to escape. But this actually works better. You killed Calvin, and I had no choice."

"In my defense, he was a big motherfucker and I had to put him down with the first try or I wasn't going to get a second one."

"Understandable," Bellamy said. He took a moment to wipe at the blood on his cheeks and chin—not his or Keo's, but Calvin's that had whipped free from Keo during their collision.

"Does Rhett know about this?" Keo asked.

"No. Any other questions?"

"Nah, that'll do." Keo reached up with his bound hands and brushed at a thick patch of blood over his right eye. "Can I at least stand up before you shoot me? I'd hate to die on my knees. It's the gentlemanly thing to do."

"Sure. It'll look weird if you were on your knees when I put a round through you anyway."

"Much obliged." Keo struggled up to his feet, but while he

was doing so Bellamy took two, then three more steps back. Keo grinned. "I feel like we've lost some trust."

"No shit," Bellamy said. He picked what looked like a shard of bone sticking to his shirt and flicked it away. "Jesus Christ."

"Talk about having a thick head, huh?"

Bellamy chortled. "What did you say to Mercer before you shot him?"

"What makes you think I said anything?"

"Jane said she heard you say something before you pulled the trigger."

"I don't know a Jane."

"She was in the Comm Room. She got out before the shit went down."

Keo shrugged. "I don't remember."

Bellamy narrowed his eyes, and Keo couldn't tell if that was confusion or anger. "You just murdered one of the most important men on the planet, and you *don't remember* what you said to him before you did it?"

"'One of the most important men on the planet?'" Keo smirked. "I think you're overvaluing him just a tad. If I had my hands free right now, I'd pinch my fingers together to further make my point."

"Fuck you," Bellamy said, and his face reddened noticeably.

Now *that* Keo had no trouble reading. Bellamy was pissed.

"Go for the head," Keo said.

"What?" Bellamy said. The Glock in his hand trembled slightly, but not enough for Keo to make up the seven or so feet that separated them at the moment. The handgun was also pointed squarely at his chest—center mass.

"Go for the head," Keo said. "One shot, one kill. I don't know if you've shot anyone before, but a body shot isn't a guarantee. A headshot—now, that's one and done. After all, as soon as you pull that trigger, everyone on the island will know and come running."

"You think anyone on this island cares about what happens to you?" Bellamy asked.

"I like to think I made an impression."

"Oh, you did; there's no doubt about that."

"Still, one shot, one kill." Keo reached up and tapped his forehead. "As evidence, I point to Mercer's brain splattered all over the Comm Room."

Bellamy's eyes narrowed even further—was that even possible?—and he lifted his hand slightly so the gun was now aimed at Keo's head. "Better?"

Keo smiled. "Watch out for the kick," he said, just before he launched himself forward and left—*then right!* It was a feint, and he was hoping to confuse Bellamy just enough to throw off his aim—

The *bang!* came faster than Keo expected, but he had been expecting it nonetheless. He twisted his body as fast as he could, but of course it wasn't fast enough. It was never going to be fast enough. He was only human, after all. Frank, or one of his blue-eyed pals, could have dodged the 9mm round easily.

But Keo wasn't a ghoul and even the fastest man alive couldn't dodge a bullet at seven (six, now?) feet, a cold, hard fact that was drilled home when the round hit him in the temple and actually spun him like a top. He slammed into the wall about the same time a streak of red splashed across the dull gray concrete.

Footsteps squeaked as Bellamy moved closer for the finishing shot, but Keo was too tired (*And bleeding. Shit, I'm bleeding.*) to turn around and confront his would-be killer. Not that it mattered. It could have been Mercer's ghost come back from the grave (or wherever it was that the island had buried him) to get its revenge, for all the crap Keo gave at the moment.

A bullet was a bullet, was a bullet.

And dead was dead, was dead.

...except when dead wasn't really dead.

Right, Frank? I could definitely use your help right now, ol' pal.

"You really thought that was going to work?" Bellamy asked from behind him. There was almost a singsong quality to his voice, as if it were all fun and games now.

"Yeah, sort of," Keo said into the wall.

"You really are too stupid to live."

"I've been called worse."

He wished he had the strength to turn around and flash one of those faux grins that was full of bravado, if just to piss Bellamy off one last time. But he didn't, so instead he stared down at the floor, at his feet, as he propped his body up against the wall with the top of his head. Blood *drip-drip-dripped* down from his right temple and made small, messy individual puddles on the floor. Sooner or later, they would merge and become one big, messy pool.

Oh, the joys of coming together, he thought, and almost laughed. But of course, nothing came out when he opened his mouth except labored breathing and what sounded dangerously like a pathetic wheeze.

On the bright side, at least he wasn't going to have to worry about the concussion he had no doubt suffered from ramming his forehead into Calvin's face. So there was that, if not a whole lot else.

See? There's always a bright side to everything.

He definitely heard himself chuckling that time, and it ended up being a spurt of uncontrollable giggling. That was probably the only reason Bellamy hadn't shot him in the back of the head yet.

"What the fuck are you laughing at?" Bellamy asked.

"Nothing, nothing," Keo said. "Sorry, sorry, private joke. You had to be there."

"Jesus Christ, you're fucked up," Bellamy said.

Fucked up? No.

Fucked? Most definitely.

Captain fucking Optimism, most indeedy!

That started another round of uncontrollable laughter, and he didn't stop even after Bellamy pressed the cold barrel of the Glock against the back of his head and pushed, because apparently this time he was determined to get the one shot, one kill down.

With nothing left to do, Keo focused on the red liquid that was *drip-drip-dripping* down the side of his face and to the floor below. He was staring so hard that his eyes started to lose focus. It surprised him that his blood would be so intensely red, and thick, like ketchup if he really concentrated hard and long enough.

He managed to close his eyes and thought of the *Trident*.

More specifically of Lara, and Carrie, and Bonnie. Shit, he should have taken them up on their offer. Bonnie, especially. How many times did you get the chance to sleep with a model at the end of the world?

Live and learn, pal. Live and...

Or not.

His legs became too wobbly to hold him up, and he fell down.

At the same time, Bellamy decided to finally pull the trigger (*Geez, man, what was the holdup? Let's get this show on the road!*) and there was a loud *bang!* that left Keo's ears ringing.

Wait. Why were his ears still ringing?

Idiot can't even shoot someone from point-blank range correctly, Keo thought before he started laughing again.

Or thought he did. All he could really be certain of was that there was a lot of blood on the floor and he was lying in it, and he was almost one-hundred percent sure most of it had come from him.

Probably...

10

GABY

With Riley's people still confined to the lower deck, there were plenty of spare rooms to choose from. She wished there could have been more time to enjoy that luxury but there wasn't, not if she wanted to leave the yacht unnoticed. It was cowardly, she knew, and he was going to be angry when he woke up, but he would get over it. She hoped, anyway.

She spent some time at the door looking in at him asleep on the bed. There was a ghost of a smile on his face, his bare torso visible in the moonlight that spilled in from the open window on the other side of the room. She had never seen him so calm, so at peace with everything. It was a rare sight, and she enjoyed it just as much as he did.

I'll see you soon, Nate. Please don't be too mad at me.

She closed the door softly, and as she walked through the empty corridor, she couldn't help but wonder how many times Will had thought that exact same thing while he was trying to get back to Song Island and Lara. She told herself it was different with her because she wasn't going to fail. Whatever happened, she would come back to Nate and start a life with him. If everything went well out there, that life would be a good one. A very good one, indeed.

Plan G. That's a hell of a name, Danny.

Hiding the preparations from Nate all day long was the hard part, but surprisingly the lying came easier. Maybe it was because she was doing this for his own good, that if he knew what she had planned he would have demanded to come with her and wouldn't take no for an answer. But after the last time, she couldn't allow that. He wasn't ready. She could see it in his movements, in his eyes. He was putting up a front, but that gunshot had taken more out of him than he wanted to admit, even now, days later. Zoe had confirmed as much.

She took the short trip to the girls' cabin on the main deck to look in on Claire, but the girl was already asleep on the large king-size bed with Elise, Vera, and Milly. Lorelei was there with them, the teenager sleeping curled up on a recliner in a corner after taking over Annie's duties. Despite the extra empty rooms, the girls hadn't branched out. Gaby guessed that had more to do with familiarity than anything.

Gaby wished she could have said she was surprised by what Annie had done, but she wasn't. Loss made people do strange things, like how she had thrown herself into Ranger training on Song Island after Josh "died," and how Lara had spent every waking day (and no doubt some of those nights, too) trying to keep them alive. Annie, meanwhile, had decided to lash out at the closest target—Will.

She stepped back into the hallway. It was better this way, anyway. If she started saying good-bye to everyone on the boat it would just make everything more difficult than it had to be. Besides, it wasn't as if she were leaving forever. She would return; she just didn't know when exactly.

On her way down to the lower decks, she fished out the bottle of pills Zoe had given her and swallowed two of the white ones.

Once upon a time she would have needed water to wash them down, but those days were long gone. Her left shoulder still throbbed from time to time, but that would lessen to a dull numbness when the meds took effect. She put a hand over it now, feeling the thick bandage under the thermal clothing. She could barely move the arm this morning, but it had improved immensely since.

"One-armed Gaby," a voice said from the shadows as she stepped out onto the exterior deck.

She glanced over at Danny, leaning against the railing nearby. He was still wearing his full tactical gear with the throat mic, and he pushed off and walked over to her.

"You should get that stenciled across your uniform," Danny said. "One-Armed Gaby. The Most Dangerous Girl Who Ever Fought With Just One Arm."

She smiled. "That's kind of long, don't you think? Besides, I'm not wearing a uniform. And neither are you."

"Hey, everyone's wearing uniforms these days, so why not us, too? I already told Carly to start making them. It'll give her something to do other than nag me. I was thinking blue with hot rod stripes. What do you think?"

"Sounds tacky."

"If by *tacky* you mean *glorious*, then yeah, it's gonna be all kinds of tacky, all right."

They walked side by side the rest of the way. There wasn't anyone else along the railing, and she had never known the *Trident* to be so quiet before. She swore she could even hear her own heartbeat. It was surprisingly calm, considering what she was about to do and where she was going.

"You ready?" Danny asked.

"As ready as I'll ever be."

"What about the arm?"

"It's good."

"Meaning?"

"It's good, Danny. Besides, I'm a rightie."

He didn't look convinced, but nodded anyway. "I should be going, not you."

"We already talked about this."

"Yeah, I know."

"Besides, I'm only there to pull security. Bonnie and Blaine will be doing all the heavy lifting. Then it'll be up to Will."

"I'm not worried about that last part. It's the everything-in-between part."

"Have faith. Will knows what he's doing."

He smirked. "I have so much faith in that boy—dead or alive or, er, dead-alive-ish—that I even took three seconds to come up with a name for his plan."

"Wow, a whole three seconds, huh?"

"It's everyone else I don't have a lot of faith in. Present company excluded, of course."

"Mercer's people?"

"Uh huh," Danny nodded.

"I know what you mean. I still feel a little queasy about allying with them after everything they did. All those towns, those people..."

She went quiet for a moment as the memories of T29 came back in a rush. The smoke, the blood, the bodies...

"But we have to do what we have to do," she said quietly. "Otherwise, we're going to be fighting this war forever. And I don't know about you, but I don't want to be doing this two or three decades from now."

Danny chuckled.

"What?" she said.

"You, thinking we'll have decades if this doesn't work."

"I guess some of Nate's optimism is rubbing off on me."

"How'd Nate-o-meter take it, by the way?"

"I didn't tell him."

"That good, huh?"

"He would have wanted to come. I couldn't let him do that. Not in his condition."

"As I recall, you were both shot."

"I took one in the shoulder. Zoe said there wasn't any lasting damage. I got lucky."

"That's one way to look at it."

"Nate, on the other hand, nearly bled to death and required emergency field surgery. Big difference."

"You and I and the moon up there know it, but he won't see it that way come morning. I imagine there'll be a lot of screaming and cursing and tears."

"Tears?"

"Silent, manly tears."

"He'll want to follow us, so you can't tell him anything. Promise me, Danny. No one can tell him."

"He'd need to torture me with pliers and at least three hookers before I spill the beans. Okay, one hooker, but she has to be really good."

They finally reached the door to the engine room, where Jolly was standing guard. He gave Gaby a *what's up?* nod.

Gaby returned it. "Hey."

"Good luck out there," Jolly said.

"Thanks."

"Enough chitchat; this isn't *The Love Connection*," Danny said, and opened the door and headed in.

Gaby followed him downstairs, then through the impossibly quiet engine room. "Your own personal mini-me, huh?"

"Jolly?" Danny said. "Good kid. Fast learner. He might make a good Ranger one of these days. Hell, if I sweat him enough, he may even be half as good as you."

"I had two Rangers training me. He's going to have to make do with one."

"Maybe not for long."

She nodded and couldn't help but smile.

Blaine and Danny had spent most of the day making the gear by hand, using the engine room to hide all the work from everyone else on the boat. They had brought down tools, supplies, and extra help as needed, and the results were now squirreled away inside two large duffel bags that looked like they might bust at the seams when Bonnie lifted them, grimacing, one in each hand.

"Heavy?" Gaby asked.

"Be glad you got the bum shoulder," Bonnie said. "But I'll manage."

The ex-model tossed one bag, then the other one, into the fifteen-foot offshore vessel tied to the back of the *Trident*. One of the bags landed with a loud *thwump*, the other one giving off a distinctive *clank!* as its contents hit the fiberglass hull.

"Good thing I've been bulking up," Bonnie said as she stepped off the swimming platform and into the swaying smaller boat. "Used to be I tried everything possible to keep my weight down."

"Muscle weight's different from fat weight," Blaine said from behind the helm.

"My aching muscles agree with you."

"Quit yer whining," Danny said, walking across the landing behind them.

Gaby glanced over as Danny handed her something wrapped in a plain brown cloth. It was easily over a foot long and heavier than it looked when she held it.

"Going-away gift," Danny said.

"What is it?" she asked.

"You can take a peek later."

"It's not a dildo, is it?"

He grinned. "I'm not saying it is, but I'm also not saying it isn't."

She smiled back and shoved the bundle into her pack. "Thanks, Danny."

"Keep in touch," Danny said, not just to her, but to Bonnie and Blaine in the boat as well. "That radio's not there for show, you know. Use it. Twice a day. Once in the morning, once before nightfall. And remember, if something goes wrong out there, you're on your own. Well, mostly. Bottom line: Try not to let anything go wrong out there."

"I can't believe I volunteered for this," Bonnie said, mostly to herself.

"That's right, you did. Sucker."

"Keep an eye on the boat until we get back," Blaine said. "I trust Maddie, but you know women and driving."

"Hey," Bonnie said.

"The man speaks the truth," Danny said. Then, to Blaine, "You want I should keep Sarah company, too?"

Blaine sighed. "She'd prefer you over me these days."

"Still trouble in paradise, huh?"

"Something like that."

"If you can, keep the other eye on my sister for me," Bonnie said to Danny. "She wasn't all that happy when I told her."

"Don't worry; I'll cuddle all the women on the boat for you guys," Danny said. "Now get the hell gone. All this sentimental crap's getting me all *Bridget Jones's Diary*."

Gaby kissed Danny on the cheek and embraced him, and he returned it with surprising enthusiasm.

"I wish I was going with you, kid," he whispered to her.

"I know," she whispered back.

"But if it's not me out there watching his back, you'd be a solid second choice." He pulled away and took a step back, both hands stuffed oddly in his pockets, like a kid who didn't know what to do with them. "Eyes wide, ears open, and guns hot. Shoot first, never mind the questions. Don't take any chances. Understand?"

Gaby nodded. "Take care of everyone."

"That's what I do."

She untied the line, keeping the fifteen-footer attached to the *Trident* before climbing onto the smaller fishing vessel. She gave Danny one last look before nodding at Blaine. The boat hummed to life, the motor catching without a problem.

Soon, they were reversing, then turning.

Danny stood at the back of the platform and watched them go, and she had never seen him look sadder or more helpless.

She waved, and he waved back.

Then Gaby hurried to the stern and sat down on one of the seats along the starboard side. She looked down at the lump resting on the floor near her legs. It was a standard size suitcase with spinner wheels that made it easy to move. The polycarbonate material gave it a nice black sheen, and though it was mostly brand new when they "borrowed" it from one of Riley's people, they had mummified it with duct tape just to make sure there weren't any holes.

"How're you doing?" Bonnie asked as she carefully maneuvered to the back, using the railing to steady herself as the craft gunned it through the darkness.

"Good," Gaby said. "You?"

"Scared shitless."

"I've been with him when he had to come up with a plan while bullets were flying over our heads. This is what he does, Bonnie. Have faith."

Bonnie pursed a nervous smile. "I have faith that you guys have faith in him, or I wouldn't be here."

"He might have changed, but he's still in there. Maybe not all of him, but some of Will is a hell of a lot better than all of a lot of other people."

Bonnie nodded and put one hand on the railing. Gaby did likewise, because no matter how many times she had been on one of these smaller boats, she could never quite shake the feeling that the next wave they hit was going to send her into the water.

She took the opportunity to glance back at the yacht, slowly fading into the endless night behind them. The only reason she could still see it at all was because of its lights, but even those were starting to blink out of existence one by one.

She thought of Nate, asleep in the cabin, oblivious to where she was right now or even that she wasn't in bed anymore. She hoped he was having a good dream. All the signs were there—that smile on his lips, the carefree sleeping posture. Those were all indicators that he wasn't reliving one of his nightmares tonight.

"You told Nate?" Bonnie asked, shouting a bit over the roar of the motor behind them.

Gaby shook her head. "He'd want to come."

"Of course he would. Kid's head over heels in love with you. The question is, do you feel the same way?"

"Yes," she said, without hesitation.

Bonnie laughed. "That was fast. I guess that answers that."

Gaby thought she might have actually blushed, and thought, *God, what are you, back in high school all over again?*

"Benny's going to be a real sad panda after hearing that," Bonnie said. "He's still holding out hope, you know. I told him it was a slim one."

"The two of you talked about me?"

"*He* talked about you. We usually ended up on guard duty together, so I was helpless to do anything but listen."

"He's a good kid."

"'Kid,'" Bonnie chuckled. "I can't believe you guys are so young."

You grow up fast or you don't grow up at all these days.

"Anyways, I'm glad you're coming with us," Bonnie said. "Blaine here's okay, but to have a real badass around..."

Gaby laughed, but felt a flush of pride, too.

She peered forward, watching as the Texas coastline started to appear out of the blackness. She didn't think she would see it again—no, that wasn't true. She was *hoping* she wouldn't see it again, and yet here she was, bandaged shoulder and all, heading right back to it.

As much as she hated returning, there was no choice because it couldn't just be Blaine and Bonnie, even though they were two of the more capable members of their group. Lara couldn't because she had an even more important role ahead of her. And Danny desperately wanted to, but he had other responsibilities now. So that left her.

Gaby remembered Danny's bundle and unslung her pack and took it out.

"What's that?" Bonnie asked.

"I don't know," Gaby said, and carefully placed the item in her lap and took out her knife and cut away the two zip ties holding the cloth in place.

Moonlight seemed to bounce off every inch of it, making it gleam in the darkness. It wasn't quite white, but it could have been mistaken for the color. It was silver, and at one point it was a cross, but had since been forged into a weapon. A cross-knife, similar to the one Danny and Will used to always carry with them. Danny had lost his back in Texas and Will, well, Will didn't need silver anymore. This one was freshly forged.

"Looks too heavy," Bonnie said.

Bonnie reached down and pulled her own knife out of its

sheath. It was also silver, and like hers and the one Blaine carried, was thinner and lighter and the blade was only half the length of the cross-knife's.

"I like ours better," Bonnie said. "Lighter, easier to cut with."

Gaby picked up Danny's gift by the grip and held it in front of her, then took a few practice swings. It was definitely heavier than the knife sheathed at her hip at the moment, but there was a nice balance to it. There was even something that acted as a pommel at the end, and cross-guards where the grip ended. The blade itself was double-edged and sharp, as was the point.

"It feels good, though," Gaby said. "I wonder when he made it?"

Bonnie put her knife away. "I remember he had one like it before. I always thought it was kind of clunky. If you're going to be carrying around something like that, a sword or machete might be a better option."

"Danny can be sentimental with his weapons."

"We're talking about the same Danny here?"

"He and Will found a pair of something like this in an abandoned apartment when The Purge happened. That's how they discovered silver kills the ghouls."

"So it was just sitting there? Waiting to be discovered?"

"Pretty much."

"Wow," Bonnie said. "I've never heard that story before. If I didn't know it was true—it is true, right?"

Gaby nodded. "It's one-hundred percent true."

"Then I wouldn't have believed it. Things like that...finding a pair of crosses—what do you call those, cross-knives?—in an abandoned building when you needed them the most..." She shook her head. "It almost makes you believe, doesn't it?"

"Believe?"

"In a higher power." Then, as if realizing what she had just said, "Not that I subscribe to something like that, but... It's a hell of a coincidence, that's all."

"Carly thinks it's providence," Gaby said. She bundled the knife back up and put it away in her pack. "Danny and Will thought it was just a stroke of good luck."

"What does Lara think?"

"We've never really talked about it in depth. I know she was raised in an atheist household, but after you've seen everything we have..."

"It's hard to keep telling yourself there's no heaven or hell," Bonnie finished for her.

"Uh huh."

"And Will, coming back..." Bonnie snapped a quick glance down at the suitcase on the floor between them. "I'm telling you, Gaby, I don't believe in anything I can't see, touch, feel, or taste, but if we survive this, and it works the way he says it will..."

"Maybe there is something out there?"

"Yeah. Maybe there is something out there, or up there," Bonnie said, and let the rest trail off.

Gaby looked forward, past Blaine standing behind the helm, and at the fast approaching coastline. It was still too dark to see any stretch of the beach, but it was starting to slowly, very slowly, come into view.

If we survive this, and if it works...

She didn't feel the dread she was expecting as land loomed in front of them. Maybe it was the presence of the suitcase—or more specifically, what was inside it—or maybe she had successfully transcended fear (*Bullshit, girl*). Of course, it could have just been Zoe's painkillers finally taking effect and making her feel invincible.

Regardless of the reason, there was a calmness at the center of her being as they skipped across the open Gulf of Mexico and back toward Texas. Gaby turned her face into the wind and leaned back in the seat, then closed her eyes completely.

She thought of Nate, oblivious to her betrayal; of Claire, asleep with the other girls in their room; and of everyone back on the *Trident*. She thought of Lara and the hard work ahead of her; of Danny, who wanted desperately to be the fourth person on the boat with them right now.

And she thought about the future.

And there would be a future, if this worked.

If this worked...

11

LARA

"What did you find out?" Lara asked.

"He was smart. Phil only approached the soldiers," Riley said. "People he knew who were ready and able to take up arms. Not counting Phil, there was Bray and Ethan in the infirmary."

"What about the two unfortunate souls that wandered down to the engine room?" Danny asked.

"Stephens and Doug," Riley said. "Phil also went to Peters and Janice and tried to recruit them."

"How do you know about Peters and Janice?" Lara asked.

"Peters came to me after everything went down, and Janice followed later. They were the only other two Phil approached."

"That you know of," Lara said, and thought, *And we all know how wrong you can be when it comes to your own people.*

But of course she didn't say that last part. Rubbing it in now wouldn't help them get to the bottom of the problem, and right now she wanted to nip this in the bud as soon as possible. There were other, more important matters on the horizon that were going to require all of her time.

"That I know of," Riley nodded. If he suspected anything else behind her statement, it didn't show on his face.

They were gathered on the *Trident*'s bridge again. It had become their go-to meeting spot because no one was supposed to be up here without permission. It allowed them to talk freely, and Lara liked being able to see what was out there with just a glance at the windshield.

Maddie was behind the helm in place of Blaine, while Danny leaned against a wall next to the small Texan. The yacht was moving again, the world beyond the wraparound screen so excruciatingly bright that Lara had trouble focusing, and she was certain the growing headache was the result of the overwhelming sunlight and not because she had barely slept at all the last few nights.

It was morning and she had eaten with the others before coming here, and she was still tired. So, so tired. Her body was drained of energy, and all she wanted to do was retreat to her cabin and lie down on her bed and reclaim all that lost sleep. She would have settled for a couple of undisturbed hours at this point.

"What about the civvies?" Danny was asking.

"They don't know what really happened or why," Riley said. "I told them Phil and the others tried to take over the boat because of the possibility we might return to Black Tide."

"They bought that?"

"Mostly."

"Not very reassuring."

"It's all I can offer."

"It'll have to do," Lara said.

"I talked to Peters and Janice," Riley said. "They've agreed not to let the others know what really went down."

"You good with that?" Danny asked. "Lying to your peeps?"

"I don't have any choice. The truth isn't going to get us any closer to our objective. Speaking of which, what's the plan when we finally reach out to Black Tide?"

"You'll tell them that we have an inside man in Texas who'll coordinate the attack for us," Lara said. "His name's Frank."

"Will is Frank."

"Yes."

"Why not just call him Will?"

Because he doesn't want me to, and because people might figure out it's my ex-boyfriend, except he's not the man he used to be.

She said instead, "He prefers Frank."

"Bottom line: I have to lie some more," Riley said.

"Practice makes perfect, right?" Danny said. "Anyhow, we know what happened the last time someone found out Willie boy's true identity."

"It's not who Will is that's important," Lara said, "it's what he knows. Who he is—Will or Frank—doesn't matter."

"The fact that he's one of them kinda matters," Riley said. "But I get your point." Then, after a brief pause, "All right. Frank it is. What else?"

"If they push for more information, we'll tell them Frank is a collaborator turncoat."

"Well, it's not *too* far from the truth," Danny said. "Kinda works, in an almost poetic sort of way."

"Not sure you know what poetic means," Maddie said.

"Words that rhyme, stanzas, and shit, right?"

"Not even close."

"Which is why poetry won't be a required curriculum in Danny's School of Badassery."

Riley ignored their back and forth, and said to Lara, "So he's gone. Will. Frank. Whatever we're calling him."

"He left last night," Lara nodded.

"And it'll be up to him. This whole thing—this entire Plan G —it all rests on his shoulders."

"He'll be there when the time is right."

"Are you sure about that? Are you absolutely certain?"

"Yes," Lara said, without hesitation.

He's never let me down before, she almost added, but didn't because it would have been a lie. Will *had* let her down before. He had promised he would come back to Song Island, and he never did.

But then he did come back, and you let him go again. So whose fault is it this time?

Maybe that was why she was so damn tired now, more so than she'd been all those months leading up to the last few days. Talking to Will, being around him, thinking about him, then letting him leave again after reentering her life in the most dramatic way possible was exhausting.

Even after watching the small vessel push off the *Trident* and drift into the blackness from the bridge last night, she still couldn't decide if she should have protested more. After all he had done to get back to her, and she had simply acquiesced and prepared for his departure. Had she *wanted* to let him go? Was that it? Was the reality of who he was—who he had become— more than she could bear?

She hated herself for thinking those thoughts, but she couldn't deny them. Will leaving had removed a heavy burden from her. She wouldn't have to explain his presence on the yacht anymore, wouldn't have to deal with more Phils opposed to his very existence.

She promised herself that once he came back, once this was all over, she'd learn to deal with who he was, because he was still Will. Whatever had happened to him, whatever he looked like and sounded like now, he was still Will.

Wasn't he?

She wasn't sure when she had closed her eyes, but when she opened them Riley was talking and looking at her: "You're that convinced he's right? About everything?"

She kneaded her forehead with her knuckles while summoning all the patience she had left. Getting annoyed with Riley's constant doubts wasn't going to do her or the plan any good. She had to convince him, because if she couldn't, what chance did she have of convincing the rest of Black Tide?

"He went through hell to get back to us," Lara said. "He almost died."

"Again," Danny said. "Dying once is a pain in the ass, but twice? Now that's hardcore."

She wasn't sure if Riley was convinced, but he nodded and glanced out the window at the bright ocean. "The best I can do is present your plan. I can't force anyone to do anything."

"And I don't want you to," Lara said. "Besides, I won't need everyone. Just enough to make a difference."

"We might be putting the cart before the horse, anyway. After all, if Rhett's already ordering everyone out of Texas, it might take a lot more than just your word to get them to commit to another fight so soon."

"Except this time we're not talking about razing women and children," Danny said. "Big difference."

"Maybe so. I'm just telling you one possibility." Riley shrugged. "Maybe I'm entirely off base and they're not as gun-shy about jumping back in as I think, and they'll readily embrace Frank's plan. After all," he added, looking over at Lara, "if you're right, then this is our best chance to take back the planet. That's something worth dying for."

"Happy thoughts, kids," Danny said. "Remember what my homeboy George S. Patton used to say: 'The object of war is not to die for your country but to make the other bastard die for his.'"

"Now that was poetic," Maddie said.

"Told you I'm all up poetry's skirt," Danny said.

"You said your good-byes?" Danny asked as they walked through the *Trident*.

"Did you?" Lara said.

"It was short and sweet, just the way we like it. If Willie Boy wasn't a top-notch conversationalist before, he's gotten even worse since."

It's his voice. Will doesn't like to talk because of his voice. He hates it. I can see it—feel it—whenever he speaks. More than anything, it reminds him that he's not the man he once was.

"Don't take this the wrong way," Lara said, "but why didn't you leave with them?"

He sighed, and she could see it in his face that it was a question he had asked himself a thousand times since Gaby and the others left on the fishing boat last night.

"Carly?" Lara said.

"Something about, 'Go with Will and I'm going to kill you,'" Danny said. "I think she meant it, too. Unless, of course, that shotgun she was holding when she said it was just for show."

"I don't blame her. You should have seen her while you were gone. I don't think she can handle you running off again."

"What can I say? I'm very lovable. Plus, I'm a wildcat in the sack."

"So Carly keeps telling me."

"Gaby's a decent replacement. Of course, she's not the genuine article, but she makes for a pretty good facsimile."

He was putting on a good act, but she could hear it in his voice that he was still tortured by staying behind.

"It's good you didn't go," she said. "I'm going to need you here when we make contact with Black Tide."

"Happy thoughts, remember? I'm sure they're not still pissed off at Riley and company."

"You don't think so?"

"Nah, they probably are. I was just trying to be optimistic."

"Captain Optimism, huh? Haven't seen him make an appearance in a while."

"I'm trying to bring him back, just like how I singlehandedly brought sexy back a few years ago."

"That was you?"

"Yup."

She smiled. "Besides, who would Jolly look up to if you're not around?"

"Yeah, there's that too."

"How's he coming, by the way?"

"Kid knows some stuff, but I'd still pick Gaby first on the playground."

"She's had Ranger training."

"I just meant because she's hot."

"Don't tell Carly that."

"Never," Danny said, and made a zipping motion over his lips.

"What kind of training did he come with?"

"Some basics back on that island of theirs, but he's probably ten percent ready. Kid's enthusiastic though, and ready to run through a wall, so that's good."

"Don't make him run through a wall, Danny."

"No promises."

"What about Nate?"

"What about him?"

"He asked me where Gaby went when I was on the bridge with Maddie, but we wouldn't tell him. I'm assuming he went to you next since you're the only other person who knows."

"Oh, he did. He even threatened to kick my ass if I didn't tell him."

"You didn't..."

"Of course not. He left fuming. Carly says he's already asked everyone in our group and will probably start in on Riley's peeps pretty soon."

"Poor kid. I know how he feels."

"He'll get over it," Danny said. "He has no choice. Adapt or perish, right?"

"Something like that," she said, even though watching Nate leave the bridge heartbroken hadn't been easy.

She had wanted to tell the young man, but Gaby was right—if he knew, Nate would just follow them out there. She knew why Gaby had left him behind, because Lara could see it in the way he walked that Nate wasn't ready. In his current condition, he would just be a liability to the mission.

They made their way through the deck, out the back door, and onto the viewing area. She leaned against the railing and let the chilly wind rake across her face, then looked out at the open seas, back toward where Texas would be.

"When was the last time you had a full night's sleep?" Danny asked.

"It's been a while."

"No time like the present to do some catching up."

"Maybe when this is all over."

"It's not going to be over for a while, Lara."

"What are you, my dad now?"

"Feel free to call me Daddy Danny if you want."

"I'll have to take a pass on that."

"Too bad Willie boy couldn't stay longer."

"Yeah."

"It was decent of him to tell us in person, though. Of course, we wouldn't have believed a single word of it if he had just passed it through Keo or someone else."

"Plan G..."

"Great name, if I do say so myself."

Danny laid his chin on the railing and stared down at some kids fishing off the aft of the yacht. To her left, the refueling ship kept pace with them, but only because the *Trident* wasn't moving anywhere close to its full speed.

"Back in Gallant, while we were hunkered down in that bank waiting for daylight, we had a nice long talk," Danny was saying.

"What did you talk about?"

"This, that, everything. Had a lot to catch up, and all that girly stuff."

"Girly stuff, huh?"

"Yup. Girly stuff. Anyways, the takeaway was that he was worried about coming back. About seeing you again since...well, you know. He didn't say it in so many ways, but I think he was afraid of how you'd react. I don't think he gave any thought to the rest of us, which should really wound my ego, but whatever. What I'm trying to get at here is, it was always about you."

She didn't reply for the longest time, and instead turned her face into another large gust of cold wind, thankful for the soothing sun rays caressing her skin.

"Thank you for seeing him off," she finally said.

"No problem. It still kinda sucks to see him leave again. But if this plan works, there's nothing to say he can't stick around. Not that I'm saying it could ever be the same for us, or for you and him."

"We'll deal with that when the time comes. For now, let's just concentrate on getting past the next couple of days."

"You think it'll work the way he says it will?"

"Are you having doubts?"

"No, but..." Danny shrugged. "I don't know. Whenever we talked about it, even before he had to switch it up when he learned about Mercer, it always felt like he was holding something back." Danny grunted and shook his head. "I'm probably just reading too much into it. You know me, always letting the ol' brain machine take over. Besides, why would he keep anything back now, after all the trouble he went through to get it to us? It doesn't make sense."

"No, it doesn't," Lara said, but her mind drifted anyway.

Was there a chance Danny could be right? Was there something Will hadn't told them about the plan? A facet of it that he didn't think they could handle, so he left it out on purpose, even from her?

"It had to be Houston, didn't it?" Danny said after a while. "But of course it had to be Houston."

She smiled. She had thought the same thing when Will told her: *Of course it would be Houston. Where else would the end come, if not where it all began for us?*

Both hers and Danny's radios squawked at the same time, bringing her back to the cold present. Maddie's voice came through the tiny speakers, and it was very obvious she could barely contain her excitement: "Lara, Danny—you wanna get back to the bridge."

"There goes your first real sleep in a month," Danny said.

"Like that was ever going to happen," Lara said. She unclipped her radio and keyed it. "What's happening, Maddie?"

"Just got a call on the designated emergency channel," Maddie said.

"Is it Gaby and Blaine? Did they run into trouble?"

"No, not them," Maddie said. "He says he's calling from Black Tide Island."

"Keo?"

"It's not Keo, but he wouldn't tell me his name. Said he'd only talk to you."

Lara exchanged a quick look with Danny, and they immediately turned and slipped back into the ghostly empty main deck.

"We're on our way," she said into the radio.

"If it's not Keo, then it has to be Keo-related," Danny said.

Lara nodded. "Has to be."

"What are the chances they sweated our number out of him?"

"I don't think so."

"No?"

"How would they even know to force it out of him in the first place?"

"Maybe through this Erin girl he was headed there with?"

"She doesn't know about the emergency channel. I haven't even told Riley." Then, when Danny gave her a surprised look, "I've only known him for a few days, Danny. And as you probably noticed, Riley's been known to make a few mistakes about personnel."

"Oh yeah, there's that," Danny said.

"It's Rhett," was the first thing Riley said when she stepped back onto the bridge with Danny. "He wouldn't tell Maddie his name, but it's him. I recognize his voice."

She was slightly out of breath when she said, "Did you talk to him?"

Riley shook his head. "He asked for you by name."

"Definitely the same guy who issued the stand-down order before," Maddie said.

Lara nodded at Maddie. "Okay. Put him on speaker." Maddie pressed a button on the dashboard while Lara picked up the microphone. She took a breath, then keyed it. "This is Lara. I hear you're looking for me."

"Someone gave me this frequency," a man said, his voice booming through the bridge's speakers for everyone to hear. Maddie was right—it was the same voice that had given the stand-down message they'd heard earlier.

"You have me at a disadvantage," Lara said. "You know my name, but I don't know yours."

"Rhett," the man said.

"Who gave you this frequency, Rhett?"

"He said he was a friend of yours."

Keo. It has to be.

"I need a name," she said.

"Keo," the man said.

Lara looked over at Danny, who grinned back at her. "I told you that boy's got nine lives. Or however many lives dolphins have."

"Dolphins?" Riley said.

"Long story," Maddie said.

"And wet," Danny added.

Lara smiled, because she couldn't help it, and then turned back to the microphone and keyed it again. "Is Keo there with you?"

"Afraid not," Rhett said. "He's currently in the brig. A little matter of murdering our commanding officer."

"Mercer," Riley said softly, as if he was afraid Rhett would hear. Or maybe he was afraid Mercer would hear?

"Put a stake in him, the man's a goner for reals," Danny said.

"I've never met the guy, but even I'm relieved," Maddie said.

"Trust me, you're not missing much. He was a typical officer ass munch."

"Mercer," Lara said into the microphone.

"Yes," Rhett said.

"Did he say why he did it?" she asked, even though she already knew the answer.

The truth was she wanted to get a feel for Rhett, wanted to dissect every word he said. More importantly, she wanted to know how he felt about Mercer's death. Maybe it was impossible to discover all those things over the radio, but it was worth a try.

"He said some people just needed killing," Rhett said through the speakers. "If you were to ask me, it was personal. Not that he admitted it."

"Why's Keo still alive if he's been captured, and if he took out Mercer?" Riley asked.

"He's a smooth talker, that Keo," Danny said. "Maybe he smooth-talked himself into a jail cell instead of a bullet to the head. Which reminds me, don't ever let him talk me into gambling with him."

Lara said into the mic, "Is this just a social call, then?"

"You're his last phone call," Rhett said. "Or last radio call, I guess. Also, he had some interesting things to tell me."

"Such as?"

"That he knows someone who knows how to defeat the ghouls. That you would know how to get in touch with this someone. He didn't give me a name, though."

Will?

"Was he right?" Rhett continued.

Lara exchanged another look with Danny, who raised a curious eyebrow, and said, "Is he talking about Willie boy?"

"I think so," Lara said. Then, into the microphone, "I might."

"You either do or you don't," Rhett said.

"That depends..."

"On?" Rhett said, the suspicion in his voice very obvious even through the radio.

"What are you going to do with that information?"

"It'll depend on what that information *is*."

Lara lowered the mic and glanced at Riley. "You know him, Rhett."

Riley nodded. "Besides Erin, he was the only other member of Mercer's command that I was mostly sure would come with me if I had asked. He's a good man. It makes perfect sense he'd be put in charge after Mercer's death. People like Rhett. He's decent, and smart, and he's no pushover. If there was a power vacuum on Black Tide, there would be a lot of people who would look to him."

"Lara?" Rhett said through the speakers. "You still there?"

She turned back to the mic. "I'm still here."

"So who's this guy with the plan?"

"His name is Frank," Lara said. "And Keo's right. Frank has a way to defeat the ghouls and take back the planet."

Rhett went quiet on the other end.

"That's some response," Danny said. "You actually made him speechless."

"It's been known to happen," Lara said. Then, to Riley, "Where would he be talking to us from?"

"The Comm Room," Riley said. "That's where all the communications equipment are."

"Hence the name," Danny said.

"So there's a chance he's by himself?" Lara asked.

"Maybe, but chances are Jane will be there with him," Riley said. "She's in charge of the room and has been since we arrived on the island. Kid's pretty good with all the gear. She was the one who figured out how you were doing that repeating message thing and replicated it for us."

"What about everyone else? The other commanders?"

Riley shook his head. "I couldn't tell you. That would depend on how much control Rhett has—"

"Lara," Rhett said, interrupting Riley.

"I'm still here," Lara said into the mic.

"That's a hell of statement you just made. Defeat the ghouls and take back the planet. The last person who promised me that ended up shot in the head by your friend in this very room I'm standing in right now."

"That's Kia, always making friends wherever he goes," Danny said.

"It's the truth," Lara said into the mic. "There is a plan, and it doesn't involve slaughtering civilians or shelling towns filled with pregnant women. This time the only things that will be hurt are the real monsters."

"So you claim."

"If you don't believe me, maybe someone else can convince you."

"Someone else?" Rhett said.

Lara looked over at Riley, then held the microphone out to him.

He stared at it, then at her. "Now?"

"No time like the present," Lara said. "He needs to hear it from a familiar, friendly voice."

"The same voice who betrayed them not very long ago..."

"Mercer's dead, remember? Things are different now for everyone. You said besides Erin, you thought you could turn Rhett. Well, here's your chance to prove that theory."

Riley sighed, then walked over and took the mic from her. He swallowed hard before keying the radio. "Rhett..."

There was no response from the other end.

"Rhett," Riley said again. "It's Riley."

"Jesus fucking Christ," Rhett finally said. "You sonofabitch."

Danny chuckled. "I don't know about you guys, but I'm getting a really good feeling about this."

12

KEO

"You head-butted a man to death," Rhett said when Keo opened his eyes. "Goddammit, Keo, you're not making this any easier for me."

"In my defense, they were going to kill me first," Keo said. "Or did I read the situation wrong?"

Rhett sighed. "You didn't."

"So what's the problem?"

"The problem is, I now have two more bodies connected to you."

"So they're both dead?"

"Yeah."

"I'll take the fall for Calvin, but what happened to Bellamy?"

"We shot him," Rhett said with a frown.

"*You* shot him?"

"No, one of my men."

Keo smirked. "Couldn't have happened to a nicer asshole."

"Don't be so goddamn cavalier. We're talking about lives here."

"Hey, better them than me."

He reached up and touched the bandage wrapped so tightly around his head that he felt like a watermelon being squeezed by a few hundred rubber bands.

A few hundred? Try a few thousand.

He could feel the rows of stitches, the ones in the very center of his forehead and the ones along the temple, underneath the gauze, but thank God there weren't any Calvin bones sticking out of him. The flesh around the impact points were probably red or black, or both, and likely made him looked like a walking ambulance, not that he wasn't already. Still, scars were better than a casket.

Getting prettier and prettier, pal. At this rate, you're going to end up looking like Lurch. Only uglier.

"Yeah, it's pretty messy up there," Rhett said with obvious amusement. "Looks like your modeling days are over."

"Eh, I was getting tired of throwing up after every meal anyway." He brought his hands back down. "By the way, I can't help but notice I'm still not dead. Not that I'm complaining, of course. Though I might feel differently if someone doesn't stop trying to jackhammer nails into my skull."

It took only a glance to know he wasn't back in the brig, but in some kind of military sickbay. Which was to say, sparsely decorated and efficiently built. There were empty beds to both sides of him and two uniformed figures worked across the room, talking over clipboards. They weren't armed, but they didn't have to be with the other two standing at the door holding M16s.

Someone had swapped out his old stained (and bloodied) clothes with one of those familiar tan uniforms with the sun emblem on white collars. No wonder his nostrils weren't instantly twitching from his own stench. He didn't have socks or shoes on, and except for the constant thrumming against his chest all the way to the very top of his head, this was probably the most comfortable he had been in a while. Of course, he didn't have a bed in the brig, so it wasn't like there was a whole lot of competition.

Rhett sat on a chair next to him, one leg casually draped over a knee. Keo couldn't decide if the other man looked worried or angry. Maybe a little of both, or maybe a third option that he couldn't figure out given the *goddamn relentless pounding in his head*.

"They said the bullet caught you in the temple and glanced off the skull underneath," Rhett said. "Took a nice chunk of skin along with it, but didn't penetrate the bone. You must be the luckiest sonofabitch alive."

Keo grinned back at Rhett.

Lucky? Maybe. He was lucky he had managed to talk Bellamy into going for a headshot instead of a surefire chest target. Or maybe "talked into" was too nice a phrase; it was more like *cajoled*.

Hey, whatever works.

"Lucky me Bellamy wasn't the best shot," Keo said.

Rhett shrugged. "Well, he was a truck driver in a previous life. We can't all be as dead-shot accurate as the great Keo."

"My legend precedes me."

"I'm talking more about your handiwork the last few days," Rhett said, leaning back in his chair, eyes never leaving Keo.

Keo looked over at the guys with M16s. He was at least reassured one of them wasn't Donovan, the guard who had let Bellamy and Calvin into the brig. "So what happened in the hallway?"

"Calvin died of his wounds before we could get him back here. Bellamy was shot when he wouldn't put down his gun."

"How did you know?"

"I went to the brig to get you, but you weren't there. Donovan confessed pretty quickly and then there was the gunshot, which told us where they took you. Bellamy was about to finish you off when we turned the corner."

"A day ago you were trying to decide whether to kill me fast or slow, and today you're running around trying to save my life. If my head didn't feel as if it were about to explode, I might just let out a nice long laugh. A guffaw, even."

"I guess if anyone deserves a good laugh, it's you." Rhett gave him what almost looked like a pitying smirk. "By the way, I got in touch with your friend Lara."

That brought a smile to Keo's lips. "She told you what a great guy I am?"

"If by *great* you mean *a royal pain in the ass*."

"But a great ass, right?"

Rhett ignored him, said, "Your friends are worried about you."

"I make very good first impressions."

"Apparently."

"You said you were coming to get me earlier. So what's the verdict? Do I get to keep being a pain in the ass?"

"I had more questions for you, mostly about your friends," Rhett said. "But no decision's been made. I guess it'll depend on what your friends have to say when they get here."

"They're coming here?" Keo said, unable to hide the surprise in his voice or on his face.

"They intercepted one of our broadcasts." He made a wry face. "Riley has been telling them our secrets."

"The prodigal son returns."

"There are some on the island who won't welcome him back."

"Is one of them you?"

"No. In a lot of ways, he opened our eyes to what we were doing. He and Erin..." Rhett pursed his lips. "I don't think we'll ever be able to repay her for her sacrifice."

"Hey, I'm the one who pulled the trigger on Mercer. Thank me."

"I'll do that by arguing for you to keep breathing."

"That'll work, too."

Rhett stood up. "Meanwhile, keep praying to whatever God you believe in. If Bellamy had moved his gun one more inch to the left, I'd be talking to a corpse right now."

"What makes you think I believe in God?"

"Everyone has to believe in something."

"I do. He has nine millimeters."

Rhett grunted and turned to go.

"Hey," Keo said. When Rhett stopped and looked back, "Can I get something to eat? Something that doesn't look like someone tossed day-old mashed potatoes into a glass of water and didn't bother to stir it?"

"I'll see what I can do. Anything else?"

"Coconut drinks? You guys have coconuts on this island, right?"

"No."

"Well, that sucks."

"I'll get you some water instead," Rhett said, and walked to the door. He said something to the two armed guards, and one of them went outside with him while the second remained behind.

Keo lay back down on the slightly hard mattress and sighed with relief. Whatever they had given him before he woke up had numbed most of his body; with the exception of the relentless throbbing coming from the halo around his head, he was as comfortable now as he'd ever been since laying eyes on Black Tide Island.

Things looked up even more when one of his doctors came over. She was in her early twenties, with light brown hair. She was just a bit taller than Lara, but shorter than Bonnie. He focused on her friendly smile. *Mary* was written across her name tag.

Way too young to be a doctor. Maybe a nurse?

"How's the head?" Mary asked.

"Pounding," Keo said.

She jotted something down on her notepad. "You were shot in the head. If a pounding headache's the worst of your problems, you're in good shape."

"I've been told I have a thick head."

Mary smiled. "That's putting it mildly. I don't think I've ever seen someone get head-butted to death before. You...really did a number on Calvin."

"Wasn't a friend of yours, was he?"

She shook her head. "I've seen him around, but no. I try to stay away from the soldiers. All that testosterone isn't good for your health."

"Tell me about it," Keo said, rubbing his bandaged forehead.

––––––––

Mary gave him some additional meds for the throbbing pain and he drifted off a few minutes later, and didn't open his eyes again until—Well, he wasn't entirely sure when he opened his eyes because there didn't seem to be any clock on the walls, and the two doctors (or one doctor and a nurse) had left while he was knocked out.

Keo grunted and tucked the pillow under him so he could (mostly) sit up on the bed. He looked across at the only other person still left in the room with him—his guard, who seemed to be staring at an old calendar on the wall to Keo's right as if it were the most fascinating thing he had ever seen in his life.

"Hey," Keo said.

The man didn't respond.

"Hey," Keo said again, louder this time.

The guy finally turned his head. "What?"

"You got a name?"

The guard tapped his name tag. Keo squinted, but he couldn't make out the letters even though they weren't that far apart. Of course, he still had a major headache and focusing on one thing was difficult, especially small letters across a room.

"You can't read English?" the guy asked.

"I can even read cursive, smartass," Keo said. "I just can't read it from here. They told you I was shot in the head, right?"

"And that you head-butted someone to death."

"That, too. So you can probably guess I'm not exactly working at one-hundred percent capacity here. Wanna help me out?"

"Henry," the guy said.

"I'm Keo."

"I heard," Henry said.

Keo nodded at the bed next to him. "Can you grab me that extra pillow, Henry?"

Henry fixed him with a suspicious look, but didn't move from his post.

"Oh, come on," Keo said. "It's not like I'm going to try anything. Didn't Rhett tell you? We're practically BFFs now."

"I doubt that's even remotely true."

"Doubt all you want, but I'd still like you to grab that extra pillow for me. I'm tired of lying down. How long has it been since Mary shot me up with those sweet, sweet meds, anyway?"

"Two hours, give or take."

"That's all?"

Henry nodded before walking over. He shifted his slung rifle from his right shoulder to his left as he did so—to take it a little more out of Keo's reach—but otherwise didn't look *too* paranoid that Keo was going to try something. Henry grabbed the pillow and handed it over, keeping a respectful distance between them before returning to the door.

"Thanks," Keo said after him.

"Sure."

"How long's your shift?"

Henry glanced down at his watch. "Another hour."

"Hey, at least you get to leave this place."

"From what I'm hearing, you won't be here very long, either."

"Back to the brig?"

"Not what I meant."

"Ah. Good news, then."

Henry resumed his post and casually switched his rifle back to his right shoulder. "Despite everything you did."

"We talking about Mercer now?"

"Who else?"

"Well, there was that incident in the hallway earlier..."

"I don't care about that," Henry said. "You didn't have any choice. They were going to kill you against Rhett's orders."

Keo stuffed the pillow under him and propped himself into a better sitting position. His head started to clear up even though the throbbing continued, though it had lessened noticeably since the last time he was awake. Instead of jackhammers trying to punch their way into his skull, the pain was now more like mallets banging away. But it was an improvement, and the best he could hope for after his most recent ordeal.

"Someone once told me there were three types of people in Mercer's army," Keo said. "The true believers, the nonbelievers, and everyone else in between. Which one are you?"

Henry didn't answer right away, but Keo didn't think he was a part of the first group. The young man didn't have the look of a Mercerian who thought Keo had killed someone he worshipped. If anything, Henry looked angry, but not that angry. Then again, considering Keo's ability to read faces, he could be completely off.

"He saved us," Henry finally said. "If it weren't for him..."

"That doesn't mean you have to slaughter innocent civilians for him. There were pregnant women and kids and old men in those towns."

"I know that," Henry said. He had come dangerously close to snapping. Then he added, in a much softer tone, "We all knew that."

"But you still went along with it."

"I...stayed behind. A lot of us who had problems with it did the same. The ones that went out there, the kill teams, were the true believers, as you call them."

"Like Bellamy and Calvin?"

Henry nodded. "They're not the only ones. That's why I'm here and Pete's outside."

"Pete?"

"The other guard. He's in the hallway."

"Two guards to keep me safe," Keo chuckled. "I told you Rhett and I are practically BFFs now."

Henry didn't say anything.

"So Rhett's in charge of this place now?" Keo asked.

"Pretty much."

"Who decided that?"

"The others, I guess."

"Did you get a vote?"

"I'm not that high up."

"How do you guys know who's up and who's down if no one wears a rank?"

"It's not that hard to figure out. Everyone knows who was in charge before and who's in charge now. We've had a year to figure it out."

"I'm not much for official rankings myself, but that sounds dangerously chaotic." When Henry didn't respond, Keo said, "So, question."

"What now?"

"What happened to my food?"

"Your food?"

"You mean no one brought me my food?"

"Not that I saw."

"Rhett promised he'd send some food over, and not that slop you guys have been feeding me in the brig."

"Maybe he forgot."

"What an asshole." Then, smiling at Henry, "You wouldn't mind—"

"Not my job," Henry interrupted.

"How about Pete?"

"Not his job, either."

"Do a guy a solid, huh? I'm starving."

Henry didn't bother with a reply.

Keo sighed. "At least tell me something, just to keep my mind off the food people keep promising but never delivering."

"What?" Henry said.

"Mary."

"What about her?"

"She single?"

"She's married."

"No shit?"

"No shit."

"I didn't see a ring on her finger."

"Maybe not technically married. It's not like there are priests around or anything. But she's shacking up with some dude. I think his name's Gary."

"Well, that sucks."

"For you, maybe."

"I thought it was fairly obvious that was what I meant," Keo said. "Now, let's figure out how to get me some food, Henry..."

It was nice to be up and about, even with the cold wind whipping at his face. Rhett had been nice enough to give him a windbreaker, socks, and boots to complete his new wardrobe, so the only thing exposed to the elements as he stood on the beach of Black Tide Island was his face. It might have been the harsh chill, with much of the breeze unhindered by the island's relatively flat land mass, or maybe lingering effects of the meds, but the throbbing in Keo's head had lessened dramatically.

Mary stood next to him, hands stuffed inside her coat's pockets while unsuccessfully trying to stop her body from shivering. Apparently she wasn't nearly as happy to be outside as he was, though as his nurse she had no choice but to follow him around in case he fell on his face.

"Can we go back inside now?" she asked after a while.

"What's the hurry?" Keo said.

"It's freezing out here!"

"It's nice weather for a walk."

"No, it's not."

"Of course it is. Come on."

Keo started down the beach, and Mary had to hurry to catch up. "Slow down, Keo!"

He didn't know why she felt the need to shout. They were close enough that he could smell her perfume. Or was that just regular feminine scent? He couldn't be sure after spending three days in that jail cell with nothing to occupy his sense of smell but his own BO.

His boots squished in the soft sand, but he stayed far enough from the incoming tide to keep from getting wet. It was nice out, but he didn't feel like getting wet, too.

They were somewhere at the back of the island, the same general vicinity where he had landed with Erin not all that long ago. The guys watching him like hawks from a distance might have even been the same men who had helped him and Erin come ashore that night. He counted two guards when he first arrived at the beach, then two more had showed up later. It wasn't like he was going anywhere without a boat in sight, so the men, as with Henry and Pete back in sickbay, were likely here more for his protection.

Which made Keo wonder: How many more true believers were out there, waiting for their chance to finish what Bellamy and Calvin had started? He'd been lucky so far, but luck was luck because it tended to come and go.

Maybe coming out here and walking around in the open wasn't such a good idea after all.

"Keo!" Mary shouted as she caught up to him.

She was already breathing hard, as if this was the most exertion she'd had in a while. And maybe it was. Mercer had brought these people to the island a long time ago, and many of them had never left. He didn't blame them for not wanting to leave, though. It was human nature not to voluntarily abandon a safe place. Lara and the others had done the same on Song Island, fighting to the very bitter end to hold onto it and only jumping ship when they no longer had any choice.

Like a few thousand ghouls coming out of a hole in the ground. Yeah, that'll make you change your mind about a place real fast.

"Henry told me you're married," Keo said.

"What?" Mary said. She gave him an odd look, as if she couldn't believe they were having this conversation. He thought she had very lovely brown eyes. "He said I was married?"

"Not married, married, but taken. By some guy named Gary."

"He said I was taken by Gary?"

"Aren't you?"

"I'm not."

"No?"

"Not that it's any of your business."

"I was just curious."

She took her hands out of her pockets and folded them across her chest for warmth.

"Cold?" he asked.

"What do you think?"

"A little body heat would fix that."

"Yeah, right," she said, and moved away until there were a couple of extra feet between them.

"Oh, come on; I don't bite. At least not if you don't want me to."

"You think you're charming, don't you?" Mary said, narrowing her eyes back at him.

"You mean it's not working?"

"Not even a little bit."

"Give me a break. I almost died today. You know what happens when you almost die?"

"No, but I'm sure you're going to tell me."

"You start thinking about what's important in life. Like a pretty nurse in a tan-colored uniform."

She shook her head, but he caught just a ghost of a smile on her lips. "I'm already seeing someone. Gary, remember?"

"I thought you said you weren't taken."

"I'm not. I'm just seeing him. There's a difference."

"Is it serious?"

"Not really," she said quickly. Then, maybe catching her mistake, "Maybe. I don't know."

That's definitely a "not really."

"Word's already gotten out about your friends," Mary said. "The ones on the way here to meet with Rhett. Something about a plan to beat the ghouls and win the war?"

Keo smiled. "Are we changing the subject?"

"Absolutely," she said, and this time didn't try to hide her smile. "Is it true?"

"Yeah. It's true."

"How?"

"I think you're going to have to wait for your commanders to tell you that."

"Tell me now."

"What do I get in return?"

"You know those pain meds I've been giving you for that raging headache you're currently experiencing? Well, sometimes they can be a little hard to locate."

"I love a woman who knows how to blackmail."

She rolled her eyes. "So what is it? What's the plan? Tell me *something.*"

"There's a guy out there who knows how they operate. He knows just about everything there is to know about them, including how to beat them. And none of it involves shelling towns with pregnant women and children."

They had stopped walking and Mary stared at him, though now she didn't look nearly as cold as before. Or at least her body wasn't trembling against the wind, even as long dark hair splayed across her pretty face.

"We can take back the planet," she said.

"That's the idea," Keo nodded.

"But *how?*"

"I'll tell you under one condition..."

She narrowed her eyes suspiciously at him. "And that is...?"

"I gotta find a cafeteria, Mary. I'm starving here."

She laughed. "Okay, Keo. Okay. Follow me."

She turned and led him back up the beach. He followed, eyes drawn irresistibly to the way her ass moved beneath her slacks.

"Are you staring at my ass?" Mary said, glancing over her shoulder back at him.

"Of course not," Keo said. "I'm insulted you would think that."

"Riiiiight," she said.

"Question, Mary."

"Oh God, what now?"

"When you said you weren't taken, how *un*taken are you?" Keo asked.

13

GABY

The morning sun beat down on them as they climbed out of the boat and made their way up the beach, careful not to step on the carcasses of sea life that had washed ashore. There wasn't very much in the way of living things to greet them, though there was plenty of grass that went all the way up to their knees and, at various points, tickled at their waists. But they had expected the open fields, having seen them last night as they sat in the fifteen-footer and waited for dawn to come.

They had taken the small craft in by trolling motor to hide their approach, then let the waves take over for about half a mile before switching to paddles. Maybe they were being too cautious (if there were such a thing these days), but the fact that everything depended on this—getting Will to where he needed to be—weighed heavily on all their shoulders. If Gaby hadn't volunteered for the mission with her eyes open, the responsibility might have been too much to bear.

She was the first one to step foot on the mushy sand, then the first one in the grass. She moved quickly and quietly, M4 in front of her and Danny's gifted cross-knife at her hip. Maybe it was a combination of Zoe's pills and adrenaline, but she hadn't felt this good in days, even weeks, and the soreness from her shoulder was barely a blip on her radar. She didn't stop until she was twenty yards up the beach and crouching in grass, her breath forming mists around her as she breathed in and out, in and out, concentrating almost as much on her surroundings as she did to control her accelerated heartbeat.

"Gaby," Blaine whispered from behind her.

She glanced back and shook her head.

He nodded, then jumped out of the boat to join Bonnie, and the two of them pulled the vessel out of the ocean. By the time they reached land, their pants, like hers, were soaked in cold water up to the knees. There was just enough green around them that if she didn't look closely she wouldn't have spotted the drab olive hull of the fifteen-footer as Bonnie tied its line to a rock, then pulled it tight to ensure it didn't go anywhere. There was very little chance they would actually need it again, but it was better to have it available in case they did.

Just in case, right, Lara?

It was strange to hope they wouldn't need the boat again, but that was exactly the best possible outcome. She had every confidence in Will's plan—even if he did have to alter it at the last minute—not only because it was Will who had engineered it, but because he had gone to such great lengths to bring it to them.

Now all we have to do is get it done...without everyone dying first.

Yeah, no pressure.

When she looked back a second time, Blaine and Bonnie had started removing items from the boat and putting them on the beach. She couldn't help but feel a little guilty about making them do all the heavy lifting. Besides her own pack, she just had her gun belt and rifle. Her job was to provide security, a task that she relished. Bonnie had gotten very good with her weapon in recent months, but she was still a notch below Danny and Gaby. Though to hear Lara tell it, none of them could touch Peters, some guy who had come aboard with Riley's crew.

Note to self: Find out if she's right when you get back.

She focused on the grass-heavy fields around her. There were no signs of civilization as far as she could see, but that was the point of choosing this spot to beach. She wasn't exactly looking forward to the long walk ahead of them, but a lot of nothing was better than even a little hint of something, especially if those somethings carried guns.

Loud grunting behind her as Blaine eased the suitcase out of the boat while Bonnie waited to lend a hand.

Gaby willed Blaine to get the piece of luggage over the side of the boat, then for Bonnie to hurry over and grab the other end.

Don't drop it into the ocean. Whatever you do, don't drop it into the ocean!

She breathed a sigh of relief when they both found firm holds and successfully made the transfer, splashing water around their ankles the whole time, before depositing the black case on dry land.

Blaine looked up and nodded at her, and Gaby returned it.

She turned back to the empty world in front of her, slinging the rifle and raising the binoculars hanging around her neck. She scanned the horizon, looking for signs—*anything*—that might indicate they weren't so alone out here after all, that maybe they had misjudged how empty the place looked while they were waiting in the ocean last night.

Nothing. There was absolutely nothing out there.

So far, so good.

She lowered the binoculars and looked back at Blaine and

Bonnie as they were slipping on their bulky packs. They already looked tired from the lack of sleep, and she wanted to tell them this was just the beginning, that the road ahead was only going to get tougher the closer they got to their ultimate destination.

But she didn't, because they already knew everything that she did. They had, after all, also volunteered when they didn't have to.

We're all idiots. All three of us.

"Good to go?" Blaine asked.

She nodded. "I don't see anything out there. We landed in a good spot."

"Nothing is good. Nothing is very good."

"You wishing you were back on the boat yet?" Bonnie asked him.

"I don't know what you're talking about. This is going to be easy. In and out, just like that."

Bonnie smirked. "Just like that, huh?"

"Yup," Blaine said. "That's my story, and I'm sticking to it. Besides, who wants to live forever?"

"I do," Bonnie said.

I wouldn't mind seeing the next couple of years myself, Gaby thought, but kept that to herself.

Bonnie and Blaine didn't just have their packs and weapons to carry, but they were also burdened with the two duffel bags— one each—and had the black suitcase between them.

"You guys need a hand?" she asked them.

"Nah, it's just like dragging around a really big piñata," Blaine said.

"Yeah, what he said," Bonnie said.

Gaby didn't quite believe them, but she nodded anyway and stood up, and weapon in front of her, began moving forward, back into Texas.

They made surprisingly good time despite having no forms of transportation except their feet. Gaby remained up front, with Blaine about ten yards (sometimes less, sometimes more, depending on the terrain) behind her. After leaving the mushier grounds around the beach, Blaine was now able to drag the suitcase by its handle, which helped them move faster. Bonnie, meanwhile, brought up the rear about twenty yards back to make sure no one was sneaking up on them. Blaine was the only one with both hands occupied, so that left Gaby and Bonnie with their rifles at the ready.

The only times they stopped was to catch their breath and drink some water, and to radio the *Trident* to let them know they had made it on land in one piece. After that, they wouldn't call again until almost nightfall. Ever since Keo had given Black Tide their designated emergency channel, Lara had switched to a secondary one, which was what they were using now to make contact.

Just in case...

It was almost noon when they finally stumbled across something that hinted at civilization—in this case, a small blacktop two-lane road that cut across the flat landscape. There were no official road signs close enough for them to see, but it was easy to pick a direction and follow it, basically keeping the Gulf of Mexico at their six o'clock.

After a while, the soothing warmth of the sun began to take its toll, and Gaby found her focus wandering slightly. There was something to be said about seemingly being the only three souls on the whole planet, with only the sounds of their footsteps against the hard earth and occasionally labored breathing to keep them company. She only wished Nate were here to enjoy it, too.

Sorry, Nate, but I couldn't let you risk it. Not after all you've been through. Don't hate me too much.

Footsteps, before Blaine appeared alongside her, the suitcase rolling behind him on its well-oiled wheels. "Anything?"

"Not much."

"I don't know about you, but I don't like the thought of walking all the way over there."

"Will said there's supposed to be a collaborator town nearby."

"And he would know, right? He's been running around out here for how long now?"

"Long enough."

"Yeah." He paused, then, "So just walk up and ask to borrow one of their trucks?"

"Sure," she smiled. "If they don't feel like being neighborly, we'll just take it by gunpoint."

"Sounds good to me," Blaine said, and drifted back until he was behind her again.

Gaby didn't change her stride. She would have slowed down if she thought the two of them couldn't keep up, but they hadn't said anything about her going too fast or too slow, so she maintained her current pace.

Except for the occasional breeze that swept across the countryside, she had difficulty remembering it was winter. Texas weather was an oddity that most Texans had come to accept, but she hadn't realized just how strange this place was until after she'd been living onboard the *Trident*. Of course, the thermal sweater she had on and the heavy load she was carrying had a little something to do with keeping the cold at bay.

Don't like Texas weather? Wait five minutes, she thought with a smile.

It was big and black and looked new if not for the blown-out front windows. There was a machine gun mounted on top of the cab, the muzzle pointed up at the cloudless sky. It was parked next to a tall elm tree, though not directly underneath the provided shade. She was looking at it from over a hundred yards and from a side angle with binoculars, and there was too much knee-high grass in her path to allow her to see much of anything around the parked vehicle.

Blaine scooted up next to her and went into a crouch a few feet to her right. He had left the suitcase and duffel bag behind to free his hands for his rifle, and he gripped it with one hand now as she handed him the glasses.

"That's a hell of a nice spot for a picnic," Blaine said as he peered through the binoculars. "What happened to its windows?"

"Looks like they were shot out," Gaby said.

Gaby glanced back at Bonnie, crouched in the grass about twenty yards behind them, rifle clutched in her hands. The two of them exchanged a brief acknowledging nod.

Then Gaby turned back to the truck. "See anything I might have missed?"

"Nope," Blaine said, lowering his hands. "Looks like a Ford. F-150 or F-250."

"Is there a difference?"

"The 1 or the 2 in front of it."

She rolled her eyes. "Okay, Danny Junior."

Blaine chuckled. "Not the worst insult I've gotten."

He turned slightly and looked through the binoculars at a wall of trees about 200 yards to their right. It was the first real group of woods they had seen since arriving on land, and they had gone around it like the plague, sticking instead to walking under the sun where it was safe.

Stay out of the dark places, girl, stay out of the dark places, she remembered telling herself.

She stared at the truck again. "What do you think?"

"I think it was smart of Danny boy to give us these," he said, tilting his rifle so that the sun glinted off the smooth steel bore of the long suppressor attached to the end of the barrel.

Her own M4, along with Bonnie's, had the same custom attachment. The extra length made the rifle somewhat unwieldy, but out here, in the open where a gunshot would travel for miles, she was glad to have the option.

"It looks pretty new," Blaine said, handing the glasses back to her. "Or someone's been keeping it clean. Good chance it's still drivable; maybe there's even some fuel in the tank depending on how long it's been out here. The blown-out windows are a problem, though."

"It's a big problem."

"The plan was always to find a ride, and here it is."

"Yeah," she said. "Here it is..."

He snapped a quick look back at Bonnie, then over to her. "We're going to have to take a chance sooner or later."

"It could be a trap."

"I don't think so," Blaine said. "No one knows we're out here. At least, no one we can't trust. And I don't see how it makes any sense for anyone to leave a truck out here on the off chance someone would walk across it."

She thought about it for a moment. Blaine wasn't wrong. There was a very small number of people who knew their itinerary, though Lara might have already told Riley and possibly Hart, his second-in-command. And Blaine was right about the other thing, too: Sooner or later they were going to need a ride.

And here it was...assuming it still ran and there was fuel in the tank. These days, those two things weren't always a given.

Finally, Gaby said, "We go at the same time. You take the

right side, and I'll take the left. Bonnie keeps an eye out for snipers, just in case."

Blaine grinned. "You sound like you've done this before."

"Once or twice."

"I'll go fill Bonnie in," Blaine said, then got up and jogged, slightly hunched over at the waist, back to Bonnie.

Gaby pulled at the straps of her pack to make sure they were tight. Her heartbeat had picked up slightly, but not nearly as much as she would have thought.

Maybe I really am getting used to all of this.

Blaine returned a few seconds later. "Ready?"

She nodded.

"Be careful," Blaine said, and was on his feet and moving forward toward the parked truck in the next breath.

She launched to her feet and was on his heels before starting to angle to the left side and didn't stop until she had put almost ten yards between them. Her eyes snapped left and right and forward, never staying still in one direction for longer than a second each time.

The country road they had been following for the last couple of hours was to her left, but there were too many fields of grass to see it at the moment. To the right of Blaine was the wall of trees, and she couldn't help but feel like eyes were watching her every movement, listening to every haggard breath she took...

Focus!

She trained her eyes back on the truck and kept moving, matching Blaine's pace.

Eighty yards...

Seventy...

She glanced left again, toward the road, but still couldn't see it. Back to the truck and the tree on the other side of it. It was a nice shaded area, the perfect spot for a pair of lovebirds to park and do whatever it was that lovebirds did. She had an image of two naked people in the truck bed popping up suddenly as they neared it.

Sixty yards left, and nothing except for the slight swaying of the branches in the background.

Fifty yards...

She sensed eyes watching her and snapped a quick look over at Blaine, but he was concentrating on their target. She looked past him, at the trees in the background.

Dark, black trees, so thick she wondered if the sun could even penetrate their crowns.

Thirty yards...

Closer now, she could see the Ford emblem up front, and there, the splashes of blood on the chrome grill.

"Blood!" she snapped, half-shouting and half-whispering.

Blaine nodded, but neither one of them stopped. Like her, he had already assumed the vehicle wasn't just sitting there on purpose. Something had happened to its occupants, and out here these days that "something" usually involved guns and blood and bodies.

She lifted her carbine and took a quick look through the red dot sight, then lowered the weapon, all the while continuously moving. Blaine hadn't stopped or slowed down to her right, and he had actually picked up his pace, which forced her to do likewise in order to keep up with him.

She finally reached the Ford and circled the front hood, sweeping the blood caked over the grill and on the dirt floor directly below.

A body.

Male. Young. Maybe in his early twenties, though it was diffi-cult to tell for sure with the blood on his face. He was crumpled on the ground and half-hidden under the front bumper, either because he had attempted to crawl to safety after being shot or his momentum had rolled him into that position after falling off the hood. The blood on the truck was clearly his because there was a hole in the side of his head.

Jesus, that's some shot.

"I got a body!" she said, using the same half-shouting and half-whispering voice.

"Back here, too," Blaine said, matching her pitch.

She rounded the truck onto the other side, where a second man sat awkwardly against the trunk of the large elm tree. He was older than the first body, with gray in his hair. His head was lolled to one side, and if not for the patch of thick red that covered his chest, turning the uniform he wore an even darker shade of black, she might have thought he was just tired and decided to sit down to take a nap. A pair of empty beer cans lay at the man's feet, and sunlight glinted off the shards of glass sprinkled around the Ford.

"I hope those beers were at least cold," Blaine said.

"I don't see a cooler," Gaby said.

Blaine made a face. "You couldn't pay me enough to drink warm beer." Then, "Your guy wearing a uniform, too?"

Gaby nodded. "They're collaborators."

Blaine glanced around at their surroundings, then hurried to the back bumper and waved at Bonnie, still hiding in the grass across the field. Gaby walked over to where the second dead man sat and quickly noticed the tree behind him.

"Blaine," she said.

He walked over. "Find something?"

She pointed at the large indentations in the trunk just above the dead man's head. There were three of them, and they had gone in deep. Gaby took out the cross-knife and picked at the bark until she could see what had caused one of the jagged holes.

"What is that?" Blaine asked.

"Bullets," Gaby said. "Someone was shooting at the tree."

"Why was something shooting at a tree?"

"It wasn't because of him," Gaby said, nodding at the dead man. "I think he was standing in front of it when he was shot. The shooter took him out by going through the two front truck windows."

"Yeah, I saw that," Blaine said, looking back at the shattered windows. "That's a Danny shot right there."

"These guys might not have even seen him when he picked them off."

"Then the sniper was shooting at someone else if it wasn't this poor bastard," Blaine said. He turned and looked around them before settling on the wall of trees in the distance. "There's a third one still out there somewhere."

"What do you think they were doing out here?"

"Beer, a nice shade... Looks like they had some downtime."

"That means the town's nearby."

"Not close enough."

"No?"

"The gunshots," Blaine said. "No one's responded to the shooting yet. These guys still look pretty fresh."

"Unless the shooter was using some kind of suppressor. We are."

"There's that," Blaine nodded, before walking around the tree to get a better look at the other side.

"Nice truck," Bonnie said as she came around the hood. Like Blaine, she had left her heavy cargo behind in the field to free her hands for her carbine.

"We got it cheap," Gaby said. "Free."

"My favorite price tag. Does it run?"

"Let's find out."

Gaby opened the passenger-side door. There was glass scattered across the seats but no blood. A two-way handheld radio lay on the dashboard, and someone had left their AR-15 behind. She looked across at the steering wheel and saw a key dangling from the ignition.

"Key," she said, before climbing inside.

She reached over and turned the key—but not all the way— and smiled when the dashboard lights turned on, along with a chime to indicate the door was open. Even better, the fuel gauge rose almost three quarters of the way before stopping.

"Hallelujah," Bonnie said, leaning in the exposed driver-side door. "I was starting to think we were going to have to walk all the way to Houston."

Blaine reappeared behind Gaby. "They couldn't have been out here for very long. Less than an hour, give or take."

Gaby climbed out of the Ford. "Did you find anything back there?"

"Some traces of the third guy," Blaine said. "My guess is, he was hiding behind the tree and the sniper tried to pick him off. After that, he ran for it." He nodded at the wooded area. "In there."

"I'd rather take my chances out here than go in there," Bonnie said, not even trying to hide the slight tremor in her voice. "Was it another collaborator?"

"Makes sense, considering the other two. The sniper was picking them off one by one." He walked around the truck to look at the first body. "He went first. Then the guy in front of the tree. Number three got the hint after that." He took in the endless fields around them. "The question is: What happened to the sniper? And who was he?"

"One of Mercer's people?" Bonnie said.

"Who cares," Gaby said. "Let's get the hell out of here before someone comes back for the truck."

"I'm all for that," Bonnie said.

Blaine and Bonnie left her to retrieve their belongings, and Gaby took another look inside the Ford—a F-150, as it turned out—and went through its glove compartment. She found a bag of jerky and a folded map of Texas, and pocketed both. There was a cooler on the passenger-side floor, and when she flipped it open found three more cans of beer, but no ice. She didn't have a lot of uses for beer, but water was water, and she tossed the cooler into the backseat.

The AR-15 leaning against the seat also went into the back, but she picked up the radio and checked the power to make sure it was still turned off. She clicked it on, but there was only silence. Gaby put it away and got out, then opened the back door to search the backseats. Boxes of supplies, MREs, and six more warm beers on the floor. There were two backpacks on the seats, each containing additional supplies and loaded magazines. Both packs had blood and what looked like bullet holes in them.

She peered out the shattered driver-side window as Bonnie and Blaine came back. The two of them looked like they were on a nervous stroll through a dangerous park, armed to the teeth and carrying their luggage for some reason.

She exited the vehicle and looked into the truck bed. There were more empty beer cans back there, though these looked as if they had been exposed to the elements for much longer than the others. There were also two ammo cans for the machine gun. She climbed up and checked the weapon.

It was a different model than the M240 they had back on the *Trident*, but it didn't take a genius to know how it operated. Every weapon was the same—the bullets went in one hole and out the other when you pulled the trigger. It was a no-brainer. The box of bullets attached underneath made the machine gun heavy when she moved it around on its tripod, which was welded to the top of the cab. There were spare casings around her feet, so someone had definitely been putting the gun to use.

From her high vantage point, Gaby took a moment to stare at

the dark woods across the field one more time, the hairs along her arms spiking at the thought of running headfirst into that thing.

"How's the view from up there?" Bonnie asked.

"Nice, but empty," Gaby said, and jumped off the truck.

"Come on; let's get the hell out of here," Blaine said, opening the back door and throwing his pack inside first. "Houston's not gonna come to us."

14

LARA

"Can you do it?"

"Yes."

"You want to at least think about it first?"

"Do you want me to at least think about it?"

"It would be nice, yes. They used to be your friends."

"They're still my friends. But not if they're trying to shoot me."

"What if I asked you to shoot first?"

Peters didn't answer that one as quickly. Lara looked across the map table and watched his expression. Peters was a tall, stocky man in his early thirties, as unassuming as they come, with short black hair poking out underneath the Houston Astros ball cap that he always seemed to have on. Or at least in the three times she'd seen him up close. The thing looked well worn, and she had no trouble whatsoever believing he had been wearing it even before The Purge. A rifle jutted out from behind his back. Some kind of bolt-action.

"I'm not saying I'm going to need you to do anything," Lara said. "We're talking worst-case scenarios."

"I understand," Peters nodded. For such a dangerous man, he was surprisingly soft-spoken, and even in a room with just the two of them she had to put some effort to hear him.

"If I need you to, can you do it?" she asked.

"Yes."

"Why?"

"Why?" he repeated.

"Why are you so willing?"

He stared back at her with hazel eyes. "I signed up with Mercer because I thought he was the right man, the right leader. But I discovered that wasn't the case, even before Riley came to me. Everyone needs to believe in something, Lara. I chose badly with Mercer, but I rectified that. Now I'm choosing to believe in you."

"Maybe you shouldn't. Maybe you're making another mistake."

"Maybe I am. And if that turns out to be the case, I'll deal with it. But for now, you asked me for my loyalty and I'm telling you that you have it, whether you think you deserve it or not."

Lara could only nod, because everything she had planned to say sounded wholly underwhelming against that response from him. She had called him to the conference room to talk about what lay ahead, but she hadn't expected this. The fact that it came from Peters made it even more astonishing, and at the same time terrifying.

The only thing she could think of to say was, "Thank you. That means a lot, Peters."

"You're welcome," he said. "Is that all you wanted to talk about?"

"Not quite." She looked down at the map, at the small speck that was supposed to represent Black Tide Island. It really was in the middle of nowhere, and they would never have gotten within a hundred miles of it if they didn't know it was even out there. "How familiar are you with the place?"

"We trained on it for months. Except for the missions into Texas, most of us spent our time there. So I know it pretty well."

"If this whole thing is a trap, how would they attack us? Where are the boats, and how fast can they hit the water and swarm us?"

"Lara, if this is a trap, Cole and the other Warthogs could strafe you before you're even within sight of Black Tide."

Well damn, Peters, at least make an attempt to lie to me! she wanted to say, but she didn't, because she knew he was right. So why wasn't she more afraid?

Peters was still looking at her closely when he shrugged. "But if you want me to work up some scenarios, I can do that."

"How soon can you have it for me?"

"I got a few hours to kill."

A few hours to kill, she thought, wondering if Peters had meant that as some kind of joke, especially considering the two bodies she knew belonged to him on the *Ocean Star.* But Peters didn't appear to be joking, not that she could really tell just by looking at the man's face.

God, I'm glad he's on my side.

"Anything else?" Peters asked when she didn't say anything.

"You said you went on missions for Mercer. What did you do on them?"

"Mostly overwatch for the scouts. Keep people—and things— from getting in their way. We were fortunate; we never really ran into any major obstacles."

"Never?"

"The few times we had run-ins, we dealt with them."

"And the collaborators never knew?"

"Not as far as we know. But it wasn't like we stayed in one place. The job was to map out their network, and once we did that, we moved on. The problem with the collaborators, and the towns themselves, is that they're largely isolated and self-sustaining organisms. Without modern technology at their disposal, they don't really have much communication with each other, with the other towns. So we were able to get away with fighting skirmishes when we couldn't avoid them and still stay under the radar."

Self-sustaining organisms, she thought. That was the last thing she expected to come out of Peters's mouth. It wasn't that she thought he was stupid—far from it, in fact—but it sounded so... What was the word? Scientific (?) coming from a man who could kill you before you even knew he was there.

"And no one ever connected the dots?" she asked.

"Apparently not."

"Okay," Lara said. "Come see me when you're done with those scenarios. I know you think they're useless, but I'd rather have something in place, just in case."

"Will do," he said, and turned to go.

"Marines, right?" she said after him.

He stopped at the door and glanced back. "Marines?"

"Danny said you used to be a Marine."

There was just a bit of a grin on his face when he answered. "No one *used* to be a Marine, Lara. You're either a Marine for life, or you never were."

"So you're a Marine."

"No. I never had much use for the regimens of modern military life. Why did Danny think I was a Marine?"

"Because of your rifle. He's only seen Marines carry it."

"Ah," Peters said, and left the conference room without another word.

Lara looked after him for a moment, almost expecting him to come back and elaborate on that answer, but of course he didn't.

She shook her head and thought again, *God, I'm glad he's on our side.*

She looked back down at the map. She didn't know what she was looking for, or if any of Peters's scenarios were going to make a bit of difference, but it felt good to be doing something during the trip.

"Lara, if this is a trap, Cole and the other Warthogs could strafe you before you're even within sight of Black Tide," Peters had said.

Tell me something I don't already know...a hundred times over.

There was no escaping it: She was taking a very big risk by going to Black Tide. As soon as they showed themselves, it would be impossible to turn away. How much did she trust Rhett? How much could you trust someone you've never met in person?

The X factor was Keo. He had trusted Rhett enough to give the man their emergency frequency in order to make contact. He wouldn't have done that without a reason. Someone who didn't know Keo might think he would have done it to save himself, but she knew better. Keo had gone to Black Tide to kill Mercer and was willing to die in order to do it. He wasn't the kind of man who would sacrifice her and the *Trident* to save his own hide.

"You better not be wrong about this, Keo," she said out loud to the empty room.

Lara didn't know how long she stared at the map, thinking about all the things that could go wrong, all the lives that were in her hands, and wondering if this wasn't the worst decision she'd ever made.

Wouldn't be the first time. And it probably won't be the last.

"Squid for your thoughts?" a voice said. She looked up at Carly, poking her head into the room. "You sleep conferencing again?"

Lara smiled at her friend. "I know, it's a real problem."

"You should see Zoe about that. There's probably a pill for it or something."

"Or something. What's up?"

Carly came in and closed the door after her. "What's up is that I've been trying to get your attention for the last half a minute or so."

"You were?"

"You were out of it," Carly said, doing jazz hands in the air. "Big, heady thoughts, huh?"

"Something like that."

"I ran across the Shootist on the way here."

"The what?"

"Peters. That's what Danny calls him. Something to do with a John Wayne movie." When Lara gave her an even more confused look, Carly sighed. "Danny's old, Lara. He knows old man stuff."

"He's not that old."

"Old enough to qualify for Medicare, if there were such things as Medicare still around." Carly leaned against the table and looked down at the spot where Black Tide would be. "By the way, speaking of being a pain in the ass, Nate's still bugging me about Gaby. I'm liable to punch that kid in the face if he asks me one more time."

"You didn't tell him, did you?"

"Of course not. That fool would just steal a boat and try to catch up to her." Carly rolled her eyes. "Kids in love in the apocalypse. What will they think of next?"

"Kids, huh? Nate's older than you."

"Semantics."

"That's not really what semantics mean."

"Shut up," Carly said. Then, "So that's it?"

Lara nodded. "That's it."

"Doesn't look like much."

"Nope."

"And we're going there."

"Uh huh."

"To ask them to join our little Scooby-Doo gang."

"That's the plan."

"What if they say no?"

"I guess we say thanks and leave."

"And they're going to just let us head off into the sunset? Remember, we are carrying around over forty people that mutinied against them. Is that the right word? Mutinied?"

Lara nodded. "You're becoming a regular Webster's Dictionary."

"What can I say? I have a lot of free time on my hands." She put a finger over Black Tide. "Doesn't look like much, does it? I can practically squish it with just one little pinky."

"It's apparently bigger in person. There's even an airfield that runs through the middle."

"Airfield means planes. Warplanes."

"Yup."

"Dangerous."

"Definitely."

"And we're still going there."

"We are."

"Because Will says we need them."

"He didn't say we need them, but he said it'd be nice to have them."

"He said that? Ghoul Will? 'It'd be nice to have them?'"

"Something like that."

"But that wasn't the original plan."

"No. He adapted."

"Adapt or perish," Carly said. "Now where have I heard that one before?" Carly looked across the table at her. "Okay, now that all the genius military talk is out of the way. How are you doing?"

"I'm fine, Carly," she said, and hoped the forced smile was at least semi-convincing.

It wasn't if the frown on her friend's face was any indication. "Danny told me you were surprisingly okay with Will leaving again so soon. But he said he understood why."

"What else did he say?"

"That he felt the same way. As much as he was happy Will was still alive—well, sort of, you know what I mean—he's not the same man who left Song Island all those months ago. Hell, he's not even a man anymore. He's...something else. That's reality. Danny says they could never go back to the way things were. It was hard for him to admit it, but Danny can be very pragmatic sometimes when he puts his mind to it. Is that the right word?"

She nodded. "He's right. Will's not the man he used to be."

"What was it like? Talking to him again?"

What was it like, Carly? Thrilling and frightening and discombobulating, all at the same time. I still can't decide even now.

"It was...strange," she said. "Will's there—he's finally back—but he's not really there. When I hear him talk, when he brings up the things from our past, it's like I'm listening to a recording of our history together. It doesn't feel real."

"I'm sorry," Carly said.

"For what?"

"For everything. I would have looked for you sooner and did all the girly stuff—you know, cry over ice cream and bad rom-coms on Blu-ray—but I knew you were busy with Black Tide and all the other stuff we're not supposed to tell anyone who hasn't been on this boat longer than a few days."

"It's okay. Really."

"Danny wanted to go, of course. With Will. But I told him he couldn't."

"He told me."

"Did he tell you why?"

"He said you wanted to be the one to tell me."

Carly sighed. "The only way I could make him stay was by telling him that I'm carrying his devil child."

Lara stared at her friend, speechless. She waited for the punchline, but Carly only smiled back at her.

"Really?" Lara finally said.

"Really," Carly nodded.

Lara hurried around the table and slipped her arms around Carly, and the other woman laughed as she hugged her back. They might have also been on the verge of tears, but at the moment neither one of them cared, though Lara did glance at the door to make sure it was closed.

"Danny hinted at it," Lara said.

"I'm surprised he managed to keep it a secret this long," Carly said. "I guess threatening him with his own shotgun worked after all."

Lara pulled back and looked down at Carly's belly. She wasn't showing yet and wouldn't for a while. "You're going to be a great mom."

"I'm going to get fat," Carly frowned.

Lara laughed. "So we'll get you a big jacket. It's winter, anyway. No one will suspect a thing."

"Yeah, but there goes my fashionista cred."

They laughed and hugged again, and this time Lara was pretty sure they were both sobbing like little girls. Good news was so hard to find these days, and after everything they had been through, she was glad there was at least one unquestionably good (*great*) thing happening in the world.

"*Daebak,*" the voice said over the radio. "Didn't think I'd ever hear from you again."

"You're a hard man to kill, Keo," Lara said. She couldn't help but smile at the sound of his voice.

"Only because I have a lot to live for. Like seeing you guys again."

Maddie was at the helm on the bridge of the *Trident,* Danny and Riley standing behind her. Black Tide wasn't even close to being in sight yet, but it was out there somewhere. The sun had begun its downward trajectory on the horizon, but they still had a couple of hours left. Sooner or later they would have to stop and anchor, because Lara had no intentions of showing up at the island in pitch darkness. Bad things happened when it was night, even out here.

"He's a regular John McClane, all right," Danny was saying. "Reminds me of me."

"Who?" Lara said.

"*Die Hard.*"

"That doesn't help."

Danny sighed. "Seriously, what did you do with all your free time when you were a kid, missy?"

"It's a movie," Riley said.

"See, here's a man with taste."

Lara turned back to the microphone. "How are they treating you over there, Keo?"

"Pretty good, all things considered," Keo said.

"Considering he blew their dear leader's brains out, I'd say that's an understatement," Maddie said.

Danny chuckled. "Yeah, ol' Keo's got himself a way with the locals, all right."

"Some guys did try to kill me earlier today," Keo was saying.

"You okay?" Lara asked.

"Nicked, but still in one piece. Well, mostly."

"Mostly is good."

"Anyway, the reason I'm calling. Rhett wanted me to assure you that he's willing and able to listen to what you have to say when you arrive, in case your extended convo with him earlier wasn't enough to convince you."

"That's awfully considerate of him."

"Yeah, Rhett's a real Southern gentleman, like that guy from that movie Danny probably knows, but don't ask him because I don't really care."

Danny grunted and mouthed something, but Lara didn't catch it.

"But considering it's almost dark," Keo was saying, "it might be a good idea to wait until tomorrow before putting the tugboat into harbor. Morning-ish, say."

"That was always the plan," Lara said.

"Brilliant minds think alike." Then, "What about our mutual friend?"

"He's in-country," Lara said, but didn't add anything else.

"And everything went...okay?"

She knew he was asking about her reunion with Will. Keo and Will had traveled together long before she ever learned Will was still alive, and sometimes she wondered what they had talked about out there as they were making their way to Sunport to link up with her.

"As can be expected," she said into the mic.

"Is that good or bad?" Keo asked.

"I'll let you know when we see each other again."

"Sounds like a plan. I'll keep both eyes out on this end, and I suggest you do the same. Not everyone's all-in with Riley coming back after that *Ocean Star* fiasco, so you're not out of the woods yet. Hell, half the people on this island still want to kill me."

"What about the other half?"

"I'd love to say they want to give me a medal, but it's more like give me an enema. With a hollow-point bullet."

"Ouch," Maddie said.

"What about Rhett?" Lara said into the mic. "What's he doing to keep you safe?"

"Whatever he can," Keo said. "But let's face it, no one looks out for my hide better than me, myself, and I. People call it selfish, but I like to think of it as basic self-preservation. Anyways, that's all I'm allowed to say. I got a couple of guys here watching me like hawks. Hawks with rifles. I don't think they'd shoot me, but why chance it, right?" There was a second or two of silence, then, "Speaking of Southern gentlemen, heeeeeeere's Rhett."

"Well, that was sweet," Rhett said through the speakers. "I almost got all teary-eyed just listening."

Danny snorted. "Me too."

"Keo's right about the clock," Lara said into the microphone. "We're running out of daylight."

"Neither one of us are going anywhere, so let's save it for tomorrow," Rhett said. "Until then, can I speak to Riley? We have a few things to hash out before he gets here. He needs to know that not everyone will be happy about it."

Lara held the mic out to Riley. "It's for you."

She and Danny stood just outside the bridge in the hallway while Riley and Rhett communicated over the radio. The door was open and they could hear snippets of conversation, mostly from Rhett's side thanks to the speakers broadcasting everything he was saying out loud.

"You think Kobe Steak was trying to give us hints back there?" Danny asked. "About not showing up until morning?"

Lara thought about it for a moment before finally shaking her head. "I think he was just being cautious and wanted to make sure we saw things the same way. I don't think he's willingly helping Rhett to lure us into an ambush."

"That didn't stop you from getting the Shootist to come up with some scenarios."

"I'm just being cautious. Just in case."

Danny grinned. "We should put that on a banner. 'Just in Case.'"

"You knit and I'll sew."

"Deal."

They continued to watch Riley on the mic while listening to Rhett's voice coming through the speakers. They seemed to be discussing names, people who Rhett thought was on their side and those who weren't there yet—or were completely opposed. None of the names made any impression on Lara.

"So I guess that settles that," Danny finally said. "We're still doing this come morning."

"Are you having doubts?" she asked.

"I'm always having doubts. Back in college, they used to call me Having Doubts Danny. Later, we shortened it to HDD, because, you know, brevity."

"Of course."

"As for doubts, well, my best friend in the world just came back from the dead as a blue-eyed ghoul. Next to that, this plan of his makes perfect, logical sense."

"Even after you thought Will might not have told us everything? Do you still think that?"

Danny thought about it for a moment before answering. "It's Will. I mean, it's not *Will*, Will. But it's still Willie boy. Ish. I have to either believe that wholeheartedly, or I'll have to question everything. And I guess I'm choosing to believe."

They returned to listening to Riley and Rhett for a moment before Lara finally said, "I hear congratulations are in order."

Danny grinned. "She finally got around to telling you, huh? I was wondering when she'd do that. Kinda got tired of you thinking I'm a chicken shit for not going back out there with Gaby and Will."

"I never thought that, Danny."

"Why not? I did."

"I'd never think that of you. Ever."

He forced a smile. "I feel it, though. That chicken shit feeling. I should be out there with them, not safe and sound on this floating bathtub."

"You're going to be a father, Danny. That's important."

"What they're doing out there is important, too."

"And it might not work," she said. "I have faith in Will, but it might not work. We can't just pretend that's not a very real possibility. But this, right here, right now with Carly, is a sure thing. That baby's going to need you whether the next few days work out like we hope or not."

Danny sighed and leaned against the wall and stared back into the bridge. "Yeah, I know. I just wish I didn't feel like such a steaming pile of crap right about now, that's all."

She put a hand on his shoulder and squeezed, and the two of them exchanged a brief half-smile.

"Welcome to the club," she said.

15

GABY

She was thinking about Nate, about how much he must be hating her right now, when she heard him coming up. That shouldn't have been possible at all—first climbing up the ladder behind her, then walking across the floor. She could even hear the rustling of the trench coat against the cold night air.

Gaby expected to feel sudden pangs of apprehension at his approach, but they weren't there. Not at the beginning, and not when he slid against the wall across the closed loft door from her and looked out at the open fields that surrounded the farm they had taken refuge in. Moonlight filtered inside the stained glass window between them, highlighting the year-old bales of hay in the back.

His face was hidden under the hoodie, the twin pulsating blue of his eyes seeming to gleam in the shadows. The flaps of the trench coat hung at his sides, revealing flashes of the matte black fabric with the mesh stretch panels that covered him from the neck down. It looked like something from the future but was really just clothing worn by extreme sports athletes to protect them from crashes, with brush guards along the upper arms and absorption panels across his torso. Danny called it a ballistic jersey and had gotten Mae and a few others to add bits here and there, but the wardrobe wouldn't stop a bullet or a knife. They did, however, hide his real identity as long as you didn't look at his face.

She did that now and couldn't tell if he was comfortable in the clothes. They were tighter than necessary because they had to hang off his thin frame, but if she didn't know better she might have just thought he was a lanky guy with a thing for black and brown leather. The eyes, of course, gave it all away, as did his face. But they had taken those things into consideration too, and he was only revealing parts of him now, to her, because there were no dangers of them being spotted by anyone else.

Gaby joined him in looking out at the long-abandoned farm, marveling at the lack of fear (she had expected *something*, but it just wasn't there) at his nearness. There was no anxiety whatsoever, and not in a million years would she ever think she could be this comfortable with a blue-eyed ghoul so close to her.

But then this wasn't just any blue-eyed ghoul. This was Will. If she were out there watching them, they could have just been two guards doing their jobs while Bonnie and Blaine rested below them. He even moved like a human, but she knew he had done that on purpose, to let her know he was coming. She had seen how fast and smooth and *silent* the blue eyes could move, and she had no doubts Will could too if he so chose.

"When did you get back?" she asked.

"Recently," he said, the hiss like a sharp knife through the stillness of the barn, though for some reason it wasn't nearly as obvious as the last time they had talked, back on the *Trident*. Was he going out of his way to lessen it?

"How did you know about this place?"

"I was here...before." He turned his head slightly, as if expecting to see something among the shadowed parts of the hay behind them. "There was a girl and a boy... They're gone now. There was a struggle and blood was spilled."

"Who were they?"

"I don't remember."

"But they were here the last time you came through. They were hiding in this barn."

"Yes." He looked back out the window, past the film of dirt over the glass panes and at the nothingness on the other side. "Nothing lasts forever."

I have a feeling we're not talking about two kids who used to call this place home anymore.

Will was hard enough to read when he could still be read, but now, she didn't have a clue what was going on inside that domed head of his.

Instead, she said what had been on her mind ever since he told them his plan: "You're connected to them. The hive mind."

"Yes."

"That's how you know so much about them. About *him.*"

"Yes."

"Who is he? Where did he come from? Where did all of them come from? I wasn't in the cities when it started, but I could see the results almost right away. Everything just went black in one night."

The questions burst out of her in one long stream, as if she had been holding them back all this time, waiting for someone who knew the answers to come around. Not that Will seemed bothered by it or the fact that she barely took a breath before she got to the end.

When he didn't answer or say anything, she continued: "You know, don't you? Who he is? Who he *really* is?"

"Just bits and pieces," Will said, "but nothing that makes a complete story."

"How?"

"When he's occupied with other matters, in other places, he becomes vulnerable. His defenses are lowered and I can sneak into his mind, see snippets of his past, some of his less guarded secrets."

"Other places?"

"The rest of the world."

"Right. Sometimes I forget we're not the only ones out there." She paused for a moment, then, "Tell me about him."

"He's old, and he's evolved over the years. Centuries."

"Centuries," she repeated.

Will nodded.

"That's a friggin' long time," Gaby said.

She didn't know why she was so surprised, because it made sense, didn't it? Did creatures that didn't die even after you cut off their heads still adhere to the laws of aging? And those were just the black eyes. The blue eyes were an almost completely different species that she knew almost nothing about except that they were even more dangerous than their black-eyed counterparts.

"If he's been around for so long, why now?" she asked.

"He had no choice."

"What's that mean?"

"We were poisoning the planet. He's already lost the oceans. Soon, he would lose the land and the air, too."

"How did he lose the oceans?"

"He believes that human progress contaminated the water, and that we were doing the same to the air and the land."

"Contaminated how? It's a big planet, Will. I've seen the water out there in the Gulf of Mexico. It doesn't look all that contaminated to me."

"I don't know. Even when he lowers his defenses, I can only glimpse his surface thoughts. Everything else is buried too deep."

"I guess it doesn't matter. At least to us, right here and now. If this works, if we do our jobs, there'll be people smarter than us who'll figure all this stuff out years from now."

He nodded.

"So he acted," Gaby said. "The Purge."

"The plan has been around for almost as long as he has, but as humanity grew and spread out, he was forced to adapt, to rethink everything. He's been building the nests, around the world, in secret for decades."

"And no one ever knew about them. How is that even possible?"

"He's had all the time in the world to prepare. He knows where to hide, how to stay unseen. They don't need very much. A drop of blood...a single body... They were content to feed on the dregs of society. The homeless. Runaways. People who wouldn't be missed."

"And then we screwed up the ocean."

"Yes..."

"What about the rain? Why doesn't that affect them?"

"The rain is purified in the atmosphere. But soon even that might not be possible as we continue to taint the Earth. We forced his hand, you see, and he had to act much sooner than he had planned. But the rate of infection took him by surprise. The cities were too dense, the people too crammed into one space. Despite his best efforts, too many were taken in the first night, and once the tide began it couldn't be completely reversed." A brief pause before he continued: "He always knew that when the end came, the bloodletting would be difficult to control without the safety nets in place. But he had no choice. The rate of human progress was simply too fast, and it was unyielding."

She had so many more questions, but before she could ask any of them, something flickered in the corner of her eye and Gaby slipped farther back behind the rotting barn wall.

"Will..."

"They haven't seen us," he said.

There were three of them—thin, gaunt, sickly-looking things —appearing from around the side of the main two-story house across the weed-covered yard from them. She didn't have to see the blacks of their eyes to know what they were as they leapt onto the front porch and vanished into the building through what remained of the door, now just a slab of wood hanging off one lone hinge. They moved through the house, skeletal figures flitting across the curtainless windows as they scoured the first floor before darting up to the second.

"I thought you said this place was safe?" she whispered.

"It was," he said, looking out the window. "They shouldn't be here."

But they are, she thought, tightening her grip on the carbine and thanking God for the silver bullets inside the magazine. That helped to calm her suddenly frayed nerves, even though she knew nothing they had on them right now would be enough if they were discovered. Because there might have only been three out there right now, but there were never "just" the ones you could see. There were always more out there, waiting patiently to converge.

The hive mind. It's that damn hive mind of theirs.

She watched the creatures moving back to the first floor and knew that as soon as they were done they were going to come out, and there would be only one place left for them to search.

"Will…"

"I know," he hissed. "Wake the others."

She pushed off the wall without arguing and slipped across the moonlit parts of the second floor until she was at the ladder. It was old and rickety and it made *too much noise* as she climbed down with the rifle slung over her back before jumping the last four rungs to the hard ground below.

Bonnie and Blaine were asleep in one of the stalls, lying on pallets covered with old stained sheets and using their packs as pillows. It was pitch dark at the back of the barn, but it was easy to make out Blaine's larger form from Bonnie's.

She woke Blaine first, nudging him on the shoulder and whispering his name.

Blaine's eyes snapped wide. "What?"

"Trouble," she whispered.

She didn't have to say any more. He was already scrambling for his weapon as she moved over to Bonnie and repeated the process.

It took longer to wake Bonnie up, and Gaby had to raise her voice just a bit too much, but finally the other woman opened her eyes and said, "It's not morning."

"Ghouls," Gaby whispered.

"Fuck me," Bonnie said, and hurried up.

"I thought he said this place was clear," Blaine said as he snatched his pack up from the floor.

"He thought it was," Gaby said, and thought, *But nothing's really "clear" out here anymore. I learned that the hard way.*

"Where is he now?" Blaine asked.

"Up—," she started to say, when a figure moved behind them and Blaine raised his M4 reflexively.

"Stay here," Will said, and then he was gone.

"Jesus Christ," Blaine whispered, lowering his weapon. "I'll never get used to the way he moves."

"What's he doing?" Bonnie asked as she slipped on her own pack and grabbed her rifle.

"I don't know," Gaby said.

She exited the stall and dodged the slivers of moonlight filtering into the building from all the rotting wood and cracks along the walls. She got a shadowy glimpse of Will just as he opened the side door.

"Will," she said.

He stopped and looked back, blue eyes glowing against the darkness. "Stay here."

"Where are you going?"

"They'll search the barn next. If they find us, more will come."

"Will," she said, but he turned and slipped outside before she could finish, and she stared at the door as it *clicked* closed after him.

Blaine appeared behind her. "Where the hell is he going? He knows we're out here because of him, right?"

"He knows," Gaby said. "I think he's going to lead them away from us."

"So where does that leave us?" Bonnie asked as she appeared beside Blaine.

"We stay put," Gaby said, "until he comes back."

"Is that wise?"

"We don't have any choice," Blaine said. "None of this works without him. So either he comes back and we proceed with the mission, or..." He left the rest go unsaid.

Or we're screwed, and all of this will have been for nothing...

By the time she got back to the second floor and peered out the loft doors, the three ghouls that were searching the main house were gone. There were no signs of them ever having been there, and for a moment she wondered if she might not have imagined the whole thing.

"How many did you see?" Blaine asked. He was occupying the same spot Will had earlier.

"Three," Gaby said.

"Just three?"

She nodded. "Just three, but where there's even one, there's usually—*Oh, Jesus.*"

They came out of the shadows and flooded across the open yard between the barn and the house. Gaby pulled farther back until she could only see a tiny sliver out the loft doors, but it was more than enough to watch them racing below her.

Blaine had done the same thing and was staring wide-eyed, his rifle clutched so tightly in front of him she could see his knuckles turning ghostly white.

There were so many of them that their number actually drowned out the sunburnt grass that had reclaimed the property in the year since their owners were taken. She might as well be looking at a moving ocean wave made of quivering pruned black flesh.

"God," Blaine whispered, "I'd forgotten how many of them there are out here."

I haven't, she thought, and said, "They're going after Will. That's why he left us. He's leading them away."

Blaine nodded and didn't say anything. Like her, he was unable to pry his eyes away from the endless horde flowing past below them. Moonlight glinted off their domed heads like flickering beacons, and they kept coming, and coming, and coming...

"There's more of them," Blaine whispered. "Over there, where we're going. You know that, right? We're walking right into a viper's nest."

She didn't say anything. Gaby recognized the long odds the moment she went over it with Lara and Danny. So she didn't know why Blaine was bringing it up now because they all knew what was out there waiting for them when they volunteered. Or at least, she did. Maybe Blaine and Bonnie didn't fully grasp the mission, but she never had any delusions it was going to be easy. Far from it.

If it works, it'll be worth it. If Will's right, three lives will be worth it...

The wave of ghouls kept coming, appearing from one side of the loft window and out the other. She willed them to keep going, despite knowing the object of their pursuit. But Will could take care of himself now that he was fully healed up. It was them she was worried about.

Don't stop now, you bastards. Don't stop—

"No, no, no *no*," Blaine hissed, because he had seen the same thing she had:

Two of the creatures had stopped almost exactly in front of the large twin barn doors and turned to face them. Not her and Blaine, but *the doors.*

"Keep going, you fucks," Blaine whispered. *"Keep going."*

But they didn't, and instead the ghouls moved toward the doors and disappeared out of their field of vision.

"Bonnie," Gaby whispered, and hurried across the floor to the ladder on the other side. She started trying to tiptoe at first, to lessen the noise, but she was moving much too slowly and began sprinting a few seconds later.

Blaine was right behind her.

Gaby was about to stab her foot down on the first rung on the ladder when she heard the unmistakable sound of a suppressed rifle shot—the *pfft!* barely audible, but with nothing else making noise inside the barn except her (and Blaine's, behind her) labored gasps against the cold air, her ears were able to pick it up.

Then a second—and a third—shot, very close together.

Pfft-Pfft!

Gaby grabbed the ladder and hurried down, this time ignoring the creaks that every single one of her steps produced, and instead of waiting until the last few rungs to jump like last time, she let go around remaining step number five and landed with a (*Too loud!*) *thump* against the hard barn floor.

She straightened up and spun around, unslinging her rifle as fast as humanly possible. Dormant pain lanced through her left shoulder, but she gritted her teeth through it. The long suppressor that added to the length of her M4's barrel still made the carbine less comfortable in her hands, but she was glad for its silent capabilities, especially with God only knew how many creatures still outside the barn right this second.

She ran forward, passing the empty stalls one by one, making a beeline for the front of the building. The first thing she saw was the big, bulky Ford F-150 parked in the largest part of the barn up front. She could just make out the tops of the twin doors on the other side of the vehicle, along with the machine gun jutting out the back like some freakish appendage—

A flicker of movement, before she realized Bonnie was crouched in front of her in the darkness, aiming her rifle at something lying on the floor about ten yards up ahead. Whatever it was, it had come inside the barn through the side entrance, the same one that Will had used earlier, which was still partially ajar. That was the only way in because they had barricaded the front entrance.

Bonnie glanced over her shoulder and hissed, "There's one more!"

Gaby was about to say *"Where?"* when a black shape the size of a small child fell out of the corner of the first floor ceiling and landed on top of Bonnie, who squeezed off two more shots as she went down. *Pfft-pfft!* as silver rounds vanished into the second floor above her.

Oh, Jesus! raced through Gaby's mind, but she was unable to put them into actual sounds as she took aim, but it was impossible to separate the creature from Bonnie because their two bodies were so entwined on the floor while lost in the shadows.

Then a startled cry—*Bonnie!*

Shoot! What are you waiting for? Shoot it!

She had to chance it, even if she couldn't be sure where Bonnie ended and the ghoul began—

There! A sliver of separation between the two forms at last!

Gaby squeezed off a shot from five feet away and the creature's head exploded like a watermelon, a chunk of it flitting across the blackened air before splattering a stall door. The ghoul's body simply toppled sideways, allowing Bonnie to grab its spindly legs, which were wrapped around her waist, and pry them free so she could scramble out from underneath the sickly frame.

"Bonnie!" Blaine hissed as he rushed past Gaby.

Bonnie seemed to have trouble standing and had to lean back against the wall for support once she was finally on her feet. Blaine reached her and grabbed her just as Bonnie's legs gave and she threatened to slide back down.

Gaby stepped over the dead ghoul and spotted the second one lying in a pile in front of the still-open side door. A cold draft invaded the barn as Gaby glimpsed blackness on the other side before she grabbed the thin slab of wood and cautiously pushed it shut with a soft *click*.

She glanced over at the front doors just to make sure they were still closed and that the two wooden beams held in place by brackets hadn't been removed. Satisfied, she hurried back to where Bonnie and Blaine were. She stepped over the first dead ghoul a second time—it was such a small creature, like a sleeping child with half of its head missing.

Blaine had guided Bonnie to the back and was crouched in front of her now. Bonnie was staring forward, eyes wide, as if she was seeing something in the shadows that neither Gaby nor Blaine could. Gaby noticed Blaine's hands, holding a rag to Bonnie's neck.

Oh, God.

Blaine looked back at her, but he didn't have to say anything.

Gaby slung her rifle and crouched next to Bonnie, then took over holding the rag against Bonnie's neck. The cloth was already heavy with wetness, because Bonnie was bleeding. A lot.

As Blaine scrambled for the first-aid kit inside his pack, Gaby leaned toward Bonnie and smiled. Or did the best she could. "Think about Jo. Think about going back home to her."

Bonnie turned to look back at her, the simple act of turning her head seemingly too much. Her face was already covered in a sheen of sweat, and Gaby used her free hand to wipe it from the other woman's forehead.

"It was too fast," Bonnie said.

"What was too fast?" Gaby asked, even though she knew the answer. She just wanted to keep Bonnie talking, because talking meant she was fighting, that she wasn't going to just sit back and take this lying down.

Fight it, Bonnie. Fight it!

"The ghoul," Bonnie said. "I got the first one, but the second was too fast."

"I know. I saw it."

"...I lost track of it when they came inside."

"It was fast, Bonnie. It was really fast."

"But you got it."

"It was a lucky shot."

"Yeah, right." Her lips curved into a barely-there smile. "You were always the better shot. I'm glad you came along."

"Wouldn't want to be anywhere else."

"Still?"

"It's boring back on the *Trident* anyway."

Another attempt at a smile from both of them.

Then Bonnie's expression turned somber. "Don't turn back, Gaby. You and Blaine have to keep going. We have to stop them now, or we never will. Finish the mission. You understand? *Finish the mission.*"

"I will," Gaby said. "*We* will. You, me, and Blaine."

"You, me, and Blaine," Bonnie repeated.

"That's right. The three of us."

"We'll finish the mission," Bonnie said, and nodded. Or tried to. "We have to finish the mission or it'll never end. This night-mare can't go on. For Jo's sake. For all of our sakes." Bonnie's voice had dropped with each word and her eyes were struggling to stay open. Gaby wasn't even sure if she was talking to her anymore.

Blaine scooted back over and she moved aside to let him treat Bonnie's wound, then, with her help, put a thick pad against the hole in Bonnie's neck and wrapped gauze around it. Blaine worked silently and quickly, but he was also applying too much pressure and Bonnie grunted with pain.

"Not too tight," Gaby said. "It's not going to help if she can't breathe."

Blaine nodded and eased up a little. He continued grit-ting his teeth and focusing on the work, doing everything possible not to look Bonnie in the eyes. Not that Bonnie was aware he was avoiding her. She was staring off again at that invisible something that neither Gaby nor Blaine could see.

"You'll be okay," Gaby said, realizing how stupid it sounded, but unable to stop herself. Or wanting to. "Think about Jo. She's going to be pissed if you don't come back. You promised her you would, right?"

Bonnie nodded.

"So make sure you do," Gaby said. "You don't want that girl mad at you. I know I don't."

Bonnie almost managed another smile. Almost. "God, I'm sleepy," she said, and closed her eyes completely. "I'm going to go to sleep now, guys. Wake me when we get to Houston."

Blaine finished and sat down on the ground and spent the

next few seconds wiping his bloody hands on his pants legs. Anything at all to avoid looking Bonnie in the eyes.

Gaby sat down next to him and watched Bonnie falling asleep, her memories of her friend Matt coming back in a flood. It had been a dank basement then, and Josh was there. It felt like such a long time ago, but she could still remember every terrifying second of it.

Neither she nor Blaine said anything for the longest time, and Gaby even forgot that not long ago there had been a horde of ghouls on the other side of the thin, rotting walls around them. None of that seemed to matter very much anymore.

Finally, after what seemed like hours but couldn't have been more than a few minutes (*Seconds?*), she whispered, "Blaine."

"I know," he whispered back, even as his body sagged, every ounce of strength seemingly sapped from his big frame.

16

KEO

He had a belly full of food (real honest-to-goodness food, not those leftovers they had been feeding him back in the brig) and a nice, comfortable bed in the facility's sickbay, and Lara and his friends were on their way. Things were definitely looking up. Of course, compared to his situation just twenty-four hours ago, simply getting a block of cheese would have been cause for celebration. And on top of that, he was pretty sure Mary was coming around.

So he should have slept through the night without a care in the world, except he opened his eyes to semidarkness and knew they were outside the door.

More than one, from the sound of it, even if they were being pretty light on their feet. But it was going to take floating in the air to escape Keo's notice, given how impossibly silent the island was at the moment. That, and the fact Mercer's true believers had already tried to kill him once already. There was absolutely no doubt in his mind that there were more of them out there, waiting to make him pay for what he had done to their dear leader.

You blow one guy's brains out and suddenly you're the bad guy. Geez.

Keo glanced down at the watch Rhett had given him. The hands didn't glow, but his eyes had adjusted enough to the darkness to see that it was just a shade over three in the morning. He grinned.

The hour of the wolf.

He slowly sat up on the bed and looked across the room at Kelly, the girl who had replaced Henry around ten o'clock yesterday. She was at her chair where he had last seen her before he drifted off to sleep, her head leaning back against the wall about a foot from the door. Her rifle lay nonchalantly across her lap, and she was snoring blissfully. They were the only two people in the entire room.

His eyes shifted back to the door. It was gray metal and stood out in the blackness. It had a lever handle and Keo waited for it to move, but it didn't.

Not yet, anyway, because he had definitely heard noises from the other side. Not the kind of sounds made by people just walking by in the hallway, either. Those would be obvious and clear. No, these were very soft and just barely audible, the result of people moving but trying not to be heard. But they couldn't help but make sounds because Keo's second guard, Jackson, was out there. Jackson had replaced Pete at the same time Kelly showed up for Henry.

Which meant Jackson was either dead or was in on it. Keo was inclined to believe the former after the last attempt on his life. Unless Rhett was a complete idiot (and nothing Keo had seen from the guy pointed to that conclusion) he would have only assigned people he could absolutely trust to guard Keo from now on. Of course, that was assuming Rhett actually knew his people as well as Keo was hoping he did, because if Jackson was in on this too, along with Kelly...

He remembered Donovan, his brig guard, opening the door for Bellamy and Calvin. He hadn't seen Donovan again since. With any luck, the guy was occupying the same cell Keo had spent time in. It would be poetic justice.

He focused on Kelly. She was definitely asleep, which either meant she didn't know what was going on or...well, she was literally sleeping on the job. The question was: What was that "job?"

He calmly swung his legs off the bed, then lowered them until his bare feet touched the cold, hard floor, and stood up—and almost fell right back down. He managed to grab the wall to steady himself first and remain upright, then spent the next few seconds trying to shake away the dizziness. Maybe it was the getting shot in the head, or having the bandages wrapped way too tightly—

Oh, who was he kidding. It was definitely the getting shot in the head from almost point-blank range that was the real culprit here. He was lucky he was even still able to stand at all after the painkillers Mary had graciously given him before leaving her shift.

He didn't move again until the stars had disappeared and he could see the concrete wall across from him. He refocused on Kelly's slumped-over form. She wasn't a bad-looking girl if she got a decent haircut. She'd been friendly enough when she tagged in for Henry and they'd even had a nice conversation about China, where she thought he was from. Keo hadn't bothered to correct her.

He had taken two steps toward Kelly—really, toward that rifle of hers—when he glimpsed shadows flitting across the narrow slit under the door, where a generous pool of artificial light spilled inside the darkened room, courtesy of the hallway beyond.

Shit.

He knew exactly what the shadows were doing without having to think about it: They were positioning themselves to enter, and there was definitely more than one. Two that he could see, possibly more hiding behind the walls either waiting for their turn or pulling security. Which meant Jackson was definitely dead.

Or in on it.

Either/or.

Voices followed—incoherent (to him, anyway) whispers—just before the door lever started to move.

Now or never!

He gave up on stealth and launched into a half-run. He made it halfway to Kelly when her eyes flew open, waking up to the sound of him running. That was bad news, because if Kelly could hear him while asleep, then there was a good chance the men lining up outside the door could, too. But that might be the least of his worries if it turned out Kelly was also a secret Mercer loyalist, because he wasn't going to reach her or the door in time. He was fast, but he wasn't *that* fast, so Keo did the only thing he could think of: He took a chance.

"The door!" he shouted about half a heartbeat before the door in question swung open to reveal two silhouetted figures standing in the open doorframe.

Kelly bolted up from the chair, at the same time grabbing her M4 rifle as it was falling off her lap. Keo braced himself for the inevitable—for Kelly to turn her weapon on him—but instead she began to spin toward the wide-open door to her right and he thought, *Oh, thank God something's going right for once!*

Either the invaders didn't know where Kelly was stationed inside the room or they had no clue she was even there, because the first man through the door was clearly searching for—and finding—him and never looked anywhere else. The hallway lights danced off the long, smooth barrel of the suppressor attached to the end of the man's submachine gun as he raised it in Keo's direction.

The *bang!* of Kelly's rifle shattered the quiet, but instead of waiting to see what happened next, Keo kept running even as the first man through the door collapsed in front of him, revealing his partner in the background. The second man was also armed with some kind of submachine gun, but he wasn't nearly as ready as the first, and his eyes went down instead of up and it took him awhile to see Keo's charging form.

So Keo kept running, except this time he was focused entirely on the door (*You picked the right guards this time, Rhett!*) even as Kelly tried to step away from the wall to get a look at the second would-be killer. The man finally glanced up and saw Keo and began to raise his weapon when Keo launched himself and barreled into the man, striking him perfectly in the chest with his shoulder.

Fuck me! Keo's mind screamed as a nuke went off inside his skull as he and his victim tumbled through the open door and into the hallway beyond. Keo landed on his chest and chin (but thank God not his forehead!) and let out a pained grunt.

The first thing he saw was Jackson slumped awkwardly nearby, back against the wall, a red line running from one side of his neck to the other, and blood dripping down his tanned uniform. The poor bastard probably never knew who had sneaked up behind him and slit his throat, or if he did, he hadn't been able to do anything to defend himself against it.

Pounding footsteps alerted Keo to a fourth person inside the hallway. He twisted his head just in time to witness a pair of fleeing boots going the other direction and he wanted to shout, *Yeah, you better run!*

But he didn't get the chance because the man he had slammed into was already scrambling to his knees in front of him. The man had dropped his weapon during the collision (*Second time's the charm!*), but instead of going for his holstered sidearm, he went for the knife in his left hip, and Keo glimpsed small strips of blood clinging to the blade's edge as it came out of its sheath.

The man was in his thirties with dark brown hair, and if there was a name on his tag, it was impossible to read with what looked like black tape placed over it.

"Fucking die!" the man spat out through clenched teeth as he lunged at Keo.

Keo rocked backward on his heels as the blade went for his chest, slashing from left to right.

It missed—*barely!*

The man didn't let his first failed attack stop him and was already moving again, bringing the combat knife—all twelve inches of it, seven of that making up the actual killing part—back up for another strike. Before he could, Keo reached forward with his left hand and grabbed the wrist with the knife and jerked the hand up, then drove his fist into the man's chest, aiming for the spot where his target's heart would be.

The assassin's face seemed to bug almost comically for a split second as his heart skipped a beat. He also lost all momentum and strength in his knife hand, which allowed Keo to push forward and invade the man's defenses and punch him in the nose. Blood splashed Keo's knuckles, but he ignored it and hit the man again. And *again.*

He didn't stop until the body went slack and fell to the floor, the knife *clanging* to the hard floor next to it.

Keo let out a sigh and sat down next to the door. He checked the hallways to make sure no one else was coming—or that the guy who had fled, returned—before allowing himself to lean against the wall to catch his breath. He thought about reaching for the dead man's weapon, but his head was pounding, not helped by the large dose of adrenaline still racing through every inch of him.

He barely noticed Kelly coming out of the door to his left.

She swept the hallway with her rifle, said something when she saw Jackson, then stepped over Keo's splayed legs and crouched next to the other guard.

Kelly didn't do something stupid, like feel for a pulse. She didn't have to. One look at Jackson's throat told her all she needed to know. Instead, she stood back up and glanced down at the second attacker. "Is he dead?"

"Not yet," Keo said.

The man just looked dead with the thick layer of blood covering most of his face, almost all of it coming from his shattered nose. But he was still very much alive, even if he was barely breathing, and didn't seem to be moving at all except for the slight rise and fall of his chest.

"Jesus, how many times did you hit him?" Kelly asked.

"Relax, he's alive. Thought Rhett might want to ask him some questions."

Kelly crouched next to the man.

"You know him?" Keo asked.

"Pollack," Kelly said. "The other guy"—she looked back into the door—"is Stans. Or *was* Stans." She poked at Pollack's name tag with the barrel of her rifle, noting the black tape over it. "Why'd they cover their names?"

"I'd guess it has something to do with that," Keo said, pointing at Pollack's right arm.

He had seen it earlier when the man was trying to slice him with the knife—a black patch with a white letter *M* written on it, surrounded by a white circle. The patch looked homemade, as if Pollack had cut out a piece from a black T-shirt and found a white permanent marker to make the emblem.

"That's new," Kelly said. She stood up and went back into the room, then came out a few seconds later. "Stans is wearing the same thing. What do you think it means?"

"Beats the shit outta me," Keo said. He was out of breath for some reason and struggled to regain his composure. "There was a third guy. He took off when Pollack and me took our argument into the hallway. I don't think he's coming back—" He stopped when he heard footsteps approaching from around the corner and quickly reached for Pollack's fallen weapon. "Spoke too soon."

"It's okay," Kelly said next to him. "I radioed in while you were out here with Pollack. They're friendlies."

"You sure?"

"Pretty sure."

Keo grunted, wondering how sure "pretty sure" was when half of the island wanted you dead. Of course, Kelly was probably not taking that into consideration when she offered up her "pretty sure."

She was right, though, when a group of tan-colored uniforms turned the corner led by Henry and Pete. The group of men jogged down the hallway toward them.

Keo relaxed his grip on the gun but was apparently smiling stupidly down at the weapon because Kelly said, sounding more than slightly annoyed, "Why are you so happy?"

"Things are looking up," he said, and ran his hands over the smooth side of the Heckler & Koch MP5SD resting comfortably in his lap.

"Goddammit, Keo, will you fucking stop killing my people?"

"Tell your people to stop fucking trying to kill me."

Rhett let out a deep sigh, though at this point Keo wasn't sure if that was frustration with him or his own people. He guessed it was probably fifty-fifty, depending on what Rhett had found out before he showed up in sickbay two hours after Pollack and Stans were carried off.

"Goddammit," Rhett said again, and resumed pacing at the foot of Keo's bed.

"What did you find out?" Keo asked.

"Like you said, they cut up black sheets and made those armbands. I don't know how many there are. Maybe half of the damn island's got black armbands hidden in their mattresses as we speak."

"So search the mattresses."

"I can't search the mattresses."

"Why not?"

"That would just escalate the problem."

"How the hell would that be escalation?"

"Because we're sitting on a powder keg. All it would take is one more Pollack or Stans or Bellamy to decide they'd rather go out in a blaze of glory, and I'll have a full-fledged civil war on my hands. When that happens, people will have to start choosing sides. Putting the place on lockdown and starting to search people's rooms will be the spark that causes that. All the other Mercer loyalists hiding out there will feel like they don't have any choice but to fight."

"Mercer would have done it."

"And look what happened to him."

"Point taken."

"I just have to limit my circle to those I can trust. And even then..."

"You can't be sure if one of them isn't informing on you to the Mercerians."

Rhett gave him a wry smile. "Mercerians?"

"Mercer loyalists." Keo shrugged. "I coined the term myself. If you wanna use it, it's gonna cost you a tribute."

Rhett walked over to a chair and sat down, and spent the next few seconds just watching Keo putting the MP5SD he had disassembled on a clean bedsheet and was now painstakingly putting back together. Both Pollack and Stans had been carrying identical weapons, though the one Stans had was noticeably more well-worn and chipped, and its inside parts as equally poorly maintained.

He thought Rhett might balk at letting him have the submachine guns, but apparently two attempts on Keo's life within two days had convinced him otherwise. The man had, in every way possible, fully committed to keeping not only Keo alive, but moving the island's inhabitants onto a new era. Keo could see the strain of that commitment on Rhett's face and wondered if he might not be having second (or hell, third) thoughts right about now.

"What did Pollack tell you?" Keo asked.

"Jack shit," Rhett said. "He's still unconscious. How many times did you hit him, anyway?"

"People need to stop asking me that. I hit the fucker enough times to get the job done. If he loses a nose over it, tough nuts."

"I guess he had it coming."

"You're damn right he did. Speaking of getting what they've got coming, what about the third guy?"

"You sure there was even a third guy?"

"I saw him take off while me and Pollack were in the hallway playing footsy."

"Did you get a look at his face?"

"Just a pair of boots running in the other direction. It was a guy, though."

"You can tell that from a pair of boots?"

"Can't you?"

Rhett shrugged, then nodded at the MP5SD. "You look like you know what you're doing with those things."

Keo put the final piece in place, then slipped the long magazine back into the weapon and laid it on the bed next to him. "I've been around a gun or two."

"No shit," Rhett said. He looked across the sickbay at the closed door. Kelly and Jackson's replacements were outside, along with two more men. "There's one good thing that came out of this..."

"I'm still alive?"

"Besides that."

Keo snorted. "What's the other thing?"

"Jackson's death isn't going to go down well with the island. The fact that they cut his throat... Jesus."

"You think the ones stuck in the middle might turn on the Mercerians after this?"

"I'm hoping. Or at least push them further over to my side."

"Let's hope." Keo stood up and slipped Pollack's gun belt around his waist and cinched it. "Thanks for letting me keep the weapons."

"Wasn't my first or second choice."

"Always happy to be everyone's third choice." Keo folded the bedsheet he had been using to clean the guns and tossed it across the room. "I don't have to tip housekeeping, do I?"

Rhett grunted.

"I'll take that as a no," Keo said. "So how does this affect the *Trident*'s arrival in—" he glanced at his watch "—soon."

"I don't know. Maybe I should call it off."

"What are the chances they might attack my friends?"

"Not your friends, but Riley and the others onboard. The... Mercerians still consider them traitors. They hate you for killing Mercer, but they don't have any love for Riley, Hart, and the others, either." He shook his head. "I'm talking about it with the others. We were already set on taking it slowly anyway, but after what happened this morning... I don't know, now."

"Don't cancel the meeting," Keo said. "You'll want to hear what Lara has to say."

"About this plan to take back the planet."

Keo nodded. "That's right."

"I have to tell you, Keo, I'm not optimistic. What can she possibly know that we haven't already considered? Or found out in the year or so that we spent scouting the collaborators in preparation for R-Day?"

"You'd be surprised what one well-placed source can find out."

"So that's it. You guys have an inside man. Am I close?"

Keo barely managed to suppress a grin. "Something like that."

"Has to be," Rhett said. "Riley hinted at it, but he wouldn't come right out and say it."

"Talk to Lara."

"I never said I wouldn't." He paused, then, "I'll tell you one thing: The fact that it's coming from her is one of the reasons so many people are pushing me to meet with your friends as soon as possible. It's not just anyone, after all. It's her. Lara. The woman on the radio. A lot of guys here still carry around iPods with her message in a loop."

"If I were you, I wouldn't mention that last part to her."

"No?"

"She doesn't like the whole messiah thing. It makes her uncomfortable."

Rhett chuckled. "That's just going to make people like her more."

Mary the pretty nurse, who in a previous life had been an EMT trainee, came to check his stitches about half an hour later. Sunrise was already filling the room, and he'd be damned if she didn't look as good in the morning as she did every other time of the day.

"Stop," she said as she unwrapped the bandages around his head.

"Stop what?" He sat on the bed as she worked. "I wasn't doing anything but being a good patient."

"You were staring at my boobs."

"It's not my fault you have very nice boobs."

"If there were still human resources around, you'd be so fired."

"Justifiable termination."

"Sit still."

"Yes, ma'am."

He sat perfectly still as she checked the stitches along his temple, then did the same for the ones on his forehead. There was a little bit of blood in both places, but as long as it wasn't pouring down his face, he wasn't too worried about it. Even so, Keo had been doing everything possible to avoid his own reflection and took it as a good sign whenever Mary (or someone else) looked at him and didn't flinch reflexively. Maybe one or two more scars would get him to Frankenstein territory, but he wasn't quite there yet.

"You've really been through a lot," Mary was saying as she picked up a fresh roll of gauze from a nearby tray. "I'm not just talking about your head. You have a broken nose, too. It doesn't look like it had the chance to heal properly."

"You're worried about me," he said, smiling up at her.

"It's my job to worry about my patients." She stopped wrapping the bandage long enough to trace the long scar that went down his cheek. She had very soft fingers. "Does this hurt?"

"Not anymore."

"But it used to."

"Nothing I couldn't handle."

"Tough guy."

"Only in front of the pretty ones."

She gave him a wry smile. "You're not going to stop, are you?"

"It can't be news to you that you're very easy on the eyes."

"Makes me think you're overcompensating for something."

"You don't think it could just be old-fashioned lust?"

"Oh, I know it's lust. But you're coming on way too strong. So what's the real story?"

Keo watched her finish her work, then pack up the medical supplies and return to a counter across the room. "I told you, almost dying gives you a new perspective on life. And I have so many friends on this island who want to keep giving and giving me those new perspectives."

She glanced back at him with a pitying smile. "I have to admit, I don't think I've ever seen a more hated man in my life."

"But half the people on this island love me for taking out Mercer for them, right?"

"Who told you that?"

"Not true? Not even a little bit?"

She shrugged. "Maybe. Most people still don't know how to feel about Mercer's death. A lot of them are still in a state of shock and confusion about recent events. You killing Mercer, Rhett recalling everyone. We don't even know if this is the end of the war we spent a year preparing for. Things are...uncertain, to say the least." Mary walked back over and handed him a small cup with two pills inside. "In case of pain. Did they bring you water?"

"Not necessary." Keo swallowed them down and handed the cup back to her. "What about you?"

"What about me?"

"Have you figured out what you're feeling about all of this?"

She smiled at him. "I'm not a Mercerian, I know that much."

He smiled back. "Word's getting around."

"It's got a certain ring to it." She sat down across from him, where Rhett had been sitting earlier, and seemed to really think about his question for a moment. Finally, she said, "Maybe grateful."

Keo was unable to hide the surprise on his face. Even Rhett hadn't gone that far.

"We all saw the pictures the scouts brought back," Mary said. "The towns, the people in them. When the planes took off, we knew what they were going there to do." She shook her head and there was genuine sadness in her eyes. "So yeah, I'm grateful for what you did, Keo. I don't have any problems admitting that. A lot of us are, even if we won't say it out loud. The truth is, not hating you for what you did is the same as condoning it, which is then the same as admitting they'd allowed themselves to be blindly led by Mercer all this time. It's...not an easy thing for people to confess, so you have to give them time."

"How much time?"

"I don't know. Maybe your friend coming here will help them get there."

"They know about Lara?"

"It's a small island, Keo," Mary said. "Secrets don't stay a secret for very long around here. You should know that by now."

"I'm beginning to realize that," Keo sighed.

17

LARA

If Rhett had been drinking water when he climbed off the twenty-footer and onto the swimming platform at the back of the *Trident*, Lara was almost certain he might have done one of those spit takes from the movies. Instead, he just stared at her for a second or two, long enough to reveal his surprise, but also to quickly recover.

"Lara," he said, extending a hand out toward her.

She shook it. "Rhett."

"You're not what I was expecting."

"Is that good or bad?"

"I don't know yet."

"Well, if it helps, you're exactly what I expected."

He reached up and rubbed his bald head. "Riley told you."

"He might have mentioned it, among other things."

"All good, I hope."

"I don't know yet."

He chuckled and she smiled before turning and leading him onto the lower deck while Nate and Jolly remained behind, watching the lone man who had guided the offshore boat over from Black Tide Island.

Lara liked having Jolly around—he made for an imposing figure clad in the stripped down urban assault vest. Nate wasn't entirely out of place next to the bigger kid, but he wasn't quite as intimidating. The extra day's rest had made Nate the healthiest he'd been since returning with Gaby and Danny, and she was glad he had given up trying to get her to reveal Gaby's location. For now, anyway. According to Carly and Maddie, he was still asking around, but doing it a little less obviously.

"You got Jolly too, huh?" Rhett was saying as they walked side by side along the boat's railing.

"He volunteered," Lara said.

"He already looks at home. But I guess it's not too hard to like living on a luxury yacht." He glanced around. "Where's Peters? I know he's around here somewhere. That guy's like a gargoyle, always perching high above you."

"You're right, he's around here somewhere."

"You had him watching us on approach, didn't you?"

"He volunteered, too."

"Of course he did." Then, "Would he have shot us if we'd tried anything?"

"Funny, but I asked him the same question."

"What did he say?"

"You know him better and longer than I do. What do you think he said?"

Rhett grunted. "That's going to help, you know."

"What's that?"

"Getting Peters on your side. People respect him. Hell, having Peters on your side's going to do more good than having Riley. You were smart to give him a home."

"Speaking of homes, I was expecting to see Keo with you."

"You didn't say he was part of the package."

"I just assumed he'd want to come back the first chance he got."

"Circumstances being what they are, I'd have a full-blown riot on my hands if I let him waltz off the island after what he did."

"So he's still your prisoner."

"Not quite."

"Then what is he?"

"I have him on lockdown for his own good." Then, when she gave him an unconvinced look, "He's not my prisoner. In fact, he's armed to the teeth."

"You let him have a gun?"

"Guns. Like I said, he's isolated at the moment, for his own good."

"Let me guess: Not everyone has been as benevolent towards him as you?"

"That's putting it mildly. You already know about the first attempt on his life. There was a second one earlier this morning."

"But he's okay…"

"He's probably busy right now trying to get into my nurse's pants, so what does that tell you?"

She smiled. "Sounds like Keo."

They walked along the railing instead of going into the deck where most of Riley's people were currently housed. Faces peered curiously out of the windows as they passed by, and Rhett stared back.

"Speaking of house arrest," Rhett said.

"Not exactly," Lara said. "We had some complications."

"You too, huh?"

"It's a dangerous world, Rhett."

"The week I've been having agrees with you."

"I'm glad you came. You made the right choice."

"That remains to be seen."

"Still, it took guts."

"So did you, coming here knowing what we have."

"Your planes..."

"Among other things."

"I guess we both know there's more at stake here than just us."

"That we do." Then, as they passed another window with civilians looking out at them, "Is everyone in there?"

"Just about everyone."

"All squeezed into this little boat?"

"It's not that little."

"Smaller than the island."

"Most things are smaller than your island."

"True enough."

"But you came here to talk about the future. So let's do that."

"All right." He paused for effect. "You told me you had a plan to beat the ghouls. I'm frankly on pins and needles waiting to hear it. Like I mentioned on the radio, the last person who claimed to have a plan, well, we all know how that one worked out."

"I'm not Mercer."

"True, you're better looking."

"Thanks, I guess."

"The fact that you're not Mercer is why I'm here, alone, and unarmed."

"That's not exactly true now, is it?"

He chuckled. "No, I guess not."

They were both taking big risks this morning. Even now, with the *Trident* adrift five miles from Black Tide, she didn't feel safe at all. She told herself she would never feel safe around Mercer's people, even if Mercer himself was no longer around to command them. These were, after all, the same men who had been razing towns full of pregnant women and children. People like that were not to be fully trusted, if she could help it.

So why are you here?

Because I don't have a choice. Because I need them. Because Will's chances go way up with them on our side.

"You have an inside man," Rhett was saying.

"What makes you say that?"

"What else could it be? Besides, Keo confirmed as much."

She nodded. "His name's Frank. He's in-country right now."

"And Riley's met him?"

"He has."

"What's he doing out there?"

"Making preparations for what's coming."

"You mean *if* we go along with your plan."

If you go along with the plan. If all of this wasn't for nothing. If we don't all die in the process.

There were a dozen more *ifs* that she could come up with, but every one of them led down the same road: Doubt. And right here and right now, she couldn't afford that.

"I think you will," she said, and the words came out so confidently that she almost fooled herself. Almost.

"What makes you so certain?" Rhett said.

"Because I'm offering you the opportunity to end this war. Really end this war in a way that doesn't include slaughtering innocent civilians."

"You're going to keep hanging that over our heads, aren't you?"

"Why shouldn't I? You did it."

He sighed. "Yeah, I guess we did."

They walked the length of the yacht in silence for a while, and she led him up one staircase at a time. She could have taken him up using the ladder at the back when he first boarded and drastically cut down their walking time, but Lara wanted to get a feel for him out here in the open, with no one else around but the two of them. She needed to know if she could *trust* this man.

"All right, I take it all back," Rhett said when they reached the final floor. "I can see you not wanting to abandon this place anytime soon. Not every day you get to call something like this your base of operations."

"It's nice," Lara said, "but it's never going to be home."

"So where is home?"

"Texas."

"Ah."

"You?"

"Kansas. I was on a business trip when the shit hit the fan," Rhett said. "What were you doing before all of this?"

You mean how old am I, don't you? she thought with a smile, and said, "At home."

"Doing what?"

"Sleeping."

"I mean, what were you *doing*. As in, your former occupation."

"Why don't you just ask it, Rhett."

"Ask what?"

"My age."

"All right. How old are you?"

"Old enough to keep everyone on this boat alive when no one else could, through more trials and tribulations than you could possibly imagine."

Rhett chortled. "You wanna ask me how old *I* am?"

"No."

"Aren't you curious?"

"Curiosity has nothing to do with it. I don't think your age matters. The only thing I care about is how capable you are and if I can trust you with the lives of my people."

"And vice versa," Rhett said. "So convince me, Lara, and I'll see what I can do to convince you back that I'm worth allying with."

It was just the two of them inside the conference room, with the morning sunlight streaming through the port window. Rhett had listened to her in silence, interrupting only when he needed clarification. In all, he broke in a total of six times.

When she was done, he leaned against the table and looked across at her as if really seeing her for the first time. She read him back, but couldn't tell whatsoever if she had convinced him or if he had concluded she was insane. The fact that he hadn't laughed in her face or turned and left was, she thought, a good sign.

Maybe.

"So that's your plan," he finally said.

She nodded. "That's our plan."

"This Frank. Can you trust him?"

"With my life," she said without hesitation.

"Even though he used to be one of them," Rhett said. It wasn't a question.

"He turned on them a long time ago," she said, marveling at how easily the lie came. But then, was it really a lie? Will *had* turned on the ghouls very early on, didn't he? "It doesn't matter what he was before; he's one of us now. I trust him enough that when the time comes, I'll be committing lives to his plan; lives that I spent a lot of time trying to protect. He's seen things no one else has. Knows things people don't even know to look for. He risked everything to get this plan to us. And now he's risking everything again by going back out there to take point." She paused to let all that sink in before continuing. "So yes, Rhett, I trust him implicitly."

"Even so, what you're talking about, it's dangerous. Hell, it's borderline suicidal."

"No more dangerous or suicidal than doing nothing. How long before they completely overrun us more than they already have?"

"Maybe it doesn't matter. You're on a boat, and I'm on an island."

"They can't get to you, but their human lackeys can. How long before they send an armada out here for you?"

"Have you looked around the Gulf of Mexico, Lara? There are no more armadas. They went around sinking every boat they could find along the marinas and shorelines a long time ago."

"They only need a dozen boats with machine guns. I've seen it, Rhett. If the blue eyes want something badly enough, they'll commit everything they have to take it. I've seen it. I've fought it. I barely survived it."

He stared at her before finally nodding. "I believe that you have."

"Besides, it's no more dangerous than sending kill teams on hit-and-run missions all over Texas."

"There is one big difference: those guys were fighting collaborators. Human beings. More importantly, a *limited* number of human beings. What we're talking about here is taking on the entire ghoul population."

"Not all of them. Just the ones in Houston."

Rhett grunted. "How many people were in Houston before all of this? A million?"

More like two million.

"The vast majority of those people are ghouls now," Rhett continued. "That's a hell of a lot to contend with, Lara, and we're going to run right into the thick of them." He shook his head. "It's almost certainly a suicide mission."

"Most of the fighting will be in the sunlight."

"But not all of it. We'll have to go into the dark eventually. That's their turf."

"Frank knows what he's doing."

"Frank's one man."

"He's also our best chance to end this. *Now.* Not a week from now. Not a month or a year. But *now*, Rhett. This is our best chance."

"You keep saying that."

"Because it's true. We don't know how long the target's going to be there. Right now, it's vulnerable. But that might change in twenty-four hours. In a week. If we don't take advantage of this opportunity, we might not get another one. Ever."

"I get that you believe everything you're saying, but what you're asking..."

"Is a lot, I know. But it's not any more than what your people were already committed to under Mercer. The only difference is, this time your bombs will be dropping on the real enemy, not kids and old men."

Rhett sighed and looked down at the map, as if the answers were down there. She could have told him it wasn't because she had lost count of the number of times she had done the exact same thing. It was just a map, and it didn't shed light on anything.

He returned his gaze to her. "Just to be clear, I can't order them to be a part of this. I wouldn't, even if I could. It'll have to be their choice."

"I'm not looking for a conscripted army. I want volunteers."

"Just volunteers?"

"I'm not ordering any of my people to do this, either. Everyone who is involved is doing so of their own free will." She thought of Nate and Danny, and added, "Some of them want to do more, but I won't let them."

"You have people anxious to get killed?"

"No. I have people who know what's at stake, who know this is our single best chance to take it all back."

"And they trust Frank."

"He's earned our trust. Over and over again."

"And you just want volunteers," Rhett said.

She nodded. "I just want volunteers."

Rhett looked back down at the map and didn't say anything for the longest time. She could almost picture the gears turning inside his head. Had she done a good enough job of selling it? Maybe. It was hard to gauge how convincing she had been. How convincing could she even be if she still had doubts about the plan herself? Even after sending Gaby, Blaine, and Bonnie out there with Will?

God, you better know what you're doing, Will.

Rhett finally stood back from the table and glanced around the room. "I can't help but notice it's only been you and me in here since I arrived. Where's Riley?"

"He's around. I asked everyone to give me time alone with you."

"You wanted to make sure you could trust me."

"And vice versa."

He sighed again. It was the sigh of a man with too much on his mind and the weight of the world on his shoulders. She knew the sound and the look because she had heard and seen it countless times from herself.

"So what do you need from us?" Rhett asked.

"Whatever you can give me," she said.

"It might not be nearly as much as you think. R-Day was a success by every stretch, but we did suffer casualties. And not everyone made it back home when I gave the recall order."

"We'll work with what you can give us. My people are very adaptable, Rhett. We were already prepared to go at this alone before we learned about what happened to Mercer."

"You're telling me you were going to do all of this by yourselves?"

"That's what I'm telling you."

"Then you're crazier than I thought."

"We've been called worse."

Rhett chuckled. "Yeah, I guess that makes two of us."

———

"Did he go for it?" Danny asked when she stepped onto the bridge.

"Maybe," she said. "He's with Riley now. Maybe Riley can nudge him to where we need him to be."

"What if they say no?" Maddie asked from behind the helm.

Lara shook her head. "I don't know, but we'll cross that bridge when we get to it."

"I don't know about you, but five miles doesn't seem like that long of a bridge when the other guy's got warplanes," Danny said, turning back to the windshield and looking out at the tiny black dot blinking in and out of existence underneath the morning sun.

Danny was right—five miles felt way, way too close given what was parked on Black Tide Island's airstrip. It was hard to believe how potentially dangerous the speck of dirt staring back at them at the moment was.

"Want me to pull back some more?" Maddie asked.

"No," Lara said. "I don't want them to think we're scared."

"Even though we are?"

"They don't have to know that. Besides, it doesn't matter if we put five or ten or fifty more miles between us. They know we're out here and they found us once before—and that time was in the dead of night. They're not going to have any difficulty locating us in broad daylight."

"Doesn't help we're the only rich man's toy floating out here for miles and miles," Danny said.

"Yeah, that too."

"By the way, while you were having your chat with Scarlett's boyfriend, Expedition 2.0 radioed in on schedule. They're on course into the...*Heart of Darkness*."

"'Heart of Darkness?'" Maddie said.

"What? Too ominous or not ominous enough?"

"As long as there isn't a fat Marlon Brando waiting on the other end."

"Well, there is something waiting on the other end, but I wouldn't call it fat, exactly."

"Did they run into any problems?" Lara asked.

"Apparently, it's smooth sailing so far," Danny said.

"Apparently?" she said, looking over at him.

He shrugged. "They didn't mention any complications."

"You didn't either when you and Gaby were trapped in Gallant with no way out. Why was that?"

"Because if you knew what kind of creek we were up at the time, you might have rushed over like a bunch of idiots and tried to rescue us. Then I'd have to save even *more* people, and even Super Danny has his limitations."

"Did you get the sense Gaby was doing the same thing when she radioed in?"

Danny thought about it. "I think she would have told me if they'd hit a snag. But she didn't, which means they're still good to go. Probably."

"I don't like probably, Danny."

"I'm sure the kid would have told us if they couldn't finish the mission. You worry too much."

"When I stop worrying, that's when you should start."

Danny smirked. "Where'd you get that from, an old T-shirt?"

"Maybe." She unclipped her radio and keyed it. "You see anything up there, Peters?"

"Ocean," Peters said through the radio. "Just a lot of ocean."

"Just a lot of ocean's good," Maddie said. "Oceans don't drop bombs on you, the last time I checked."

Lara glanced up at the ceiling, not that she could see Peters somewhere up there. The man had apparently found a good enough perch that even Rhett and his driver hadn't spotted him when they were approaching the *Trident* earlier.

"That guy's like a gargoyle, always perching high above you," Rhett had said about Peters earlier.

Thank God he's our gargoyle now.

Danny was looking at her. "You spent a lot of one-on-one time with Rhett Butler. Anything we should be worried about?"

"You mean, does he have squirrelly eyes?" Lara smiled.

"Something like that."

"I never got the sense that he was being dishonest. If he's lying—playing some kind of game—then he's very good at hiding it. Besides, he came here and he didn't have to do that."

"Riley also vouched for him," Maddie said.

"And we all know what a great judge of character Riley is," Danny said.

"Riley's word matters, but Keo's matters more," Lara said. "He wouldn't have okayed Rhett if he didn't think we could trust him. But just in case, keep us ready to move at a moment's notice, Maddie."

Maddie nodded. "I got one foot on the gas pedal, boss lady—"

A brilliant white flash from the horizon cut Maddie short. Lara didn't have to turn her head to get an eyeful because she was already staring at the spot where the light had come from—it was directly in front of her.

Black Tide Island.

She was still trying to process the sight when a loud *BOOM!* washed across the ocean and over the boat.

"That was an explosion," Danny said, walking toward the windshield. "Something just went off on Black Tide. Something *big*."

18

KEO

If he hadn't almost died twice (*three times?*) in just the last few days alone, Keo would have been able to appreciate the quiet of Black Tide Island a little more. But he was intimately aware of the situation—Rhett was on the *Trident* and he was, essentially, left by himself in sickbay, with God only knew how many men waiting for the opportunity to take their shots at him.

Well, he wasn't really alone. There were two guards in the hallway immediately outside his door and two more nearby. But Keo was not the kind of guy who relied on other people—in his experience, strangers tended to let you down more than they helped—and if not for the presence of the MP5SD leaning against the wall to his right, within easy reach, he might have been on his feet pacing instead of lying in bed.

The second submachine gun lay on the next bed over, along with the gun belt and Glock he had taken from Pollack. It felt good to be armed again. Hell, overly armed, if you really wanted to get technical about it, but Keo wasn't about to moan about having too many weapons after having gone without for so long.

Rhett had orders for him to stay inside where it was (supposedly) safe, which meant no more wandering out onto the beach for some fresh air. Keo would think Rhett was being overly paranoid if there hadn't already been two attempts on his life. Rhett might not have come right out and said it, but he clearly seemed to think a third attempt was just waiting in the wings. Keo wasn't about to disagree, even if being stuck inside the medicinal-smelling sickbay was getting old pretty fast.

Keo busied himself by taking inventory of his bullets for the fifth time in the last hour. It wasn't like he had anything else to do. Both MP5SDs yielded fully loaded thirty-round magazines since neither one of his would-be killers had managed to get a single shot off last night. The bad news was that he didn't have any spares. He had thought about asking Rhett for some but hadn't felt like pushing his luck. Being able to keep the guns was already more than he could have hoped for; keeping the belt and sidearm too was a bonus.

Besides, thirty rounds apiece meant a total of sixty, and Keo had gotten by with much less. Like zero-bullets-at-his-disposal less. So he was definitely not going to complain. At least, not out loud.

It was already eight in the morning, and the sun was forcing its way into the room through the high window. Although Mary had claimed the doctor was supposed to show up to check on him by now, the man hadn't done so in the hour since she left. That left Keo to wonder if she had gotten her boss's schedule wrong or if someone had held the man back. Not that he needed a doctor at the moment. Everything throbbed occasionally, but he'd never felt more alive, even if he didn't look the part. Besides, there were plenty of bottles in the drawers and cabinets around him if he was feeling adventurous.

He couldn't see the *Trident* from the room's lone high window because the sickbay was on the wrong side of the island. He couldn't see much of anything really except for blue skies.

But they were out there, with Lara meeting with Rhett. It was only a matter of time before Rhett came back, and whether he had agreed to pitch Frank's plan to the other islanders or not, Keo was gone after that. He wasn't looking forward to a confrontation if Rhett said no, but Keo was tired of asking people for permission.

Have German guns, will swim.

Hopefully he wouldn't have to swim too far to get back to the *Trident*. What were the chances Lara would immediately leave without him if Rhett turned her down?

He was still trying to figure that one out when the door opened and Henry stepped inside. Keo glimpsed Vern, one of his newer guards standing in the hallway with Kelly.

"Glad you're up," Henry said. "Saves me the trouble of waking you."

"I was never asleep," Keo said. "Hard to have nice dreams when half the people on this island want you dead."

"You're being dramatic. It's more like one-third."

"Hurray for me. Rhett come back yet?"

"Not yet."

"So what is this, a social call? You miss our chats, Henry?"

"Cameron wants to see you."

"I don't know who that is."

"Rhett put her in charge while he's gone. Come on." He nodded at the MP5SDs. "Just bring one of those, and be careful where you point it."

Keo slung one of the submachine guns and walked over to Henry. "Trust me, I don't go around pointing my muzzle at people unless I plan on pulling the trigger."

"Yeah, well, not everyone's ready to accept the sight of you walking around with a gun yet. Let's not give them any excuses to see you as a threat."

"Since when did they need an excuse? Besides, the people on

this island should be used to me doing things they don't approve of by now."

"I guess we'll find out."

Keo followed Henry to the door. "I was just going to bring one anyway. What do I look like, a redneck with a gun fetish?"

Henry chuckled. "I don't think anyone's ever going to mistake you for a redneck, Keo."

In the hallway, Keo locked eyes with Kelly. She appeared rested and had changed clothes, and for some reason was prettier than he remembered or had initially thought when they first met. Of course, people tended to look more attractive to him after they had saved his life, and Kelly had definitely done that last night.

"Now that's a look I didn't think I'd ever see," Kelly said.

"Heckler & Koch is the latest accessory fad in Paris this year," Keo said.

"Yeah? I gotta get me one."

"Maybe in pink?"

"Why, is that your favorite color?"

Keo smirked. "It's not *not* my favorite color."

Besides Vern and Kelly, there were two other soldiers waiting outside. One of them was named Mallory, but Keo had never caught the other one's name. Henry started heading down the hallway and everyone followed, with Keo and Kelly behind him. He guessed Henry was one of Rhett's more loyal men and had been put in charge of the guards, though all of it was confusing to Keo without proper ranks on uniforms. It made him appreciate the obvious hierarchy of the U.S. military just a little bit more.

They walked for a while and turned two corners.

A few minutes later and after two more empty stretches of hallway, Keo asked, "How big is this place?"

"Big enough," Henry said.

"That's big."

"I know, right?"

"I can talk to you all day, Henry."

"You're welcome."

"So where are we going?"

"I told you, Cameron wants to see you."

"But *where.*"

Henry tossed a quick look back at him. "Why? You afraid I'm luring you into another trap?"

"You'll forgive me if I'm not in the most trusting mood."

"I don't blame you after last night," Kelly said beside him. "But this isn't that. Cameron just wants some help."

"Help?" Keo said.

"People have gone missing," Henry said. "As far as we know, it happened after Pollock and Stans's attempt on your life."

"Mercerians," Keo said.

"I like the name," Kelly smiled. "It kind of fits with what they did with the black armband, with the *M* and everything."

"Creative types, huh?"

"That's one description for them."

"Whatever you wanna call them, we have people looking, but they're coming up empty," Henry said.

"And how can I help?" Keo said. "Do I look like a bloodhound to you? I've been locked in solitary all morning. I didn't even know for sure the *Trident* had arrived until you told me. I don't know anything about what's happening on this little jovial island of yours."

"I don't know what she thinks you can do, but Cameron asked for you, and I'm assuming she'll let you know when we get there. So just chill and stop with the questions. You're starting to get on my nerves."

Keo smiled. "So *this* is what it takes to get on your nerves?"

Henry chose to ignore him and kept walking through the empty corridor, with Keo, Kelly, and the other two following behind. After a while, Keo was starting to get the impression he had wholly underestimated the size of Black Tide.

"By the way," Kelly said next to him, "I've been meaning to ask: What kind of name is Keo, anyway?"

"Brad was taken," Keo said.

"Huh?"

"That's what Brad said."

Cameron was in her late forties, graying around the temples, and looked like someone's grandmother instead of the woman in charge of Black Tide while Rhett was away on the *Trident*. She looked up at Keo with a tired face that told him she hadn't gotten a whole lot of sleep recently. She was bent over a table with a map of the island inside what looked like a command center. There was a bigger version of the map on one of the walls, but the one on the table had small green figurines placed strategically over it. Toy soldiers, the kind you'd find in a kid's room.

For the first time since he arrived, Keo got a good idea of what Black Tide actually looked like from an aerial view, including the interconnected buildings that made up the base. He had been kept in the brig on the east wing, while the quarters and the Comm Room were in the middle sections. And just minutes ago they had walked through the west wing, which had a noticeably higher presence of soldiers and armed people going in and out of operations-centric rooms.

"So you're him," Cameron said. "The man who destroyed everything we've been planning for the last year with one bullet."

"You say it like it's a bad thing," Keo said.

"It is, for some people."

"Are you one of those 'some people?'"

Cameron shrugged and gave him a tired look—which was to

say her expression didn't change since he stepped inside the room. "I'm just trying to keep people alive. If calling off the war brings everyone home, then all the better."

"So we have that in common."

"Was that why you killed Mercer? To stop the war?"

"What do you think?"

"You don't look like the savior type."

"I can be very deceptive."

Henry and Kelly had stayed outside in the hallway with the other two, so Keo walked over to Cameron by himself. There had been three others in the room when he arrived, but after Cameron sent them off, it was just the two of them in a place designed to accommodate twenty, maybe more, comfortably. There were no windows, but the lights were bright enough for Keo to see every worry line on Cameron's face.

"When was the last time you slept?" Keo asked.

"I can't remember." Cameron waved a dismissive hand. "But I didn't ask you here to talk about my sleeping habits. What did Henry tell you?"

"He was short on specifics."

"The specifics is that as of right now we're missing nine people."

"Define 'missing.'"

"As in, unable to confirm their whereabouts. They didn't report in for duty this morning, and when people were sent to their quarters, they weren't there."

"Mercer loyalists."

"Possibly. Rhett and I talked about searching the rooms for those black armbands Pollack and Stans were wearing, but we decided against it."

"He told me. Something about not wanting to set off a powder keg."

"We were being cautious. But now..."

"Now you have nine guys with guns somewhere on the island hiding from you."

"That's it in a nutshell."

"Did you find any black armbands in their quarters?"

"No."

"Have you told Rhett?"

"Not yet."

"Why not?"

"Because nothing's happened yet. Right now it's just nine missing people. Maybe they snuck off the island after news of what happened to Pollack and Stans reached them."

"And why would they do that?"

"They know we have Pollack, that he's still alive. Maybe they're afraid he might break and start naming names."

"Lots of maybes."

She nodded. "Too many."

"Did he? Pollack. Did he break?"

"He hasn't said a word since he woke up this morning. I don't think he's going to, either."

"You should tell Rhett about the missing men."

"Not yet."

"You don't think this is something he'd want to know?"

"I don't want to interrupt what's happening on the *Trident* right now. What they're talking about over there—what's eventually decided—might very well change the course of humanity."

Overstatement much? Keo thought, but he quickly realized she wasn't entirely wrong or that far off the mark. Lara and Rhett were, at this very moment, talking about Frank's plan, which if it worked *could* save mankind.

Okay, maybe not too much overstating it, after all.

"He told you what the meeting's about," Keo said.

"Word gets around."

"So I've heard," Keo said, remembering Mary's words not too long ago:

"It's a small island, Keo. Secrets don't stay a secret for very long around here."

He wondered how much the missing Mercerians knew and if this was their reaction to it. That thought made him a bit uneasy, and suddenly he was less concerned about what they were planning to do to him and more about Lara and his friends on the *Trident*.

"I'll call him when I have something substantial to tell him other than that I can't find a few missing people," Cameron was saying.

"So that's your problem," Keo said.

"That's my problem."

"And why am I here? How can I help?"

Cameron stared at him from across the table for a moment. He thought she might be trying to read his face. and he wanted to tell her *good luck* seeing through the scars and the bandage around his head. Even Keo wouldn't be able to read his own face —that is, if he'd let himself see his own reflection, which he still hadn't yet.

"Rhett told me what you did," Cameron said. "How you did it. I don't just mean with Mercer, but with the others, too."

"I was defending myself."

"I'm not accusing you, Keo. But there's a reason Rhett decided to let you have those weapons. The ones that are missing —all nine of them—were in Texas when they were recalled. They were all part of Mercer's kill teams."

"What are you getting at? That they're dangerous? Not news, Cameron."

"The point is, they've killed before. Henry, Vern, and the others—even Kelly, before last night—haven't. There's a reason some of us stayed on the island and others, like Pollack and Stans, volunteered to go out there to run around killing collaborators."

"Spell it out," Keo said. "I don't have all day."

"Don't be an asshole."

"Hey, only one person can tell me not to be an asshole, and you're not her."

Cameron clenched her teeth, a clear sign she'd rather not say what was coming next but apparently had no choice. Watching her discomfort was almost enough to make Keo do a little chuckling, but he somehow refrained himself.

"I need you to help me find the missing men, and if necessary, kill them," Cameron said.

Keo would have let out a laugh if he hadn't already guessed what Cameron wanted from him minutes ago. Instead, his only thought was, *The more things change, blah blah blah.*

"Well?" Cameron said, still watching his face.

"Well, what?"

"Will you do it?"

"Are you saying I have a choice?"

"You didn't twenty-four hours ago. But as of this morning you do, per Rhett's orders."

"You should still call Rhett," Keo said.

Cameron looked down at the two-way radio sitting on the edge of the table between them. "Not until I have something concrete to tell him."

"You just asked me to murder some of your people. You don't think that's concrete enough?"

"I didn't tell you to murder anyone," Cameron said, and he could almost picture cartoony steam venting from her ears as she glared at him. "I just need your help to find—"

The room shook as a massive *BOOM!* washed across the island. Keo spun in the direction of the explosion (*Outside the building!*) even as the floor under him trembled and the toy soldiers on the table toppled.

When he turned back around, Cameron already had the radio in her hand and was almost shouting into it: "What's happening? Someone tell me what's happening out there!"

"An explosion!" someone shouted back through the radio. Male, the man's voice labored; he was clearly running and talking at the same time. "It's the fuel station! Someone just blew up the fuel station!"

"Jesus Christ," Cameron whispered.

"Jet fuel?" Keo asked.

"No. Those are stored separately from the gas we use for the boats. They're at the hangar on the opposite side of the island."

"The docks!" the same man shouted through the radio. "The fire's spreading to the docks!"

"The boats!" someone else shouted. A woman this time. "Cameron, the boats are still tied to the docks!"

"Put out the fire!" Cameron shouted into the radio. "This is Cameron, to everyone listening right now: Get to the docks and put out that fire! Save as many boats as you can! Now, goddammit; everyone get down there now!"

The docks, Keo thought. *Why the hell would someone blow up the docks?*

The boats, of course, were moored there, but what was the point of setting them on fire? To sink them? Why would Mercerians want to sink the boats? They were eventually going to need them to get off the island. That is, if they wanted off the island.

Did they want off the island?

Voices were shouting through the radio, too many for Keo to even begin to decipher what they were saying. Cameron had put the two-way back down between a couple of fallen soldiers and was staring at it, maybe just as confused about what everyone was shouting. After a while it all started to sound like gibberish, and except for repeated words like *fire* and *docks,* he had no clue what was happening out there.

Why the hell would the Mercerians want to destroy the docks? Why—

"It's a trick," Keo said.

"What?" Cameron said, looking up at him.

"The explosion. It's a trick."

"I don't understand..."

"They set the docks on fire because they knew it was important to the island. To everyone. So what happens? Everyone runs straight there to fight the fire. It's a *trick,* Cameron. Do you see?"

Cameron stared at him as if she didn't quite understand what he was saying. Or maybe she did, but she just found it too difficult to believe.

"Cameron," a voice said. Keo looked over at Henry, standing in the open doorway. "Should we go too?"

"No, stay where you are," Keo said.

"What?" Henry turned to Keo, as if surprised to hear his voice. It didn't take him long to ignore Keo and turn back to Cameron. "Cameron, what are your orders—" he started to say, when there was a second explosion—except this one was closer and much louder because it was *right outside the room.*

Keo was looking at Henry when the other man vanished in a torrent of shrapnel, just as a third *BOOM* rang out about half a heartbeat after the second explosion, the force of the nearby blast knocking Keo off balance and into the table. Cameron grabbed onto the edges on the other side as toy soldiers spilled to the floor; the radio joined them a second later, chaotic voices still shouting through its speakers.

Grenades. Those were goddamn grenades in the hallway!

He pushed off the table and was running to the door even before Cameron had righted herself. He unslung the MP5SD just as he reached the opening, doing his very best to pretend he couldn't see the frag damage all along the frame or the bloody red chunks of Henry that had been left behind.

He slid the last few feet, stopping just before the toes of his boots touched a pink fleshy lump that might have been a hand sticking to the floor. Smoke and explosive powder stung his nostrils even before he leaned out and looked left, glimpsing bodies (*no, not bodies, body* parts) everywhere.

Kelly had been out there when he last saw her. The same Kelly who had saved his life last night, and who this morning looked much prettier than he remembered.

But Keo didn't get a chance to look for Kelly or anyone else, because as soon as he stuck his head out, he spotted them: Four figures moving down the hallway, picking their way through the remains of bodies that had been left in the wake of the two exploding grenades. Keo's head was still ringing from being so close to the explosions, but there was nothing wrong with his eyes. All four men were wearing green and black camo paint over their faces, looking for all intents and purposes like killers on the warpath.

They spotted him a split-second later and one of them stopped and lifted his AR, and as he did so Keo glimpsed a black band wrapped tightly around his right arm between the elbow and the shoulder.

Keo already had his weapon up, and he shot the man in the chest, the suppressed gunshot absurdly gentle against the death and destruction around him. It was an easy shot from less than thirty meters, and the man should have gone down, but instead he stumbled backward. Another man, behind him, reached out to catch his comrade.

Body armor?

Keo didn't get a chance to squeeze off a second shot because two of the four men stepped forward and opened up, the clatter of automatic rifles firing in the narrow hallway like a cascade of thunderclaps. Bullets *pek-pek-peked!* off the concrete walls and *ping-ping-pinged!* against the metal doorframe, and Keo jerked his head back into the room as erupting pieces of the building flicked at his face and pelted his clothing.

"Keo!" Cameron, shouting from behind him.

"Mercerians!" he shouted back over the rain of gunfire.

He took five steps away from the exploding opening before darting to his left where he flattened his back against the wall next to the door. Even though he had the hallway on the other side, he felt safe enough with the thick slab of concrete between him and them. They weren't going to get through the wall unless they had a rocket on them, and frankly if they were carrying that to this party, they deserved his scalp for being so goddamn well prepared.

He glanced over at Cameron, who had a pistol in one hand and was crouched behind the table. He hadn't noticed it before, but the table was almost in the very center of the room (by design, he guessed), which also lined Cameron up directly with the damaged door and gave her a perfect view when the first Mercerian stepped into the doorway, his tan uniform and painted face flashing across the thin slit where the door hung on its hinges for Keo to see.

Keo hadn't even gotten the chance to react when there were two shots—*pop-pop!*—from Cameron. Keo opened his mouth to scream out *"They're wearing body armor, aim for the head!"* when there was a hellacious burst of return gunfire and the map table splintered, and large pieces of it buzzed across the room.

The Mercerian kept firing in Cameron's direction, his rifle bucking in his hands as he stepped through the door—

Keo shot him in the head with the MP5SD, the *pfft!* of his single shot comical against the loud racket of the man's AR. But barely audible or not, the suppressed shot did its job and the

9mm round blew the man's brains out the other side of his temple. This time Keo's target went down.

Even as the shooter was falling, Keo had spun out from behind the door, at the same time switching the fire selector on the submachine gun to full-auto. He hated to do it because he only had the one magazine (*Should have brought the other one too, dammit!*), but there was no other choice, not with three more armed assholes out there—

No, not out there, but *in the doorway*.

Two of them at least, watching as their friend collapsed in a heap in front of them. By the time they looked up, Keo had squeezed his trigger and stitched the opening from left to right, firing diagonally from bottom to top.

The first couple of shots *ping-ping!* off the metal doorframe but the rest found their marks, shattering a leg, a kneecap, then slamming into body armor before continuing up and up. One of the Mercerians' faces turned mushy red even as he somehow squeezed his own trigger and his rifle raked the floor to Keo's right, sending small chunks of concrete into the air before dotting the wall across the room.

One of the men fell, only to scream when his blown knee slammed into the hard floor, but even that scream was cut short when he toppled face-first. The second one simply fell, a bloody red lump where his face used to be. Keo ignored the horrific sight and kept moving until he was on the opposite side of the doorway and was pushing against the wall. He quickly slung the now-empty submachine gun and drew the Glock.

He waited for the fourth man to try his luck, but the guy either figured out that all of this was a lost cause and ran for it, or he was biding his time. Either way, no one else poked their head through the opening.

Keo leaned toward the door to listen for footsteps, for the tell-tale squeak of boots against the hallway floor, but all he could hear was his own racing heartbeat and a series of gunshots. The latter wasn't coming from immediately outside, but rather from other parts of the facility. There was a hell of a gun battle going on somewhere out there.

He pulled away from the door and slowed down his breathing. His nose twitched at the stench of blood and smoke and gunpowder in the air.

A groan came from behind him and Keo looked over. The man who had screamed when he slammed his shattered kneecap into the floor was trying to raise himself back up. He dripped blood with every labored breath, and Keo didn't think the man had enough strength left to fully—No, the guy was stronger than he looked, and somehow managed to crawl back to his knees.

Keo shot him in the back of the head.

Then he spent the next few seconds listening to the gunfire in the other parts of the building. Keo's position also allowed him to get a better look at what was left of the map table and Cameron lying behind it. She wasn't moving, which was no surprise since there was enough blood pumping out of her neck and chest to make a small kiddie pool. He wished he could have said he felt something, but the truth was he barely knew her, and people dying around him was starting to become a regular occurrence.

It was different with Henry and Kelly, though. Especially Kelly. She had saved his life last night, goddammit. Maybe she was still alive in the hallway. He hadn't exactly spent a lot of time looking—the bodies and blood and body parts had gone by in a blur—so there was a chance she might have survived. Henry definitely hadn't, but Kelly, maybe...

Say it one more time and you might actually believe it, pal. They tossed two grenades out there. Two grenades. Nothing's going to survive that. Nothing.

He sighed and waited, but if the fourth guy was still out there he was being very, very quiet, which allowed Keo to hear the ongoing gunfight on the other parts of the island. Was it his imagination or was the whole thing coming toward him? It sure as hell sounded like it.

And him without a fully-loaded submachine gun.

Keo holstered his Glock and grabbed one of the dead Mercerian's AR. It was way too light, but luckily the dead men came with waists full of ammo pouches. Keo grabbed one, loaded the rifle, then stuffed two spares into his back pocket.

Outside the door, somewhere close by, the *pop-pop-pop* of automatic gunfire continued, and this time he was definitely certain it had crept closer toward his position.

Here we go again...

19

LARA

"Peters, what do you see?"

"I got targets," Peter answered through the radio. "Too many targets."

"Don't shoot unless you're sure."

"That's the problem. I don't think I can be sure."

"Explain."

"It's the uniforms. They're all wearing identical uniforms. I can't be absolutely sure, but some of them might be wearing camo on their faces, too."

Lara exchanged a look with Maddie even as the *Trident* moved closer toward Black Tide Island. There was something inherently very wrong with what they were doing at the moment —moving *toward* the sound of gunfire instead of *away* from it. And yet she hadn't been nearly as hesitant about giving the order as she should have been, a realization that made her more than a little worried.

"What did Keo call them, Mercerians?" Maddie said.

Lara nodded (*Who else could it be?*) before keying the radio again. "We're treading dangerous territory here. Don't take a shot unless you can be absolutely sure they're targeting the *Trident*. Otherwise, let Rhett deal with it."

"Roger that," Peters said through the radio.

"We're close enough, Maddie," Lara said. "Let's not make ourselves too tempting a target in case they decide to turn their guns on us."

Maddie manipulated the controls and the boat slowed. "You think they're still on the island? The ones that caused the explosion?"

"I don't think they're going anywhere. If they were, they wouldn't have blown up the docks."

"Good point. Kinda hard to swim all the way back to Texas from here. Of course, Keo probably could."

"Probably," Lara said, and managed a small smile.

The engine might have cut off, but the ocean currents continued to push them forward. Black Tide loomed in front of them—500 yards or so. They were close enough that she could see the gray smoke billowing into the sky on the other side of the island. That would be where the docks were, the source of the explosion they had heard earlier. It was also the reason Rhett, Riley, Hart, and a few others were on the two speeding boats headed back now.

"You think this is a good idea?" Maddie asked. Like Lara, she was looking after the boats as they carved their way toward the island. "Letting Riley and Hart go back now?"

"It wasn't my call. They wanted to go." Lara keyed the radio again. "Peters."

"Yeah," Peters answered.

"Can you hear anything?"

"Like what?"

"Anything at all that tells us what's happening over there, who's doing all the shooting. Anything."

Peters didn't answer for a few seconds. Then, "The gunshots have stopped. Or I can't hear them anymore."

If anyone could hear shooting it would be Peters, who was still somewhere on top of the *Trident* right now with his sniper rifle. Inside the bridge, they could see almost everything out there, especially with binoculars, but hearing what was happening was an entirely different story.

Lara said into the radio, "Danny."

"Yeah!" Danny shouted back, his reply almost completely lost in the loud roar of wind and boat motors.

"The shooting seems to have stopped."

"I'll take your word for it! I can't hear shit down here."

"Be careful."

"Careful's my middle name!"

"That guy has more middle names than a porn star," Maddie said.

She couldn't see Danny on one of the two boats speeding back toward land, but he would be on the same vessel as Hart and Riley. Without Danny onboard, she should have felt a little uncomfortable putting the *Trident*'s security in the hands of Peters and Jolly, two men who had been a part of Mercer's army only a few days ago, except she wasn't. It was easy to trust Peters —she had looked into the man's eyes, knew what he had done and could do, and believed with every ounce of her being that he didn't do anything he didn't want to, including following her orders. And he wanted to, which was the amazing part.

"That's going to help, you know," Rhett had said about Peters. *"People respect him. Hell, having Peters on your side's going to do more good than having Riley."*

As for Jolly, who was standing outside the bridge in the hallway right now, Danny was vouching for him, and Danny was better at reading other men than she would ever be. Besides, she was pretty sure the young man had an almost teacher's pet-like crush on her, which made her feel old.

That's because you are old, and getting older every day.

Her radio squawked loudly, and Danny shouted through it, "Beaching now!"

Good luck, she thought, but didn't bother to shout it back over the radio. Danny wouldn't have heard her anyway because he— along with Hart, Riley, and Rhett—had already driven their boats up onto Black Tide and were jumping over the sides and onto the sand.

The first thing the four men would see would be the bodies. There were three that Lara could make out through binoculars— or she thought they looked like bodies, anyway. The truth was, given the distance and (lack of) clarity, she could have been staring at three deformed logs that had washed ashore.

Except she knew better. Those were bodies, victims of the prolonged gunfire that had erupted after the explosion. She was at least comforted that this time it wasn't happening onboard the yacht, though the fact that Keo was still out there tempered that quickly, and what were the chances that this didn't have anything to do with him?

Almost as likely as Keo not being able to handle himself in all that mess.

Danny and the other three black silhouettes were racing up the beach now. They were moving at a steady pace when one of them paused for a moment next to one of the bodies, maybe to check it for vital signs. But the man was back on his feet a few seconds later and running to catch up with the other three.

Lara focused her binoculars on the stacks of smoke rising lazily into the cloudless sky from the other side of the island. The fire had either been contained or had stopped its spread because the rest of Black Tide looked untouched by the explosion and resulting blaze.

She thought about telling Maddie to go around Black Tide to get a better look, but decided against it. There were still no guarantees that the same people who had torched the docks weren't still around. The last thing she wanted was to risk the *Trident* against something more than just small arms fire. What if they had used a grenade launcher on the docks? Or maybe even an RPG? According to Rhett, the island had its own armory built up from an entire year of constant stocking.

"Peters," Lara said into the radio. "Anything?"

"They're in the weeds," Peters said.

He was referring to Danny and the others. She had lost sight of them once they left the beach behind. She could just make out rows of gleaming metal in the background—the military facilities that stretched across the length of the island.

"They must have taken the fighting indoors," Peters continued.

"Can you hear gunfire?"

"No. But if they're inside the facilities, I wouldn't. The walls are concrete and metal."

"All right. Keep your eyes open."

"Roger that," Peters said.

Maddie glanced over. "Anxious?"

Lara gritted her teeth. "I hate standing here helpless."

With nothing to do, they stood on the bridge in silence and looked out the wraparound front windshield and waited.

It was an agonizing full minute, which later became two...then five.

Five minutes became ten...

"You want me to move closer?" Maddie finally asked. Lara could hear it in the other woman's voice—Maddie was hoping for the go ahead.

"No," Lara said, despite wanting desperately to give the small Texan her *yes*.

It was almost an agonizing half hour later when they finally heard from Danny again: "Sorry to keep you waiting, ladies. And Peters."

"Danny," Lara said. "What's the situation?"

"It's under control. They were trying to retake the facilities. Fortunately they had the decency to concentrate their bad guy planning to the command area, left the civvies section mostly untouched."

"Who were they?"

"One guess."

"Mercer loyalists?"

"Bingo-schmingo," Danny said. "Or Mercerians, as Keystone calls them."

"Speaking of which, did you find Keo?"

"Yeah, he was in the middle of it, but you probably already figured that one out."

Lara exchanged a quick *of course* look with Maddie.

"He's uglier than I remembered, but still relatively in one piece," Danny said.

"Relatively?" Lara said.

"Like I said, way uglier, so who knows what's going on with that dude that isn't immediately obvious to the human eye."

"What about Rhett and the others?"

"All good. We caught those Mercerian troublemakers while they were retreating through the hallway. It wasn't pretty. I guess you could say not all of them's going to get an open casket funeral."

"And the docks?"

"Rhett says his people secured it. Or, well, what's left of it."

"How bad was it?"

"No official body count yet. You probably can't hear it, but

Rhett's giving a speech over the intercom right now. Pretty rousing little sucker too, from the reactions I'm seeing on the faces of some of the civvies."

"What's he saying?"

"He's telling them what happened, who's responsible, and how many people are dead as a result. Don't tell anyone, but I think he's playing a little fast and loose with that last number. Anyway, I think this could be it, kiddo."

"'It?'"

"The last gasp of Mercer's ghost," Danny said. "After this, I don't think anyone's going to want to be caught dead calling themselves Mercerians. When the crowd turns on you, that's when you know your Amateur Night at the Apollo's *finito.*"

There was no one waiting for her on the beach when she arrived alone on the tender. Not that she expected anyone to be, since she hadn't told Danny or Rhett that she was even coming. But she had to see it in person, if just to familiarize herself with Black Tide and its inhabitants. These were the people she was going to have to win over in order to give Will's plan every possible chance of success.

When she climbed out of her small boat, people in civilian clothes were removing the three bodies she had seen from the bridge of the *Trident*. They had draped sheets over the dead men and were carrying them away while soldiers in tan uniforms stood watch along the beach. No one tried to stop her, or even seemed to notice her.

She walked through the group of civilians and soldiers, stepping around the blood in the sand where she could and over them when she couldn't. Lara recognized the looks on the faces of the people closest to her—they were still shell-shocked by what had happened and seemed to almost be moving on automatic pilot. The soldiers looked more alert, though not by very much.

She took her time traveling up the beach, the mushy sand sinking under her boots with every step. Finally, she reached the grass and got her first real good look at the connecting metal structures that made up Black Tide's facilities. A stripped down version of an airfield separated her and the buildings, but at the moment there were no planes in sight. She guessed they were probably housed in hangars at the other end of the island.

There were spent shell casings on the ground, along the path that was used to walk between the beach and buildings, and scattered in the untended fields. Some were old, but most were unmistakably very new and still glinting against the morning sunlight. Fresh splashes of blood clung to the taller stalks of grass.

Black Tide was eerily serene in the aftermath of the gun battle, with only a few scattered whispered conversations on the beach. Some of the people she passed by gave her a slight acknowledging nod, but no one stopped to question her presence.

She was halfway to the buildings when a familiar voice said, "As I live and breathe, *the* Lara walks amongst us."

She stopped and glanced over. "You've looked better."

"Story of my life," Keo said, smiling back at her.

He was sitting against a tree, some kind of submachine gun leaning against the trunk next to him. The weapon looked similar to the one he had been carrying when they first met. An MP-something.

She wasn't surprised at all to see that he had collected extra scars, most noticeably the stitches across the middle of his forehead where the skin was still black and purple. A thick bandage, held in place by tape, stuck out from his right temple like some kind of abnormal third ear. Other than that, he looked like the Keo she remembered from their last meeting on the *Ocean Star*, and the sight of him very much alive and sitting there casually watching her back brought a smile to her lips.

She walked over to him. "I heard you went and got yourself shot in the head."

"My legend precedes me."

"You look pretty good for a guy who was shot in the head."

"There's some debate about that."

"You're alive."

"Since you put it that way, yeah, never felt better."

She nodded at the submachine gun next to him. "I also see that someone let you have your toys back."

"It's a decent replacement. Sort of just fell into my lap, too."

"Oh, I don't believe that at all."

"You're too paranoid. Just because people are constantly trying to kill you doesn't mean *everyone's* trying to kill you."

"Now you're starting to make almost as much sense as Danny."

"That doesn't sound like a compliment."

"Depends on your perspective. But I don't see anyone trying to kill you now, so I take it you've made nice with everyone here?"

"The ones still alive, anyway." He picked up a can of beer and drank from it, then made a face. "Tastes like dog piss."

"So stop drinking it."

"Can't. Free beer. I never turn down free beer."

She sat down against the tree next to him and sighed as a fresh, cool breeze whipped across the island and over them. Keo had chosen an excellent spot, one that allowed him to see almost everything, including a long stretch of the beach. She could see the tender she had arrived in from here, which meant he had been watching her all this time and didn't say anything until she was almost past him.

"Can I have some of that?" she asked.

He passed the can over. "You're not going to like it."

"Let me be the judge of that."

"Suit yourself."

"Can't be that bad," she said, and took a small sip...before spitting it back out. "Jesus."

"Told ya."

She handed the beer back to him. "How can you even drink this?"

"It was either this or water." He drank from it again before making the same face. "A guy can only drink so much water before he wants something different."

A couple of civilians walked past them, sticking to the path. Neither one of them glanced over in their direction.

"Thank you," Lara said.

"For what?" Keo said.

"You saved our lives. That night, when Mercer's warplane found us..."

"Eh, I had nothing else better to do anyway."

"I mean it, Keo. Thank you. Elise and Carly and everyone else on the *Trident* thanks you, too."

He nodded, as if she'd just told him thanks for mowing the lawn, and gulped down the last of the warm beer before folding the can between his palms and tossing it into the grass. "What about you? You doing okay?"

"Why wouldn't I be?"

"Frank."

She sighed and leaned back against the tree and closed her eyes and enjoyed the wind against her skin. It had been so long since she allowed herself to just sit still and do nothing. How long ago had it been since she had an entire day where she wasn't making a decision that could cost people their lives?

Too long. It had been too damn long.

She opened her eyes and stared up at the cloudless blue sky.

"He's in Texas waiting for me to convince what's left of Mercer's people to go back to war."

"I don't mean that," Keo said. "I mean, are *you* okay after Frank's return?"

"I'm okay, Keo." It was probably a little too quick of an answer, but if Keo doubted her, he didn't pursue it.

He said instead, "I think they're ready to be convinced."

She followed his gaze to the beach, where a half dozen civilians were milling around in small groups. They were looking out at the *Trident*, adrift at sea in the near distance.

"What if I can't?" she asked.

"You will," he said.

"You sound like him."

"Who?"

"Will. Frank. He's sure I can do it, too."

"He's right."

She glanced over at him. "Why?"

He smiled again, and she thought it was probably the most earnest, not-smartass smile she had ever gotten from him. "Because it's easy to believe in you, Lara."

"Why?" she asked again. Then, before he could answer, "*Why?*"

"I don't know what to tell you. It's just something that is, not something you can put into words. Some people might call it destiny. Some might call it fate. You can call it whatever you want. It just is."

"I don't believe in fate or destiny."

"Providence, then?"

"My parents would have a stroke if they heard that."

"Not believers, huh?"

"Not much, no."

"Maybe you should start. It's never too late."

She shook her head and looked back at the beach. "When did you start turning into a hippie?"

"Like I've been trying to tell people, after you've almost died as many times as I have, you start wondering about things you didn't use to."

"Sounds dangerous for a man like you."

"Oh yeah. Spending three days in a jail cell by yourself while stewing in your own juices, waiting for people to decide whether they're going to kill you fast or slow, doesn't help either. You start thinking about all kinds of crazy things."

"And after all that, you're still alive."

"What can I say? I didn't want to be accused of being an asshole by some chick with a fancy yacht."

Lara smiled to herself. "She sounds like a real bitch."

"She has her moments."

They watched two men in tan uniforms walk by. One of them glanced over, saw that she was looking at him, and quickly turned away. They continued on up the path, but she could almost sense them doing everything humanly possible not to stop and look over again.

Next to her, Keo chuckled. "Like I said, they're ready. Not all of them, mind you, but maybe enough."

She closed her eyes and concentrated on the wind in her hair, the feel of the breeze against her skin.

She didn't want this. She'd never wanted this. The fact that everyone seemed to be convinced she could do something she had no experience in, or ever dreamed of doing in this life or any other, made it all the more...what was the word? Aggravating? Annoying? Absolutely terrifying?

"How freaked out are you right now?" Keo asked.

"What makes you think I am?"

"If people started treating me like I'm the second coming, I'd be pretty freaked out right about now."

She pursed a smile. "Maybe a ten."

"It's human nature, you know. This need for a savior. That's why they gave themselves to Mercer so willingly and went along with his insane plan for a whole year. They knew what it was, but they went along with it because everyone needs something to believe in. Or someone."

His words brought back what Peters had said, that she still couldn't get over:

"Everyone needs to believe in something, Lara. I chose badly with Mercer, but I rectified that. Now I'm choosing to believe in you."

"Why me?" she asked now.

"Why not you?" Keo said.

"What if you're wrong? What if Will's wrong? What if everyone's wrong about me?"

"We're not, though."

"What *if*."

"But we're not," he insisted. "You took charge on the island, knowing bad men with guns were coming right at you. You stood your ground and you led. Then you did it again on the boat. You could have folded and hid in your room at any time, but you didn't. Instead, you took command. That was instinct, Lara. Not everyone has those kinds of instincts, but you do."

She watched two women in civilian clothes walking along the path in front of them. They were doing their very best not to look over at her, but she could tell they wanted to badly.

"Keo," she said after a while.

"Yeah?" Keo said next to her.

"If I'm able to convince them, I'm going to need someone to lead them. Danny can't do it."

"What's wrong with Danny boy? I saw him a few minutes ago. He looks like he's still got all his arms and legs."

"Carly's pregnant."

"Ah."

"I need someone to take over for him."

"Okay," Keo said.

"Don't you want to at least think about it?"

"Nah."

"I think you should at least think about it."

"You said you need me to do this, right?"

"Yes. Besides Danny, you're the only one I trust to get this done."

"Okay, then. Consider it done." There was a *snap!* as he opened another can of fizz-less beer. "Want some?"

She shook her head and gave him an amused smile. "How many of those do you have?"

"They got cases of the stuff in storage," Keo said. He took a sip and made the same face. "Unfortunately, they all taste like warm piss."

The Comm Room was smaller than the bridge on the *Trident*, but the gear that lined one side of the wall was more sophisticated. Right now she was only concerned with the microphone that Jane, the young woman in charge of the room, had handed to her and said, "Whenever you're ready."

Lara nodded back before looking over at Riley and Rhett standing nearby. Under the room's artificial light, Rhett looked as if he had aged ten years since she first saw him this morning. Riley just looked anxious.

Behind her, Danny leaned against a wall next to the open door, spooning meat from a can of SPAM as if he hadn't eaten in weeks.

"Any suggestions?" she asked him.

"Speak from the heart," Danny said. "Wherever that is."

"Thanks for that."

"Any time."

She turned to Keo, sitting on a chair in a corner. He had found another can of warm beer and was balancing it on one knee as he looked back at her. If not for the scars and bruises, he could easily have been mistaken for the guest at someone's backyard Fourth of July party, a man without a care in the world.

"What about you?" she asked.

"Have a sip; it'll loosen you up," Keo said, holding up the can in offering.

"No thanks. I learned my lesson the first time."

"Your loss," he said, and took a drink. "Christ, this thing sucks."

"So why do you keep drinking it?" Danny asked.

"It was either this or water."

"Now that's one fine answer."

Lara looked back at Jane. The young woman was smiling at her, as if she knew something Lara didn't. Lara had seen that same expression on other faces, including Jolly and a few others she'd passed in the hallways on her way here.

She should have been terrified of what she was about to do, what all of them were asking her to do. For God's sake, what did she know about leading people? About convincing traumatized soldiers to voluntarily go back to war when they had already been through so much?

This is insane. This is completely and utterly insane.

But she nodded at Jane anyway. "Okay."

Jane turned around in her chair and pressed a button on the dashboard. "You're connected to the intercom. Hit the transmit lever and you'll go live."

She took a breath, then keyed the microphone and raised it to her lips.

"This is Lara." She paused, closed her eyes for a bit, then

opened them again. "Some of you may know who I am. I'm no one special. I'm just like you, trying to survive this madness the best way I know how. But things are different now. For me. For you. For all of us."

She hesitated, but this time didn't depress the transmit lever.

"I came here to ask for your help. I need your help...to put an end to this fear that consumes me every time I close my eyes and try to go to sleep. This endless nightmare that we're all living in. Right now, as I speak, we are making preparations for an attack on the enemy. The *real* enemy. The ghouls. The nightcrawlers. Whatever you want to call them. The things that hide in the shadows and stalk us night after night after relentless night. There is a plan to end this, to save everyone. But I need your help."

Another pause. It was so much easier when she was practicing the speech in her head. Now, having to say it out loud with everyone watching and listening...

"It won't be easy. I won't lie to you. It's going to take determination and blood and sweat and tears. But if you help me, if we come together under this single purpose, I believe we can strike a crippling blow against the enemy and take back the night."

She took a breath.

One second, two...

"We're going to be holding meetings for as long as it takes. Everyone is welcome to attend and ask questions. Ask anything. Ask *everything*. Nothing is off the table. Nothing will be held back. But you don't have to come. This is voluntary. I won't force you to meet with me, and neither will Rhett or anyone else. If you show up, it will be because you want to. Because like me, you look out there and you're tired of living in fear."

She was drained, emotionally and physically, and even keeping the transmit lever pressed seemed to take a lot out of her.

She took another deep breath and let time slip by.

One second, two, three...

"Forget about Mercer. Forget about his war, or what happened today with those loyal to him. This isn't about him or them. This isn't even about us. This is about your children, or the children you'll have one day. Your children's children. For all the generations that are going to come after us. This is for them. Don't let them inherit a world where they have to hide from the monsters like we did."

Another deep breath.

"We've lost people. Every single one of us. Friends. Family. Loved ones. We've all suffered and made sacrifices. We've done things that we aren't proud of. I've been there. I've done all of them and more. Every single one of us has. None of us are angels. We're just survivors trying to keep going the best way we know how. We've made mistakes along the way. Terrible mistakes. We've put our faith in people who didn't deserve it."

She thought about Mercer, about Will, Keo, about Carly and the kids...

"The past is the past, and it can't be undone. But in the here and now, we can affect the future. Because this is it. This is the chance we've been waiting for. What we do or don't do in the next few days will decide the path of humanity for generations to come. This is the opportunity we've all been waiting for."

She released the transmit lever and took a breath.

One second, two...five...

"There is a plan to strike back at the enemy—the *real* enemy—and end this nightmare once and for all. But I need your help..."

20

GABY

She was making sure the locks on the suitcase were in place for the third time in the last hour when Blaine finally returned to the barn. He was wiping dirt off his hands, and despite the fact they were all wearing mostly dark clothing, she could still make out the specks of dry blood on his shirt and under his chin. He tossed the shovel with the chipped wooden handle near the shelf where he had found it this morning and dug out a water bottle from his pack.

"You okay?" she asked.

"Gave her a nice spot under a tree about fifty yards from here," Blaine said. "Took a while. The ground is a lot harder than it looks."

"I could have helped."

"Not with that shoulder. Besides, you're going to be carrying her load from now on; might as well save it for that."

She nodded and picked up her pack and slung it on. The duffel bag that Bonnie had been carrying since they reinserted into Texas sat nearby, and she picked that up and tossed it into the backseat of the Ford. Blaine did the same with his bag before walking to the suitcase, kicking at the empty rolls of duct tape she had used to seal the piece of luggage.

"How are we for gas?" she asked.

He shook his head. "Keep an eye out for a replacement. Our best bet is to find a car that still has some usable gas left."

"What are the chances of that?"

"We found this one, didn't we?"

"We got lucky."

"Yeah, well, maybe we'll keep getting lucky."

Tell Bonnie that, she thought as she helped him lift the suitcase and shove it into the backseat.

"You radio the *Trident* yet?" Blaine asked.

"I did."

"Did you tell them about Bonnie?"

"No. I just told them we were still on course."

Blaine nodded solemnly. "The mission was always to get Will to where he needs to be. We're still ahead of schedule when it comes to that, so nothing's changed. Any news from Black Tide?"

"They made contact, and the guy in charge's supposed to show up and meet with Lara."

"She'll get it done."

"She didn't sound all that confident."

"She'll get it done," Blaine repeated without a shred of doubt.

She nodded. She wanted to share his confidence, but too many things had already gone wrong for her to be absolutely certain. She didn't say it out loud, though. Blaine didn't need to hear them, and frankly, neither did she.

Blaine walked around the Ford truck while Gaby went back for her rifle. She picked it up and paused, staring down at Bonnie's M4 leaning nearby. There was blood on the grip and some on the barrel; she hadn't noticed them last night, but they were clear now in the morning light.

"Kid," Blaine called from the other side of the truck.

"What about Bonnie's rifle?"

"Leave it. Maybe someone will find some use for it later."

Gaby hurried to the front doors and threw them open. Sunlight pierced the barn and she blinked against the brightness, and for a moment—just a very brief moment—let herself be lost in the welcoming heat.

Then she turned around and climbed into the Ford as Blaine fired up the engine.

"How far?" she asked, glancing over at the fuel gauge.

"Not far enough," he said, and put the car in gear.

"Not far enough" turned out to be twenty miles short of their ultimate destination. Or, at least, that was according to one of the signs on the highway where the Ford eventually slowed down, groaned for a few seconds, then simply stopped working.

Even so, she had to be happy; they had made pretty good time despite having to constantly use back and smaller country roads to avoid detection. Simply taking the on-ramp onto the freeway was out of the question, as tempting as it was. There were too many potential dangers to worry about, and all it would take was one prolonged skirmish with a collaborator patrol—or one of Mercer's kill teams—to not just delay them but grind the mission to a halt. And they couldn't afford that. Not now. Not after losing Bonnie just to get this far.

They spent the next three hours inside a small town called Henley looking for a replacement vehicle, or at the very least still-usable fuel. Despite being a small hole in the middle of nowhere, Henley had two gas stations. They pried the storage tank lid open on one of them, and Blaine peered down with a flashlight.

"Give me some good news, Blaine," Gaby said.

He shook his head. "It's gone bad. The color's too dark and"—he wrinkled his nose—"the air's sour."

It was the same with the second gas station on the other side of town. Fortunately, Henley was a small community and the "other side" was only a leisurely ten-minute walk away.

"What now?" she asked as Blaine stood up and clicked off his flashlight.

He looked around, then nodded at the garage attached to the station's store. "Check in there. Maybe someone was smart enough to sock away extra gas with some kind of stabilizer."

"Really?" she said doubtfully.

He shrugged. "It's the countryside. People are smarter out here."

"If you say so. What are you going to do?"

"We passed by a used car lot a few streets back. Maybe they'll have something we can use."

"Good luck."

"I'll need it," Blaine said, and was turning to go when she heard it: *A car engine.*

"Blaine!" she snapped.

But he had heard it too and spun around and darted back toward her before she could even get his name completely out. "Garage!" he hissed.

They had plenty of time to jog across the station. Sound traveled these days, especially in a place as dead as Henley, and the car could have been a mile or two—or five—away when they heard it.

She was glad they had left the bags and suitcase in the Ford, which they had pushed off of the road and into someone's attached garage. Without the added weight, she was able to move faster and they reached the side building while the sound of car engine was still far off. In fact, they didn't really have to run at all and she felt a little silly while trying to catch her breath.

The room was just dark enough to give her pause as she opened the door, sunlight spilling inside for possibly the first time in a year. She waited to hear shuffling—telltale signs there were creatures inside—but there was just the haggard rush of air expelling from hers and Blaine's lungs. The smell that hit her was spilled motor oil and old chemicals and not the foul stench of undead things that shouldn't exist.

After five seconds inside the semidarkness with no attacks from the shadowed corners, she breathed easier and moved toward the steel metal front door and peered out the small windows at the top.

Blaine appeared next to her. "They're still a long way off."

"What are the chances they found the Ford?"

"I don't think so. Or at least they better hope not."

He was referring to Will. The garage they had stashed him and the Ford in was pitch-dark, which meant anyone who found him would be making the biggest mistake of their lives, just like the two poor bastards who had tried to kill him back on the *Trident*.

"Best-case scenario is it's just a patrol," Blaine said. "They'll show up, look around, then leave."

"And worst case?"

"We weren't as careful as we thought, and they saw us. Or heard us."

He was right. Just as they could hear the car coming long before they could see it, it wouldn't have been difficult for someone else to pick up the Ford's engine from many miles away.

"Here it comes," Blaine said.

A white truck with *GMC* in big red letters on its front grill turned the corner. She thought (*hoped*) it might go right past them, but the vehicle slowed down and changed to the right lane —toward the entrance into the gas station.

"Shit," Blaine said.

"They know we're here."

"Or maybe they're stopping for gas."

"You don't think they already know the gas here isn't good anymore?"

He sighed. "Maybe they know we're here," he said, and pulled away from the small window and unslung his pack.

"What are you doing?"

"Suppressors," Blaine said.

She understood and did the same, searching through her pack for the long metal accessory, then screwing it onto the barrel of her carbine.

"Just occurred to me," Blaine said, "but that GMC looks like a fine replacement, don't you think?"

"I hadn't thought of that."

He grinned. "That's what I'm here for. The brains."

"If you'd told me that beforehand, I wouldn't have volunteered."

Blaine chuckled and she smiled, then turned around and peeked out the window at the white truck as it stopped in the wide-open parking lot spaces in front of the gas pumps, to the left of the garage. She said a little silent prayer at the lack of a mounted machine gun in the back, though a man did appear from behind the cab to stretch his arms like he had just woken up from a good nap.

"Collaborators," Blaine said.

She nodded, noting the black uniform the man standing up in the truck bed was wearing. Of course they would be collaborators. Who else would be driving around out here like they owned the place?

Two more uniformed figures climbed out of the vehicle. The driver was a tall man and his passenger was a woman with a ponytail. They both wore gun belts, though only the man reached back into their truck and pulled out an AK-47. The third man, who remained standing in the truck bed, had also picked up a Kalashnikov and slung it, all the while shielding his eyes from the sun above.

There was just enough distance—about twenty yards—and brightness for Gaby to make out the names on their uniforms. Not that she wanted to know anyway. It was easier to just think of them as obstacles to be taken out.

"This is it?" the driver asked the woman.

"This is it," the woman said. "There're only two gas stations in Henley."

"One-horse town," the third man said.

"Not even one horse," the woman said.

The driver walked over to the gas pumps and flicked absently at the nozzles with the barrel of his rifle. "You sure you heard a car, Cory?" he called back to the truck.

Cory, the one in the truck bed, nodded. "It was definitely a car. Heard it clear as a bell."

"It was probably one of ours," the woman said.

"Maybe, but you wanted to detour to check, so don't blame me if we come up with goose eggs."

"You're a better shot than me, right?" Blaine said in a low voice next to her.

"Yeah," Gaby said.

"You answered that pretty fast."

"Why, did I hurt your feelings?"

"A little bit."

"Too bad. I'll take the two at the truck. You take the driver."

"Or I take the driver and one of the two at the truck."

"Okay, sure," she said. "*After* you take the driver."

"Sounds like a plan."

By the time they maneuvered in the darkness back to the side door and pushed it open (*Quietly!*), she was afraid the three collaborators might have moved from their last position.

But they hadn't: The driver was still at the gas pumps, though he had slung his rifle and placed his hands on his hips as he scanned the town. The woman hadn't bothered to wander away from the truck and was leaning against the hood, looking bored. Cory had produced a pair of binoculars and was peering through them with his back turned to the garage. The three of them looked so disinterested in their surroundings, at the potential dangers hiding in all the buildings, that she almost felt sorry for them.

Gaby stepped out of the garage first, and once she did that there was nowhere to hide, because there were no other structures or covers on this side of the business. She took one, two, three, *four* steps away from the opening door to give Blaine the freedom to exit and move without her blocking his path. Pebbles on the cement floor *crunched* (*Too loudly!*) under her boots with each step, and she glimpsed Blaine out of the corner of her right eye as he hurried forward to get to the corner in order to see his man at the gas pumps.

The woman at the truck either heard her or Blaine's footsteps, because she turned her head—almost lazily—around.

Twenty yards. Easy peasy.

She didn't think about the woman as a *woman*—a fellow human being—and instead just saw her as what she truly was: a target. That made it easy for Gaby to pull the trigger and instantly ignore the sight of the woman dropping, or the fresh splatter of blood on the hood of the white vehicle.

She swung the rifle over, lining up her second shot at Cory, still standing in the truck bed. Because of the suppressor on the M4, Cory hadn't heard the gunshot, or if he did he didn't process it fast enough.

By the time Cory sensed that something was wrong—maybe he saw the woman falling down out the corner of his eye—and began to turn around, lowering the binoculars as he did so, Gaby shot him in the chest and the young man vanished behind the cab like some kind of magic act.

Gaby hadn't stopped moving for a single second since exiting the garage. She rushed toward the GMC, the carbine in front of her the entire time, one eye fixed on the red dot sight. She snapped a look at the woman on the parking lot floor, then at the cab again, waiting for Cory to poke his head back up and shout out, "*Surprise!*"

She didn't worry about Blaine or wonder if he had taken care of his target. She trusted that he had (*Don't let me down, Blaine!*) and didn't waste the second or two it would have taken to check. If she was wrong she would be dead in the next few seconds anyway, and when those seconds went by and she was still on her feet, she took it as a very good sign.

The female collaborator was also still alive and staring at Gaby as she neared. Their eyes locked—the woman had light blue eyes and an impish nose—and Gaby expected her to reach for her holstered sidearm, but she didn't. Instead, she kept one hand pressed against her right shoulder, a few inches higher and slightly to the right of where Gaby had aimed for.

Gaby felt a pang of annoyance at having missed her shot. It wasn't really a miss, but it wasn't a killing shot either, and if the woman had been able to summon the wherewithal to draw her pistol and open up, maybe she or Blaine, or both, might be bleeding on the ground right about now. She wanted to blame it on the adrenaline, or the fact that she was moving and shooting at the same time, but neither explanation did anything to temper the irritation.

She grabbed the Glock from the woman's holster and threw it across the parking lot. Another time and place and she might have saved the weapon, but she was already carrying too much to add another two pounds.

The woman continued to stare up at her, eyes blinking

rapidly as if she was having difficulty focusing. *Ashley* was written on her name tag. Gaby ignored the confused stare and finally checked on Blaine.

The big man had rounded the gas pumps and was standing over the truck's driver, who had managed to unsling his AK-47 but never got the chance to use it. Blaine looked up from the crumpled body and nodded at her.

Gaby turned her focus back on the GMC and peered into the truck bed. Cory lay awkwardly on his side, blood pumping out of the hole in his chest—right where she had aimed for.

One out of two ain't bad.

She returned to Ashley, who was still staring at her as if afraid to look away for fear something might happen if she ever lost sight of Gaby even for a second. Blood trickled out between Ashley's fingers; her face had paled noticeably, the energy sapping from her with every passing second and labored breath.

"I guess Cory was right after all," Ashley said, her lips curling into something that almost resembled a wry smile.

"I guess so," Gaby said.

She stood over the woman, who looked to be in her late twenties. The ponytail was pulled much too tightly and it stretched her forehead, giving her a severe look that wasn't entirely attractive.

"You shot me," the woman said.

"Yes, I did."

"Cory?"

"He's dead."

"Shit."

"Yeah," Gaby said.

Blaine finally appeared next to them and took in the woman. "How many more of you are out there?"

"A lot more," Ashley said.

"Where are they?" Gaby asked.

"Wouldn't you like to know," the other woman said, and again, that barely credible attempt at a defiant smile.

Gaby crouched and unslung her pack and opened it. She pulled out a white box and set it down on the concrete parking lot between them. It was a first-aid kit Zoe had put together before they left the *Trident*, and Ashley's eyes zeroed in on it.

"It's not a life-threatening wound," Gaby said. "But it will be without proper treatment. I don't think anyone's coming here to rescue you, do you? At least, not in time."

Ashley sighed. "What do you want?"

"You know what we want. Information."

"I can't give you that."

"Of course you can."

"How you figure?"

"You're a survivor," Gaby said, staring back at Ashley. "I know the type. I've run across more than a few of you. You don't care about them. You're just wearing that uniform because it keeps you alive."

Ashley didn't say anything, but she also didn't look away from Gaby, either. Blaine, meanwhile, was staying very quiet next to them.

"It's a pretty easy trade," Gaby said. "Information, in exchange for tending to your wound. What you do after that is your business."

"They'll want to know what happened to Cory and Drake," Ashley said.

"So tell them the truth. *After* we part company."

"Just like that, huh?"

"Where we're going, it's not going to matter who or what you tell about us."

Ashley narrowed her eyes, maybe wondering how much she could trust Gaby. Finally, she said, "What are you, sixteen?"

"I'm the one with the first-aid kit."

"That's a fair point," Ashley said. Then, nodding, "All right."

Gaby opened the box and spread out the contents on the floor. "You said there were more of you out here. How many more between us and Houston?"

"Everyone," Ashley said.

"What do you mean, everyone?" Blaine said.

"I mean everyone who can get there by tonight, who isn't already locked down in the towns."

Gaby exchanged a look with Blaine before turning back to Ashley. "Why?"

"I don't know," Ashley said. "I just do what I'm told. We were headed to the city and were taking a break on the side of the road when Cory heard your car."

She pried Ashley's hand away from her shoulder and pressed down with a sterile bandage, then took out a small pair of scissors and began cutting away enough of the shirt uniform to get at the wound underneath. Ashley grunted but didn't put up any fight.

"No peeking," the collaborator said instead to Blaine.

"Don't worry; you don't have anything I haven't seen before," Blaine said.

Gaby might have put more pressure than necessary against Ashley's wound, and maybe the woman thought the same thing because she glared at her. Gaby ignored the hard look and went to work.

The wound wasn't nearly as bad as it looked, and the bullet hadn't hit anything vital. In fact, it was almost at the same spot where she had been shot not all that long ago. Just remembering that made Gaby's own left shoulder throb slightly, and she made a mental note to take another one of Zoe's painkillers (*maybe two*) before the day was over.

"How many are we talking about?" Gaby asked.

"Hard to answer, since I don't know everyone," Ashley said.

"That you know of."

"A couple thousand."

"A couple *thousand?*" Blaine said, not even trying to hide his surprise.

"I told you, it's everyone who isn't already locked down keeping the towns safe," Ashley said. "They're ordering every patrol across the state to converge on the city." She shrugged her good shoulder. "Something big is happening, but I guess I'll never find out now."

"You'll live," Gaby said.

"Why?" Ashely asked.

"Why what?"

"Why are you saving me?"

"Because we had a deal."

Ashley nodded, but by the look on her face, she didn't entirely believe Gaby. "You're going there, aren't you? Into Houston?"

Gaby didn't answer her and neither did Blaine.

"Damn," Ashley said. "The party of the century and I'm gonna miss it."

"You believe her?" Lara asked through the radio.

"I don't think she's lying," Gaby said. "She has no reason to."

"Are you sure about that?"

She thought about Mason, about Josh...

"Every collaborator I've ever come into contact with other than Josh weren't true believers," Gaby said. "They were opportunists. Ashley is one of them. She does what she's ordered so she can keep surviving. No more, no less."

Lara didn't reply right away, and Gaby took the moment to glance out the office window at Ashley outside. The collaborator sat in the back of the GMC, parked inside the garage of an auto body shop two blocks from the gas station. There was enough natural light coming through the windows that they weren't sitting in complete darkness. Ashley's head was tilted against her chest, the effects of the sedative Gaby had given her—not because she wanted to spare the woman any pain, but because a sedated hostage was easier to handle than a fully alert one. Ashley's hands and legs were bound with duct tape and she was sitting in the same spot where Cory had fallen (and bled) after being shot, but if that made her uncomfortable when they put her back there, Ashley hadn't said a peep.

There were scuffling noises as Blaine's boots moved around on the roof above her. He was waiting for signs that Ashley had lied, that there were other collaborators out there who would come looking for them. Gaby didn't think she was lying, though, but it was better to be safe than sorry.

They had transferred everything from the Ford over to the GMC Sierra, including Will. Gaby wondered what Ashley's reaction would be if she knew just how close she was sitting right now to a blue-eyed ghoul. Someone like Ashley wasn't "chosen," the way Josh or Mason had been, so she would never have come into close contact with the creatures. Gaby knew intimately how unnerving that introduction could be.

"Unnerving?" That's one way to put it.

More like "horrifying."

"As long as you're sure," Lara was saying through the radio.

"I am," Gaby said. "What about what she said? Does it change anything?"

"Maybe," Lara said. "We were already prepared to clash with the 200 or so Will had seen patrolling the city even before we found out about Mercer. But a couple of thousand... It makes getting Mercer's people onboard even more important. I'll talk to Danny and Keo, see what they think. God knows they have a lot more experience in battlefield tactics than I do. Whatever happens, we'll do what we always do. We'll adapt."

Gaby smiled to herself. "Adapt or perish."

"Exactly. And speaking of adapting, are you in any immediate danger out there?"

"I don't think so. The group we stumbled across was on its own. According to Ashley, no one's looking for them. They're calling all the collaborators to the city, and I don't think they're going to waste time sending out search parties for a truck that didn't make it. Even if they did, we're in a good place here. They'd have to literally run into us to find us."

"How is everyone? Bonnie and Blaine?"

Bonnie...

She must have been quiet for too long, because Lara said, "Gaby, what happened?"

"Bonnie's dead," Gaby said.

"What happened? When?"

"Last night. Two of them found us where we were hiding. I guess it wasn't nearly as abandoned as Will thought. But it would have been worse if he hadn't been there and led the rest of them away."

This time it was Lara's turn to be silent. As she waited, Gaby was glad there was an office—as small and cramped and crowded with junk as it was—for some privacy. She didn't like the idea of saying all of this out there where Ashley could overhear, even in her sedative-laden condition. Not because she was afraid Ashley would escape and snitch on them, but because it was none of her damn business.

"What about you and Blaine?" Lara finally said. "How are you guys *really* doing out there?"

"We're fine. I wasn't lying about that part."

"And Will?"

"He's fine, too. Don't worry about us, Lara."

"I can't help it. It's my job to worry about you. About everyone."

Gaby could hear the stress in Lara's voice even over the radio. The kind of pressure her friend was under all these months and to this very day was something Gaby couldn't possibly imagine, or ever want to.

"How are things progressing on your end?" Gaby asked.

"It's...coming along," Lara said. "I won't know anything until later tonight. And maybe not even then."

"Where are the winds blowing?"

"The winds are very hard to read right now, but I think there's a chance. It'll depend on how much the last few days have taken out of them. Not just fighting Mercer's war, but the aftermath of his death. A lot has gone on since. With us, with them..."

"But there *is* a chance."

"There's a chance, yes, or I would have told you to come home right now, especially after what happened to Bonnie."

"What are you going to tell Jo?"

"The truth. That Bonnie died a hero, that she sacrificed herself to ensure the mission's success."

Gaby nodded to the empty, silent room and remembered Bonnie's last words:

"Don't turn back, Gaby. You and Blaine have to keep going. We have to stop them now, or we never will. Finish Will's mission. You understand? Finish the mission."

We'll finish it, Bonnie, don't you worry, she thought. *We'll goddamn finish it or die trying.*

21

KEO

"You're handsomer every time I see you, Keo. What's your secret?"

"A good personality. People skills. All that good stuff."

"Maybe you should go easy on that good stuff because you're running out of places to put bandages."

"Always more below the neck, Doc."

"Let's not go there."

"That's what she said."

Zoe smirked. "What's the gossip around the island water cooler? Did Lara's speech go over well?"

"From what I'm hearing from my well-placed sources, it's about fifty-fifty," Keo said.

"Is that good?"

"It's not bad."

Zoe deftly placed a new bandage over his temple and taped it into place. "I thought the island had their own doctors."

"They're a little busy right now."

"Right. The shooting this morning."

More like "the attempted coup d'état this morning."

"Uh huh," he said.

"Was it as bad as I've heard?"

"Most of the injuries are from the docks. Burns and shrapnel."

"What about all that shooting?"

"Dead people don't need doctors, Doc."

"Oh." Zoe moved to his forehead to check on the stitches, then went about cleaning and covering them with a new bandage. "So there's a fifty percent chance Black Tide might decide to pitch in?"

"I wouldn't bet on the whole island, but maybe just enough to give Frank's plan a boost."

"You mean Will."

"Uh huh."

She finished up, then snapped off the surgical gloves before putting her instruments away. "How many were willing to meet with Lara?"

"When I was there, a few hundred had shown up."

"Soldiers?"

"And some civilians."

"Why do we need civilians for this?"

"You win wars with fighters, but they can't do their job without support from everyone else, Doc. Mercer understood that when he set up the FOBs. I'll say this for him: He was a maniac, but he knew what he was doing."

"Then maybe you shouldn't have killed him."

"He started it."

"Yes, he did."

Zoe pushed her cart back to the corner where she kept all the other medical equipment. She looked over at him and he thought she wanted to say something—or ask something—but didn't. Instead, she began putting the roll of gauze away.

Keo slipped his jacket back on and zipped it up. He had

forgotten how cold it could get on the *Trident*. The island by comparison felt warmer despite not having a whole lot of nature to block the winds. Then again, maybe it was all that tropical scenery.

"What's on your mind, Doc?" Keo asked.

Zoe stopped what she was doing and turned around. She leaned against the counter and didn't say anything right away.

"I won't bite," Keo said.

"What do you think?" she finally asked.

"About what?"

"Plan G. Lara and the islanders. Can it all work? You've been out there. More than any of us. You've seen more."

"You were at the camps."

"I was, but it's not the same. I was sheltered, and mostly around other people."

Keo sat back down on a stool. "To be honest with you, I don't know. But that's the thing…"

"What is?"

"I know what I don't know." When she gave him a quizzical look, he continued: "I've never been a leader. It was never my thing. I've always taken orders, did what was necessary. I guess when you've been doing that for as long as I have, you start developing the ability to tell when someone is full of bullshit. Like a sixth sense. You have to, because they're sending you to what could potentially be your death."

"So what is your sense telling you about all this? Are we just setting ourselves up for failure? For more dead friends?"

"I think…" He stopped himself. He was sure he had the answer, but suddenly realized now that he didn't and maybe he never had.

Zoe watched him patiently from across the room.

"I don't know," Keo said. "But Frank believes in the plan, and

I haven't seen or heard anything about the guy that leads me to think he's talking out of his ass. You know what he is now, right?"

She nodded.

"He believes it can save Lara," Keo continued. "And that guy —or thing, or it, or whatever you want to call him now—is alive almost purely because of that driving need to protect her."

"He loves her. He'll always love her."

"That seems like the safest bet in history." Keo stood up. "So what I'm saying is, I guess, yeah, I think it could all work, but it's not going to be easy. It's going to take a lot of doing, but I've seen Frank in action. That guy, he can do things."

Zoe nodded, and he saw the relief on her face.

"A year ago, all of this would have been beyond my pay grade," Keo said. "But I've seen things that can't be explained; hell, that defy logic, even. You can't help but start entertaining wild possibilities after that."

"But it's so risky."

"Life is risky, Doc. Especially these days. At least there's a big ass pot of gold at the end of this rainbow."

She nodded again and seemed to be talking mostly to herself when she said, "And we could use a win. God, can we use a win. We've already lost so much already. Carrie, and now Bonnie..."

Keo stared at her. "What about Carrie and Bonnie?"

"What?"

"You said, 'Carrie, and now Bonnie.' What did you mean by that?"

Zoe's face paled. "You don't know..."

"Know what?"

"Oh God, no one's told you..."

"Told me *what*, Doc?"

He vividly remembered Carrie, back on Song Island, trying to convince him to stay. They were preparing for an attack at the time, and he wanted no part of it—especially one on behalf of a bunch of strangers.

"*It's not about the island,*" she had said. "*It's about the people on it. It's always been about the people. Stay with us, Keo. There might not be anything for you out there, but there's something here, now.*"

She hadn't come out and said it, but he'd known what she meant. She was talking about herself, asking him to stay with her. In the months after she had followed up with hints, but he had always been too focused on getting to Gillian to take her up on her offer. He had regretted it ever since.

Then there was Bonnie...

But it was always about Gillian...until it wasn't anymore.

Keo gritted his teeth and thumbed a bullet out of the magazine and flicked it into the air, then watched it drop all the way down to the water three decks below. He had a great view of Black Tide nearby as well as the surrounding Gulf of Mexico from the rear of the *Trident*. The cool wind and solitude, along with the slowly creeping orange glow of evening, made the place ideal to be alone with his thoughts.

Another 9mm round shot into the air before gravity pulled it back down, turning end over end as it vanished out of view and, a second later, the soft and barely audible *ploomp* as it landed in the water below.

"Those things cost money, you know," Lara said as she appeared next to him. She leaned against the railing and looked down at the same patch of blue water.

"I'm replacing them with silver ammo," he said.

"Smart, but that still doesn't mean you can literally just throw bullets away. Every bullet counts."

"My bad."

"My bad?" she smiled.

"Don't people say that anymore?"

"I don't think people ever said that, Keo. At least not anyone over ten."

"You learn something new every day." He nodded at the beach in front of them. "What's going on over there?"

People were milling along the sand. Most of them were civilians, but there were a few soldiers among them. He saw handshakes, talking, and laughing. A few might have even been embracing.

"Riley's people," Lara said. "I asked them to go back, to put in a good word for us."

"Looks like they're getting along. Like that little uprising on the *Ocean Star* never happened."

Ploomp! as another round dropped into the water below.

"I guess they realized it wasn't about them after all; it was always about Mercer," Lara said. "About his war. In a lot of ways, Riley did them all a favor by opening their eyes."

"That's what I keep hearing."

"Funny how things work out. Not all that long ago, one of them almost killed Riley for it. Now he's helping Rhett organize the meetings on the island, trying to convince them to do it all over again. It feels wrong somehow."

"Soldiers fight, Lara. Even if they weren't soldiers before this, they are now. The ones who don't have the stomach for it will stay home. The ones that do will come with us. Yours, Mercer's, or Frank's war. It doesn't matter, really."

"Maybe you're right. I still have a hard time thinking about this from a military perspective."

"You'll come around," Keo said. "Speaking of which, shouldn't you be over there right now?"

"What do you think I've been doing since noon? I'm

exhausted, Keo. I think I might have met and talked with every single person on that island."

"I told Doc we're looking at a fifty-fifty chance we'll get enough volunteers to give Frank's plan the best shot at success."

"You were being generous."

"Was I?"

"I'd kill for fifty-fifty. It's more like forty-sixty. Maybe thirty-seventy."

"Still good odds. I've done with worse."

"For you, maybe. For us mere mortals, it's not nearly enough. But we should get a better idea by the end of tonight. I wish I could give them more time, but we're running out of it. Will's going to be in position soon, and we need to be there for him."

"How many do you need?"

"All or most of the pilots. Some of the tankers. And a lot of the support people."

"I think you'll get it. Or most of it."

"You think so?"

He thumbed loose another 9mm bullet. "Your speech over the intercom was pretty convincing. I got goose bumps."

"I didn't know you had goose bumps to get, Keo."

"It's either that or I'm coming down with the flu. Considering my run of luck these days, who knows."

She gave him an amused glance. "What are you talking about? You're still alive, aren't you? When I last saw you on the *Ocean Star*, I thought that was the last time we'd ever talk."

"Oh, ye of little faith."

"I should have known better. Next time, I will."

Keo flicked another round into the ocean. "So, lowballing it at thirty-seventy, huh?"

"Around there. I just hope they can get over the fact that I'm a twenty-something medical school dropout trying to convince them to fight another war after everything they've been through."

"In your defense, you're only a dropout because the world ended."

She laughed, and Keo smiled.

He couldn't remember the last time he'd heard her laugh—if ever. *Had* she ever laughed before while he was around, before he left to find Gillian? Not that she ever had a whole lot to be happy about. Will had been missing all that time, and there was all the work involved with training everyone and keeping the *Trident* afloat. Even now, he had no idea how she was doing it, shouldering all the responsibility on so little sleep and rest.

She looked as tired today as she did back then. The number on her birth certificate might have said twenty-six years, but he was looking at a much older woman. It wasn't in the worry lines or the bags under her eyes, but in the way she leaned against the railing, as if she needed the extra support.

"That's what people keep reminding me," she said. "College dropout by way of the apocalypse, getting ready for a war."

"It's true."

"Still, Mom would be so disappointed."

"That you're a dropout, or that you're about to launch another war?"

"Both."

She looked across the water at the beach and the civilians still gathered there. It really did look like one big happy reunion, and he found himself watching along with her in silence for a while.

Finally, she said, "What are you going to do after this, Keo?"

You mean if I'm still alive? he thought, but said, "I have no idea. I haven't thought that far ahead."

"No plans?"

"Not a one."

"That makes two of us."

"What about Frank?"

"What about him?"

"If this works out the way he says it will..."

"I don't know if it'll be possible to go back to the way it was. Everything's so..."

"Fucked up?"

She smiled. "Different. Everything's so different."

"That would have been my second guess." Keo slipped the empty magazine back into the MP5SD and slung the weapon. "I'm just sorry I wasn't around when you asked for volunteers to go out there with Frank. Or around when everything else happened onboard the boat."

Lara sighed. "Zoe told me. I'm sorry, Keo. I was looking for the right time to tell you myself, but with everything happening at the island... I'm sorry you had to learn about Carrie and Bonnie this way."

"Don't sweat it. You had a lot on your plate."

"I know you were close to both of them. I don't know what else to say except I'm sorry."

"I'm more worried about Lorelei and Jo."

"Lorelei took it hard. She threw herself into helping with guard duty as a way to cope. I have Carly and Sarah and the others keeping a close eye on her."

"And Jo?"

"Jo..." Lara pursed her lips. "I haven't gotten around to telling her yet. How do you tell someone their sister isn't coming back?"

"You want me to do it?"

Lara shook her head. "No. It's my responsibility. I'm the one who sent Bonnie out there."

"She volunteered. All three of them did."

"That doesn't matter." She looked off at the setting sun in the distance. "First Carrie, now Bonnie. And it's not going to stop. There are going to be more casualties before this is over."

Keo didn't say anything. He didn't know what to say anyway,

and the silence, with only the calming back and forth of the waves against the anchored *Trident,* was almost therapeutic.

Their peace and quiet was only broken when Elise and Vera and a couple of the other kids appeared along the railing two decks below them. The kids looked off at the island's long stretch of beach, pointing and talking excitedly amongst themselves.

"They've been bugging me about going over," Lara said. "I think they miss the beach we had back at Song Island."

"Why haven't you let them?"

"Because I can't protect them out there. I can't be everywhere at once. Neither can Carly nor Sarah. They're safest here, onboard with us. For now."

"You sent Riley's people back there."

"They're not Elise and Vera."

He nodded. "Pretty soon they'll have company."

"You know something I don't?"

"Danny. He's going to be a daddy, remember?"

That brought a smile to her lips. "I'm still trying to wrap my head around that concept."

"That poor kid," Keo said. "That poor, poor kid."

Lara laughed, and Keo smiled.

"You're coming home."

No. Not home. It had stopped being home over a year ago when the world crumbled and the cities blacked out and he found salvation elsewhere. Home wasn't a place of brick and mortar or cement. Home was her.

Lara.

"You belong here."

The voice had grown in strength after that first night back on land, when he had to lead the black eyes away from Gaby and the others. He had only been partially successful and two of them—the slowest among the horde—had lagged behind. The woman died as a result of that failure.

That left two.

"You've always belonged here."

He couldn't let that happen again. Not with Gaby's life at stake. She was one of the reasons he was doing this. The reason he was taking the fight to Mabry. Back to where it all began one cold, dark night.

"It's good you've finally accepted it."

He was the beginning and the end, the nothing and the everything. Nowhere, and everywhere.

"You didn't think you'd be able to slip through unnoticed, did you?"

No. He never had any delusions he would be able to make it back to the city without being seen, felt, or sensed. Mabry had spied him through the black eyes as he led them away from the barn, into the woods, and out the other side. But they were slow things, dumb things, and he outmaneuvered them with minimal effort and destroyed the ones that got close enough to pose any danger.

"Or maybe you're still lying to yourself."

He wanted to answer, wanted to shout back in defiance. But he didn't, because it was a trick, an attempt to lure him out of hiding. Once he exposed himself to the stream of consciousness that linked the brood to Mabry, there would be no secrets left between them. It was already difficult enough to stay hidden this close to the city, having to move in the daytime.

"Lying to them."

The sun made him defenseless and weak and reliant on others. Unlike all the other times when he was here, in the darkness, when he was alone and fast, and though Mabry always knew he was close, he could never locate him.

"Lying to her."

It wasn't just Mabry out there probing, picking at the defenses he had erected to protect his mind and his sanity. He could feel them—the other blue eyes. The ones that had remained in the city to protect him. To protect Mabry. They were reaching out, too. Searching, waiting for him to make a mistake. Just one mistake so they could pounce.

"Come home."

Home? No, not home. His home was wherever she was.

"I'll see you soon..."

The desire to come out of the suitcase was like an itch he desperately wanted to scratch, that continued to grow with every passing second. Finally, finally, Blaine unwound the layers of duct tape and pulled the zipper, and he emerged. He could have broken through—it wouldn't have taken very much effort at all—but that would have damaged the transportation and forced them to repair it, and they might need it again for another day.

Blaine flinched at the sight of him—it would have been imperceptible to the human eye—and the big man's heartbeat increased marginally, though they might as well be firecrackers to his hypersensitive ears. The clothing he wore helped to ease Blaine's mind, but it would never be enough. Because whatever he did, whatever he hid underneath, he would never truly be the man they remembered. He wasn't a man at all anymore.

"Sorry about that," Blaine said. "Had to take care of the prisoner first. Make sure she didn't see you."

He nodded, not that he cared if the woman saw him or not.

"Place's secure," Blaine continued. "So tomorrow we either get moving or run back to the shoreline, huh? I'm not sure which one I'm hoping for, to be perfectly honest with you." An awkward grin. "Still waiting for word from Lara."

The right response eluded him, so he chose to stay silent instead. It was difficult talking to Blaine and the others. They didn't know him as well as Lara did. As well as Danny or Gaby. Or maybe he just didn't care enough.

"What now?" Blaine asked. "We just wait it out?"

"Yes," he hissed.

"I guess it's gonna be a long night. Good thing the truck seats are comfortable. Not to mention warm. Not that you need warmth, right?" Another attempt at a smile that went awry from the very beginning. "Of course not. I keep forgetting where you've been spending your days."

There was a slight quiver in Blaine's voice, the uncertainty that comes with allying yourself with a blue-eyed ghoul. He understood and decided to take mercy on them both by leaving Blaine and gliding across the oil-slicked garage floor.

Gaby was in the office at the back, and he slipped through the open door. She looked up from the desk where she had placed her disassembled rifle on white rags and was running a tooth-brush through the metal parts. She was biting down on a small flashlight to see with, and she removed it now and placed it next to her.

A flush of pride at how much she had grown, proof that what he used to be—*who* he once was—had mattered. But the unwanted emotion was only temporary and quickly diffused by the large amount of exposed silver on the desk. He wrinkled his nose and wanted to spit out the taste, like knives against his tongue.

"Blaine's still nervous around you; that's why he's blabbing so much," Gaby said. "It's going to take him a while to get used to it. The others, too."

"I know," he said.

"Haven't heard back from Lara yet, if that's what you're going to ask."

He nodded, even though that piece of information was unnecessary because he could hear everything while inside the suitcase.

"But I think it's going to be good news," Gaby continued. "Lara can be pretty convincing when she needs to be, but I prob-ably don't have to tell you that."

"She'll convince them," he said. "She was born to lead. She just didn't know it until now."

"I hope you're right, because there's a lot of bad guys out there for us to take on all by ourselves."

"We wouldn't have been alone."

"I know. We'd have help. Still, I'd feel better about this mission if there were a couple of tanks and Warthogs lending a hand."

"She'll convince them."

"I hope so." Gaby stopped what she was doing and turned around in her chair. Green eyes fixed on him and he saw no traces of fear or hesitation. "Regardless of what happens with Lara, or on Black Tide, when you get right down to it, it's all going to come down to you. So you better be right, Will. After what we went through to get this far..." She stopped short before continuing: "You better be right."

He nodded.

"Then why do I keep getting this feeling you're not telling me everything? That you're holding something back? Not just from me, but from Lara too?" She stared at him with none of the reluctance or apprehension that Blaine still couldn't overcome, and might never be able to. "Tell me you've told us everything, Will. Tell me the truth."

"I've told you everything," he lied.

"Everything," she repeated.

"Everything," he lied again.

She nodded and sat back in the chair. "So what now? Sit here until Lara radios back with news?"

"Yes."

"I hate waiting. Have I told you that?"

"Maybe..."

"You don't remember?"

He shook his head.

"I guess it's not important. You only remember the important things, right?"

"Yes."

"That makes sense. Everything else is just a pain in the ass." She swiveled around to the desk and picked up the pieces and continued working. "Do you remember all those times on the island?" A smile creased her lips. "When you and Danny taught me all of this? Those were still some of the best days of my life."

The memories weren't there. Not in their entirety, anyway. There were flashes, visions that came and went. Some were more cohesive than others; but many were just fragments, reminders that they served no purpose other than to cloud his mind and divert him from the truly important things.

"Danny wanted to come," Gaby was saying. "You know why he didn't, right?"

"Yes."

"You do?" she said, unable to hide her surprise.

He knew, because he could hear everything on the boat even while shuttered away inside the cabin below deck. If not the actual sounds that made up the conversations, then the vibrations that resulted and traveled along the ship's hull. It was one of the many talents he had developed very early on after his transformation—to hear without actually hearing. But he didn't know how to put those things into words, just like he didn't know how to explain the hundreds (thousands?) of other things the change had bestowed upon him—the gifts that came from the curse.

So he only hissed, "Yes."

"I keep forgetting how different you are from the run-of-the-mill ghoul. Are all the other blue eyes like you?"

"Not like me."

"You know what I mean. I know they're not like you. Thank God for that. I meant in terms of everything else."

"Yes."

"What about Mabry? He's blue-eyed too, isn't he?"

"Yes...and no."

She gave him a quizzical look. "What's that mean?"

"He's more."

"More how?" she asked.

He's the everything, and the nothing. The nowhere, and the everywhere.

The beginning...and the end.

———————

The town was empty as he made his way through it, slipping around buildings and up and down rooftops. He could see and smell evidence that they had been here many times before, doing what they did best—searching, always searching—but there wasn't a single black eyes in the area tonight.

The humans were gathered along the highways that led into the city. A dozen here, another dozen behind them, and more still that he couldn't see, on the other sides of the city. The stink of fear clung to their pores underneath their black uniforms, trails of sweat behind the gas masks despite the cold. Anxiety radiated off them, the knowledge that they had been summoned here to take up positions against...something.

"You're close now, aren't you? Yes. You are. You're very close."

Like all the other times, he didn't answer. Instead, he glided through the night underneath, over and around the highway. It would be so easy to reach out and kill the human traitors, but he resisted the urge.

Not here, not now.

Besides, they didn't matter. Only the plan mattered. The mission.

Plan G, as Danny called it.

"That's everything?" Lara had asked him, back on the boat. *"That's the plan? All of it?"*

"Yes," he had lied.

The city loomed in front of him now, its buildings dark and proud under the moonlight, like sentries watching for signs of his encroachment.

"You're so, so close."

The voice had gotten stronger, more insistent. It took everything he had to quell it as he scaled down the side of the building. He expected the blue eyes that guarded the city to come out in search of him, but they remained where they were.

In there, with Mabry. Always with Mabry.

"Come closer."

It didn't take him long to reach the edge of the city, even taking every precaution. He didn't worry about the humans and concentrated on the overwhelming presence of the brood before him. He could feel their unease, taste the uncertainty in the air around them. There were so many, packed into one place. Every building, every home, every office. The side and back streets were empty when they shouldn't have been, but the emptiness was a lie, an obvious ploy to lure him in.

They knew he was coming, because Mabry knew.

Thousands. Hundreds of thousands.

Millions...

He retreated. Slowly at first, then faster.

And faster still...

"Gaby."

She opened groggy eyes while her hand instinctively moved an inch or two closer to the rifle leaning against the desk she had laid her head on to sleep.

"You're back," she said, her voice barely a whisper, even as she pulled her hand away from the weapon.

"Yes," he hissed.

She opened a bottle of water and took a drink. "I'm never going to get used to how quiet you can move. Even with all that stuff on. What were you doing out there?"

"Scouting."

She smiled. "Danny was right. You can take the man out of the Ranger, but you can't take the Ranger out of the man. So what did you find out?"

"Nothing new."

"What about the collaborators?"

"They've arrived."

"Where, exactly?"

"Everywhere."

"That's not good."

"They don't matter."

"Right. The plan." She ran her fingers through her hair. "So Ashley wasn't lying after all."

"No."

"I didn't think she was anyway."

"Lara?" he asked.

She shook her head. "I haven't heard back from them yet." She glanced at her watch. "It's only a few minutes past midnight, and she did say this was probably going to go all the way till morning." The chair creaked as she leaned back on it and let out a yawn. "Do you ever get tired?"

"Not anymore."

"But you can get hurt. Like back at Gallant."

"Yes."

"You can die, too." She added quickly, uncertainly, "Again, I mean."

He nodded. "Yes."

"I feel like Blaine sometimes. As much as I've gotten used to being around you—this new you—there are still things I'm never going to understand, and I'm not sure if I really want to."

"Gaby," he said.

She looked over at him, suddenly alarmed by the tone of his voice. "What is it? What's wrong?"

"The woman."

"What woman?"

"The collaborator."

"What about her?"

"I need her."

"You need her?"

"Yes."

There was a moment of confusion on her face, but it was quickly replaced by understanding.

Then something else, something... Disgust? Fear? Or maybe it was resignation, an acceptance of the way things were. The way *he* was.

"I need her," he said again.

"Are you hurt?" she asked quietly, as if afraid Blaine and the woman would overhear outside the office.

"No."

"Then why?"

"I need more. I need to be stronger."

"What about back on the *Trident?*"

"It wasn't enough."

"Because of what happened at Gallant?"

"Yes," he lied. "Because of what happened at Gallant."

She looked past him and out the window—at the truck, but mostly for the woman in the backseat, whom she couldn't see from her angle but knew was out there.

Her eyes finally returned to him. "Is there another way?"

"No..."

"There has to be..."

"There isn't."

Her face darkened, anger replacing the uncertainty. "Then

why are you telling me this? You could have just taken her. It's not like Blaine or I could have stopped you."

"You needed to know."

"Needed to know what, Will?"

"Who I am. What I am."

She sighed, then nodded and turned back to the desk, and said quietly, "Then I guess you should do what you have to do."

Blaine was asleep in the front seat of the truck when he opened the door and took the woman out. Her eyes flew wide and she might have screamed, except his hand was over her mouth before she could utter a single noise and he carried her out of the side door and into the darkness.

He took her far from the garage, far from Gaby, before laying her down on a rooftop. Her eyes, as wide as he had ever seen a pair of eyes, focused on him instantly and every inch of her body shook uncontrollably and never stopped.

"Please," she whispered.

"I'm sorry," he said.

It seemed like the thing to say, even though he didn't mean it. He didn't know this woman, but he had no ill feelings toward her. She was simply there and he needed the precious liquid pumping through her veins.

"Please. *Please*," she said.

"I'm sorry," he said again.

"But I did everything you wanted. I even *killed* for you."

"Not for me."

"I don't understand..."

"You don't have to," he hissed, and bent over her.

She whimpered as he bit down. Her hands clutched at him,

fingernails digging into his skin. He didn't feel it and continued to feed, drawing the life force out of her one slurp at a time.

Over and over and over, until she stopped thrashing and lay still in his arms.

I'm sorry, he thought, but the words sounded hollow even in his mind, so he concentrated on the feeding instead.

She tasted sweeter than the two from the *Trident*, and for a moment—just a moment—he allowed himself to savor her in the way he was meant to. The way Mabry always intended him to.

"*Come closer*," Mabry beckoned somewhere in the back of his mind. "*Come closer...*"

BOOK THREE

THE LAST RODEO

23

KEO

"Excuse me, but I thought I just heard you say there might be *millions* of those bloodsucking things in Houston right now, waiting for us to walk right up to their front door and ring the dinner bell. But that couldn't have been right, because what suicidal moron would volunteer for something like that?"

Keo grinned to himself. He had to admit, Peele had a way with words for someone who looked like he should be filling out people's tax forms and not volunteering to lead the tank portion of an attack on the enemy position. Then again, Keo had met plenty of people who didn't look like they could defend themselves, but proved otherwise when the chips were down. Peele may or may not be one of those folks, but he was certainly asking all the right questions.

"And how do we even know this Frank guy will be there?" Peele continued. "For all we know, he might not even make it into position. And then what? We'll be slugging it out with a few thousand—you did say thousands, right?—collaborators who probably came better armed this time after what we did to them during R-Day."

Because Frank is a blue-eyed ghoul. Because he can go where we can't. Because if you knew the truth about ol' Frank, you'd piss your pants.

"Frank will be there," Lara said. "He's the most sure-thing part of this plan. It's everyone else you should be worried about."

"Who is he?" Cole asked. The pilot stood with his arms across his chest like he didn't want to be there.

And yet here he was, along with Peele and Alex, another one of the tankers. Of the three, Cole stood out. He was, after all, the guy who had been doing Warthog strafing runs all across Texas ever since Mercer's war began. Of the three pilots on Black Tide, he had been the only one to volunteer. It made perfect sense to Keo that Cole would be here. Only the grizzled veteran would be able to shake off what he had done in Mercer's name in such a short turnaround. It wouldn't surprise Keo at all if the other two were too disillusioned to ever climb back into a cockpit ever again, though to hear Cole tell it, he was on the verge of convincing at least one to join the fun.

It's all fun and games until the bullets fly, right, boys?

They were inside a large room in the command area of Black Tide's facility. It didn't have the size of the earlier room where Keo had met with Cameron, but then it also wasn't riddled with bullets and blood. It was big enough to accommodate all eight of them, including the two R's—Rhett and Riley—while still leaving room for a few more bodies.

"The kind of intel he's sending back takes a lot of work for one man," Cole continued. "And you say he's been out there this entire time. So who exactly is this guy, that he's able to do all of this?"

Keo couldn't tell if that was suspicion in Cole's voice or just straightforward curiosity. Maybe it was a little of both, and from the looks on Alex's and Peele's faces, it was a question that was also on their minds.

"He was an Army Ranger before all of this," Lara said. Her voice was steady and confident, and if Keo didn't know any better, he would swear she didn't have a single doubt about Frank or his plans. "He served in Afghanistan, then was part of a SWAT unit. When I tell you that he's the most sure-thing part of this plan, I'm not exaggerating. This is what he does. And he's very good at it."

Alex and Peele exchanged a quick look, but Cole remained unmoved. Or, at least, Keo couldn't read anything on that lined face of his.

"Why didn't you say that before?" Alex said. He was the youngest by far—twenty-two, if that, with dark blond hair. Keo thought he looked a bit like Danny, if Danny were shorter and learned to shut up once or twice.

"A Ranger," Peele said. "That explains a lot."

Lara looked over at Danny, standing next to her behind the table with the map of Texas. That was a signal for him to pitch in.

"We served in Afghanistan together," Danny said. "He's a good bloke. Smart as a whip. The guy excels at SERE and you should take everything he sends back as gospel. I can't count the number of times I've put my life in his hands. A lot of people have. Lara, Keystone Cops over there, to name just a few who wouldn't be here if not for him."

"If his intel is correct, that just confirms we'll be running into a buzz saw," Cole said.

"Speak for yourself," Peele said. "You'll be in the sky. We'll be the ones on the ground with all those collaborator assholes."

"You volunteered, remember?" Rhett said. He had kept quiet while Lara did the briefing, and this was the first time he had spoken up in almost twenty minutes. Keo had almost forgotten he was even in the room with them. Then again, he wondered if anyone remembered *he* was present, since he hadn't said a word since the meeting began.

"I know that, Rhett," Peele said. "But I didn't know *this* was what we're going up against."

"It doesn't matter how many are out there," Lara said. "I'm not asking you to win. Your objective—your only objective—is to keep them away from Willie Boy while they finish the mission."

"That's this guy Frank's group?" Alex said. "Codename Willie Boy?"

"Yes."

"Who came up with that, anyway?"

"I did," Danny said.

"What's it mean?" Alex asked. "I get that we're Rolling Thunder and Cole's Eagle, but what the hell's a Willie Boy?"

"Trade secret. Maybe I'll tell you when this is over."

"So we'll just be a distraction," Peele said, still focused almost entirely on Lara. "Keep as many of them off Willie Boy's back as possible?"

"Yes," Lara nodded.

"For how long?"

"As long as you can."

"What if we're forced to retreat?"

"As long as you can," Lara repeated. "I'm not asking you to sacrifice yourselves. We just need to give Willie Boy every single second possible."

That seemed to appease Peele somewhat, and he nodded. He had a good ten years on Alex, but looked young next to the aging Cole.

"While they'll be busy with you on the ground and Eagle in the air, Striker will assist Willie Boy," Lara said. "Together, they'll complete the mission."

"Just like that?" Cole said.

"Just like that," Danny said. "What, it should be harder?"

"Is it really going to be that easy?" Alex asked. He sounded doubtful, but Keo thought he heard a little bit of hope in there as well.

"It won't be that easy," Lara said. "None of this is going to be easy in the slightest."

She stared at all three of them, one after another, and gave time for her words to sink in. Keo had to admit, it was the right play. It was the same as telling them that she wasn't hiding anything, that she wasn't going to bullshit them about how hard all of this was going to be.

"Everyone will have to do their part," Lara finally continued. "We need to give Willie Boy every chance in the world to succeed. That means holding on for as long as you can. *As long as you can.*"

"How does it work?" Alex asked. "Not the plan, but everything else."

"The ghouls share a hive-like mind. This King Ghoul, as Danny calls it, controls them through a psychic link. Don't ask me how it all works, it just does. You've all been out there; you've seen them for yourselves. The things we don't know about them could fill a book. But we know enough, thanks to Frank."

"It's all supernatural shit," Rhett said. "I stopped trying to understand them a long time ago." He gazed across the table at Lara. "If she says killing King Ghoul takes them out, then I believe her."

Lara nodded gratefully back at him.

"I've seen it up close and personal," Danny said. "I've gone toe-to-toe with them. And I'm not talking about your garden-variety black eyes."

"The blue eyes," Riley said.

"We've heard stories about them," Peele said. His voice had dropped noticeably for some reason. "They lord over the towns, keep the blood pumping."

"They do that, and then some," Danny said. "The important

takeaway is that they run the show. They use the black eyes like marionettes. Cut the strings by taking out the baby blues, and the puppets go down for the count."

"How?" Cole asked.

"That's for history and scientific folks to figure out. I just know that when you snuff out one of them, every black-eyed ghoul in the area just stops."

"Just stops?" Peele said.

"Like they ran out of batteries or something."

"That's...insane."

"Right, because this whole year has been so sane," Keo said. It was the first time he had spoken, and they all turned to look at him. "I've seen the same things Danny has, up close and way too personal for my liking. You take out one of the blue eyes, and the rest don't know what the hell to do. Imagine what happens when you remove King Ghoul. The one that controls them all. The head of the snake."

"Think of it like a military chain of command," Danny said. "At the bottom you have the grunts—the black eyes. They make up the vast majority of the ghouls out there. The baby blues are the COs and NCOs rolled into one—they run every aspect of the daily grind. And up at the very top—"

"King Ghoul," Cole said.

Keo watched the veteran's face carefully. Cole might have been the only pilot to volunteer so far, but he had come into this room with a lot of doubts, and from the looks of it, Keo had a hunch he would eventually leave with less.

"Exactamundo," Danny said. "Cut off the head and the tentacles flail around all dramatic like, then they eventually die. That's what Frank found out while he was out there. Trust me when I tell you, he went through hell and back just to get this information to us. He sure as hell didn't do it for the LOLs."

"And now he's back out there again," Lara said, picking up after Danny.

It was almost as if the two of them had rehearsed it, but of course Keo knew better because he had been with them for the last five hours on the *Trident*, coming up with the plan.

She continued: "He's moving into position, and when the time is right, Frank will kill King Ghoul."

"How?" Peele asked.

"It doesn't matter how. What matters is that he'll be the one to do it, with a lot of help from us. From you and Cole, and Keo over there. He can't do this alone. If this is going to work, he's going to need all of us to throw everything we have at the city."

Alex and Peele exchanged another quick look, and this time Cole joined them.

"What do you think?" Alex asked, looking across at Rhett.

"I think this is our chance," Rhett said. "Lara and her people know more about these things than all of us combined. Mercer had us so concerned with the collaborators, with the towns, that sometimes I think he forgot who the real enemy was. Lara and her people never did. I think we need to grab this opportunity before it's gone, because we might not get another shot at these fuckers."

Keo watched the faces carefully, and he was almost certain Alex was completely convinced. Peele still had some way to go, but he was headed there. As for Cole...the pilot could have been thinking about a cheeseburger, for all Keo could decipher from his facial expression.

"There's some good news," Keo said.

"Spill the beans, Kerosene," Danny said.

Keo got up and walked over to the table. He leaned over the map and made a circle around the city of Houston. "They're calling every available patrol unit to help secure the roads into the city. That leaves everything else"—he circled the rest of the state—"wide open."

"Meaning?" Peele asked.

"Meaning, when we reinsert back into Texas and start moving toward the target, there won't be any opposition until we reach Houston itself. Or if there's any along the way, it'll be but a shadow of what they could have thrown at us. Will we run into a patrol or two out there? Maybe. Maybe not. But it won't be as many as we were going to before they recalled everyone to help guard Houston. So in a way, Head Ghoul—or King Ghoul, or whatever it's called—did us a big favor and it doesn't even know it."

"Even if all that's true, there's gonna be a hell of a lot of opposition once we do reach the city limits," Peele said. "Truthfully, I can shell those black-eyed fuckers all day, but the other type of enemy does tend to shoot back. The tanks can withstand a lot of damage, but if what your people are saying is true and there are a couple thousand collaborator assholes waiting for us..." He shook his head. "Man, I wish we had more tanks."

"What about you, Cole?" Alex asked, looking eagerly across at the former airman. "What are you thinking?"

Good question, Keo thought, turning to observe the grizzled veteran himself.

"It's going to be more dangerous for you boys down there," Cole said. "Like you said, Peele, I'll be in the sky. Unless the bad guys have learned to fly since R-Day, I'll have the airspace all to myself."

"So you're in?" Peele asked.

Cole pursed his lips, but he nodded, if almost reluctantly. "After what we've done, even if it was in another man's name, I don't see how I can *not* do this." He paused, before continuing: "If you're asking me to tell you what to do, I'm not going to do that. That's for every man to decide for himself. But I got markers on my soul, boys. We all do, after R-Day. I figure we owe it to ourselves to try to make up for that. It's not going to magically erase every horrible thing we did out there, but maybe it'll help me get some sleep in the nights to come."

It was a damn fine speech, and even Lara and Danny were impressed by it. The fact that it had come from Cole meant even more to the other islanders from the looks on their faces.

Leave it to the old guy to bring it home.

"Are you guys in?" Rhett asked, looking across at the tankers.

Alex hesitated and looked to Peele.

"Yeah," Peele nodded. "I'm in."

"Then I guess I'm in, too," Alex said.

"Good," Lara said, as if she never had a single shred of doubt that this was exactly how the meeting would end up.

Damn, she's good at this.

Lara glanced down at her watch. "Go back to your people and fill them in. Then try to get some sleep. Tomorrow's going to be a long day for all of us."

Lara and Danny went back to the *Trident*, but instead of going with them, Keo decided to stay behind and wander the halls of Black Tide even though it was well after three in the morning. He had never really had much luck getting shut-eye the night before a big assignment, and this was definitely the biggest he had ever been given by a long shot.

"See the world. Kill some people. Make some money."

That was the old motto, for a simpler time. Which was funny to think of them as that, but looking back, everything was so much more black and white when he was pulling the trigger for the organization. Nowadays he was coming up with mission plans and volunteering for work that no one was going to pay him a single dime for, and if he were to not come back, probably only a few people would even care.

Lara would be one of them. Maybe Danny too, and Lorelei. He would have been able to add Carrie and Bonnie to that list, once upon a time, but that wasn't possible anymore.

Rhett's people had done a great job cleaning the hallways after the running firefight yesterday. Except for the area around the command wing, the rest of the buildings looked almost untouched, and he wouldn't have known a shootout had taken place if he hadn't been right in the middle of it.

It was late, and he hadn't stumbled across a single soul until he reached the civilian section. There, a man and a woman were engaged in quiet conversation when he turned the corner. As he walked past them, the woman followed him with her eyes.

He was almost at the other end of the corridor when she finally said, "Hey."

Keo stopped and glanced back.

"You're Keo," the woman said.

"Who?" Keo said.

"Keo. The guy who killed Mercer."

"Wrong guy."

"You sure?"

"I'd know my own name."

"What is your name?"

"Ken."

She clearly didn't believe him. "Where'd you get all of that, Ken?" she asked, making a circle in front of her face with her hand.

"Went for a swim and jumped smack into a pile of rocks."

"Really."

"Uh huh. It's dangerous out there, so you guys might want to be careful when you're skinny dipping later on tonight."

He turned and went around the corner.

"That was him," he heard the woman say.

"He said it wasn't him," the man said.

"Seriously? Who gets those scars from jumping into the ocean?"

Keo smiled to himself and kept going.

The infirmary door was closed, but not locked. There were no guards standing outside, but there were bloodstains on the floor and walls from the last time someone had tried to kill him. He guessed Rhett's people hadn't gotten around to cleaning up this part of the facility yet.

He opened the door and leaned in, then took a moment to let his eyes adjust to the semidarkness. A single stream of moonlight splashed in from the high window, and Keo could just make out the figures occupying the beds. The wounded from this morning's coup attempt.

A figure sitting at a desk turned around. Male, wearing a white coat, and not who Keo was hoping to find.

"Help you?" the man asked.

"I'm looking for Mary."

"Her shift was up three hours ago."

"Communal quarters?"

"She has her own room now."

"You wouldn't happen to know which one, would you?"

The man squinted through the darkness at him. "Do I know you?"

"Keo."

The man chuckled. "I should have known with that face."

Keo sighed. "You got a number for me or not, pal?"

"What time is it?" Mary asked when he knocked on her door and she opened it and peered out, blinking rapidly against the hallway light.

The room behind her was darkened, but it was the exact same décor as Mercer's had been the night Keo came for him. He guessed every single private quarter in the place was identical, with a small bed in the rear and very little in the way of aesthetics.

More importantly, a quick glance inside the room didn't reveal a second figure.

Half-asleep or not, Mary noticed and rolled her eyes. "Yes, I'm alone."

"I didn't say anything."

"Uh huh."

"Gary?"

"So you came here looking for Gary?"

He smiled. "No."

She took a step back and held the door open for him. "Wanna come in?"

"Yes, please."

"Just to sleep."

"I'm insulted you think I'm here for anything but."

She smirked and closed the door behind him.

"Nice place," Keo said. "The guy at the infirmary told me you just moved in."

"A lot of the private quarters opened up after this afternoon, and they let me choose one. I guess being one of a handful of people who know their way around a wound helps. Though I wouldn't have had the opportunity if it weren't for you."

The cot squeaked as he sat down. "Me?"

"Yeah, you." She walked over. "I don't know who it used to

belong to, but he was a Mercer loyalist. I found his black armband hiding under the pillow." She sat down next to him and yawned. "I'm really tired, Keo. It's been a long day."

"Then you should go back to sleep."

"You staying?"

"It's an awfully small bed."

"We'll make it work."

She lay down on her side and turned her back to him. Keo followed her lead, and she scooted over until their bodies were pressed front to back.

"Keo," she said. "Go to sleep."

"I didn't say or do anything."

"I can feel little Keo stirring."

"Little?"

"Tame him now, or you'll be sleeping on that very hard floor."

"Speaking of hard—"

"*Keo!*"

"All right, all right," he said. "Sleep only."

She reached back and patted his hands, and he slid them around her waist and pulled her tightly against him. He inhaled her scent, and even though he knew she had been much too busy today to take a shower, he couldn't fathom how she could still smell so wonderful.

"You're leaving, aren't you?" she whispered, not sounding nearly as tired as she had seconds ago.

"I thought you wanted to sleep?"

"Answer the question."

"Tomorrow morning."

"That's only a few hours from now."

"Uh huh."

"I heard not a lot of people volunteered."

"Enough did."

"Are you sure?"

"Yeah."

"You're one of them."

"I am."

"Why you?"

"Why not me?"

She didn't answer right away, and he could feel the slight rise and fall of her heartbeat even from behind. Finally, she said, "You're crazy. You're all crazy. After everything Mercer put us through, to jump right back into another fight so soon..."

"This might be the last one we ever have to fight. That's worth a little risk, isn't it?"

"That's the problem, Keo..."

"What is?"

"You know why there are wars with Roman numerals in human history?"

"Crazy Germans?"

"No, because they're leaving room for more. Because there will never be a 'war to end all wars.' There will just be sequels. That's why they put Roman numerals at the end of wars."

Keo didn't know what to say, so he didn't say anything. He'd never been much of a historian—staying alive one day at a time, one gig at a time, had always been more important than what some old guys did before he was born.

But he had to admit, Mary made a good point. Did he really think this was going to be the end of the struggle? Even if, by some miracle, Frank's plan actually worked out the way he said it would, would there be no more wars for him to fight? No more skirmishes to survive? No more bad guys (*Haha, look who's calling other people bad guys now. Cute.*) for him to nip in the bud?

"Go to sleep," Mary whispered, the tiredness returning to her voice. "You'll need all the rest you can get."

He closed his eyes and felt her body relaxing even further against him as she dozed off moments later.

Keo followed ten minutes after that.

In his dreams, there was asphalt and bullets and blood. In the middle of it all were pulsating blue eyes, so blue and bright that it was like staring into the sun itself...

24

GABY

This is what you get for ditching Nate. This is your punishment. And you deserve it. Every stinky chunk of it.

She sighed as one foot and then the other sank into the thick, muddy water.

No, not water. Not even close to water. She *wished* it were water.

For a second she was afraid she would keep sinking, that the unholy mess (*That's a nice word for it*) would just swallow her up, but the liquids finally settled around her knees even though the ripples extended farther out and bumped harmlessly against the brick walls around her.

I can't believe I'm down here. This is so disgusting.

Even with the mask firmly in place over the lower half of her face, the still-exposed parts of her skin tingled against the tainted air. She concentrated on regulating her breathing (*In and out, in and out*) and focused on seeing the world in a sea of green provided by the night-vision goggles. The extra effort helped to keep her mind distracted, and for just a second or two she almost managed to convince herself she wasn't standing knee-high in a sea of year-old waste.

Year-old? God, I hope it's only a year old.

Her heart was racing at double its normal speed, and she could hear every single breath she took like aftershocks against her earlobes. She snapped her eyes shut and fought for control, willing herself to slow down, to let the mask's filter do its work, and pretend she was somewhere else at that moment.

"Gaby."

She opened her eyes to the sound of Blaine's voice behind and slightly above her. "Yeah."

"You went quiet there for a moment."

"Sorry. What did you say?"

"What's the verdict down there?"

"It stinks. What do you think?"

Blaine chuckled. "I'm coming down."

"The more the merrier."

She took a couple of steps forward and swept the narrow passageway with the M4, the laser pointer underneath the barrel providing an exact guide of where the bullet would go if she fired. She tuned out the *clank-clank* of Blaine's boots moving down the rusted metal ladder behind her while getting a better look at her surroundings.

The only saving grace to standing in a major city's sewer system was the size—the round-shaped tunnel was over ten feet wide and tall, like a giant straw made of brick and concrete, except the floor was flat against the soles of her boots. Condensation *drip-drip-dripped* around her, the *plops* that landed adding to the filth like drawn-out raindrops. Despite the generous size of the place, she would have still felt a stab of claustrophobia if not for the fact she could see every crack and puddle of water thanks to the NVG.

"Sorry, kid," Blaine said when he hopped the last rung behind her and splashed parts of her clothing with the water.

"It's okay; I can't smell it."

"You sure about that? Even with this thing on, I'm getting some serious whiffs."

"Sure? No, but that's my story and I'm sticking to it."

Blaine chuckled again, and she smiled. The levity helped to ease her mind somewhat. She remembered all those times when Danny and Will joked their way through a bad situation. This definitely qualified as one of those, though no one was shooting at them and *there was nothing hiding in the darkness.*

There you go. Jinx it, why don't you?

"Where did he go?" Blaine asked.

He had gone on ahead of them after coming down first and ensuring there was nothing waiting down here. The last time she saw him was almost two minutes ago when he disappeared around a bend in the tunnel in front of her.

"Scouting ahead," she said.

"He's good at that."

"It's what he does."

"I should have spent more time with you guys back on the island. One of my biggest regrets."

"You can always ask Danny when we get back. He's already training Jolly."

"Yeah, I'll do that," Blaine said.

Soft sloshing sounds from in front of her broke through their chatter, and Gaby lifted her rifle, as did Blaine, who had moved to stand beside her. She sneaked a quick look over at him, at the single lens protruding out from in front of his face like a freakishly long third eye, complemented by the breathing apparatus over his mouth. The only thing on Blaine's face (and hers) that was still exposed to the climate was his forehead, and it was

already damp with something that looked like dirt and soot and...
other things.

Her finger tightened against her carbine's trigger, and she
thanked God for silver bullets when he appeared around the
bend, his movements so light and effortless that if not for the
trench coat, she didn't think he would have created any ripples in
the water at all. Gaby still couldn't decide how to feel about
seeing him in that black leather getup, with the hoodie covering
most of his face and those glowing blue eyes peeking out at her.

He carried the remaining duffel bag—the heavier of the two—
behind his back as if it weighed little more than a feather. They
had left the other bag behind since she and Blaine were now
wearing its contents.

Gaby lowered her rifle. "Anything?"

"Nothing," he said (*hissed*).

"How far?" Blaine asked.

"Far enough," he said, and turned back around.

Gaby exchanged a quick look with Blaine, but all she could
see was his NVG lens staring back at her. He looked a bit like a
bipedal insect, albeit one with a rifle.

"Ladies first," Blaine said.

Will had begun moving again, and she fell in behind him.
Blaine carried the radio in his pack, the bulk making him look like
a hunchback. If he was having trouble with the extra weight, he
hadn't said a word.

The mask that covered her mouth had a fleece portion that
extended all the way down the length of her neck. It was comfortable enough to wear for long periods (and it was going to have to
be) and although she told Blaine she couldn't smell the (mostly)
liquefied waste around her, it was very much a lie. There was
simply too much of it to ignore completely, and it probably didn't
help that her eyes had begun to sting and the exposed parts of her
face continued to tingle, a constant reminder of where she was.

God, if I never have to do this again in a hundred lifetimes...

She picked up her pace until she had caught up to Will. From behind, with the trench coat dragging over the water's surface, she wouldn't have been able to tell that he wasn't the Will she remembered. Even his hands were covered in tight black gloves, and there was absolutely nothing about him to give away that he wasn't human. At least, from the back. Every now and then she heard the distinctive *clanking* of the objects inside the duffel bag slung over his back.

"Will," she said.

He didn't answer verbally and didn't stop, but she caught a slight turn of his head in response.

"Why aren't they down here?" she asked. "It's pitch-dark. Sunlight doesn't even know this place exists."

"They don't need it," he said. "The city is theirs."

So even the monsters don't want to come down here. So what does that make us, exactly?

Filthy, that's what.

He didn't say anything else, and the only sounds were her breathing and the *drip-drip-drip* around them. After a while, he pulled slightly ahead of her.

She slowed her pace until Blaine caught up. "Is it me, or is he going slow on purpose?" Blaine asked.

"Maybe," she said. "But if he wanted us to move faster, I'm sure he would have said so."

"Any idea where we're going, exactly? Which part of the city?"

"He didn't say. I guess we'll find out when we get there."

Blaine sighed. "If I knew we were going to be down here literally walking in people's shit, I'm not sure I would have volunteered. What about you?"

"I probably would have still."

"Yeah, who am I kidding? I would have, too."

"I guess we're both idiots."

"Yup."

They walked on in silence, the filthy water displacing and reforming around them and, gradually, she became aware of what sounded like animals moving on the other side of cracks along the walls. Condensation continued to *drip-drip-drip* in front and behind them, and the only thing louder than her filtered breathing was the *thump-thump-thump* of her heartbeat.

"If this works, you think they'll give us medals?" Blaine said after a while. "Maybe write songs about us?"

"Songs?" she said, smiling behind the mask.

"I'd like a song about me," Blaine said wistfully. "That would be cool..."

She wasn't sure how long after they climbed down into the sewer system that she started to notice the air had gotten warmer and sweat was starting to form around her temple and drip down the corners of the NVG and mask. It was so quiet down here, with the only sounds coming from their breathing and movements—and the occasional scratching noises from behind the curved walls—that it was difficult to tell how much time had passed.

Gaby snapped a quick look at her watch every now and then, but time seemed to be standing still and didn't explain why her legs were getting tired and she was moving slower. She didn't fully grasp just how much her pace had flagged until Will began putting more distance between them, even though he didn't seem to be moving any faster than before. If anything, he was holding back just to ensure he didn't outwalk her and Blaine.

She wanted to ask him to stop so she could rest, but she didn't. She refused to do so because Blaine wasn't complaining, and he was carrying more pounds on his back than she was. But at least there was one benefit to her growing fatigue: her shoulder wasn't giving her any problems, either thanks to having numbed over or the result of Zoe's painkillers. She wasn't going to be throwing softball pitches with her left arm anytime soon, but this was the next best thing.

Finally, Will began to slow down before stopping completely ten feet in front of them.

Gaby said a silent prayer, but also reflexively tightened her grip around the carbine. "Something wrong?"

"No," Will said. "We should rest."

"Are we almost there?"

"No." He pointed to his right. "I'll be back."

He continued on, disappearing around another turn in the tunnel.

Gaby walked over and glanced at where he had pointed. It was another raised platform carved into the side of the tunnel, about five inches above the water line, similar to their original point of entry. There was also a rust-covered ladder at the back.

"Where's he headed off to?" Blaine asked as he appeared next to her.

"He didn't say."

"So he can see in the dark, huh?"

"You didn't know that?"

"I figured they had good night eyes—because, you know, that's their natural environment and everything—but I didn't know it was that good."

"Now you know," Gaby said, and climbed up the platform.

Once up, she was reaching instinctively for her mask when she stopped herself just in time.

Right. The sewage.

She kept the mask on but took off the night-vision goggles. There was just enough light inside the tunnel to see the thick films of filth dripping from her pants legs. She didn't even want to think about how badly she was going to smell for days to come, or how many showers it was going to take just to get enough of the stench off her to be bearable to herself, never mind to others. She pictured Nate laughing at her discomfort, her punishment for leaving him behind in the middle of the night.

She walked all the way to the back of the narrow platform and glanced up at the manhole covering above them. It was sealed tight, but there were small holes (for fingers or tools to remove the metal lid, if necessary) all along it that allowed slivers of morning sunlight to rain down on them, but not enough to brighten the tunnel.

Blaine unslung his pack and let out a loud sigh of relief as he settled on the damp concrete floor next to her. Like her, he reached for his mask, but thought better of it and left it on, and only removed his NVG. She sat down next to him and didn't know how tired her legs were until she wasn't standing on them anymore.

"You think he told us to rest because he knew we were tired?" Blaine asked.

"Maybe. Were you tired?"

"Hell yeah. My legs are killing me. But at least I'm not lugging around that thing he has over his back. I didn't know he was that strong, either."

"They all are." She thought about the farmhouse in Louisiana. "And fast. You need to remember that if you ever come face-to-face with one of them."

"How fast?"

"However fast you've made them out to be in your mind, increase it by a hundred times and you'll come close."

"You're kidding..."

"No."

"Noted, then." Blaine leaned his head back against the wall

and shook his pants legs and watched the thick sludge dripping off the fabric. "You've seen them—fought them. What's it like?"

"It's...not something I want to ever do again, if I can help it."

"Silver doesn't do anything, but a bullet to the head is all it takes?"

"Yes."

"Crazy how that works. All that speed and strength and night vision, and all it takes is one bullet to the head to put them down."

"It's not as easy as it sounds, Blaine."

"Right. Because they're fast."

"They're really, really fast."

"Fast," Blaine repeated. "Gotcha."

I hope you never have to find out for yourself, Gaby thought as she stared into the pitch darkness of the tunnel and wondered if hell was being trapped down here without night vision, and alone.

Time had a way of slipping by when you were moving through a dark tunnel lit up in a sea of green fluorescent. After a while, she started ignoring the scratches coming from between the cracks to her left and right (and she swore at one point, above her) and the constant stirring of sewage around her ankles. The brief rest had done her legs good, and they walked the next few hours without stopping.

It was difficult to judge if they were making good time without being able to see where they were at any given moment. Even the occasional presence of platforms to their right wasn't much help since they seemed to show up at almost random intervals. The only upside was the presence of sunlight raiding the tunnel from the manhole coverings above the platforms, so each time they reached one it was an exhilarating reminder that there was a world beyond this hellhole she was currently trapped in.

Will continued to come and go, and once he vanished and didn't return until almost thirty minutes later, which was about twenty-five minutes more than his longest previous disappearing act. She had spent most of it trying to decide whether to retreat or race ahead in search of him, and each time she thought she had made a decision she had to remind herself that this was his plan, that he knew what he was doing, that *God, I hope he knows what he's doing or we're all going to die down here, and I do not want to die down here.*

But then he would come back, and she would breathe a sigh of relief and was glad the mask hid most of it. Even though, when she thought about it, he probably heard her reaction anyway, given his hypersensitive hearing.

Another time the green colors of her NVG found him standing in front of them. He was so still she thought it was a mannequin at first...until he moved slightly. She had no idea what he was doing—maybe he was listening for something.

Each time he left them, the tunnel seemed to get smaller and more claustrophobic, and the water colder and tougher until it was like fighting through mud. When he was with them, Will kept his position in front the entire time, the bottom half of his coat growing thicker as it sponged up more of the tunnel's contents. Not that the extra weight slowed him down even a tiny bit. But as his coat became more and more bloated, she was reminded that she was also knee-deep in the same disgusting filth, and no wonder her own pants were starting to feel heavier, and heavier...

Blaine stayed silent for most of the trek, and she only knew he was still back there at all because she could hear him moving around. The big man never lagged too far behind, but he was more active than her, mostly because he wasn't always walking forward; he occasionally turned and walked backward to make sure nothing was sneaking up on them. She could always tell when he did this because the ripples around her increased noticeably.

Eventually, after what seemed like half a day, Will indicated another platform in front of them before disappearing up ahead into the shadows.

"I think that means we get to rest again," Gaby said.

"He's a prince, that guy," Blaine said.

They climbed up the platform, and this time both she and Blaine had to pull off their masks in order to eat and drink from their rations. She did the best she could to breathe through her mouth the entire time, but that was a tricky thing when she had to bite and swallow, too.

She was gagging by the time she gratefully slipped the breathing apparatus back on, thinking, *Never again. Jesus lord, don't ever let me do something this ungodly stupid ever again.*

Blaine, next to her, let out a large breath as soon as his own mask snapped into place. "Jesus Christ. Let's make a pact to shoot each other in the head if we ever decide to do something like this a second time."

"I don't think we're going to have to. Either we make this work the first time, or there won't be a second time."

"I didn't say to bum me out, kid."

She smiled at him before realizing he couldn't see with the entire lower half of her face covered up. "I've been meaning to ask: What did Sarah say when you told her you volunteered?"

"She told me good luck."

"That's it?"

He shrugged. "We're not really seeing each other anymore."

"You said that before. What happened?"

"We grew apart, that's all. It happens. We're both adults, so no point in living in misery if it's not going to work."

"I'm sorry, Blaine."

"Hey, it was a good run. We were good for each other...until we weren't anymore." He stared off at nothing in particular for a moment. Then: "What about you and Nate?"

What about me and Nate? Good question, and I wish I had a better answer.

"I don't know," she said. "I guess it'll depend on whether he shoots me on sight for leaving him in the middle of the night when I see him again."

Blaine chuckled. "The only thing that kid's going to do when he sees you again is run over and grab you in a big bear hug."

"You think so?"

"Trust me. I know guys. I'm one of them."

"I've noticed."

"Yeah, the kid loves you. That's not the kind of thing that comes every day. You should hold onto it."

Gaby nodded. She knew about Blaine and his own past. Before Sarah, there had been another woman whom he had found after The Purge, only to lose.

We've all lost something. Someone. But we keep going. That's what makes us survivors.

Next to her, Blaine had stood up and slipped his heavy pack back on. "Anyways, what is this, a mission or a Doctor Phil counseling session?"

"Can't it be both?" she said, standing up alongside him.

"God, no."

He climbed down first and she followed.

They hadn't gone more than a few yards when she spotted Will's cloaked figure standing up ahead. When he turned around, his eyes were a dull blue-green against her night vision.

"What's wrong?" she asked, making up the rest of the distance between them.

"We're almost there," Will said.

Thank God. I was beginning to think this damn tunnel would never end.

"Already?" she said instead, doing her best to hide her relief.

"Soon."

She stared at him for a moment. There was something about the way he was looking at her—as if he didn't even see her at all.

"What's wrong, Will?" she asked.

"Nothing," he said, and turned and started forward again.

She hurried after him. "Will. What is it? What aren't you telling me?"

But he didn't stop, and kept walking, and soon he had extended his lead without any effort at all.

She gave up trying to catch him, and soon Blaine was walking next to her.

"What was that about?" he asked.

"I don't know," Gaby said, trying to remember the look on Will's face. There was something about it that scared her, because it looked like it scared *him.*

"Maybe it's because we're getting closer," Blaine said. "That's what he said, right?"

She nodded.

"It could be that hive mind thing," Blaine added. "Lara said he could hear them and vice versa. Maybe the closer he gets to them, the more it's affecting him."

"Maybe..."

Up ahead, Will had come to a sudden stop again.

"What now?" Blaine asked.

Will's head was craned slightly toward the ceiling, and she was about to ask what was happening when she felt it.

Oh.

She couldn't hear or see the cause of the aftershocks from down here—at least, not yet—but she had no difficulty feeling it through the rippling in the water around her and the slight tremors in the floor underneath her boots. More evidence came from the small layers of dust that broke off and drifted down from the curved ceiling above them.

And then, just like that, it was gone.

"Was that what I think it was?" Blaine asked next to her.

She nodded, then sought out Will's pulsating blue eyes, now peering back at her from the darkness.

"It's started," he said.

25

LARA

"He pulled a Gaby on me, Lara. That *asshole*."

Lara had to fight back a smile, but was mostly unsuccessful and hoped her friend didn't see it. Carly had been saying the same thing since they left the *Trident*. Lara was inclined to blame it on all the coffee they had drank—she'd had two herself, each one packed with as much sugar as she could stomach—but knew better. Carly was angry for a very good reason.

"He Gaby'd me, Lara," Carly had said as soon as she saw her. "That asshole snuck off while I was still asleep. He *snuck off*."

"I'm sorry," she had said, and she was.

If she knew what Danny was planning, she would have tried to stop him, for all the good it would have done. Danny was still tortured about letting Gaby go with Will, essentially taking his place. The news of Bonnie's death might have been the last straw for him. A child on the way or not, Danny couldn't stay behind again.

And she knew exactly how he felt. There was something very wrong about being here, safe on the island, while her friends were out there risking their lives. Gaby and Blaine with Will, Danny and Keo with the strike team.

I should be out there with them.

With him...

"What exactly are you going to do out there?" Keo had asked when she brought the topic up last night, while they were in the conference room onboard the *Trident* coming up with, essentially, the battle plan to sell to Rhett's people.

"Something," she had said. "I would be doing something."

"No offense, but you'd just get in the way," Keo had said, with that seriousness that was rare for him. "This is what I do, Lara. Let me do my job, and you do yours."

He had said it with such straightforwardness, as if he were telling her the ocean was blue, that she didn't know whether to be angry or grateful.

And Danny had stood there during their back and forth and hadn't said a word. Looking back now, she had a feeling she understood why. Keo's words didn't just work on her, but it had with Danny too, because like Keo, this was what he did: Danny was a soldier.

I should have known he would do this. I should have seen it coming.

"That shithead," Carly was saying next to her. "He promised me, Lara. He promised me he wouldn't go."

"Did he say anything last night?" Lara asked.

"He didn't say a damn thing. He came back from your meeting and went straight to sleep." Carly sighed. "Normally Danny leaving me alone in the early mornings is a good thing, but this time... *That shithead!*"

Carly was still fuming as they walked through the facility's hallway. The place was strangely empty, as if everyone knew what was about to happen today and decided to stay out of it by hiding in their quarters. Except for her and Carly, there was just

Jolly behind them, keeping a respectable distance. Lara had grudgingly let the young man follow her to Black Tide, but she was still embarrassed to have an armed escort, even if it was just one man.

"We should just nuke the whole city," Carly was saying. "Drop a big one and take them all out, King Ghoul and all. That would keep Danny from having to go in there."

"You have a nuke stashed away you haven't told me about?" Lara said.

"Well, no."

"Then there's that whole radiation fallout mess. We kinda want to reuse Texas after this, Carly."

"Stop making too much sense. Anyway, Danny deserves to get a little radiation roast for what he did." Carly narrowed her eyes at her. "And you swear you don't know anything about it?"

"I swear I didn't know what he was going to do," Lara said, looking her friend back in the eyes.

Carly nodded and sighed heavily again. "I hate him so much right now."

"No you don't."

"You're right, I don't, and that makes it worse."

They turned the last corner and approached the Comm Room, which had two guards outside. They both stood a little straighter when they saw her, and the only thing missing was a salute.

I'll never get used to this. Never.

Lara did her best not to let her discomfort show on her face and gave both men a pursed smile.

"You ready for this?" Carly asked next to her.

"As ready as I'll ever be," Lara said.

"I'm not sure I even want to be here. Should I be here?"

"I need a friendly face with me, Carly. Everyone else is out there."

"Okay, then, let's do this."

One of the men opened the door for her, and she stepped inside with Carly. Jolly didn't follow them in.

Rhett and Riley were already there, along with Jane, the young woman who manned the communications equipment. The two men were standing in front of a wall with a large map of Texas taped in place. The banner was a new addition and was already heavily annotated with colored markers. Houston was circled, as were multiple points along the Texas shoreline.

Riley looked over. "Got a good night's sleep?"

"No, but I had a lot of coffee," Lara said.

"That makes three of us."

"Four," Carly said.

"We drank about a gallon of the stuff," Rhett said. "So if I need to call a bathroom break, you'll know why."

"You guys have bathrooms in this place?" Carly asked.

"Yes, but you have to look for them."

"This is Carly," Lara said. "Danny's, uh..." She looked over at Carly.

"The mother of his demon spawn," Carly said, and shook Rhett's and Riley's hands.

"I heard he went out with Striker this morning," Riley said. "That was a surprise. I thought he was sitting this one out."

Carly grunted, but didn't say anything.

"That's what we thought," Lara said. "But apparently he had other ideas."

"Gotta say, I'm glad to have him out there," Rhett said. "You can never have too many Rangers on your side."

"He's not going to be on your side for very long, because when he comes back, I'm going to kill him," Carly said.

"She doesn't mean that," Lara said.

"The hell I don't."

"Where are we now?" Lara asked the two men.

"We're on course to hit the target by noon," Riley said. He pointed out the locations on the map as he talked. "Eagle One and Two are ahead of everyone, as expected. We're expecting real-time reconnaissance from them very soon. Striker's getting ready to lift off as we speak, and Rolling Thunder's already inland and is reporting no troubles so far."

"No one's tried to stop them?"

"According to Rolling Thunder, the regular patrols all seem to be MIA. They haven't run across a single collaborator, on foot or on a technical. Looks like Keo was right, which should make the road to Houston mostly uneventful for the teams."

"Uneventful is good," Lara nodded.

"A good news, bad news situation if I've ever seen one," Rhett said. "The teams won't have to fight their way to the equipment they hid while they were pulling back, but there's going to be a hell of a lot of personnel waiting at the roadblocks."

"Have you heard from Willie Boy?" Riley asked.

Lara walked over to the map and looked it over. "I talked to them last night. They were already moving into position while we were all trying to sleep."

"How will we know when they've made it there?"

"Striker will make contact."

"You have an awful lot of trust in this Frank guy," Rhett said.

He died and came back for us. For me. How do you not have faith in someone who did that for you? she thought, but said, "You would too, if you knew him as well as we did."

Next to her, Riley kept quiet but shuffled his feet slightly.

"Willie Boy will be in position when the time comes," Lara continued. "Everyone else just has to play their part."

"They'll get it done," Riley said.

"Is it going to be enough?" Carly asked. "The ones that volunteered. Are they enough?"

Lara looked back at her and pursed a smile. "God, I hope so."

"Eagle One to Black Tide. Over."

Rhett picked up the microphone and keyed it. "We read you loud and clear, Cole. What's it look like up there?"

"Empty," Cole said, his voice piped through the room's speakers. "I'm confirming the earlier scouting reports that collaborators have stopped their daily patrols around the southeast part of the state and begun to amass around the Houston city limits."

"How many are we talking about?"

"A few hundred per each defensive position, concentrated around the major arteries into the city."

"God, that sounds like a lot," Carly said quietly.

Because it is a lot, Lara thought, remembering the size of a city like Houston and all the many ways in and out of it.

"What kind of weapons are you seeing?" Rhett was asking into the mic.

"Technicals, machine guns," Cole answered. "No heavy firepower from what we can see from up here, but they could be hiding it, waiting to bring them out when Rolling Thunder gets closer."

"I thought for sure they'd have added some tanks to their arsenal after what we did to them," Riley said.

"Maybe we gave them too much credit," Rhett said. Then, back to the mic: "Wheeler. What's your take?"

Wheeler was the pilot of the second Warthog, codenamed Eagle Two. Cole had been telling the truth last night when he told them he was on the verge of convincing a second pilot to join him.

"Ditto what Cole's reporting," a second male voice said through the speakers. "They've got perimeters pretty well set up. Roadblocks with cars on the highways, along the feeder roads.

Everything into the city. Haven't taken a shot at us yet, so I don't know what they're waiting for."

"Don't jinx it, kid," Cole said.

Wheeler laughed. "Sorry about that, old timer."

"You got an ETA on Rolling Thunder?" Cole asked.

"Two hours," Rhett said. "How are you for fuel?"

"We're good to go. Eagle One out."

"Eagle Two out," Wheeler said.

"They know we have planes," Riley said. "So why no anti-aircraft measures?"

"Maybe Rhett's right; maybe we give them too much credit," Lara said. "They're just civilians, after all. They don't have the added benefit of Army Rangers helping them prepare for a battle. According to Willie Boy, they weren't summoned to Houston until two days ago. That's not a lot of time to hunt down and drag something like anti-aircraft weapons into position."

God, you're getting good at lying to people, Lara thought, marveling at just how calmly and confidently she had said everything.

"There are easier ways to shoot down planes," Rhett said. "A few of the smarter ones began arming themselves with shoulder-fired missiles after R-Day. Those things are point-and-shoot, and one of them could just as easily lock onto an A-10."

"Do Cole and Wheeler know that?" Lara asked.

"Cole's an old pro; I didn't need to tell him. Wheeler would have done the same thing since they'll be flying in formation most of the time, and Cole wouldn't let him make himself an easy target."

"What about the tanks?"

"Dodging rockets comes with the territory. They'll deal with it. After R-Day, they have experience doing exactly that."

"You said they were only two hours away. I didn't know they could move that fast."

"The M1 Abrams are faster than you think, especially when they can open up on a highway."

Lara checked her watch. "What about Striker?"

"They'll be taking off from the *Erin* soon," Riley said.

Lara smiled at the name. Rhett's people had rechristened the *Ocean Star* to *Erin* in honor of the woman who had brought Keo to Black Tide. According to Danny, renaming FOBs after lost heroes was a common thing in the military.

"How good is the pilot that's going to be flying them in?" Lara asked.

"He's the best we have," Rhett said. "He trained the other three helicopter pilots. If anyone can get Striker to where they need to be, it's him." Rhett looked over at Carly when he added, "Don't worry. They're in good hands."

Carly didn't answer, and Lara walked over and put a hand on her friend's arm and squeezed. She could feel the tension radiating from almost every inch of Carly's body.

"He's got Keo with him," Lara said. "He'll be fine. They both will."

"I know," Carly nodded back before giving Lara a pained smile. "I'm still going to kick him in the balls when he gets back, though."

Lara couldn't help but smile. "I'll hold him for you."

———

"The rig definitely looks better in the daytime," Keo said through the radio. "The name change was a nice touch, too."

"That was Rhett's idea," Lara said. "Where's Danny?"

"He ran away when I told him I was going to contact you guys before takeoff," Keo said. "I have no idea why."

Lara glanced over at Carly. "I guess Danny's smarter than he looks."

Carly sighed. "Only until I smash him in the head with his own boots."

Lara turned back to the microphone. "Are you guys ready?"

"As ready as we'll ever be," Keo said. "Lots of raw nerves, but they'll get over it. I would be extremely doubtful this thing is going to work if I didn't know Frank as well as I do. The guy knows his stuff."

"What about you?"

"Not my first time on the roller coaster. Besides, who else is going to make sure this thing actually works? Danny boy's a bit rusty. I guess that's what happens when you start playing house with redheads."

"I'm going to kick Keo's ass, too," Carly said.

"Carly sends her love," Lara said into the mic.

"I'm sure she does," Keo chuckled. "Tell her not to worry. I'll keep Ranger boy alive long enough for him to come home and get his just desserts. I'm expecting at least a couple of kicks to the groin area."

"*At least* once," Carly nodded.

"Do me one favor, though?" Keo said.

"Anything," Lara said.

"I can't get Danny to promise to name his kid after me, so how about rechristening the *Trident* to the *Keo*? That has a nice ring to it."

Lara smiled. "I'll think about it."

"Sweet."

"I always wanted to ride around on my very own Keo," Carly said. Then, before Lara could repeat it over the radio, *"Don't say that."*

Lara didn't, and said instead, "Bring everyone back home, Keo."

"I'll do my very damn best," Keo said.

Next to her, Jane had snapped to attention. She was wearing a headset and leaning over the controls.

"I have to go, Keo," Lara said into the mic. "Good luck."

"Luck's got nothing to do with it," Keo said, "but thanks anyway. Striker out."

A second later, their connection went silent.

Rhett had walked over and taken the headset from Jane. He adjusted the mic and spoke into it. "Roger that. Continue on course and keep us updated." Lara waited for Rhett to remove the headset and look in her direction. "Rolling Thunder. They're halfway to the city and are still reporting zero enemy contact."

"Where did you hide those tanks, anyway?" Carly asked.

"We had an entire year to plan this, remember?" Rhett said. "There are contingencies for contingencies. We scouted the entire state from east to west, south to north. There are whole swaths of Texas that the ghouls don't waste their time searching because there's nothing there. Say what you will about Mercer, but he made damn sure we were ready for a long campaign. He always saw this as a crusade that wasn't going to end in our lifetime."

"That's the right word for it: crusade," Riley said solemnly.

Lara walked back to the map and looked it over. "Rolling Thunder is moving too fast. They'll reach Houston before Striker does."

"We had factored in opposition on the roads," Rhett said. "The lack of that is putting them ahead of schedule."

"Tell them to slow down. The last thing we want is for them to get there too soon and get bogged down in premature skirmishes."

"Danny hates it when his skirmishes start prematurely," Carly said.

Lara smiled back at her before turning to Rhett. "I've been

thinking about them. The collaborators. Maybe there's a way to cut down their numbers."

"How?" Rhett asked.

"I'm going to ask them."

"Ask them?" Riley said. "Ask them what?"

"To leave the battlefield." Riley and Rhett exchanged a look, but she ignored them and turned to Jane. "We had a program on the *Trident* that allowed us to broadcast a recorded message through all the frequencies. It cycled automatically and repeated the message. Riley told me you came up with something similar?"

"Like what you did with your broadcasts," Jane said.

Lara nodded. "Yes."

"Mercer had me look into how you guys were doing that. It took a while, but fortunately I had a lot of time on my hands."

"What are you thinking, boss lady?" Carly asked.

"I want to give them a choice," Lara said. "Keo once told me about a collaborator town where people were secretly listening to our broadcasts. Maybe it wasn't just confined to that one town; maybe there are others out there still tuned in."

"You want to broadcast to the collaborators ringing Houston?" Rhett asked.

"Yes." Then, before she could hear the doubting words she knew were coming from the two men in the room with them, "I know they're not all just going to throw down their weapons and walk away at the sound of my voice. I'm not that delusional. They've been committed to their ghoul masters for a year now, and it won't be easy to turn them."

"Then what's the point?" Rhett said.

"The point is trying to save lives."

"Theirs?"

"Ours, theirs. If I can convince even one of them to leave their posts, that's one less person for our people to fight."

"She's right," Riley said. "Even if we can get just a handful to leave, it'll be worth it. One less gun to deal with."

Rhett didn't look convinced. "So what are you going to say?"

"I'll think of something," Lara said.

"Whatever you do, don't mention that they're traitors to the human race," Carly said. "People hate it when you call them that."

"I'll keep that in mind, Carly, thanks."

"Hey, that's what I'm here for. That, and glowing."

"You're definitely glowing," Riley said.

"Back off, Romeo; I'm already spoken for," Carly said. "At least, until I strangle Danny to death when he comes home."

Jane handed her the microphone. "Whenever you're ready. I'll record the message, loop it, then run it through the program and send it out into the world on multiple frequencies at the same time, so that way we'll increase the chances of someone hearing it."

"You improved on our program," Lara said.

The young woman blushed a bit. "Like I said, I had a lot of time on my hands. There is still stuff in here I don't know how to use."

"No pressure," Carly said from the back of the room. "It's not like it's my baby daddy's life at stake, or anything."

"Thanks, Carly," Lara said.

"You're welcome, boss lady."

Lara took a deep breath, then keyed the transmit lever.

"This message goes out to all the men and women guarding the roads into Houston. My name is Lara. Some of you may know who I am. I was there at the beginning, just like all of you. I survived when so many didn't, and a day doesn't go by that I don't think about everything and everyone I've lost."

She depressed the transmit lever and looked back at Carly.

Her friend nodded. "Good start."

Lara turned back to the mic before keying it again:

"I did what I had to in order to survive, just like all of you. It's not my place to judge your actions; I can't put myself in your shoes. What I can do is tell you that the past is the past. What matters is what we do from here on out. Some of you may know what's headed your way, but you might not know why, because *they* won't tell you. But I will."

Another pause, then:

"Listen carefully, because I'm about to tell you everything they don't want you to know…"

26

KEO

Take out some bad guys. Kill some monsters. Save the world.

Keo would have laughed if he really thought about it, but the truth was he was beyond the point of no return. If he had any doubts about that, all he had to do was look out the hatch and down at the shadow of the chopper as they glided across the rippling blue surface of the Gulf of Mexico.

Way too late for doubts now, pal.

"She's going to kill you when you get back!" Keo said, shouting over the engine to be heard.

"Fuck off!" Danny shouted back.

Danny sat on the other side of the bench, with warm bodies between them. They probably didn't really have to shout back and forth, but it was the natural thing to do when you were flying around in a very loud helicopter.

"I'm going to tell her you convinced me to tag along," Danny shouted. "That you begged and begged until I gave in."

"Yeah, she'll buy that."

"She definitely will. I have her under my thumb."

"You're that good in the sack, huh?"

"I'm the best, buddy. Back in college, they used to call me Danny Best. You know why?"

"I'm sure you're going to tell me."

"Because I'm *that* good."

Keo grinned. "Just keep telling yourself that!"

"What do you think I've been doing since we climbed onboard this spinning machine of death?" Then, when the others looked over at him in response, "Oops, did I just say that last part out loud? I meant, this totally non-dangerous-looking contraption! Yeah, that's the ticket."

"Smooth!" Keo said.

They had been airborne for less than ten minutes, and Keo's butt was already going to sleep on him. It was so much easier the last time he was in a helicopter, or maybe it was the constant (and multiple) throbbing pain that kept him from feeling the discomfort that time. He didn't have any excuses now, even though being squeezed into the back with seven other guys, with enough guns and ammo to arm a small Third World country *clank-clank-clanking* on the metal floor around their legs, was a pretty big pain in the ass.

But at least he had the window seat, which gave him something to look at other than James's young and way-too-handsome face all morning long. The blond kid looked wired, as if he had spent more time drinking coffee than sleeping the last twenty-four hours. Keo was used to seeing people getting jacked up for operations, but something about the way James was gripping his AR (so tight that his knuckles were actually turning pale white) between his legs made Keo just a little bit nervous.

"Relax, kid!" Keo shouted across to James.

James wasn't really a kid, and Keo seemed to remember the other man telling him he was twenty...something back on the

Ocean Star. Keo had been a little occupied with other things to actually commit it to memory at the time.

Probably twenty-something...going on thirty-something, from the looks of it.

James flashed him the most unconvincing of grins. "I am!"

Yeah, right.

"I thought you've been out there before?" Keo asked.

"I have," James said, "but it wasn't like this."

"Like what?"

"Before, we did everything possible to avoid them. That was the job. This time, we're going straight at them." He shook his head. "Not the same."

Apparently the others felt the same way, because no one had really said much except for a few throwaway chitchat lines about the weather when they boarded. The nervous energy thrummed all around Keo, even from the pilots up front. Keo and Danny's brief burst of back-and-forth had been the longest conversation since the chopper took off.

They were riding in a Sikorsky MH-60T Jayhawk, one that was designed for the United States Coast Guard, except the orange and white colors had been changed to dull tan to match Mercer's army. It was plenty big enough to haul around two pilots and eight passengers, and wasn't the same one he and Erin had flown in before; that one was also a Sikorsky, but he distinctively remembered that the interiors were different.

Keo took a moment to look at the faces in the back of the chopper with him. They were young and old, almost all men except for one woman. Danny was on the other side, and the ex-Ranger had his eyes partially closed and looked as if he were napping, much to the chagrin of the others.

He glanced out the open hatch as a flock of birds shadowed them from a distance. He thought of Mary, who was awake and already at the infirmary before he had even woken up this morning and made his way back to the *Trident*, where Danny was waiting for him all geared up with his M4A1 slung.

"Let's get the hell out of here before Carly wakes up," was the first thing out of Danny's mouth.

A flurry of movement, as the copilot turned around in his seat and handed a headset to Danny. "Take a listen to this!"

Danny opened his eyes. "What is it?"

"It's going out on all the frequencies. Looks like a little psyops at work."

Danny took the headset and slipped it over his ears. He listened in silence while Keo and the others looked on.

"Psyops?" James said. "I didn't know we were doing that."

"Me neither," Keo said.

After about a minute, Danny pulled off the headset and leaned in Keo's direction. "Take a peep, take a peepers."

Keo took the gear from him and slipped it on. "What is it?"

"Just listen."

Keo did, and smiled.

Lara.

"...We're coming to kill them. To kill *it*. The true monster that lives inside the city, that is responsible for all of this. It calls itself Mabry. Yes, the devil has a name, and its death will end our collective nightmare. Our forces won't engage unless fired upon, so I'm asking you to get out of their way, to let them into the city so they can do what they have to do. For us. For you. For everyone. I'm asking you to be a part of the solution. I'm asking you to join us. This is our planet. Help us take it back. Don't fight us. *Help us.*"

There was a brief pause, then the message repeated itself from the beginning:

"This message goes out to all the men and women guarding the roads into Houston. My name is Lara. Some of you may know who I am. I was there at the beginning, just like all of you. I survived when so many didn't, and a day doesn't go by that I don't think about everything and everyone I've lost. I did what I had to in order to survive, just like all of you. It's not my place to judge your actions; I can't put myself in your shoes. What I can do is tell you that the past is the past. What matters is what we do from here on out. Some of you may know what's headed your way, but you might not know why, because *they* won't tell you. But I will…"

Keo pulled the headset off. "You think it'll work?" he shouted across at Danny.

The ex-Ranger shrugged. "Couldn't hurt. They already know we're coming. Might as well see how many we can peel off."

James was staring at him intently, and Keo took pity on the kid and handed him the headset. The young man quickly slipped it on.

"Hey," a voice said.

Keo turned to the big guy sitting next to him; he had a goatee and a bald head that looked freshly shaved. An M249 light machine gun was perched between his legs, and *Vince* was stenciled across his uniform's name tag.

"Yeah?" Keo said.

"What's she like?" Vince asked.

"Who?"

"Lara."

"What do you wanna know?"

"I saw her on the island, but I never got the chance to talk to her. I was going to introduce myself at the meeting last night, but there were too many people in front of me and I could tell she was getting tired of answering questions."

"Well, aren't you sweet," Danny said. "Barf."

"She's the toughest woman I know," Keo said. "She's got a good head on her shoulders. A lot of people wouldn't be alive now if it weren't for her."

"I'm one of them," Vince said.

"Yeah?"

Vince nodded. "I wasn't like most of these guys. I didn't join up with Mercer until much later. I was out there by myself, barely getting by. Running out of food, water, ammo, you name it. There were five of us in the beginning, and by the end there was just me. I was about to give up, you know, end it all myself instead of waiting for those bloodsuckers. Then one day I hear this voice coming through the radio. It wasn't even mine. The radio, I mean. One of the guys was always playing with it, hoping to hear something, but he never did."

Vince paused and seemed to relive the memory. Keo noticed that the others were listening, some more actively than others. Even Danny, on the other side of the bench, was watching as Vince told his story.

"Anyway," Vince continued, "this voice comes through the radio. Telling me about silver, about all the other stuff I didn't know. But more than that, telling me to keep fighting. I still remember what she said. 'If you're hearing this message, you are not alone. Stay strong, stay smart, and adapt. We owe it to those we've lost to keep fighting, to never give up. Good luck.'"

"You remembered all that?" Danny asked.

"Yup," Vince said. Then he grinned almost shyly. "It wasn't hard. That message played over and over. I must have heard it a thousand times. Her voice... It's not even about the silver or the other stuff. You don't know how it feels to have someone out there talking to you, even if they weren't really talking to you. Just reaching out, telling you there's hope. That you're not alone." Vince paused again before continuing. "Anyway, that's why I was hoping to meet her last night."

"You can, when we get back," Keo said.

"Yeah, I'm definitely doing that. Whatever it takes this time."

"When you do see her, you might wanna edit out the part

where you wanna make beautiful babies with her," Danny said. "She gets a little squeamish about that sort of thing."

The others laughed, but Vince shrugged it off with, "Screw you, man," though he didn't sound all that offended.

"Just a thought," Danny said before leaning back against his seat.

"I mean it, though," Vince said, turning back to Keo. "First thing I'll do when I get back is find a way to thank her. I know a bunch of guys who feel the same way."

"I'll introduce you," Keo said.

"You guys good friends?"

"Not as good as that guy," Keo said, nodding in Danny's direction.

"Cool," Vince said, and sat back looking very pleased.

"What about me?" James said, taking off the headset.

Keo looked across at him. "What about you?"

"I never got the chance to meet her, either."

"You were on the oil rig when she was there."

"Things were kind of hectic back then."

"Weren't you also on the *Trident?*"

"Yeah, but I didn't know who she was then. And plus, people were pointing guns at each other. It wasn't the best time to make introductions."

"Okay, sure, you too, then."

"Hey," someone else said. It was the only woman in the group: *Angie.* "I wouldn't mind a proper intro myself. And unlike these guys, I won't be trying to convince her to make beautiful babies with me."

Keo grinned across at Danny. "You hear that?"

"Yeah, yeah," Danny said. "We'll see what we can do, kids."

"Anyone else?" Keo asked.

One other person raised their hand...then another one. That left only one more—a large lump of a human being sitting between Angie and James. He had shaggy blond hair and shoulders that would have made him a lot of money in the NFL.

"What about you?" Danny asked him.

The man with *Hanson* written on his name tag said, "What about me?"

"You don't want a piece of this action, big fella?"

"Not interested."

"No? Then why'd you volunteer? You do know this is an all-volunteer mission, right?"

Hanson tapped the M249 sitting between his legs. "Your friend ain't got nothing to do with it. I spent a year making silver bullets. Now I'm finally going to get to use them. That's why."

"Perfectly logical, albeit somewhat scary, reason," Danny said.

Hanson just grinned back at him.

There were three of them, all tan-colored M1 Abramses moving northwest on the long stretch of State Highway 288 in almost a single (though somewhat jagged) line. There was absolutely nothing but flat country and farmland flanking them, and would be for a long time until they neared Houston. There was no traffic for the tanks to worry about, but they were clearly moving slower than their forty-five miles per hour max speed. Not that a car or two (or a dozen) would have slowed them down even a little bit. He'd seen those monsters do plenty of damage against unwanted obstructions. Smartly, there was no one manning the machine gun turret just in case there were snipers out there.

"Three?" Keo said to Danny. "When did we get three? I thought it was just Peele and Alex?"

The ex-Ranger nodded. "Third crew threw in at the last minute. It's our lucky day, Canoe."

"That's one way to look at it."

"Hey, chin up. We're riding into battle. What more could you possibly ask for?"

"Oh, I could think of plenty."

Danny chuckled. "Now you're just being greedy. This is what we do. Let's just enjoy the ride."

Keo looked across at James, noticing that the younger man had taken something out of his pocket and had put it on one of his fingers.

"When's the big day?" Keo asked.

James looked up. "What?"

Keo nodded at the ring on his finger.

"Oh," James said. "We got married this morning, before I left for the *Erin*." He twirled the ring nervously. It was a plain gold band, but Keo didn't think its value was in how much it cost. "She didn't want me to wear it. You know, so I wouldn't lose it. What do you think?"

"It's a nice ring."

"No, I mean, should I put it away? So I won't lose it?"

Keo shrugged. "I wouldn't worry about it. It's plain-looking enough you could probably find a thousand of them in a jewelry store to replace it if you did lose it. She'd never know the difference."

"She had this one saved up for a while now—or at least that's what she said—and I'd hate to lose it."

Danny leaned forward and looked over at James. "Don't sweat it, kid. If you want, I'll chop it off your finger and take it back to her so she can give it to the next guy."

"Hey, fuck you," James said.

"Was it something I said?"

"Maybe," Keo said.

"Sheesh, everyone's so sensitive these days," Danny said.

The pilots broke away from the highway long before they saw the city in the distance. The advance scouting by the Warthogs had given them a pretty good idea of where the enemy positions were, and the Jayhawk had rerouted its approach to the target site accordingly.

Out the helicopter's hatch, the flat lands and fields of the Texas countryside had given way to concrete and buildings. The smaller towns on the outskirts of Houston looked frozen in time, vehicles still parked where their owners had abandoned them. There was a peacefulness about the scenery, a calmness that might not have looked so different a year ago even when there were people around. Wasn't that the reason most people moved out here in the first place? For the peace and quiet?

He was staring at a McDonald's golden arch, wondering how much longer it was going to stay up there, when he glimpsed figures moving around on the rooftops of a nearby Wallbys. He hadn't fully processed what he was seeing before they opened fire, bullets punching into the hull above his head, the *ping-ping-ping!* like firecrackers going off next to his ear.

"Contact!" Keo shouted even as he jerked his head away from the opening. "Collaborators at five o'clock!"

Thank God he was strapped to the bench, or Keo might have been thrown out the hatch when the big Sikorsky pitched left, then right, even as the *pop-pop-pop* from below faded against the engine's roar.

Vince had grabbed ahold of Keo while the helicopter was throwing them around and putting distance between them and the shooters. "Whoa, man, you hit?"

"I'm good, I'm good," Keo said, righting himself. "I'm good..."

"I guess they definitely know we're coming now," James said across from him.

"Yeah, I think that's a pretty safe assumption, kid."

Danny unbuckled his seat belt and leaned toward the cockpit. "How much farther?"

The copilot glanced back. "Ten minutes!"

Danny nodded, then swept the faces around him. "Listen up!"

They turned to look at him.

"You've all been briefed on the mission," Danny shouted, even though he really didn't have to. Keo guessed it was mostly to get everyone's undivided attention. "You know how this is going to go down. The bird's going to insert us right up the target's skirt. There may or may not be a hornet's nest of bad guys waiting to make us wish we hadn't volunteered. You can take one thing to the bank: It's going to get hairy real fast, and you're going to be scared—hell, you wouldn't be human if you weren't—but you'll have to push through it and do your job. Whatever happens, *do your job*, and we all go home happy little campers with a great story to tell the kids. Fuck up, and we carry you back in a body bag. *Comprende?*"

The others nodded back at him.

"Good." Danny turned to Keo. "You got the ball, Kemosabe. Try not to get me killed, huh? I got the world's hottest redhead and a bun in the oven waiting for me at home."

"No promises," Keo said.

Danny grinned, then sat back down.

No pressure, Keo thought, staring at the faces looking back at him and wondering whatever in the hell possessed him to agree to lead this mission.

Oh, who was he kidding? He knew exactly what he was doing out here. It was because she had asked him to.

"Besides Danny, you're the only one I trust to do this. To get this done."

How the hell was he going to say no to that? He could have,

sure, but he didn't want to. It wasn't often people told him they needed him to do something and didn't threaten to put a bullet in him if he didn't. All she had to do was ask.

You're going soft, pal. Real soft.

Keo sighed to himself and refocused on the faces looking back at him.

Vince to his left, close enough that they rubbed shoulders every time one of them took a breath. Then there was Mackey, squeezed between Vince and Danny. James, directly across from him, with the mountain of a man, Hanson, immediately to his right. Angie after that, and, across from Danny, Delaware, who looked more like a Florida with his dark tan.

Keo smiled back at them. It wasn't hard. He had mastered the fake smile a long time ago.

Up front, the copilot threw another quick look into the back. "Hold onto your panties, ladies; we got incoming!"

Keo turned his head and looked out the hatch as both Warthogs appeared outside, staying alongside them just long enough for him to catch a glimpse of the shark's teeth painted on the front of both jets, the "mouth" opening wide where the Avenger rotary cannon was positioned. Instead of the U.S. star insignia on the side, there was the familiar sun emblem with the rays shooting outward.

The twin-engine planes were close enough that the Sikorsky actually tilted slightly as it was caught in their wake. Keo also reflexively grabbed onto the hatch, forgetting for a moment that he was still buckled in.

One of the Warthogs veered right while the second one kept straight ahead.

"I'm glad those things are on our side," Vince said beside him.

"Yeah," Keo said. "Let's hope they're enough."

Or this is going to be one short mission, he thought, but didn't think Vince or the others needed to hear that last part.

Keo kept his eyes outside the hatch as the main downtown area of Houston appeared in the distance. The sun was high in the sky, a great ball throwing a sea of brightness against the towering skyscrapers. Monuments to mankind's greatness, now probably teeming with tens of thousands of ghouls. Could they see the aircraft gliding across the cityscape right now? He could imagine their frenzied state, wanting desperately to attack, to swarm with their numbers but held back by an invisible enemy.

He looked across at James, still playing with his wedding band. "Hey."

James glanced up and tried to smile—and failed miserably.

"You'll do fine," Keo said. "Don't wander off, and don't do anything I don't do. Stay close to me or Danny at all times."

James nodded, but it looked too halfhearted.

"*Stay close,*" Keo said again.

"Okay."

"It's okay, you know. Everyone's nervous their first time."

"Were you?"

"I was fucking terrified. But I got over it."

James nodded again, and this time Keo almost believed the kid wasn't scared shitless. Almost.

"What about me?" Vince asked, clutching and unclutching the machine gun between his legs. "Any words of wisdom?"

"Yeah," Keo said. "Shoot everything that isn't us."

"That's it?"

"Danny, you got some advice for him?" Keo shouted across the bench.

"Yeah," Danny said, leaning forward, "if you absolutely must shoot someone, go for Lego My Keo over there. After all, he's ugly and no one's going to miss him."

"Thanks for that, pal," Keo said.

Danny grinned back at him, just as two massive *BOOMS!*

shattered the afternoon air, both explosions coming from directly ahead of them.

It was quickly followed by the familiar roar of a 30mm cannon, firing to their right:

Broooooooooooorrrrttttttttt!

27

GABY

They were close. She could feel it, an overwhelming sense of dread—the kind that made it hard to breathe even with the mask keeping (most) of the smell around her at bay—growing with every step. It had gotten worse in the last hour or so, and as if to confirm her suspicions, the attack finally began.

The narrow, claustrophobic world they had been stuck in for what seemed like an entire lifetime shook and the cracks widened, dust and dirt falling from the walls in sheets as the first bomb detonated, followed not long after by the second. Then a third and a fourth, sending aftershocks across the entire length of the tunnel.

They stopped moving to listen to the buildings crumbling, the *pek-pek-pek* of falling debris easily heard even from all the way down here.

"Jesus Christ," Blaine said. "That last couple sounded way too close."

A big chunk of the ceiling came loose and *plopped* into the thick sewage water in front of her, creating ripples around her knees. She had hoped the water would start to get shallower the farther into the city they went, but there was no such luck. If anything, it seemed to get denser, and each footstep took just a little bit more effort. Of course, it could have just been that she was more tired now than when they had begun the trek.

Will was standing about ten feet in front of them, looking forward as if the tunnel (seemingly) coming apart around him wasn't worth his attention. It was nothing new—if anything, he was doing that more and more often. He was here, with them in the sewer system, but not *really* here.

"Will," she said.

He glanced over, blue eyes glowing against the green of her night-vision goggles.

"Is this all going according to plan?" she asked.

"Yes," he hissed.

She clutched the rifle tighter. "What—"

Brooooooooooorrrrttttttttt!

Every inch of her body trembled at the noise and it took a second—five seconds—before it passed.

"Jesus, I hate that sound," she whispered. "I fucking *hate* that sound."

"Is that it?" Blaine asked, water sloshing around his boots as he moved closer. "Are those the Warthogs you were telling me about?"

"Yeah. I still hear them in my nightmares."

"At least they're on our side this time."

"'They?'"

"Doesn't it sound like there's more than one of them up there?"

"Maybe, I don't—"

Will was looking at them.

"What is it?" she asked.

"We have to go," Will said before turning and continuing on.

They followed, while beyond the tunnel walls the continued

brooooooooooorrrrtttttttt! of the Warthog sent shivers up and down her spine. This one sounded farther from their position than the previous, which meant the planes were constantly on the move as they engaged enemy targets across the city. Or at least, that was the plan.

God, I hope it's all going according to plan up there...

"You're right," Blaine said, "they do sound like Godzilla...on crack."

"It's worse when they're right on top of you."

"What kind of guns are they using?"

"Danny says they're 30mm Gatling guns. By the time you hear the noise, the bullets have already landed. And if they're shooting at you..."

"You're already dead."

"Uh huh."

"Like I said, glad they're on our side."

"Yeah," she said quietly, still not fully one-hundred percent in agreement.

The loosened parts of the tunnel were starting to fall at a quicker rate around them now. Something *pek!* off her NVG and bounced into the water. Will had put a little more space between them, and she had to keep biting her tongue to ask him to slow down. She picked up her pace instead, and Blaine did likewise next to her.

"Damn, that sounded way closer," Blaine said when another *brooooooooooorrrrtttttttt!* filtered through the thick concrete walls.

"It's definitely closer," Gaby said.

"So it wasn't just me."

"No."

"Good to know. Being down here for so long—how long has it been now?—I'm not sure I can trust my instincts anymore."

You and me both.

Will had slowed down, allowing them to catch up. Seeing his unpanicked state (was he even capable of panicking anymore?) always put her mind at ease, and she had to keep reminding herself that this was all going according to plan. His plan.

God, she hoped this was all going according to plan.

She kept one eye glued to Will's black-shaped form about fifteen yards in front of them and the other on the walls and ceiling, waiting for the tunnel to come tumbling down and bury them down here where no one would ever find them.

Way to think happy thoughts, girl.

"I didn't think she had it in her," Blaine was saying.

"Who?" Gaby said.

"Lara. When we had to abandon Song Island, I didn't think she could keep it together, much less take command the way she did. She really proved me wrong."

"I think she proved everyone wrong, including herself."

"Funny how things work out."

She understood why he was talking. It wasn't because any of this was important, because they weren't. He was doing it because it helped to keep his mind off what was happening up there and the continuous trembling around them whenever one of the planes came too close to their position. And each time the Warthogs did that, she trembled slightly, thankful it was too dark for Blaine to see unless he was staring right at her.

"Lara thought she was going to be a doctor," Blaine was saying. "I thought I was going to go from one dead-end job to dead-end job until the day I died. Now look at us."

"Is that a good thing?" she asked.

He chuckled. "I don't know. But what about you? I bet you had choices."

"I always just thought I'd go to college and see what happened after that."

"So it's safe to say you never thought you'd be carrying an M4 while knee-deep in, literally, shit?"

She smiled underneath the mask. "That's an affirmative."

Small-arms fire.

They had begun about ten minutes ago and didn't sound as if they were going to be stopping anytime soon. Instead, they got louder as she, Blaine, and Will continued to trudge their way through the sewer, which meant of course they were moving *toward* the gunfire.

Will was somewhere in front of her, though she had lost sight of him when she craned her neck to look up at the ceiling (*for just a moment*) to make sure it wasn't going to cave in on her. Every now and then she would hear one of the Warthogs doing another strafing run from somewhere else in the city, the familiar roar of their guns reaching her all the way down here, as if seeking her out and asking her, *Hey, you remember us?*

Yes, she remembered them. She would never forget them for as long as she lived...however that turned out to be.

Positive thoughts. Think positive thoughts.

And then Will disappeared.

"Where'd he go?" Blaine said as he stepped up beside her.

"I don't know," she said, fighting back the panic in her voice.

"I wish he'd tell us first before he does one of his vanishing acts."

And I wish I was back on the Trident *with Nate*, she thought, when her night vision picked up something in the water in front of them.

It was floating on top of the sludge: A trench coat.

"What is that?" Blaine asked.

She knew the answer even before she reached forward and

picked up the fabric with the barrel of her carbine, the long suppressor at the end giving her a pole with which to work with. The cloth was heavy, its natural color buried underneath the layers of filth. It was shredded in spots, just like Will's trench coat had been when he led the ghouls away from them at the barn a few nights back.

"This ain't good," Blaine said, lifting his rifle until it was in firing position.

Above them, the gunfire continued, the *pop-pop-pop* of automatic rifle, interspersed with barrages of *brap-brap-brap* from a machine gun, coming from seemingly every direction now. It was a full-blown war zone up there.

"Gaby," a voice said.

The hairs on the back of her neck spiked as he appeared out of thin air in front of her.

"Jesus Christ," Blaine whispered. "I think I just had my first stroke."

She didn't give voice to it, but Gaby felt the same way. She always knew Will could be extremely (*impossibly*) quiet when he wanted to be, but to come and go without her or Blaine even noticing, while the three of them were trapped down here in the close confines of the tunnel and knee-deep in sewage?

How does he do that?

Will hadn't just taken off the coat, she saw, but had ditched the backpack he had been carrying. The reason for that was easy to see: he didn't need it anymore because he was now wearing its contents.

The "gauntlets," as Danny called them, covered both of Will's hands and extended almost all the way up to the elbows where they were clasped in place by a combination of leather and metal straps. Studs gleamed against her night vision, jutting out of the gloves from where his knuckles would be—essentially silver spikes, each one almost three-quarters of an inch long. He wore identical foot-long knives on his thighs, the handles covered in thick black duct tape for better gripping. The blades themselves were silver which, while not fatal to Will, was to the black eyes. A smooth, black matte ballistic helmet covered his entire head, his eyes hidden behind tinted goggles built into the piece.

The addition of the helmet to the ballistic jersey made him look like a motocross racer geared for the ride of his life; or maybe an extra from one of those post-apocalyptic movies, wandering wastelands looking for unsuspecting victims. The getup was unquestionably intimidating, even though its main purpose was to hide his identity as well as give him the tools he'd need for close-quarter survival against ghouls.

Close-quarter. Like being stuck in a sewer tunnel.

She couldn't tell at all that he wasn't just another man by looking at him. Maybe he was a little too obviously lanky, but the wardrobe hid his skeletal shape underneath it. The whole thing should have been heavy—she would know, having carried all of that in the duffel bag for a time herself—but Will moved in them as if they weighed nothing.

"Sweet threads," Blaine said. "Gotta get Mae and the gals to make me one of those when we get back."

Gaby almost smiled, except the shooting above them had increased in intensity and it drew her attention instead. It was still just the *pop-pop-pop* of small arms, along with the *brap-brap-brap* of machine gun fire. There were no signs of the Warthogs, and she couldn't decide whether to be glad or worried by that fact.

She looked back at Will. "How much farther?"

"Almost there," he said, and turned and continued on.

With his helmet on, she had to strain to hear him. His voice also didn't sound nearly as hissy.

She and Blaine followed him down the tunnel again, and with each step the gunfire above them (In front of them? Behind them? She swore it sounded as if it were coming from every direction now.) seemed to get louder and faster, more intense as the back-and-forth continued unabated.

Jesus. What's going on up there?

"Listen to that," Blaine was saying. "Like World War III times ten."

"It's the strike team," she said. "Striker. Looks like they're already here."

"So shouldn't we, I don't know, hurry?"

She glanced at Will for confirmation. If he had heard Blaine, it hadn't pushed him to go any faster.

He knows what he's doing. Just follow his lead.

But then, creeping into her consciousness, *God, I hope he knows what he's doing, because Blaine's right; it sounds like World War III times ten up there.*

"What's our code name?" Blaine was asking.

"What?" she said.

"That's Striker up there. The tanks are Rolling Thunder, right?"

"Uh huh. Lara told me when I talked to her before we came down here."

"So what's our code name? Do we even have one?"

"Willie Boy."

"Willie Boy?" Blaine repeated, staring at her as if he thought she was trying to prank him. "Seriously?"

"Seriously."

"That's...not nearly as cool as Striker or Rolling Thunder. What's about the Warthogs flying around up there?"

"Eagle."

"Yeah, Willie Boy's definitely not nearly as cool." He sighed. "Do I even need to ask who came up with it?"

She smiled to herself under the mask. Inane chatter with Blaine helped to keep her mind off the viciousness of the gun battle above them. It also kept her from screaming at Will to *hurry. Hurry before everyone is dead while waiting for us!*

She wondered if she might have actually said that last part aloud, because suddenly Will stopped and turned around, and Gaby saw her own reflection in the helmet's goggles.

"What is it?" she said.

"Here," he said.

"Here?" she repeated.

The helmet bobbed up and down. "We'll need help to go farther."

He turned his head and she followed it to another platform carved into the side of the tunnel about ten feet in front of her. Small streaks of sunlight became visible when she took a few steps forward.

"This is it?" Blaine asked behind her.

"This is it," she nodded.

"About friggin' time."

Definitely about friggin' goddamn time, she thought, listening to the hellacious gunfire above them.

Turning to Blaine, she said, "Ladies first."

Blaine grunted. "You're Danny now, is that it?"

"He's like a virus. Infecting everyone around him."

"They have shots for that, I hear," Blaine said as he climbed up the platform, waste dripping from his pants legs.

Even though she couldn't smell it, seeing the sewage sloughing off Blaine's clothes made her gag slightly. She fought through it and followed him up. As she straightened, clutching her rifle, she glanced behind her.

Will had turned around again and was now looking down the tunnel, as if he could see something up there that she couldn't even with the NVG.

Trust him. You have to trust him.

She and Blaine turned their backs on the dark tunnel and

looked up at the round metal object at the end of the ladder embedded into the wall. Long streaks of sunlight slivered through the ventilation holes, partially distorting her night vision. Here, on the platform and standing directly below the grate, the gunfire was even louder, the *pop-pop-pop* more immediate, and she thought she could even hear the *clink-clink-clink* of bullet casings flicking across...concrete pavement?

Where the hell were they, exactly?

Blaine went into a crouch and unslung his pack. She watched him frantically dig around before he found what he was looking for and pull it out: a two-way portable radio.

Blaine turned the gear on and, glancing up at the covering, keyed it. "Striker, come in. Striker, this is"—he might have cringed a little when he said—"Willie Boy. Can you hear me? Answer if you can hear me." When no one answered, he said louder, "Striker, Striker, this is Willie Boy, do you read—"

"Yeah, yeah, I heard you the first time," a familiar voice said through the radio.

Keo.

Gaby couldn't help but grin to herself, even as the rattle of gunfire echoed from the other end of the connection. There were so many and they were overlapping, sounding more like hail slamming into a metal roof.

"Took your sweet ass time," Keo said through the radio. "We got tangos coming at us in waves over here. What's your position?"

"We're right below you," Blaine said. "Whenever you're ready."

"Coming to you!"

Blaine stood up and put the radio away, then snatched up his carbine and took a step back from the ladder. Gaby positioned herself next to him, her own M4 pointed up at the grate above them.

Keo had said *"Coming to you!"* but he hadn't said when he would get there, or how far he had been when they made contact.

So they waited ten seconds.

Then twenty seconds...

Thirty...

Gaby exchanged a puzzled look with Blaine and wondered if he found staring at her NVG just as comical as she did staring at his.

"He said he was coming to us, right?" Blaine asked.

She nodded. "That's what I heard."

"So where is he?"

"Give them more time. Sounds like they have their hands full up there."

"Sure, why not?" Blaine said. "It's not like we got anywhere else better to be."

"No hot dates, huh?"

"Nope. What about you?"

"Maybe a hot shower after this."

"Or a hundred."

"Or a hundred," she nodded.

Gaby looked over her shoulder, expecting to find Will standing behind them, but he was gone. *Again.*

Dammit, Will, I wish you'd stop doing that.

She refocused on the manhole lid above them instead. It still hadn't moved since the last time she looked, though she thought she could see shadows flitting across the ventilation holes this time.

"Where's Will?" Blaine asked.

"I don't know. He left again."

"I wish he'd stop doing that."

She smiled to herself behind her mask. "Yeah."

She glanced over, hoping to see that he had returned, but there was still just empty space back there. The fact that all of this depended on him and he was nowhere to be found left her more than just a little terrified—

"Gaby," Blaine said.

She turned around and was going to ask *What?* but she didn't have to because she could see it:

The round covering above them had started to move...

28

KEO

The HC Dome was over 200 feet high and the length of one and a half football fields. According to Danny, the place was originally built for a capacity of 40,000 before it was expanded in recent years to 60,000. It was where the local professional sports teams played their games, and in its time the Dome (because that was what it was—a stadium with a giant dome on top) was the first of its kind but had since been surpassed by more high-tech sports arenas in recent decades.

Keo didn't know a thing about the place or what used to go on within its round-shaped walls, and he would never find out because the first time he laid eyes on it, the structure was missing the thing that gave it its name, along with a large chunk of everything else. There was just a pile of rubble where the gargantuan building used to be, the result of two massive cluster bombs dropped by an A-10 that had preceded their arrival.

Plumes of gray and white ash smoke still filled the sky above the jagged skeletal remains, while the Warthogs had begun dropping smaller payloads on the surrounding buildings when the Sikorsky touched down in one of the many parking lots that circled the area. The pilots chose their LZ wisely—in a no-parking zone toward the top half of the lot. There was a surprising mass of cars waiting for them, signs that there had been some kind of concert or game here the night of The Purge.

They were far enough from the crumbling dome—200 meters, give or take—that he didn't reach for the breathing mask to protect himself from the spreading clouds of pulverized cement and concrete. He was the first one off the MH-60T Jayhawk and blinked against the sun (*Day is good. Day is very good!*) and proceeded to sweep the area with the MP5SD while peering through the red dot sight, Lara's voice going through his head from the briefing last night:

"Other than the Dome itself, Eagle will take out the nests around the area. Frank says that's where the bulk of the blue eyes will be. If we can take them out—all or most of them—it'll make his job a lot easier."

He'd gotten three breaths out when a missile slashed over his head and impacted an apartment complex across the street. The resulting explosion sent a sea of brick and smoke and God knew what else into the air.

Ghouls. He was looking at ghoul body parts.

Now that's something you don't see every day!

James, the second person off the Jayhawk behind him, saw the building go up and said breathlessly, "Holy fuck."

"You good?" Keo asked, shouting to be heard over the *whup-whup-whup* of the rotor blades above their heads.

James nodded back, but his face didn't look "good" at all.

Tough it out, kid, Keo thought while shouting, "Don't stray! Understand? Stick to the group!"

Another nod, this one much more assured.

The Warthog that had devastated the building had veered off, traveling miles in the blink of an eye, and Keo heard the *brooooooooooorrrrtttttttttt!* of its Gatlin gun, like some man-made monstrosity cursing its creation, as the warplane razed something on a highway well beyond Keo's line of sight.

"What's it doing?" James shouted.

"Keeping collaborators off our ass!" Keo shouted back.

Brooooooooooorrrrttttttttt!

Brooooooooooorrrrttttttttt!

Damn, he was loving that sound!

He spun back to the chopper and smacked the younger man on the shoulder, shouting, "Give me security!" as a second Warthog swooped by overhead, the wave of its flight path like a gust of hurricane wind ripping across both their faces, overwhelming even the helicopter's rotors for a moment.

To his credit, James did exactly as he was told, racing away from the Jayhawk while Vince and Hanson hopped down after him. Keo pointed at them, then at the four-lane road that led into the parking area from a nearby frontage road.

"Take up positions!" Keo shouted. "That's where they'll be coming first!"

Vince and Hanson nodded and jogged off, each man resting his machine gun across the hood of a different vehicle facing the south entrance. Keo took a moment to pull out his binoculars and swept the highway in the near distance, the same one the Warthog had strafed earlier. He searched for the moving vehicles he knew would be coming as soon as the collaborators figured out where their helicopter was going.

BOOM! from behind him, as a Warthog fired another missile into a building to the right of the HC Dome. It looked big enough to be an arena, but maybe his perspective was somewhat warped by being at ground level. Even as the structure began to fall apart, a second missile—*BOOM!*—took out the walls that were still standing.

Keo was too far away to make out any details, but he thought he might have heard what sounded like screams (?) coming from the collapsing building.

"*Eagle needs to take out these buildings around the Dome,*" Lara had said, staring across the map at Cole. "*Use everything you have on them and save the Gatling gun to push back any collaborator reinforcements that will be rushing to Striker's position.*"

To hear her giving the orders, he could almost believe she had come up with every single part of the plan herself, that it wasn't her, him, and Danny who had hashed everything out on the *Trident* before heading over to Black Tide. But that was the one thing about Lara he always admired: When she committed, the woman really committed.

"Hey, Coaster!" someone shouted behind him.

He glanced back at Danny, heading to his position from the other side of the helicopter. He was already pulling on a thin white mask over his mouth, and like Keo, James, and everyone else, was shouldering a large pack.

"I've heard of silent but deadly, but never loud and deadly!" Danny shouted.

Keo was going to ask him what he was talking about, and why he was putting on the mask, when the stench hit him.

Jesus Christ!

It came from seemingly nowhere and overwhelmed him in the blink of an eye. Keo was used to the stench of vaporized ghouls—or, at least, he thought he was—but he wasn't at all prepared for this level of assault on his senses, as what must have been thousands of dead (*again?*) ghouls were exposed to the sun.

He reached into his pocket and took out the mask and snapped it over his mouth, even as his eyes stung and began to water, and if not for the continued *whup-whup-whupping* of the chopper blades above them, he wasn't sure if he could keep this morning's breakfast down.

Danny crouched next to him, the Ranger's heavily modified

M4A1 resting casually atop one bent knee. "You know, I used to come here all the time with our mutual friend. Watched the home team take on the bad guys and drank enough beer to barf out a small swimming pool."

"Bad guys?" Keo said.

"Yeah, everyone who isn't on the home team are the bad guys."

"Of course."

Danny glanced back at the remains of the HC Dome. "Had a lot of good times in there."

"Not anymore!"

Danny sighed. "Don't rub salt in the wound, Kilometer. That's just mean."

A sudden massive gust of wind made them both glance up just as one of the Warthogs came back around. Keo stared at the empty slots under its wings as it swooped past them and headed toward a long stretch of highway in the distance.

"Looks like it blew its load all over the place," Danny said. "I hate it when that happens."

"That happen often?" Keo asked.

"Once or twice. Let's hope he stocked up on those sweet, sweet 30mm rounds, otherwise this is going to be one very short trip to the ol' Dome. Speaking of which—" Danny said and pointed.

"I see it!" Keo shouted.

He got up and jogged over to where Vince had stationed himself, his M249's bipod perched on the hood of a Jeep Wrangler. He patted the big man on the shoulder and pointed at a vehicle barreling down the frontage road from the highway. "Incoming!"

Vince nodded and repositioned his machine gun. "Weapons free?"

"Wait until it gets closer!"

He snapped a quick look at Hanson, positioned fifteen meters to his right, his own MG mounted on the hood of a red sedan. He didn't have to shout across at Hanson, who had already seen the approaching vehicle and turned to face it, too.

Keo took a moment to take in the scene.

Danny was still crouched next to the Sikorsky behind him, with James nearby; Danny may or may not be saying something to the kid. Angie, Mackey, and Delaware were on the other side of the aircraft; they looked alert and ready—or at least as much as they could with the rotors sending a continuous blast of wind against their backs and faces while they tried not to gag on the stench of dead ghouls that continued to swarm them from every side.

He turned back at the approaching enemy—some kind of truck—moving fast toward them, and soon would be turning into the street that ran parallel to the stadium. There was just the one car, so either the guy had been sent here to find out what they were doing, or more likely, it was the only collaborator that had survived one of the Warthog's recent strafing runs along the highway to reach its destination.

Not that it mattered. One truck, even a technical (though it was still too far off at the moment for Keo to be absolutely sure that was a machine gun mounted on top of its cab) wasn't going to do much against two waiting MGs.

A tap on his shoulder made him glance back at Danny, who shouted, "I told the chopper to take off! They're just sitting ducks out here!"

Keo nodded and watched the Jayhawk as it began lifting up, and up...

"Fingers crossed they don't wander off too far and forget about us!" Danny said, and Keo was pretty sure he was grinning like an idiot behind his mask.

"Not funny!" Keo said.

"You just need a sense of humor, that's all!"

"I got plenty of that. You're just not funny!"

"Hey, do I go to where you work and heckle you?"

Without the helicopter's presence on the ground with them, Keo could suddenly hear his own racing heartbeat again, not to mention the growing acrid stench of dead ghouls wafting across the parking lot from the Dome and surrounding buildings. The Warthogs had taken down everything they could before running dry of bombs, but that left over a dozen or so apartments still standing around them.

Too many. Still way too many.

"Frank says that's where the bulk of the blue eyes will be. If we can take them out—all or most of them—it'll make his job a lot easier," Lara had said.

If, if, if, Keo thought. *My life is full of ifs these days.*

They had positioned themselves in a rough semicircle, with Vince and Hanson facing the south—where the parking lot connected to the main point of entry—while James and Delaware watched the east, with Angie and Mackey facing west. Keo didn't have to worry about north—there was nothing back there except the craggy remains of the HC Dome, and nothing was coming out of that. At least, not while the sun was on their side.

He turned around when someone opened up, the *brap-brap-brap* filling the void left behind by the helicopter's rotors.

Vince was firing as the collaborator truck finally turned into the parking lot. The vehicle was a Chevy, and it was big and red and moving fast. *Too* fast, because either they didn't know what was waiting for them, or they weren't afraid.

Should have been a little more afraid, boys.

Vince was slightly perched over his SAW, controlling it with two hands as the weapon's bipod seemed to dance and spent shell casings *clink-clink-clinked* onto the hood of the Wrangler and bounced off and onto the concrete floor around his feet.

The enemy vehicle hadn't made it very far into the lot—a hundred meters, give or take—when Vince's rounds caught it in the grill and spiderwebbed its windshield. Keo glimpsed a man in the back holding on for dear life as the driver lost control. The Chevy rammed into a parked sedan, and the man in the back looked as if he had been fired out of a cannon and disappeared between two other parked cars.

"Ouch," Danny said. Without the helicopter blasting wind in their faces and ears, he no longer had to shout. "Poor bastard."

"Fuck him," Keo said.

"Harsh!"

Keo didn't have a chance to see what became of the driver and his passenger, because carbines began *pop-pop-popping* to the right of him. He spun in that direction as Angie and Mackey fired on two trucks coming from the west side of the parking lot. They had fired much too soon because both vehicles were still too far away, and they were just throwing rounds downrange and not hitting their targets, though they were doing plenty of (unnecessary) damage to everything else

"They're abandoning the perimeters and converging on us," Danny said before getting up and jogging over to Angie and Mackey's position. Keo watched the ex-Ranger tap Angie on the shoulder. "Hold your fire. Let them get closer. Those bullets cost money, you know."

Angie and Mackey stopped shooting and slid down behind the car they had been using as cover.

"Hanson!" Danny shouted. "You're with me!"

Hanson picked up his M249 and jogged over to Danny, the big man carrying the MG as if it were a toy and not something that weighed almost twenty pounds empty. The two of them set the weapon up on the hood of a car next to the one Angie and Mackey were using.

Keo checked in on their east side. James and Delaware were

supposed to be watching that direction, but they were too busy staring anxiously at the two vehicles coming at them from the west.

"Hey, eyes forward!" Keo shouted.

The two men snapped out of it and turned back around just as a fresh torrent of gunfire exploded from the west. Hanson had opened up with his SAW before Angie and Mackey joined in. Danny was directing Hanson's fire, but not shooting himself.

The collaborators were almost within a hundred meters when the closest truck was ripped to shreds by machine-gun fire. The vehicle slowed down, then slammed into a lamppost, cutting it in half as someone—maybe the driver—slammed into the windshield headfirst and left a bloody stain behind.

The second truck kept coming, though for some reason it seemed much slower than the first. A uniformed man was swiveling around an MG welded in the truck bed and began opening up on the car Angie and Mackey were hiding behind, the *ping-ping-ping!* of rounds hitting the sedan's other side like out-of-control pinball machines.

Danny was shouting, but his voice was lost in the continuous roar of Hanson's M249, busy pouring everything at the approaching vehicle. The twin MGs going off at the same time— literally firing at one another—created the kind of strange cacophony of noise and rhythm that Keo had never seen replicated anywhere except on the battlefield.

"Keo!" someone shouted.

Keo looked back at Vince, staring at him. He didn't have to hear what Vince was going to say next to know what he wanted.

"Stay where you are!" Keo shouted at him.

Vince gritted his teeth, but stayed put.

Now that the vehicle was closer—fifty meters and closing!— Keo saw why it wasn't stopping: It had armor plates on its front grill and sides, and there might have been two (*two?*) slabs of glass over its front windshield. The tires were massive to accommodate the extra weight, which also explained why it was moving so damn slow.

But slow or not, the technical wasn't going to stop because Hanson's machine-gun rounds were landing but ricocheting off the metal plates. Danny had begun firing too, now that the enemy vehicle was closer, for all the good it did.

Keo was about to turn back to Vince and give him the okay to join the fray when a gust of wind slammed into him, and a split-second later the unstoppable enemy vehicle speeding toward them simply evaporated against a flood of 30mm rounds pouring down from the sky.

Then came the delayed *brooooooooooorrrrtttttttttt!* as the A-10 swept past the parking lot and kept going, and Keo remembered Vince saying back in the helicopter as they were approaching the city, *"Jesus Christ, I'm glad those things are on our side."*

No shit, pal. No shit!

The devastated vehicle actually kept moving for a while on its oversize tires, even though there was absolutely nothing left of it but a carcass. Then it simply rolled to a stop. There were no signs of the driver or his mates, and Keo was glad he couldn't see what had become of them.

He didn't have a lot of time to process the destruction anyway, because he heard Vince shouting from behind him, "Incoming! We got more incoming!"

Keo turned around and cursed under his breath.

Collaborators. Two sets of them, converging on the south entrance from two separate directions.

He counted two—four—*six*.

"Hanson!" Keo shouted. "Get your ass back into position!"

"Yeah, Hanson, move that sweet ass!" Danny chimed in.

Hanson was struggling to reload his machine gun when Keo called his name. The man grunted, snapped a new ammo box into place, then lifted the heavy weapon and jogged back to his old spot. Keo couldn't fathom how he was carrying all that load and didn't seem to be even breaking a sweat.

"James, Mackey!" Keo shouted.

Neither James nor Mackey needed Keo to say the rest. They stumbled to their feet and ran over, James leaning against the trunk of the Wrangler while Mackey joined Hanson at the sedan.

Behind him, Danny shouted, "Angie, Rhode Island—stay where you are!"

"It's Delaware!" Delaware shouted.

"Close enough!" Danny said before running over to Keo's position. "Any word from Willie Boy?"

Keo shook his head. "Not a peep."

"That means they're still on their way."

"They've been on their way here for two days now."

"Hey, you can't rush Plan G. Didn't anyone tell you that?" Danny slipped a new magazine into his carbine. "And to think, I almost missed out on this!"

"Lucky you!"

"I know, right? Good things really do happen to good people!"

Keo snorted, then turned around just as the collaborator trucks began pouring inside the parking lot. "Pick a target and keep shooting until they stop moving!"

"Brilliant strategy!" Danny laughed as he stood up and began shooting over the vehicles in their path. "George Not-So Patton this guy!"

Danny's laughter was quickly drowned out by the *ping-ping-ping* of rounds hitting automobiles, interspersed with the *brap-brap-brap* of machine guns and the *pop-pop-pop* of carbines. Keo had been through plenty of battlefields, but he had to admit he'd never had to fight in a place congested with this many cars. Glass shattered all around them and he was pretty sure tanks were being punctured because he could suddenly smell gasoline over the still-lingering acrid stench of dead ghouls.

Keo darted over to Vince's position and opened fire with the MP5SD, his suppressed gunfire comically quiet against all the clatter of unsuppressed weapons around him. If he had any ideas about getting a good chuckle out of that, though, the sight of six— five now, with one having just stopped, its windshield riddled with bullets and blood—collaborator trucks coming toward them ended that notion.

Then, without warning, four of the remaining five broke off from the main pathway, leaving just one to come straight up the middle at them. Two went east and two more went west, the drivers bent low over their steering wheels while the men in the back simultaneously hung on and fired their mounted MGs.

The continuous roar of small arms fire and light machine guns was dizzying, fraying Keo's senses to the point where he couldn't even feel the adrenaline that he knew must be surging through his veins right about now. It always happened during a stand-up gunfight, and this was as stand-up a gunfight as he'd ever been in.

Danny appeared next to him, his M4A1 clattering loudly, but he somehow managed to shout over it anyway: "Where the hell are those A-10s?"

"Maybe they're out of bullets!" Keo shouted back.

"Hell of a time to be running out of bullets! Remind me to give them a stern talking to after this! Spankings may be in order, too!"

"You got it!"

Keo focused on a white GMC zig-zagging its way around the parking lot, squeezing between stalled cars when it could and slamming grill-first to move them when it couldn't. He couldn't see how many men were in the vehicle—not that it mattered, because the only one worth keeping an eye on was the uniformed guy behind the machine gun.

Finally the GMC seemed to jerk off course about fifty meters from their position and buried its nose into the side of a gray Prius. It hadn't stopped for more than a second before Vince stitched the side with 5.56 rounds. Keo couldn't see the collaborator in the back or any of the ones in the front, so they were either dead or out of the fight. Either/or worked for him just fine.

Just as Keo was turning to pick up the remaining vehicle coming from the east side, it slammed on its brakes about sixty meters away and people lunged out of the truck. James had stopped firing to reload, and Keo stepped over next to him and emptied the rest of his magazine into the black Nissan with white stripes, but he had no clear target and was just wasting bullets. It was a good thing, he told himself, that he'd brought plenty this time.

He didn't stop shooting until James had finished reloading and began firing to his left. Keo went down into a crouch and was reaching for a fresh magazine when a body to his right jerked and collapsed to the parking lot floor.

Vince!

Keo slung his submachine gun and hurried over. He leaned over the big man and was reaching for him when he saw Vince's wide-open eyes staring up at the cloudless sky, a surprisingly small thin trail of blood trickling out of a hole in his forehead.

One down...

He glanced up at Danny, now crouched across the open space next to Hanson. Danny was reloading and watching Keo, who shook his head. Danny let out a silent sigh, then nodded to his left—Keo's right.

Keo looked over at Mackey, on the ground next to the trunk of another vehicle that looked like it had been shredded by a few hundred rounds. The barrage had taken Mackey with it, blood pooling over his chest and under him.

Two down...

Keo stood up and snapped a quick look over the Wrangler: One of the collaborator trucks had been stopped by their weapons fire, but the other one, taking a cue from their comrades, had abandoned their bullet-riddled vehicle and taken cover behind the parked cars that dotted the lot about seventy meters away. They were now exchanging fire with Hanson, James, and Danny.

He ducked back down, bullets *zip-zip-zipping* over his head, and maneuvered over Vince's body and was preparing to take over his SAW, still perched on the hood of the Wrangler, when the radio clipped to his hip squawked and a familiar voice said, just barely audible through the roar of gunfire, "Striker, come in. Striker, this is Willie Boy."

Keo stayed down behind the hood and took out the radio, even as Blaine continued calling out through the two-way: "Can you hear me? Answer if you can hear me. Striker, Striker, this is Willie Boy, do you read—"

He keyed the radio and interrupted Blaine. "Yeah, yeah, I heard you the first time." Keo glanced over at Danny, who was watching him back and simultaneously reloading his rifle. "Took your sweet ass time," Keo said into the radio. "We got tangos coming at us in waves over here. What's your position?"

"We're right below you," Blaine said. "Whenever you're ready."

About fucking time.

"Coming to you!" he shouted.

Danny got up and streaked over, keeping low as bullets buzzed over his head. "Willie Boy?"

"They're in position and waiting for us!" Keo shouted.

"About fucking time."

"What I said."

"Well, what are you waiting for? An engraved invitation?"

"Cover me!"

"Gee, I was just going to do my nails, but since you asked so nicely..." Danny stood up and resumed shooting, and somewhere between when he pulled the trigger and when he stopped firing, he managed to shout out, "Go! We'll be right behind you once we take care of these pecker heads!"

"James, you're with me!" Keo shouted, and darted across the open space.

James was immediately on his heels, both of them keeping low as they raced out of their area of operation and across the parking lot. Keo led him into the open, the strangling smell of vaporized ghouls getting thicker with every step closer to the rubble that used to be the HC Dome.

"Christ!" James shouted behind him, just as something *zipped!* over Keo's head.

Too close!

They finally reached their objective while still far from the remains of the domed sports building: A manhole covering out in the open near the very end of the parking lot.

Keo snapped a quick look left, then right, just in case there were more collaborators trying to outflank them. As bad as having to survive a dozen technicals was, it could—and would—have been worse if they didn't have the tanks and A-10s to lend a hand. A hell of a lot worse.

"This is it?" James asked, sliding to a stop next to him.

"This is it," Keo said, and crouched on one side of the round metal object embedded in the concrete floor while James scooted over to the opposite side.

The young man looked across at him and swallowed.

"You okay?" Keo asked.

"No," James said. "I should have stayed on the island with my wife."

Keo had a humdinger of a retort, something even Danny would have been proud of, except before he could say it there was a thunderous *THOOM!* from behind him.

He glanced up just in time to see a fireball falling out of the sky in the distance.

29

WILL

Silver.

There was silver everywhere.

If he remembered how to gag, he might have.

The ones that clung to his hips and stuck out from the gauntlets over his hands were the worst of them. But the silver in all the weapons around him was just as bad.

Silver.

So much silver.

He was grateful for the helmet, because it hid his discomfort. He pushed through it, flexing his fingers underneath the gloves, knowing that he would need them very soon. Not yet, but soon, because this was the end of the line. The tunnel continued and bent left, but he didn't need to go left; he needed to go straight.

They came down the ladder one by one. Racing heartbeats and gasping breaths pounded in his ears, followed by gasps as the smell hit them. It was such a human response, and for a moment he was glad he was beyond all of it.

"Oh God," the young blond who came down first said as he

reached up to make sure the mask was still firmly placed over his mouth. "I think I'm going to throw up."

"Not yet, kid," Blaine said. "How bad is it up there?"

"It could be worse," a familiar voice said as its owner skipped the remaining rungs and leaped down to the platform. "Make room, there's more coming."

"Sounds like you guys got a hell of a party going on up there," Gaby said.

"A handful of technicals, but it could have been a lot worse."

"Mercer's army came through after all?"

"Looks like it. But our luck might have run out. I saw an aircraft go down. Not sure if it was our ride out of here or one of the Thunderbolts."

"You're fucking me," Blaine said.

"Nope."

"Well, shit."

"Ditto," the man said (What was his name? It was there, just underneath the surface— *There*. Keo. His name was Keo.) as he and the blond unslung their packs and pulled out night-vision goggles and snapped them on.

"You guys okay?" Gaby asked.

"We took some casualties," Keo said, "but in one piece, for the most part."

"We'll wait for the others. Go ahead with Wi—Frank."

Keo climbed off the platform and sighed when the sewage sloshed around his knees.

"I think I'm going to throw up again," the blond said as he stepped down beside Keo.

"Keep it together," Keo said before looking up the tunnel, allowing his artificial third eye to adjust to the darkness. "Long time no see."

"Yes," he said, grateful that the helmet obscured his voice and tamed the hiss.

"Nice outfit."

"Danny."

"Of course Danny."

"That's him?" the kid asked. No, not a kid. Just young.

"That's him," Keo said. "Frank, James. James, Frank. Now that that's out of the way, let's get to work so we can all get the hell out of this literal steaming pile of shit."

Behind them, another figure climbed down onto the platform, the *clank-clank* of boots on the metal rungs even louder than the continued gunfire from above. Another familiar voice, urging the figure on, "Move faster, Hanson! Or do you want me to go down there and give you a hand, princess?"

"Hey, I'm going as fast as I can!" a gruff voice answered. "You try climbing with fifty pounds of gear!"

"Excuses, excuses!" the familiar voice said.

"I got you," Blaine said, and helped the climber off the steps.

They made room for a woman. She was wounded, and he licked his lips at the taste of fresh blood in the air.

"You're hurt," Blaine said.

"I'll live," the woman said. "It's just a scratch."

"Looks like a hell of a lot more than a scratch to me. Can you walk?"

"She's a big girl, she'll be fine," the familiar voice said, just before its owner landed on the platform. *Danny.* He pinched his nose and his voice was muffled when he said, "I've heard of being knee-deep in shit before, but this takes the cake."

"Don't mention cake," Blaine said.

"Where's Delaware?" the woman who wasn't Gaby asked.

Danny shook his head.

"Shit," the big man with the machine gun said.

Danny turned to Gaby. "Hey there, kid."

"What are you doing here?" Gaby asked. "Aren't you supposed to be back on the *Trident*, safe and sound?"

"And what, miss all this fun?" He pulled his night-vision goggles out from his pack and slipped it on. The newcomers did the same. "Well, let's get this show on the road. I got places to be and babies to watch being born."

Danny hopped down the platform and walked over to where he stood with Keo. He couldn't see the man's lips behind the mask, but he assumed Danny was grinning at him.

"Nice, if I do say so myself," Danny said. "I should open my own fashion line when this is all over."

"This getup's your handiwork, too?" Keo asked.

"Most of it. The ladies helped with the sewing and such. My hands are way too manly for that sort of stuff."

"What about the guys chasing you?" Blaine asked as he and Gaby walked over to them, the other two newcomers following behind.

"I doubt they'll come down after us," Keo said. "It'd be almost suicide, and I don't think they're that stupid."

"Someone's being overly optimistic," Danny said.

"But just in case, James and Angie, stay behind on the platform. Shoot anyone that tries to come down after us."

"Go; we got this," the woman said.

Danny walked over and nodded at him.

"You shouldn't be here," he said.

"Can't let you hog all the glory," Danny said. "Okay, Willie boy, it's your show. Lead the way."

All eyes turned to him, the faces he didn't recognize staring the hardest.

"Let's go," he said, and turned back into the dark tunnel.

They moved silently, labored breathing pushing against their masks. Adrenaline coursed through their veins, increasing their already rapid heartbeats. Every one of their steps sounded like crashing ocean waves against his ears even through the thick wall of the helmet.

He knew exactly where to go because he had planned it to the exact step, and stopped when they came to the section of the wall where the tunnel curved left. There was nothing here to indicate that this section was anything special, but he knew better, because he could *feel* and *smell* and *hear* them on the other side.

"Here?" Keo asked.

He pointed.

"I'll take it that's a yes," Danny said. He stepped forward and unslung his pack. "Just like old times, huh?"

"Not quite."

"Close enough. So this is your big plan."

He nodded.

"What's the matter, sewer rat got your tongue?" Danny asked.

"Be careful," he said.

"Aw, I didn't think you still cared." Danny glanced back at the others. "You boys might want to make some room. It's been a while since I've done this, and I'm definitely not paying for any missing eyes or ears."

His nostrils twitched at the smell of plastic and chemicals as Danny brought out the pack's true contents.

"I hope this tunnel was built to city specs," Danny said as he began attaching the malleable material to the wall, creating an almost door-shape design above where the water ended. "Or, er, hopefully they didn't. Whichever one keeps it from falling on our heads."

"Don't jinx it, man," the big man said from the back.

"I'm just kidding, Hanson, relax. I know exactly what I'm doing." Then, slightly under his breath, "Mostly."

Behind him, Gaby and the others took a few tentative steps back. Their pulse accelerated further, the force of their breath against their masks increasing accordingly. Although it was cold, damp sweat covered their skin from head to toe and dripped down to the filthy water around their knees.

As they watched Danny work, Gaby said, "This is it. The end of the line. I didn't think we'd ever get here."

"Didn't think I'd ever be alive to see this, either," the big man, Hanson, said. "That's him? Frank?"

"That's him."

"What's with the wardrobe?"

"Protection."

"From what?"

"What's on the other side of that wall."

"What *is* on the other side of that wall?"

"Glory, boys," Danny said, standing up. He looked back at them. "When I mentioned you should all take a few steps back, what I really meant was, keep going until I say stop."

Tentative steps as they started backing up again. Danny followed, unfurling a bright yellow cord from a spool as he backpedaled.

"Is the tunnel going to hold?" Gaby asked.

"Should," Danny said.

"Should?"

"There's not enough C-4 to take out the whole place, just enough to punch a big hole in the wall for us to go through. So it *should*, theoretically, hold."

Gaby sighed. "I hope you're right."

"Yeah, me too."

"Man, I don't like the sound of that," the young blond said.

When they had put enough room between them and the turn up ahead, Danny flashed them one last look and chuckled. "Remember, you guys volunteered for this."

"We're all going to fucking die down here," Blaine said from somewhere in the back.

"That's the spirit," Danny said. Then, as the others lined up and hugged the wall behind him, Danny turned to him. "You sure about this?"

He nodded. "Do it."

"I told you Carly's pregnant?"

"I know."

"Of course you do. We're still thinking about a name. Got any suggestions?"

He shook his head.

"Still the chatterbox, I see," Danny said. Then, holding the trigger in front of him, "All right. Enough of this awkward reunion. Fire in the—"

"Wait, you're not going to count to three?" Keo asked.

"Three schmee," Danny said, and there was a *click!* followed by a *BOOM!* as the tunnel shook around them.

Loose chunks of brick *plopped* into the water, and a thick mist like some kind of living thing extended out of the blast with rubbery fingers. He didn't need the helmet or the clothing to protect him against the flood, but he wiped at the goggles as they appeared...a moving forest of black eyes and frail limbs.

Too many.

Had he miscalculated? Or had Mabry summoned more down here since the last time?

There were so many he could barely make out any spaces between their twisting and gyrating forms as they surged forward toward the opening where the wall used to be and through the hole.

It took him a second—maybe less—to make the decision.

There were too many—simply too many—and the others would never survive to reach the other side.

He stepped forward, alone, and into the spreading clouds.

He had removed the helmet because it was too cumbersome and he didn't need to conceal his identity anymore. He could move faster without it, and even though the extra weight was minimal, he needed everything he had—speed, strength, and agility—at their absolute fullest as he waded into the abyss.

There were a lot more of them than he had expected, that had survived the bombings, and they poured down the darkened hallway, so many that they were almost climbing on top of one another to reach him. He didn't hesitate and stepped into them, the silver studs over his knuckles doing tremendous damage with every swing regardless of direction.

He punched through chests and heads and smashed bones, and this time they didn't get back up when he felled one—two—a *hundred* of them. The silver was toxic to them and they collapsed, screaming in his mind, and somewhere, beyond, the blue eyes shouted through the hive, *"Stop him! Kill him! Don't let him advance!"*

But they couldn't stop him. They never could before, and not now.

They flopped by the wayside, dying (*again*) as they fell, one by one by one. Soon, he began to smell the fear emanating from their pores, glimpse the horror on their faces and in their hollowed eyes as he continued cutting a swath through their numbers.

And yet they came, one after another after another, because they had no choice. This was what they did. They were the first line of defense.

Screams roared inside his mind, but he didn't try to shut them out. There was no time—not even a second to waste on something so trivial.

"Stop him!"

And they kept coming, an endless surge of black eyes and limbs. The never-ending *clacking* of bones against the concrete floor as he smashed and tore and ripped through them two, three —*five* at a time. Still they came, pushing against his exterior, but doing almost no damage. He would have felt sorry for them if he could muster the emotion.

Behind him, shouting and gunfire echoed. Keo, Danny, Gaby, and the others. To help them would mean going back, and he couldn't do that. He was too far in now that retreating would mean total and complete failure.

And he was close to the end. So, so close.

"Kill him!"

This wasn't part of the plan, but it would have to be. Maybe he always knew it would be him alone at the very end, despite all his preparations. Despite his friends, despite Mercer's tanks and planes. Who else could survive this? Who else could break through the onslaught of flesh and bone and teeth?

So he kept moving, pushing forward, doing whatever it took. He shut out the gunfire from behind him and wished them well, because there was more at stake than just a few men and women in a tunnel. A lot more.

"Tear him limb from limb!"

He fought and gained ground inch by inch by inch. The hallways blurred and he lost track of how far or long he had traveled. They were all identical—dark and dirty and swamped in the stench of the dead. There was no light, but that didn't matter because he didn't need light to see anyway. He could have closed his eyes and simply relied on his other senses. There were so many beating against him, from all sides, that he couldn't move his arms in any direction without striking one, two, *a dozen* of the creatures.

And still they came.

"Don't let him advance!"

And he punched and kicked and struck and tore and ripped and severed.

And still they came...

They seemed never ending, relentless in their need to push him back, to stop his momentum. But if they expected him to be cowed by their continued onslaught, they were sadly mistaken.

He pushed on, striking blow after blow, because he couldn't stop.

Not now, not when he was so close.

"Stop him! STOP HIM!!"

There were five of them, their blue eyes pulsating in the shadows. They had been waiting here all this time, commanding the black eyes to attack. It was a smart strategy, he realized as he turned the corner.

He was tired and the gauntlets had ripped to shreds, each and every one of the silver studs dull and unusable, little more than stumps now. The seams of the gloves were beyond loose, and it would have taken too much effort to hold onto them, so he relaxed his fingers and let them drop to the floor.

Black blood oozed from his arms and legs and face, splattering the already filthy floor. Most of it wasn't his, though some was. Teeth bites and missing flesh covered his limbs and neck, but nothing that would slow him down.

They stood watching him.

Waiting, unmoving, maybe trying to gauge his remaining strength.

And there, behind them, was the steel door. *He* was on the other side.

But not yet. That would come later.

He always knew there would be obstacles. The planes had taken away most of them, but not all. He had expected this, so there wasn't really disappointment as he turned the corner.

He imagined Danny's voice in his head: *"Five? That's plenty manageable, buddy!"*

The blue eyes hadn't moved or looked away since he showed himself. Sports memorabilia littered the floor between them; torn posters and murals of men in bright costumes covered the walls. Memories of champions from the past.

"Look at him," they said, their five voices sounding as one inside his head.

"He wears clothes..."

"He wants to be human again..."

"Why?"

"Pathetic."

"We'll be doing him a favor..."

"...putting him out of his misery..."

"Yes..."

"Doing him a favor..."

"He's pathetic."

"...not worth all the attention."

"...pathetic..."

"Why don't you just die?"

No, he thought, forcing the single word—calm and measured, but full of defiance—back at them.

They looked stunned by it.

"Finally, he talks," they said.

"Finally, he gives in."

"...he should have a long time ago..."

"Saved himself the pain..."

"...the misery..."

"Stupid..."

"Too late now."

"He's going to die..."

"...should never have come here..."

"You fool."

No, he thought again, and began walking toward them.

The first knife slid free, then the other. His nostrils flared at the taste of fresh, untouched silver, but he pushed through like he always did.

The creatures snickered at the sight of the blades.

He clutched the handles tight, tighter. His only advantage. Whatever happened, he couldn't lose them. The thing that left him gagging would now save his life, so long as he never relinquished them.

And he wouldn't.

For them.

For her.

"*Silver,*" they said inside his head. "*He uses the enemy's weapon against us.*"

"*...still wants to be human...*"

"*We'll show him...*"

"*...what it means to be human...*"

"*Weak...*"

"*Frail...*"

"*He'll break easily...*"

"*...like before...*"

"*Do you remember?*"

Yes. He remembered the pain. Every second of it. The days of healing from his wounds on the *Trident*. Having to drink from the two men, then later, the female. He told himself he hadn't wanted to, that he needed them in order to regain his strength.

He had been telling himself that for a while now.

"*You'll die here,*" they said, watching him approach.

"*Alone...*"

"*Then we'll come for her...*"

"*...Lara...*"

"*Such a pretty name...*"

"*We'll play with her...*"

"Until she begs us to stop..."

"But we won't..."

"Oh no, we won't..."

"...no matter how many times she begs."

He smiled back at them.

They frowned in response, confused.

"Come then," they said. *"Come, and do your worst."*

"Welcome home."

It was fast. They were all fast. But the first one wasn't fast *enough*, and he stabbed it in the chest and listened to it roar inside his head. It thrashed against the blade that he used to impale it to the wall, but before it could pull itself free, he plunged the other knife into the side of its head and it simply and immediately stopped moving.

"It's been a long time coming."

The air rippled behind him, signaling another impending attack. He dropped and the fist intended for him missed by an inch and cratered the wall instead. Specks of concrete pelted him, but he ignored it and spun while in a slight crouch, and lunged, driving both blades into the creature's stomach. It squealed, but before the others could come to its rescue, he slashed upward with both knives and severed its body into three sections. It stumbled back, and while its arms drooped from what remained of its torso, he stabbed it under the chin and drove the blade all the way up into its brain.

"You should have come sooner."

He sensed the hesitation in the remaining three even as they attacked at once, converging at him from three different sides. He backpedaled, their blows glancing off his chest and head and face, but he shook them off. They were strong—as strong as him—but they were using fists whereas he had knives.

"*What took you so long?*"

He slashed, the blade slicing through its target without any resistance. The arm fell off, but its owner ignored it and reached for his throat. He cut again and its other arm flopped to the floor, and this time it paused for the smallest of nanoseconds before stumbling, even as the other two leaped over it to get at him. He saw them coming but didn't react fast enough, and they pummeled him to the blood-slicked floor.

"*Why did you waste so much time?*"

They were on top of him, one holding his legs in vise-like grips while the other straddled his chest, pinning him to the hard pavement. There was no triumph on its face, no wasted emotion as it cocked back its fist to deliver the killing blow, when he drove the knife into the side of its head. Its eyes widened even as life sapped from them and it toppled off him.

"*Why did you have to keep fighting your nature?*"

He got his legs under the second one and launched it into the air. It slammed into the ceiling and came crashing down along with crumbs of loosened plaster. It was scrambling back up, but before it could straighten on buckling legs, he threw one of the knives and caught it in the forehead, and it collapsed back to the floor and remained still.

"*Always fighting.*"

He staggered to his feet and walked the short distance over to the ghoul. He pulled the knife out of its still form, then decapitated the head of the last creature, the one without the arms sitting against the wall. There was a spark of defiance in its eyes just before it simply ceased to exist.

"*Kate was right about one thing...*"

Finally, finally, he allowed himself a moment to rest, even as thick coagulated blood *drip-drip-dripped* off the blades, their rhythm intoxicating to his still-enflamed senses. Everything around him was slick with blood—the walls, the floor, the ceiling, even him. His muscles were sore and every inch of him ached.

"You're persistent. Resilient. A born fighter."

His strength was sapped, his mind spinning, and just standing was a chore. He raised a hand and leaned against a wall to keep his legs from giving up on him. He couldn't shut out the pain because that would mean paralyzing himself, and he couldn't do that.

Not now. Not now...

"You would have made such a fine addition."

He had never felt more human since his transformation, and he didn't know if he should be exhilarated or alarmed by the sudden realization. He had blocked out all the sounds from behind him, where the hallways connected to the tunnel. Keo and Danny and Gaby. They were still back there, somewhere. He longed to turn around and go save them.

But he couldn't. He couldn't...

"Maybe I always knew it would end this way. Even back then, in that nothing town outside the bank. Do you remember?"

Yes, he remembered. He didn't even have to dig very far. He recalled that night in that small town, inside the bank. A chaotic twenty-four hours as he and Danny fought for their lives, and the lives of their friends. One of many times they had been forced to rely on everything they had while praying to an unseen God that neither one of them actually believed in.

Yes, he thought, pushing his response into the hive mind. *I remember.*

"There you are. It's good to hear your voice again. You've shut me out for so long."

Enjoy it. It'll be the last thing you hear.

Mabry laughed inside his head.

He glared at the metal door up the hallway. There was

nothing between him and it now, and it beckoned him like a siren.

"*You've come this far, so finish the journey.*"

He gripped the knives and began walking toward the door.

"*Welcome home...my son.*"

"What the fuck! Where did Frank go?"

"Did anyone see him?"

"Holy shit!"

"What the fuck do we do now?"

"What the *fuck* do we do now?"

There was too much smoke and pulverized concrete trying to get into his eyes and nostrils and mouth, despite having the mask and NVG on, for Keo to pinpoint who was shouting out what questions. It could have been one or two or all of them at the same time. His ears were still ringing from the blast, so that didn't help at all. Behind the lens of the night-vision goggles, the thick mist on the other side of the tunnel looked like a living thing with tendrils reaching out for him.

Frank had disappeared into the expanding clouds, his dark shape there one second and gone the next. Keo struggled to see even with the artificial assist, though breathing was easier thanks to the mask. He was stumbling backward, trying to regain his footing because he swore the ground was still trembling in the aftermath of Danny's C4. The only thing he was certain of was the pounding headache inside his skull, reminding him of all the punishment his poor head had endured the last few days.

Right. Like I needed the reminder!

But Danny had done his job—he had carved a hole in the wall for Frank to go through without bringing the entire structure down on top of them. The problem was that Frank had gone without them.

What the fuck, Frank? This wasn't the plan!

A warm body pushed against his back and a familiar voice (*Gaby*) shouted very close to his ear, "Keo! Will's gone! What happened to Will?"

"He went inside!" someone answered. Male. *Danny.* "That dumbass! We were supposed to go in together!"

"Inside? Inside where?" Gaby asked.

"Where do you think, kid!"

"Why—" Gaby started to ask when someone opened fire, the *brap-brap-brap* of a machine gun like a series of thunderclaps slamming off the dripping walls around them.

"There goes the neighborhood!" Danny shouted.

"Back, back!" Keo shouted. "Get the fuck back now!"

"Oh, ya think?" Danny said, sounding very dangerously close to laughing.

They came out of the smoke—thin figures slightly hunched over, obsidian eyes like polished gems against the green field of his NVG. They were moving fast, racing through the sludge, some actually clinging to the walls and a few of them were on the ceiling, but how was that even possible? When had they learned to do that? Could they always do that?

A red laser dot flashed across the first wave of ghouls as the *brap-brap-brap* continued to rain death and bodies fell, *plopping* into the water one by one by one. But if Keo thought that was going to stop them, he was sadly mistaken, because more of them rushed out of the swirling smoke, like nightmares coming to life before his very eyes.

"Back, back!" Keo shouted again, flicking the fire selector on his MP5SD to full-auto with one hand while turning on the laser pointer attached to the bottom of the barrel with the other.

"Wait, which direction should we go again?" Danny asked, and this time he really was laughing. "I'm so confused!"

Keo couldn't help himself and grinned behind his mask. He didn't know if he liked the ex-Ranger or was *this* close to turning around and kicking him in the face.

He was still deciding when he squeezed off a burst and three ghouls flopped into the thick sludge. With the NVG and the silver rounds going exactly where the laser pointer directed them, he couldn't miss, and neither could any of the others shooting to the left and right of him. Their bullets punched through weak flesh and hit one, two, sometimes three bodies behind the first target.

It was the literal definition of a shooting gallery, except this one was endless and each falling creature only opened up a new space for the one behind them. They kept coming, like rabid dogs splashing the sewage filth that threatened to swallow up their tiny forms. Keo swore a few of them actually disappeared under the water where they were trampled by the others. Bodies began floating around them, looking more like unreal papier-mâché than beings that were, once upon a time, men and women.

The only thing that saved them from being overrun in the very first seconds of the hole's creation was the size of the tunnel. Not that he had ever been down here before—or, thank God, any place even remotely similar—but Keo was surprised by how roomy it was. But maybe roomy was a matter of perspective, because for the endless horde trying to get at him, the man-made cavern wasn't nearly wide or tall enough, and the black eyes were starting to slam into each other and the walls as they surged forward all at once.

Keo continued to backpedal, not wasting a second to glance back to check where he was going and trusting everyone else to keep moving. Then he was past Hanson, who had stopped firing his M249 for some reason.

"Keep firing, Hanson!" Keo shouted.

Hanson shook his head and dropped the machine gun, then unslung his carbine. "I'm out!"

"Whatever happened to the magic ammo box?" Danny shouted.

"No such thing!" Hanson said.

"Now you tell me!" Danny said as he backed up on the other side of Hanson while firing nonstop with his M4A1.

Keo squeezed off a long volley into the oncoming tide of blackened creatures and watched a group of them drop and vanish into the water, but their sickly forms weren't nearly heavy enough to cause them to sink and they simply floated back up... only to be crushed under by a new wave of ghouls trying to get by.

There was no order, no semblance of control with the monsters. The sight of them vomiting forth out of the dark tunnel without end should have terrified Keo, but instead it made him chuckle to himself.

A girl. You know that, right? You're here because a girl asked you to.

Man you're getting soft!

"I'm out!" Keo shouted, and ejected the magazine and scrambled for a new one.

"You want me to reload for you?" Danny shouted. "Go go go!"

Keo turned and ran, kicking up filthy water over his clothes, and some got high enough to splash his mask, but he was beyond caring or even aware of the smell at that point. He reloaded as he ran while Danny and Hanson and Gaby fired into the throng behind him.

A new round of gunfire, these coming from *in front* of him, made him look up.

Angie, James, and Blaine were retreating *toward him*, firing into a new wall of ghouls surging from the other side of the tunnel.

"Fuck me," Keo said under his breath.

Blaine either heard him or sensed him, and glanced over his shoulder while fumbling to reload his own weapon. "They're behind us!"

Gee, thanks for that newsflash, Blaine.

Keo wanted to laugh, but he raced forward and took Blaine's place in the middle of the trio and unloaded his new magazine into the twisting sea of bodies and jet-black flesh and eyes instead.

Angie was firing to his left, a sewage-covered bandage wrapped tightly around her right hip. If she was in any pain, Keo couldn't see it on her face as she backed up and shouted, "I'm out, I'm out!"

Blaine had snapped a fresh magazine into his M4 and begun firing again, standing to Keo's right. "What happened?" he shouted. "Where's Will?"

"He's gone!" Keo shouted back.

"Gone? What do you mean, gone?"

"Poof! Gone! We gotta get to the platform and get the fuck back to the surface!"

"There's no fucking way we're getting to the platform now!"

"Fuck!" Keo shouted.

Keo couldn't even see where the platform was anymore. There was just bodies. Moving and twisting black bodies as ghoul after ghoul scrambled up the tunnel, trampling and climbing and crawling over one another.

"Back up!" Keo shouted. "Back the fuck up!"

Angie and James reappeared to his left and right, Angie hobbling on her bad leg. But she gritted through it and shouted, "Go! Go!"

Keo and Blaine turned and went, reloading as they did while Angie and James covered their retreat.

Behind him—now in front of him—were Danny, Gaby, and Hanson, the flashes of their weapons lighting the dark tunnel in staccato flashes, each one giving Keo a good view of a sea of crooked and butchered teeth and gnarled flesh. The creatures were still coming, but slowly, their advance hindered by their own vast numbers and the quickly forming piles of bodies of their dead that began soaking up the sewage water, creating a sickening wall of bloated corpses that slowed their progress.

Jesus Christ, if I never have to see anything like this again in fifty lifetimes...

The ghouls were slowing, but they weren't stopping. Which was a problem because Danny, Gaby, and Hanson were backing up toward Keo and pretty soon they were going to be pressed up against him and there would be nowhere to retreat.

Ten meters...

Nine...

Danny stopped shooting and backpedaled away from Gaby and Hanson to reload. He threw a quick glance over his shoulder, and Keo saw that he had removed his mask. "Let me guess: The exit's no good?'

"Yup!" Keo shouted back.

"Well, that sucks!" He finished reloading and pulled back the charging handle. "Man, Carly is so going to kick my ass when they find me down here covered in shit! Talk about being in double-deep shit!"

Danny spun around and opened up on the fresh wave of incoming horde, even as Gaby stumbled past him, trying to reload and run at the same time, only to discover that there weren't a lot of places for her to run to. The look on her face as she saw what was back there was one of pure horror, and for a split second she locked eyes with Keo.

Then someone screamed, and Keo turned back around in time to see James disappearing into the mass of limbs. The ghouls flowed over him as if he were little more than a speed bump, and Keo watched helplessly as Angie, instead of retreating, ran forward and began hitting the closest ghoul with the stock of her rifle.

Keo wanted to shout *You idiot! Get back here!* but he never got the chance. Instead, he watched with almost morbid fascination as an undead thing's head caved in under Angie's brutal assault. But the creature didn't go down, and instead its hands grabbed Angie and pulled her in like a mother would a child for an intimate embrace.

"Blaine!" Keo shouted.

The big man had finished reloading and immediately started firing into the very spot where Angie and James had disappeared. Keo couldn't figure out if he was doing that to spare the two of them from being turned or—

"Blaine!" Keo shouted again. "Get back here!"

But Blaine didn't move, and kept firing, even as the horde converged on him. Keo cursed under his breath and took one, then two steps back toward Blaine, determined to grab him and drag his ass back whether he wanted it or not, when Blaine's legs seemed to give out from under him and he disappeared into the water. The last Keo saw of him was the barrel of his rifle sinking but still firing into the ceiling, bringing down chunks of the brick and mortar on top of the ghouls that had begun to overwhelm the spot he had been standing in just seconds ago.

"Blaine!" Gaby shouted, racing forward while firing her rifle.

Keo reached out just as she was about to pass him by and grabbed her by the elbow and yanked her back. She nearly lost her balance and fell, but he managed to keep her upright enough to begin dragging her back with him. "He's gone! He's gone!"

Gaby struggled against him, but Keo kept dragging her backward, even as she continued to squeeze off round after round into the trudging horde. There were now so many bodies in the water that every step the creatures took meant they had to push away a half-dozen dead ghouls blocking their path. Keo didn't want to think about where James and Angie and Blaine were in that quickly growing graveyard.

"I'm empty!" Hanson shouted from behind him.

"Go!" Danny shouted.

Their voices were so close—much closer than Keo had expected—that it made him look back to be sure, and found himself staring right into Hanson's NVG from less than a meter away.

"We're fucked!" Hanson shouted at Danny. "We're outta space!"

"Shut up and reload!" Danny shouted back.

Keo spun back around and put another burst through the nearest four ghouls, watching them fall and almost-sink before the next wave was on top of them. Gaby was free again and was unloading her M4 next to him, the *plop-plop-plop* of their bullet casings hitting the water echoing off the walls of the tunnel, which seemed to have constricted inward since the last time he looked.

He had been running back and forth with such wild abandon that there were clumps of things on his face and over the NVG lens, but Keo could still see and what he saw, as dirt-smeared as it was, wasn't something he wanted to bear witness to in the last few seconds of his life.

He took a step back and sprayed, then did it again. Gaby was mirroring his movements, though he was pretty sure she wasn't aware of it. Not that it did any good because there were simply *too goddamn many of them.*

So many that the water was rising as it became stuffed with their corpses, and despite the fact that every one of their bullets chopped their way through two, three, sometimes four of the damn things, there was such an unlimited number that it didn't do any good at all. The only results were that they kept backing up, and Keo was very aware that Danny and Hanson behind him were doing the exact same thing, and pretty soon there would be no place for any of them to go.

"Keo!" Gaby shouted next to him. "What now?"

He snapped a quick look at her, but saw only the NVG tube staring back at him as she dropped her rifle into the water—it sank and didn't come back up—and drew her sidearm and began shooting.

What now? Good question.

There was no *what now.* This was the plan. Get Frank through the wall and follow him under the HC Dome and finish off Mabry. They always knew Frank would have to do most of the work—he was, after all, stronger and faster than all of them combined—but they would assist him, because that was the plan.

Frank's plan and Danny's stupid name for it.

Plan G.

Oh, to have a backup plan.

Plan H? he thought, and wanted to laugh out loud, but of course he was too busy shooting and so was Gaby next to him, and Danny and Hanson were behind him doing the same thing.

There was no path forward and no road back. They had come to a complete standstill in the tunnel, somewhere between the platform in front of them and the hole in the wall behind them. Darkness was closing in from both sides, though the creatures had begun to slow even further because of the sheer number of dead bodies in their path.

"Fuck fuck fuck!" Hanson was shouting behind him.

"Get a new vocabulary, Hanson!" Danny said, laughing as he did so.

"Fuck you!"

"Sorry, already married! But if you wanna buy me dinner first, I might think about it!"

Danny laughed again, and for some reason Hanson joined right in.

Keo had switched back to semi-auto to conserve ammo. He didn't need to know he was down to his last magazine. The lightness around his waist was all the evidence he needed. Pretty soon he'd be down to his pistol, just like Gaby, who had just reloaded a second time—

Click! as the MP5SD went empty.

Keo slung it instead of just dumping it into the water the way Hanson had done with his M249 earlier. After all, you didn't find a whole lot of Heckler & Koches lying around Texas these days, and Keo was a man who appreciated good firearms—even if they were empty and were only going to be useful as a blunting instrument in the next few minutes.

Minutes? We're being a little optimistic, aren't we?

Try seconds, pal!

He squeezed the trigger on the Sig Sauer again and again, and though the handgun didn't have a laser pointer, it didn't matter because the ghouls had gotten so close that he didn't even have to aim to take out one, two, three with a single shot. Another time and another place and the kill ratio per bullet would have made him a happy man, but right now all it did was open space for another one or two or *five* to take a fallen undead thing's place.

And they kept coming...and coming...

"Keo!" Gaby shouted next to him.

He ignored her and reloaded.

"Keo!" she shouted again.

He finally glanced over and saw that she had stopped shooting. The Glock was back in its holster and she was palming something in her left hand. The parts of the oblong object that he could see behind her clutching fingers gleamed green against his NVG.

He stared at her—or at her night vision—and they didn't have to say anything. He knew exactly what she was going to do.

Keo pulled the mask off his face—retching smell be damned—and grinned back at her. "Do it!"

She pulled off her own mask and smiled back, then took a step closer to him even as she slipped her right index finger into the grenade's pin.

Behind him, Danny and Hanson had stopped shooting, either because they were out of bullets or dead. He could have turned around and made sure, but at the moment he didn't want to find out. Besides, it wasn't going to matter anyway in the next second or so.

"Do it!" he shouted at Gaby.

She nodded and started to pull the pin—

"Wait!" he screamed, and Gaby was maybe half a heartbeat from finishing the pulling motion when she stopped.

Keo looked up from the frag device in Gaby's hand and down the tunnel, and stared right into the twin black eyes of a ghoul. It was so close that Keo almost let out an involuntary gasp, but he didn't because he was too busy taking aim with the Sig Sauer and was on the verge of pulling the trigger—except he didn't.

Because it was quiet.

The tunnel had gone completely and terrifyingly *silent*.

The creature in front of him looked frozen in place, even as its twin blackened eyes stared at him. (*Jesus Christ, how did he get so close?*) Except there was something wrong with its eyes—they were hollow and lifeless like all the rest, but that wasn't it. It looked almost like it was in some kind of a trance.

And it wasn't alone. The ghoul standing immediately to its right, and the one immediately to its left had also gone still and lifeless. The same was true for the legion of hunched over forms behind them.

The only noise in the entire tunnel, other than Keo's racing heartbeat—and that of Gaby's to his right—came from the *drip-drip-drip* of condensation around them.

"Keo?" Gaby whispered. She was still clutching the grenade in her left hand, still in mid-pull with her right.

"I don't know," Keo said.

He stared at the ghoul standing less than a foot from his face. It was looking at him, but he didn't think the creature actually saw him, as if he had simply stopped existing in its universe. So what the hell was it looking at?

The same was true for the others. They looked in his and Gaby's direction, but not *at* them.

Keo took a quick step away from the closest ghoul and glanced behind him. He saw the back of Danny's head, the Ranger's right fist holding a Glock at his side. Next to him, Hanson was gripping his knife, the silver blade gleaming against the fluorescent green of Keo's night vision.

But it was the sight in front of the two men that made Keo stare for more than a few seconds. The ghouls on that side of the tunnel were standing like permanently frozen stalks of grass jutting out of the filthy water, staring at Danny and Hanson (and Keo now) but not seeing them.

Danny shot a quick look back at him and whispered, "What the hell did you say to them?"

"I didn't say shit," Keo whispered back.

"It's him," Gaby said. "It has to be him."

Keo glanced over at her, saw that she had taken her finger away from the grenade pin and was holding it nonthreateningly at her side, and had drawn that weird cross-knife with her right hand.

"Him who?" he asked.

"Will," she said. "This is him. He's doing this."

"How?"

"I don't know."

Keo looked over his shoulder again and saw Danny watching him back, equally as confused. The fact that Danny didn't have a single smart-ass thing to say was more stunning than the ghouls simply just stopping.

"Um, maybe we should, uh, go?" Hanson said.

"Big man's got good ideas," Danny said.

Keo turned back around and tried to locate the platform down the tunnel through all the still bodies, but there were so many of them and even with the NVG, all he could see were bloated corpses in the water and motionless ghouls—

There.

There was just enough of a sliver in the creatures' ranks that he was able to make out the edge of the platform twenty meters away.

Twenty goddamn meters away.

"You first, Kemosabe," Danny said behind him.

"Why me?" Keo said.

"You're closer."

"Not by much."

"Still, closer."

Keo sighed. "I fucking hate you."

"You don't mean that," Danny said, and Keo could imagine him grinning when he did.

"Be careful," Gaby whispered next to him.

He nodded.

Be careful. Right.

Keo took a big breath—didn't even smell the filth that was his entire world at the moment—and took one step, then another one, around the undead thing that was almost on top of him. He maneuvered around the ghoul, then another one, then two more until he had reached the wall. He hugged it with his back and slid more than he walked forward down the length of the tunnel. He jostled a ghoul (actually heard Gaby gasping behind him), but the stick-thin figure didn't seem to notice, so he kept going.

He didn't look back at the others until he was a third of the way to the platform and saw all three of them watching him. Hanson was sweating profusely, and Gaby and Danny were either mesmerized by his every movement or about to vomit. Keo knew exactly what they were feeling, and he tightened his grip further on his Sig Sauer at his side.

Then he resumed sliding his way through the limbs and wet bodies.

About halfway to the platform, he was unable to keep moving in the same manner and had to step forward, then around one, two, then three of the creatures. It was impossible to go around them without bumping into them, which he did again and again, and each time he swore his luck was going to run out, but it never did.

The ghouls continued to ignore him and stared off, even as he rubbed up against them and had to push floating bodies out of his path and into them. There were so many and they were so small he felt like an adult trying to make his way through a field of children.

Finally (*finally!*) he reached his destination and climbed up onto the platform. He spent a moment to strip off his NVG before stepping forward and craning his head up while leading with the Sig Sauer in both hands. He expected a head or two to stare back down at him from topside, but there was only the round covering still in place. Keo might have actually let out a loud, involuntary sigh as the brilliant rays of sunlight caressed his face.

He moved back to the platform's edge and was able to see the others easily over the domed heads of the creatures between them. He waved them over.

Gaby moved first, then Hanson, with Danny coming last.

Keo hurried back to the ladder, afraid his luck was going to run out *any second now*, and started climbing. Every step took him closer toward the sunlight and away from the filth of the sewer. After not smelling the stink of the tunnel for so long, he was starting to lose his tolerance. Or maybe it was the fresh air filtering through the gaps in the round lid above him, reminding him there was another world beyond this stinking hellhole.

He finally reached the top and pushed the heavy metal covering up with one hand before sliding it completely out of the way. He held his breath for the sound of a gun discharging, but his head was still attached to his shoulders a second—two, and even three seconds later—so he kept moving, sticking first his head up into the euphoric brightness, then the rest of him.

He climbed out into the sunlight, realized he had been holding his breath for the last thirty or so seconds, and finally gave himself permission to breathe again as he rolled away from the round hole. He swallowed in a lungful of fresh air (*God bless you, fresh air!*) as he pushed himself up on one knee and raised the 9mm.

Footprints and splatters of dried blood covered the area around the opening, but there were no signs of anyone living or dead. He looked toward the parking lot, where they had carved an LZ for the Sikorsky earlier and come under fire, but only saw bullet-riddled cars and no collaborator presence.

Keo turned around when he heard Gaby coming up behind him, then reached down and pulled her out of the sewer. She had been holding her breath too, and Gaby finally sucked in a large lungful when she collapsed on the pavement and stayed down there for a while.

He hurried over to help Hanson up. The big man was halfway out of the hole when Keo looked past him and down at the platform below.

"Hanson," Keo said, "where's Danny?"

Hanson gave him a confused look, then stopped climbing and glanced down. "He was right behind me."

"So where is he?"

Hanson shook his head, mumbled something incoherent, then started climbing back down.

"Hanson!" Keo hissed, but Hanson didn't respond.

"What is it?" Gaby asked. She had picked herself up and was holding her Glock at her side while looking around at the parking lot. "Where's Danny?"

"I don't know," Keo said. He stayed at the opening, looking after Hanson as the last of Mercer's men hopped down the ladder and craned his head (hesitantly, very hesitantly) back into the tunnel he had just escaped from.

"Keo," Gaby said. "What's happening?"

"I don't know," Keo said.

Hanson came back, got on the ladder, and began climbing up with surprising speed for a man his size. Keo scooted away as Hanson reached the opening, and Keo grabbed his proffered arm and pulled him out.

"Where's Danny?" Gaby asked.

Hanson shook his head. "He's not down there."

"What the fuck does that mean?" Keo asked.

"Just that," Hanson said. "He's not in the tunnel." The big man shook his head, looking, Keo guessed, probably as bewildered as he and Gaby were at the moment. "He's gone."

"So here you are. At last. Tell me: Am I everything you imagined?"

Mabry's voice was everywhere—inside his head and outside. The duality of it was jarring, and it took him a moment to adjust. Fortunately he had enough experience shielding himself from unwanted voices and was able to limit the effects on his senses. Even Mabry's hiss was comforting, which shouldn't have been possible but was.

"All that effort to avoid me. To run away. Only to come here. So much time wasted for nothing."

Mabry didn't resemble the creature he had seen outside the Cleveland bank all those months ago. The ghoul was taller, his chest fuller, and his shoulders broader. The blue of the eyes so incandescent that he couldn't look away even if he wanted to, and he didn't for fear of losing track of his target, his mission.

Make it count! a voice that wasn't Mabry's echoed inside his head. The words came tumbling from the past, at a time when he was surrounded by sand and blood, heat and cold. Danny had been there. He didn't remember much, but he remembered enough. Was it Danny's voice? He couldn't be sure.

Danny...

He was back there, in the tunnel. With Gaby and Keo, and Mercer's men. Maybe dead. Maybe barely alive. He couldn't hear or feel them because he couldn't afford to extend his senses beyond the room. Everything he had, every ounce of willpower, was focused on Mabry. In this room, right here, right now.

His mission. His final mission.

"Tell me," Mabry said, "was it worth it? Was all of this worth it?"

"Yes," he said.

Mabry smiled. A true smile, the kind the other blue eyes could never quite master no matter how hard they tried—how hard *he* tried. "It must be fate, then. Or maybe you think it's providence. That night in the apartment, when you stumbled across the silver. You, of all people. A man who doesn't believe. And yet, and yet, it was there when you needed it most."

"Coincidence," he said.

Mabry laughed. It was dry and humorless, and it reverberated off the walls and the interior of his skull. He willed himself to ignore it, to push through.

Concentrate.

Concentrate!

"I've been alive too long to believe in coincidences," Mabry said. "There was a time when I was a nonbeliever like you. But that was long ago. You wouldn't believe the things I've seen, the things I've witnessed men do—the things *I've* done to get this far."

There was an entire room between them, and it should have been difficult to hear Mabry's soft (*soothing*) exterior voice, but it wasn't. The air around him hummed, the sensations both warm and cool, stale and fresh—at once freezing and scorching.

It didn't make any sense. Nothing made any sense.

Concentrate!

"Men were never meant to have dominion over the planet," Mabry said. "They're too destructive for their own good. They poison the oceans with their filth, and they would have done the same to the sky before I stopped them. It's not their fault, really. It's in their nature to destroy."

His nostrils flared at the stench of human bodies. Too many to count even if he had wasted the second or two it would have taken to do so. They were shoved inside the lockers that lined the walls around him and hung from heavy metal hooks. Men and women, old and young. Frail and naked, resembling black-eyed ghouls, but not there yet. They were very much still alive, and if they were lucky, they wouldn't know what was happening to them, that Mabry fed on them whenever he needed the blood that flowed through their veins.

He licked his lips involuntarily.

No, this wasn't him. He wasn't one of them. He wasn't like Mabry.

No.

"I knew the time would come," Mabry continued. "All I had to do was wait. But I've always been patient. You learn to be when you've survived for as long as I have. Time loses its power when age and disease no longer matter."

"Everything dies," he said.

Mabry's lips creased again. Even standing so far apart (*so near*), the two of them bathed in absolute darkness, he could see the gentle (*caring*) smile. "Do you really think it's going to be that easy? That you would come here, kill me, and save everyone? Save your beloved Lara?"

No, he thought, and tightened his grip around the hilts of the knives hanging at his sides. If their silver blades nauseated Mabry as much as they did him, the ghoul didn't show it for even a split second.

"You didn't even tell her the truth," Mabry said. "Not all of it. What does that say about your commitment?"

He had told her enough. Told Danny and Gaby enough. They didn't need to know everything. Not yet, anyway.

"Do you know how many have stood where you are now?" Mabry continued. "And I've survived them all. Every single one of them. What makes you different? What makes you special?"

He couldn't help himself, and the corners of his lips curled into a smile (or at least, what he thought was a good version of one).

Mabry cocked his head slightly to one side. "Kate. You think because she turned you, that this time it'll be different. This time you'll succeed where all the others have failed. You and your two little knives."

He refused to stop smiling.

"I've braved armies," Mabry said. "I've mastered monstrosi ties the likes of which you couldn't imagine. Untold lives have been cast against me, but I've always continued on while they fell and rotted into the ground."

"This time it'll be different," he hissed.

"That's what the others thought, too. But it never is. Maybe fate brought you here, maybe it was providence lending a hand. Whatever it was—whatever it is—it'll all be for nothing. Humanity's days have come and gone. Lay down the knives and embrace it. I still have room for you by my side."

"No."

Another sigh, this one slightly more impatient than the last. "You should have come home earlier. I would have sent people for your beloved and brought her to you, given you the happy ending you so desperately crave."

"You'll never touch her. You'll never get close to her."

"We'll see about that. When we're done here, I'll send for her. It doesn't matter how far she hides from me. I'll find her—somehow, some way—and bring her here. I've already reserved a spot. And whenever I feed on her, I'll think of you, and how silly you were, how wrong Kate was about you."

"No."

"You won't have a choice. You never did. Neither will she. None of you ever did. You think you know how long I've been planning this? Putting all the pieces into place? You don't have a clue. You'll never truly grasp the complexity of it; you couldn't possibly appreciate how much patience and planning and effort it took to get this far."

"Shut up," he said. "You talk too much."

A hint of anger flared across Mabry's eyes. "Show some respect."

"You don't deserve it."

The razor-thin smile returned to Mabry's lips. "I should have taken you outside the bank. It would have been mercy. For both of us. All it would have taken was a few hundred more of my children."

"You made a mistake."

"Yes. I did. I thought I saw something in you, something Kate thought she saw, too. But we were both wrong."

"She's dead. Kate."

"Yes, she is. You took her from me."

"You can join her."

"No, I won't. Every mistake can be rectified, but you will never find peace with your precious Lara. You will never find peace anywhere, because you will never leave this room alive."

"We'll see."

He gripped the hilt of the knives even tighter and took the first step across the room.

"*Come then,*" Mabry said, and this time the ghoul's voice

thrummed, hollow and lifeless, inside his head. *"Show me what you've learned. Show me how you'll succeed where whole armies have failed. Show me."*

His walk became a run—faster, faster, *faster*—and he was on the other side of the room in the blink of an eye, and slashing—

—and missed!

He had been fast. As fast as he had ever been. Faster than he thought he was capable of—and it hadn't been enough. It hadn't even been close.

"Pathetic," Mabry said.

He shut off the pain receptors to his left arm as soon as Mabry grabbed it by the wrist and broke it, and the knife clattered harmlessly to the hard floor.

"This is it?"

He hacked away with the remaining blade, but Mabry jerked his head back and the blade missed again, and again, and *again.*

"This is all you have?"

His chest quaked against Mabry's open palm, bone and muscle quivering against the impact. But there was no pain, just numbness.

"You woke me up for this?"

He swung the knife in desperation at Mabry's neck, but the ghoul effortlessly sidestepped it and got ahold of his arm, snapping it at the elbow.

"How sad."

The second knife fell away as he stumbled back. Long—impossibly long—and warm fingers snatched him around the throat before he could retreat too far, and flung him across the room into one of the lockers. He collapsed to the floor, the warm body hanging in the locker coming loose from the impact and collapsing on top of him.

"Kate spoke so highly of you."

He struggled to stand, but it was difficult with arms that

didn't—and couldn't—obey his commands. At least he couldn't feel the pain.

"She would be disappointed by this effort."

He managed to stand and attempted to refocus on Mabry as the air around him shifted and then the ghoul was there, in front of him and grabbing him by the throat again and slamming him into the locker. Metal fragments stabbed through his back, and blood splashed the cold concrete.

"I expected more from you," Mabry said, and smashed him into the locker, twisted sharp metal spearing his back and drawing more blood.

"I expected more fight."

And again, into the remains of the locker. *Bam!*

"I expected more spirit."

Bam!

"But Kate was wrong."

Bam!

"And so was I."

Bam!

"You're just another husk."

Bam!

"And that's all you'll ever be."

The fingers finally, mercifully released him and he slid to the floor, a heap of shattered bones and ripped flesh. Blood pooled under him. Too much blood. All his. His senses were out of control, and he couldn't focus on any one thing.

"You're not who I thought you were," Mabry said, talking aloud now. "Maybe you never were. I welcomed you to my side, but maybe I shouldn't have." Thin lips formed a frown, the disappointment radiating from every pore of the creature's blackened flesh. "You don't deserve it."

"Yes," he said, forcing the word out through a sheet of blood that dripped down his face from the open gashes along his skull. He didn't feel any pain, but he knew it was there.

His body was broken. Everything was broken.

"Yes?" Mabry said, standing over him.

Blood dripped from the ghoul's fingers, the rhythmic *drip-drip-drip* as intoxicating as what poured out of his back, his thighs, and his arms where the sharp edges of the locker had dug deep enough to slice bone.

"Yes," he said again.

Mabry bent and grabbed him by the throat and lifted him effortlessly into the air. He had no strength left to resist. The ghoul held him in place as if he were nothing—and maybe he was nothing.

Concentrate! the voice from somewhere in his past shouted. *Make it count! This is it! Make it count! You won't get another chance!*

You won't get another chance!

He thought of Lara. It was always Lara at the back of his mind, even in his lowest of low moments. She was always there— a radiant glow, waiting to bring him back from the abyss, back to where things mattered.

Except there was something wrong with his memory of her this time. She wasn't quite as easy to see, the crystal blue of her eyes not quite as bright, and he began to lose his way.

Lara. *Lara!*

"Yes?" Mabry said, leaning forward. "Yes what, Will?"

"You're right," he said. Croaked. Whispered?

"About what?"

"I can't beat you."

"No, you can't. You never could. And you never will."

"I can't beat you..."

"You said that already," Mabry said. "So what made you think you ever could?"

"I can't beat you," he said for the third time.

Mabry sighed and his face softened. It was such a human emotion for such an inhuman creature. Even his grip seemed to lessen out of mercy, though the ghoul didn't let him down.

"Good-bye, Will. Go with the knowledge that you won't be alone for very long. She'll join you—your precious Lara. Then Danny and Gaby and the others will follow. In the years to come, we'll train the rest to serve us, and in time they won't remember any other life. It will be *glorious*."

Now, he thought. *Now, now*, now!

He'd heard the footsteps when they were still in the hallway while Mabry was talking, gloating. By the time he tasted the bitter bite of new silver in the air, the figure had slipped inside the room through the open door and was running—and running *fast*—at Mabry.

But it wasn't fast enough.

Mabry spun and struck, and the dark figure flew across the room and crashed into the lockers on the other side.

In that split second, he reached out and grabbed Mabry's arm, the one still holding him in the air, and pulled himself forward and toward the ghoul. It was difficult because of his mangled hands, and getting a good grip was impossible, so he wrapped his shattered appendages around Mabry's arm instead and kicked out and backward at the wall behind him for leverage.

Mabry turned, eyes enlarging—not in fear, no, he was beyond that—as he lunged forward. If Mabry knew what he was going to do, he didn't stop him in time. Despite everything—his superior speed, his impossible strength—Mabry entertained a brief moment of indecision, of confusion.

That was just enough time for Will—

(*My name is Will!*)

—to open his mouth, extending his jaw as wide as it would go —*and even wider still*—before biting down, his teeth tearing through flesh and then the cranium itself. It was surprisingly weak and flimsy, for all the power it was sheltering, but even so two of Will's teeth, then a third and a fourth and a *fifth* shattered against the frontal bone as he made contact.

And he kept pushing and pushing until *he was through* and finally, *finally* tasted the mushy thing underneath.

Mabry screamed, and a mind-numbing explosion of pain erupted inside Will's mind. It echoed and burst and reformed and imploded again and again, even as Will tasted flesh in his mouth and blood dripped from his teeth. And this time it wasn't just his blood.

He collapsed to the floor in a pile of pulverized bones and speared flesh as Mabry stumbled. The ghoul's legs gave way and he dropped to his knees, hands groping at the chunk of missing flesh and bone even as he continued to scream inside Will's head, his pain and misery piercing the river of consciousness that linked the two of them—that linked all of them.

Listen, Will thought, projecting his voice out into the hive mind. *Listen!*

And they did. He could sense the fear in the ones inside the tunnel just beyond the dome, from the others nesting inside the buildings around them, desperately waiting for nightfall. More than that, he could feel the ones in the other parts of the city, the state, and beyond, every single one of them watching and listening and witnessing Mabry's fury and pain.

The images and sounds of the encounter had started broadcasting when Will first confronted the five blue-eyed ghouls, when he brought down his mental defenses and rejoined the brood, and the link remained intact when he showed himself to Mabry.

And they had listened and watched and felt every blow and pain, including the fight that proved not to be much of a fight after all. They were seeing and hearing everything he was, and the signal only got stronger as more of them plugged in.

One became two, two became four, and on and on until the numbers reached the tens of thousands, then the millions, and *more*.

He could sense the blue eyes trying to take control, trying to demand the hive's attention, and failing miserably. The brood was enraptured by the sight of Mabry's agony, the undeniable sound of his pain.

Listen! Will shouted. *Do you see? Can you hear it? Can you feel it? Listen!*

Mabry continued to scream, the full extent of his pain beyond anything Will had ever experienced. And he had done that. He had attacked and conquered the father—the beginning and the end, the nothing and the everything, the nowhere and the everywhere—and left him bruised and bleeding and *dying*.

Will rolled the meaty, gooey substance he had found with his teeth around in his mouth before finally swallowing it down. He savored the taste clinging to the roots of his shattered and bleeding mouth, not because he wanted to, but because he wanted them—*all* of them—to see and know it along with him.

I did this, he said without saying it. *I did this!*

Blood oozed down the corners of his mouth and dripped from his chin as he stood up—rising slowly, but rising nonetheless. His legs weren't working correctly, but they obeyed him enough to carry him forward, toward Mabry, and he stood over the kneeling ghoul, whose voice continued to cry out in his mind.

The ghoul looked up at him and its thin lips quivered, though no words came out. Its eyes seemed to have dulled, more ash than blue now. There was an emptiness about the way it looked up at him, at once defiant and yet weak.

Do you see it? he said into the hive mind. *Look at him. Do you see it?*

Then Will shoved his fist through the open hole in Mabry's forehead, and the spongey black and blue-veined thing on the other side offered no resistance whatsoever. He pulled his hand out as the ghoul collapsed to the floor and lay still, and Mabry's cries faded from his mind.

Will walked back to the lockers, finding renewed strength from a place he couldn't fathom, and sat down. He leaned against a pair of dangling feet and watched the black-clad human figure reappear, dragging one leg behind him as he approached tentatively.

The man stepped over Mabry's body, then came over to crouch next to Will. Bright red blood covered the lower half of his face, and his breathing was ragged and slightly out of control, but he was also grinning.

"How many times have I told you not to run off all by your little lonesome like that, huh?" Danny said. "Now look at you. All bleeding and broken and shit. By the way, that was gross. You *bit his fucking head off.* That's got to be the most fucking gross thing I've ever seen in my life, man."

"I...adapted," Will said. His voice came out odd, the result of broken teeth. Maybe he had just mumbled the words, though Danny seemed to understand him fine.

"So taking a literal bite out of the bad guy wasn't part of the original plan, huh?"

"No."

"But it worked. That's all that matters, right? Plan G is officially in the books."

"Not over," he said. It was easier to say as few words as possible. There was no pain—he was beyond feeling pain at the moment—but the damage was severe all over.

Danny glanced back at Mabry's body, then at the open door. He gripped the knife in his fist. A cross-knife with a silver blade. "What the hell are you talking about? The plan was to kill King

Ghoul, and it's game over. Cut off the head and the body dies. Right?"

"No."

"No? What do you mean, no?" Danny narrowed his eyes at him. "You lied, didn't you? You lied to us. Lara. Me. Everyone."

"Yes."

"You *dick*."

"Not over."

"Now what?"

"Help me. Up."

"And then?"

"Finish it," Will said. "One more. Thing. Left. Then...it's over."

Danny sighed, wrapping his arms around Will's thin frame. "It's time to get a new wardrobe, by the way. You look like a hobo. And oh, have I mentioned you're bleeding? Like, a lot?"

"I know."

"What the hell's wrong with your body?"

"Broken."

"That explains it."

"Doesn't matter."

"Oh, I'd say it matters, dude."

"Doesn't matter. One more. Left. Then...over."

Will felt them stirring finally—the creatures in the tunnel beyond the hallway. The black eyes. A few hundred here, a few thousand out there, and the millions (*billions*) beyond. They waited, confused and agitated.

But mostly confused.

My children, Will projected. *My brood. The father is dead. But you're not alone. You'll never be alone.*

"You wanna give me some directions here?" Danny said as he pulled them up from the floor with some effort.

"Outside," Will said.

"It's still day out there."

"Yes."

"Yes?"

"Outside."

"You are aware that you're still all spindly and shit? Or did you lie about that, too?"

"No."

"So what then, Mr. Mushy Mouth?"

"Help me. Danny. Stop. Talking."

"Might as well tell me to stop breathing," Danny said as he half walked and half dragged the both of them to the door. "By the way, I think one of my legs is broken, thanks for asking."

"You'll. Be. Fine."

"Shows what you know. I'm pretty sure one of my kidneys flew out of my mouth when that thing hit me, too. Is that possible? Can you lose a kidney through your mouth? Christ, you're bleeding a lot. I'm drowning in this stuff. By the way, I'm having a kid. Did I tell you that? God, you're bleeding a lot. It's like a friggin' Free Ketchup for Everyone Day back here."

"Danny..."

"So this is it, huh?"

"I'm sorry."

"What do you have to be sorry for? I'm the one dragging your skinny ass around, Mister Hobo. I'm the one doing all the work. But then, what else is new?"

"Sorry. Danny. I'm...sorry."

"Sorry's not gonna fix this, man. You thought about what *I'm* gonna do without someone to try my awesome jokes on first?"

"You'll. Do. Fine. All...of you. Look. After. Her. For...me."

Danny didn't say anything.

"Danny..."

"Yeah, yeah," Danny said. "It's not like I got anything else better to do, you selfish prick."

Will smiled. A true smile this time, he was sure of it, as his friend led him to the door one step at a time.

He could sense the black eyes out there, in the tunnel, waiting for them. For *him*. The confusion lingered among them, but there was something else that hadn't been there before: a growing anticipation, almost excitement.

Follow me, Will thought, pushing his voice into the hive mind. He heard it reverberate through the stream of consciousness, from one mind to the next, to the next. *Don't be afraid. There's nothing to fear.*

"No!" the blue eyes shouted, their voices rising from the ranks of the brood. They were desperate, demanding attention. "*Don't listen to the traitor! Ignore him!*"

Will continued projecting, because he could feel it: He had them. The black eyes were listening to him, and him only.

I'll show you the way, he said, his voice growing with confidence as it expanded further and further, to more and more minds.

Follow me, he said, trumping the fading voices of the blue eyes as the hive, as one, turned to him.

Follow me, he called out, his voice soothing and comforting, the way Mabry's had been before him. *The father's dead, but you're not alone. You'll never be alone.*

Follow me, and I'll show you the way back to the light...

32

LARA

"We've engaged the enemy. I repeat: We've engaged the enemy."

The calm voice coming through the Comm Room's speakers belonged to Peele, the man in charge of the three tanks that were at this very moment butting up against the main roadblock into Houston. Peele and Rolling Thunder's goal was less to actually break through and more to keep the collaborators from leaving their posts and interfering with Striker's mission, which was to link up with Willie Boy and take the fight directly to Mabry. A year ago that kind of tactical planning would have made Lara question who she was; these days, it was just another decision that she hoped didn't get too many people killed.

You're responsible for this. You sent them out there. Your friends, strangers, even the man you love.

You did this. You did this.

Rhett had the microphone and spoke into it: "How many are we talking about, Rolling Thunder?"

"Don't know; didn't get the chance to take a roll call," Peele said through the speakers. "I'll get right on it as soon as they stop shooting at us."

"Small arms?"

"Looks like a couple of LAWS—Shit!" Then, to someone else, presumably in the tank with him, "Jesus Christ, Larry, watch where you're going! I don't wanna be eating a rocket right about now!"

"Laws what?" Carly said quietly next to her.

"Light Anti-Armor Weapons System," Lara said. "Shoulder-mounted single-shot anti-tank weapons, basically."

"And you know this how?"

"Danny. He thought they'd have something like that."

They stood behind Jane, who was planted in front of all the communications gear in the room, while Riley and Rhett remained in front of the big map. The two men were constantly marking locations of where the forces were—theirs, the enemies, and a big circle in red marker around where the HC Dome was to the southwest of the city, away from Downtown area. She had stared at that spot so many times today that she thought she could remember every single parking lot and tenement building or highway around it.

Anxiety radiated from Carly next to her, and Lara knew exactly what her friend was feeling. It wasn't just that their loved ones and friends were out there in danger, but that they couldn't do anything about it except to stand here and listen, helpless to affect what was happening in Houston right now because it was out of their hands.

God, please, don't die. Please, don't die because of me.

"Okay, okay," Peele was saying through the speakers. Lara wasn't sure who he was talking to, and neither was Rhett by the look on his face.

"Peele, you okay?" Rhett asked.

"Hell no," Peele said. "They're coming from everywhere. The only reason we're still in one piece is because of the armor."

Then, shouting, "Back up, back up! Alex, for God's sake, watch where you're shooting!"

Riley looked across the room at her. "I'm not sure how long Peele's going to last out there. He sounds pretty rattled."

"They have to last a lot longer," Lara said, and thought, *Please don't die, please don't die.* Then, as confidently as she could muster, "Without them, the collaborators are all going to converge on the HC Dome. We need to give Striker as much time as possible to get down there and assist Willie Boy with their mission."

"Willie Boy," Carly said, shaking her head. "Let me guess: Danny came up with these code names?"

Lara managed a smile. "Yeah."

"Well, at least Rolling Thunder and Eagle sound cool."

Lara leaned forward and put a hand on Jane's shoulder. "Can you get the A-1os on the radio for me?"

Jane nodded and flicked switches on the dashboard, then adjusted her headset's mic and spoke into it: "Eagle One, Eagle Two, this is Black Tide. Eagle One, Eagle Two, can you read me?" She paused for a moment, then picked up a second microphone and handed it to Lara. "It's Eagle One. Cole."

Lara took the mic while Jane hit another switch, and they heard Cole's voice through the speakers.

"—crazy down there," Cole was saying. "There's a swarm of technicals buzzing around Rolling Thunder. They look like ants trying to bite a lumbering elephant."

"Now that's a sight," Carly said.

"Cole," Lara said, "I need you to keep any collaborators that are breaking away from the roadblocks from converging on the Dome."

"I hear ya, and that's what Eagle Two and me've been doing all day," Cole said. "But not all the bad guys are getting the hint; some of them look pretty stubborn. We're doing all we can to convince them otherwise, but there's just two of us trying to cover an entire city."

"Do the best you can, Eagle One."

"Understood, Black Tide. We'll do our best."

"Thank you, Cole."

"Yes, ma'am," Cole said.

"Now that's a gentleman," Carly said.

"How are you for ammo?" Rhett said into the mic.

"Not good," Cole said. "I'm down to just the Avenger. I'm doing my best to conserve ammo, but it's going to run dry sooner rather than later."

"What about Eagle Two?"

"Wheeler's in the same boat."

"Ask him if he saw anyone abandoning the fight," Carly said. "You know, in case Lara's plea worked."

Rhett relayed the question, and Cole answered: "A dozen or so vehicles took off when Rolling Thunder showed up. I was about to blast them, but they were obviously hightailing it so I held off."

"A dozen or so technicals," Riley said, smiling slightly. "That's something."

"That's a dozen less assholes trying to kill my Danny," Carly said. "That's more than something."

"The true believers are staying behind," Rhett said. "The ones slugging it out with Peele and the rest of Rolling Thunder right now. Only true believers would think you can go head-to-head with tanks. You gotta be pretty goddamn committed."

"Straight-jacket type of commitment?" Carly asked.

"Not to them. There's no turning back for them. It's all-in or nothing."

Lara watched Rhett for a moment, wondering if he was talking about the collaborators out there fighting with Peele and the others, or if he was referring to people closer to home.

She was still thinking about Rhett's words when Cole shouted through the speakers, "No, goddammit, no!"

"What happened?" Lara said into the mic. "Cole, what happened?"

"Wheeler," Cole said. "Shit!"

"What happened to Wheeler?"

"His Warthog just went down. Jesus Christ. They've been trying to tag us with shoulder-mounted launchers all day, but—Jesus! How the hell did they manage to get Wheeler? I warned that little punk not to make it too easy on them. Dammit!"

"Without two Warthogs up there keeping them honest, those technicals are going to start converging on the Dome," Riley said.

Lara keyed her mic. "Eagle One, I need you to do a flyby of the Dome. I need an update on Striker."

"I'm almost there," Cole said. He sounded calm again, but maybe that was just the transmission hiding his emotions. "Okay, I see... I see tangos in the open, but our boys are MIA."

"MIA? Explain."

"I don't see any action down there. Either they're all dead or they made it underground."

Lara looked back at Carly.

"Dead or underground," Carly sighed. "We're hoping for the latter, right?"

Lara nodded, as Rhett said into his own mic: "What else do you see, Cole?"

"Wait, wait," Cole said. "Okay, okay, I'm pretty sure Striker's underground. I see tangos moving toward one of the manhole coverings. Give me a sec; I'm going to make sure no one follows them down."

Cole went silent for five seconds...

Seven...

Ten...

Then he was back: "That's it, guys, that's my last bullet. I'll stick around, buzz the area, and try to draw some of their fire. I don't know how long until they figure out I'm running on fumes and start ignoring me, though."

"Be careful, Cole," Rhett said.

"Roger that, Black Tide. Eagle One out."

"Tough old coot," Carly said. "Reminds me of my dad, if my dad was a former airman with suicidal tendencies."

Riley looked across the room at Lara. "That's it. They're in the tunnel. Nothing we can do now but wait."

She nodded, not quite sure what she was feeling. Maybe it was relief that Keo and Danny had made it to Will, or possibly terror because she knew what was waiting for them down there.

Please don't die. God, please don't die because of my decisions.

The thought weighed her down and sapped the energy from her, and she was already so damn tired. All the days of not sleeping, the nights of worrying about Will and everyone onboard the *Trident* came back in a rush to punish her, and she had to sit down in a chair next to Jane or else she might have collapsed in a heap.

When was the last time she had just sat down? She didn't know the answer to that question and couldn't even begin to come up with one. Her eyelids were suddenly heavy, and she could feel something out there, calling to her.

What?

She wanted to fight it, wanted to resist. There was too much work to do, too many lives out there hanging in the balance.

Will. Gaby and Blaine and Danny.

She couldn't allow herself to close her eyes...

Maybe just for one second.

I'll close my eyes for just one second...

When she opened her eyes, she was standing on a beach. She had no shoes on and she was smiling as cool water gently lapped at her toes. The sand was very white—much whiter than she remembered Black Tide having—and there was a nice breeze. A perfect breeze, in fact. She had let her hair down and it lifted and swayed with the wind, and for some reason it seemed to be longer than it should have been.

She looked around her.

She wasn't standing on Black Tide Island. She would remember this stretch of beach anywhere, but these days it usually only appeared in her dreams because she could no longer actually go there anymore. In her dreams, where things were perfect and she could live as a twenty-something woman without the weight of the world on her shoulders.

There, the solar-powered lampposts that ringed the island. And there, the long cobblestone walkway where, once upon a time, armed men had attempted to rush only to be met at the other end by violence. The very same violence that she had orchestrated in a bid to keep the island.

But there were no bodies there now. No blood and no bullet casings to mark one long, bad night. And there were no beached vessels loaded with killers trying to kill her and her friends.

There was just...her, back on Song Island.

This is a dream.

It was in the way the wind caressed her cheeks, the warmth of the water against her feet. The sun shone brightly in a cloudless sky and it was all perfect, which was how she knew it wasn't real. The closest she had ever come to perfection was here, on this place months ago, when she had someone to share it with.

What am I doing here?

She glimpsed a figure in the distance, walking toward her. He was so far (*How is he so far?*) that she couldn't make out any details, but she knew it was a man by the shape of his shoulders.

He was wearing slacks, the legs rolled up to his knees; a bright-colored Hawaiian shirt meshed perfectly with their surroundings.

Perfectly. There's that word again.

She shielded her eyes to get a better look, but she already knew who it was before the man ever reached her. Even that didn't make any sense because when she first saw him he appeared to be on the other side of the island, except now he was only twenty yards away.

Then ten...

Then stopping in front of her.

"Will," she said, whispering his name as if she were afraid he would evaporate into nothingness if she said it too loudly.

He was the Will she remembered. A *human* Will. The one with the deep brown eyes that made her trust him back when they first met, even though she shouldn't have trusted any man after what she had been through.

It was Will.

It was her Will.

She leaped into his arms and he grabbed her in a tight embrace. Then he was laughing when she pulled back and began kissing him on the forehead, on the nose, on the cheeks, on the lips. He kissed her back urgently, hands gripping her tightly. She ran her fingers through his hair—short, perfectly cut, as if he'd just come from the barber—and refused to let him go, too afraid he would leave her again if she did.

She didn't know how long they stayed that way—hugging, kissing, laughing on the sand—but it had to be minutes. Maybe longer than that. She wasn't sure because time felt slippery, as if days could go by and she'd never notice, or ever need to stop to eat and drink and sleep. Not while she had him back.

Which was how she knew it was a dream.

She pulled away but refused to let him go. Dream or not, he looked and felt and tasted *so real* that a part of her wanted desperately not to care, to just go with it; take everything she could get before it slipped away again.

But she didn't listen to the voice because she wasn't the same person she was when they first met. She had changed over the months since meeting him, since losing him, since...

...losing him...

"Will," she said softly. "This is a dream."

He smiled at her. "I just wanted to see you again as the man you remembered."

"I don't think I ever remembered you in a Hawaiian shirt."

He laughed. It was loud and hearty and her heart filled up hearing it, because the Will she knew was reserved and thoughtful and he rarely just let it out like he was doing now. And she beamed, because his laughter was so wonderful and she couldn't get enough.

"No," he said, "but I thought it would be a nice touch."

"It is," she said. "It is."

She kissed him on the lips again. Softly, gently, afraid of breaking him.

"Will," she said, the sound of his name like music to her ears. "How are you doing this?"

"We're connected. We've always been connected."

"Always?"

"Always."

"So why didn't you do this before?"

"Because once I make the first connection, I won't be able to sever it. I'll always be there at the back of your mind. It can be... uncomfortable for some people."

"Like you and Kate."

He nodded. "But it was never this powerful with her. What you and I have..." He was glowing in the sunlight, the smile frozen on his lips, contagious. "It's stronger than with anyone else."

"So what does this mean?"

His smile faded.

"Will," she said, the joy draining from her until there was just that empty hole in her soul again. "What does this mean for us? For you, out there in the real world?"

"I lied to you."

"About what?"

"Mabry. I lied when I said killing him would reverse the infection. There is no reversal, Lara. What's done can't be undone."

Her arms came loose and she pulled away from him, taking one, then two steps back in the sand. The water continued to lap at her feet but she barely noticed it now, too consumed by the whirlwind of emotions ripping through.

"You lied to me," she said. "You lied to me..."

"I'm sorry."

"What else did you lie about?"

"Not everything. I can end this nightmare by killing Mabry. I can give you and humanity a second chance. A real, fighting chance."

"How?"

"I told you about him. How Mabry's the beginning and the end. The everything and the nothing. The nowhere and the everywhere. He exists in here." Will tapped his temple. "Even when he's not there, he's there. We come from him, Lara. All of us."

"The ghouls..."

"Yes."

She saw the sadness in his eyes, but there was also something else there that hadn't been before: *Acceptance.*

"Every ghoul comes from him," Will continued. "His blood flows through our veins. In so many ways, he gave birth to us. He's our father."

"Your father?"

"It's how they look at it. The brood. They are his children. They obey him without question. They go to sleep with his voice in their heads, and wake up with it comforting them. He is the everything, and the nothing. Everywhere, and nowhere. The beginning...and the end."

"What's happening at the Dome right now, Will? Where are you?"

"Still there. Danny's with me. He's helping me to finish it."

"How can you be there and here at the same time?"

"This is just a dream, Lara. You were right. It's a shared connection between the two of us. A bubble that exists outside of time."

She shook her head. She didn't understand any of it and she didn't care to try, because he had lied to her. He told her he could save them and himself, and he had *lied to her*.

But slowly, very slowly, the anger slipped away, because she knew why he had done it. Because she would never have agreed to the plan if it meant he wouldn't return, wouldn't come back to her even if it wasn't as the man she loved.

He did it for you. Everything he's done, it's been for you, you stupid girl.

She walked back to him. She put her hand on his cheek, and he closed his eyes and leaned into it. She smiled and held him there, enjoying the warmth of his skin. It was so unlike the last time they had made contact, below deck on the *Trident*. He wasn't the Will he once was then—or the Will he was now.

"Will I remember any of this when I wake up?" she asked.

"Do you want to?"

"Yes. Very much."

"Then you will. The same way I remembered my dreams with Kate. It lingers. Always. That's why I never joined with you before. It can be disturbing always having another consciousness at the back of your mind. And our bond is so much stronger..."

"Then why now?"

He smiled at her, and it was genuine and touching, and the sadness had left his eyes, replaced by happiness. "I wanted to see you again. I wanted to explain why I lied, why I did what I did. But most of all, I wanted to tell you that I love you."

She put her other hand on his other cheek and held him steady. Even as her mind processed everything he had said—the magnitude behind his words—she clung onto him for as long as possible.

"You're leaving me," she whispered. "You're leaving me again."

"I have to," he whispered back, covering her hands with his and squeezing, hard. "It's the only way."

"Why?"

"Because Mabry's dead. I killed him. His death will leave a hole, and someone has to fill it."

"You."

"Yes. They saw me kill him. They heard him crying in pain before his last moments."

"You overthrew him," she said, and pursed a smile at the thought.

"It was the only way to make them listen. To make them pay attention. Not all of them will do it—obey me—but enough will to make a difference in the days to come. Enough to give you and everyone a fresh start."

"And what about you?"

He squeezed her hand even tighter, then leaned forward and kissed her on the forehead.

"Will," she whispered. "What about you?"

"I have to show them," he whispered. "They won't do it unless I show them that there's nothing to fear. It's the only way."

"Why you?"

"Because...I love you."

He pulled away, but she wouldn't let him go. She held onto his hands, but he somehow slipped through anyway and stepped back, and back...

"Will," she said. "Don't go."

"It's the only way it'll work," he said. "I have to show them. I have to lead them."

"Do something *else*."

"I would if I could, you must know that. But this is the only way."

"Will, no."

He stopped, but the dozen or so feet between them might as well be an ocean. The sun played tricks with her eyes, and she could barely make out his face for some reason. She wanted to run over to him, to hold onto him and never let go, but her legs refused to obey her.

Move! Why won't you move?

"Lara," he said, the sound of her name on his lips filled with so much joy that her heart ached just to hear it. "Take care of our friends. Take care of Danny. Take care of everyone for me."

She held out a hand toward him, pleading for him to take it. "Don't go."

"I have to."

"No..."

"I love you. I'll always love you."

She tried to force her legs to move, but they wouldn't, even as Will got smaller, slipping further and further away from her.

"You have more important things to do now," he said. Though it shouldn't have been possible with the crashing waves and the growing distance, she could hear his voice just fine, as if he were standing right next to her and not slowly but surely vanishing before her eyes. "They're going to come to you, ask you to lead them. You should, because you can. You're stronger than you think you are. Even now, after all you've done, all you've accomplished, you're still capable of so much more. I believe in you, Lara. Now you have to keep believing in yourself."

"Stop!" she screamed. "Will, stop!"

But he didn't, and he turned, and continued walking away.

As the waves splashed against her bare feet and the wind whipped at her hair, she knew he was never coming back, that this would be it—the final time she got to see him. Not just as the Will she always remembered and loved, but the new Will too, the one in Houston right now with Danny.

He was leaving her...and this time he wouldn't come back.

———

She opened her eyes to Keo's voice coming through the speakers, the sound of helicopter blades *whup-whup-whupping* in the background.

"I can't believe what I'm seeing. They're just... They're just walking out of the buildings and into the sun. Jesus, there's so many of them. I had no idea there were so many... God, what is this? What's happening?"

She looked over at Carly, standing next to her, one hand gripping the headrest of her chair so tightly that her fingers were ghost-white.

Rhett had the microphone and said into it, "Eagle One, can you confirm what Striker's seeing?"

"Striker's right; I'm seeing the same thing," Cole said. "There are just ashes down there. Ashes and bones. It's like a graveyard. And they're still coming out of the buildings. Every single building in the city. God*damn*. They're just walking outside and dying by the hundreds, thousands..."

"I have to show them," Will had said. *"They won't do it unless I show them that there's nothing to fear. It's the only way."*

"Rolling Thunder," Rhett said into the mic, "can you confirm what they're seeing?"

"Fuck yeah, I can," Peele said. He sounded almost delirious. "When they started coming out of the buildings, I thought for sure we were fucked. But they're just dead. Again. Whatever. You know what I mean. They're just stepping outside and burning and *poof*, like that, gone. Never seen anything like it. Jesus Fuck."

"That man's got a way with words," Carly said, and Lara wasn't sure if her friend was going to cry or laugh, or do both.

Lara reached for the second mic. "Keo, can you hear me?"

"Loud and clear," Keo said.

"What about Gaby and Blaine? What about Danny?"

"Gaby's right beside me..."

She waited for him to add Danny's and Blaine's names, but he didn't. In fact, he didn't say anything else.

"Keo," she said, too afraid to say the rest of it.

"Blaine didn't make it," Keo said. "And Danny's MIA."

Lara glanced over at Carly, her friend's face as pale as she had ever seen it.

"We lost sight of him when we were hightailing it out of the tunnel," Keo said. "Gaby thinks he went back for Frank. But I don't know."

"What *do* you know?"

"Nothing. Nothing for sure. We're circling now, heading back to the Dome."

Lara leaned into the mic, but she didn't say anything right away. She dreaded what she was going to say next, with the dream still fresh in her mind. Even now she could taste the crisp air, hear the wave coming onto the beach and lapping at her toes...

"I have to show them... It's the only way."

"Keo," she said into the mic, "what happened to Frank?"

"I don't know," Keo said. "It was chaotic down there. Chances are he's with Danny like Gaby says, so when we find one we'll find the other, too."

"Gaby's right; Danny would never just leave him," Carly said quietly behind her.

"We're circling the HC Dome now," Keo said through the radio.

"Collaborators?" Lara asked.

"They're bugging out. Whatever's left of them, anyway. They can see what's happening just as we can. The ghouls coming out of the buildings, then frying in the sun. There are bones everywhere, Lara. Jesus Christ, there are piles of bones everywhere."

"Find them," Lara said. "Find them, Keo."

"I will," Keo said, and there wasn't a single shred of doubt in his voice. "One way or another, we're not leaving empty-handed, I can fucking guarantee you that."

Carrie. Bonnie. And Blaine.

Maybe she should have been happy it wasn't more. How close had Gaby, Keo, and Danny come to joining that list? How many others had lost their lives helping Will do what he needed to do in order to save them? To save all of them?

She thought of them. Her friends...

Blaine, whom she knew longer than the others, but Bonnie had become a good friend. Carrie too, in her own way. But she would miss Blaine most of all, and maybe that was why she had avoided going to the bridge when she made her way back to the *Trident*, because everything in there reminded her of him.

But she knew she needed to be back on the yacht. More than

that, she *wanted* to be here. There wasn't the feeling of triumph she was hoping for as Peele and the others confirmed what they had initially seen—that the ghouls had simply stepped out of their hiding places to burn in the sun.

"*I have to show them,*" Will had said. "*They won't do it unless I show them that there's nothing to fear. It's the only way.*"

But there was a lightness in her, brought forth by a sense of accomplishment. There wasn't quite the pangs of regret and guilt from her losses that she had been fully prepared to confront, even though she continued to feel it in her very soul.

Carrie. Bonnie. Blaine...and Will.

And who else whose names she didn't know? Even now, Riley and Rhett were trying to get a head count of the people they had lost in the mission. The tankers, Wheeler, the members of Keo and Danny's Striker team...

She was leaning against the railing on the main deck, watching Elise, Vera, Jenny, and some of the other kids running around on Black Tide's beach in the near distance, when her radio's squawk broke in through the serenity of the moment.

"Where are you?" she asked.

"Ten minutes out," Danny answered. "I heard you were looking for me. What can I do you for?"

Danny was putting on an act, but she appreciated it anyway, and said, "Are you okay?"

"In one piece. At least until I get back there and Carly tears me a new one."

"Justifiable homicide, some would say."

"No arguments from me," Danny said. Then, quietly, "About Will..."

"I know, Danny."

He didn't say anything right away. Then: "How?"

"I'll tell you when you get back here. Are you sure you're okay?"

"Broken leg, maybe a punctured lung. Whatever. I'll get by."

"I know you will."

"He didn't, you know," Danny said. "Will. He didn't suffer at the end. Of course, I could have just misread that stupid smile on his face."

"He was smiling..."

"Yeah. A big ol' grin. I don't think I've ever seen Willie boy smile that big in my life. Like he was going on vacation with three high-priced escorts or something equally awesome fantastic super duper."

Lara couldn't help but smile. "Did he say anything?"

"He told me to look after you, on account of how you're always getting into trouble and whatnot. So, that's on my plate."

"Sorry about that."

"Eh, that's why God gave me an extra arm, amirite?" Then, without missing a beat, "By the way, I think we should try to convince Keo to stick around. That guy's pretty useful. Ugly as sin with those scars of his, but pretty useful in a pinch."

Somewhere on Danny's side of the connection, she heard Keo's voice: "Hey, you know I'm sitting right here, right?"

"Did you hear that?" Danny said. "Some weird buzzing noise. Shoo, fly, shoo!"

"Tell her about the other thing," Keo shouted in the background.

"What other thing?" Lara asked.

"Keester had a thought," Danny said. "I know, dangerous, right? But it might be worth spending a sleepless night or two on it."

"What is it?"

"The time zone differences."

"Time zones?"

"Willie boy timed it to kill the black eyes in our area, when it was still bright and shiny out. What Kilo was wondering was, what about in the rest of the world, where it was dark when Will sent out the call? Are those buggers still going to follow through, even after knowing what happened to the others? And they would know, right? With that whole connected hive mind of theirs?"

Lara didn't answer him right away. She didn't know how to, because the mere thought that all of this might have been for nothing, that for every million or so ghouls Will's death (*again*) had erased from the world there was still countless more out there, made her want to retch.

"I know, sorry to poop on the party," Danny said through the radio. "I told Kimbo Slice over here he was being a real buzzkill."

"Tomorrow," she said finally. "We'll find out what's happening out in the rest of the world when people start talking again. For now, let's just enjoy this."

"Sounds like a plan."

"Hurry back. I'll be waiting on the *Trident*."

"Roger that," Danny said. "Striker and company outro."

Lara put the radio away and continued leaning against the railing.

Was it possible? Could Will's sacrifice have been in vain?

No, she couldn't believe it. She *wouldn't* believe it. Will would have known about something like that. He would have taken it—along with countless other factors she hadn't even thought about or realized even existed—into consideration when he came up with his plan.

Right?

Elise and Vera were in the water now, trying to splash Jenny and the other kids. They had decided to team up and looked to have victory well in hand.

She thought of what Will had said on the beach, in the dream that only she would ever know about.

"Take care of our friends. Take care of Danny. Take care of everyone for me."

She would do that. She would take care of their friends and everyone else who needed her help.

She would do it, because she had it in her.

And because she wanted to.

Lara smiled again and looked up at the sun. It was bright. As bright as she had ever seen it. How was it so bright? It didn't matter, as long as it was there and she could close her eyes and let the warmth wash over her.

And she did that now, and thought about her next move...

EPILOGUE

"This is Lara, and if you're listening to this, then you've survived the unimaginable. It doesn't matter how you did it, just that you did when so many didn't. By now you've seen the endless piles of bones outside and you've heard the rumors. They're true. All of them. We've struck a crippling blow against the ghouls, but it's not over. It's far from over. They're still out there, along with the blue-eyed ones. But they don't control us anymore, and we know how to defeat them. It's their turn to be afraid. We're going to organize and we're going to hunt them down and destroy every single one of them, and they're going to find out that the night is no longer theirs. Make no mistake, this is the chance we've been waiting for—this is the start of a new beginning. For all of us. Because we're in this together, whether we called ourselves collaborators or rebels, or didn't call ourselves anything at all in the last year. None of it matters. Not anymore. A lot of very good and brave people paid the ultimate sacrifice to give us this second chance. Don't waste it like we did before with endless bickering and petty grievances. Let the past die with the past. This is our chance to make the world ours again. Help me—join me—and we'll take it back. I'm Lara, and I'm a survivor. If you're listening to this, then so are you..."

Made in the USA
Monee, IL
11 November 2022

17580094R00281